I0667299

# Goliath Book Rating

This book is rated **SFA**: *Suitable for all*

Content: Fiction/Thriller/Surreal/Comedic
Violence: Only on people who deserve it
Swearing: Occasional, mild
Nudity or sexual content: Implied only
Made-up words: 44
Page turnability: 7.26 GBI (adjusted)

This information has been compiled by the Goliath Corporation
Public Readership, Information and Certification Bureau.
Reading of banned books is forbidden by law.

**Goliath.** For all you'll ever read™

# Lost
## in a
# Good Book

ALSO BY JASPER FFORDE

*The Eyre Affair*

THURSDAY NEXT

IN

# Lost in a Good Book

A NOVEL

## Jasper Fforde

VIKING

VIKING
Published by the Penguin Group
Penguin Putnam Inc., 375 Hudson Street,
New York, New York 10014, U.S.A.
Penguin Books Ltd, 80 Strand, London WC2R 0RL, England
Penguin Books Australia Ltd, 250 Camberwell Road, Camberwell,
Victoria 3124, Australia
Penguin Books Canada Ltd, 10 Alcorn Avenue, Toronto, Ontario, Canada M4V 3B2
Penguin Books India (P) Ltd, 11 Community Centre, Panchsheel Park,
New Delhi—110 017, India
Penguin Books (N.Z.) Ltd, Cnr Rosedale and Airborne Roads, Albany,
Auckland, New Zealand
Penguin Books (South Africa) (Pty) Ltd, 24 Sturdee Avenue,
Rosebank, Johannesburg 2196, South Africa

Penguin Books Ltd, Registered Offices:
Harmondsworth, Middlesex, England

First American edition
Published in 2003 by Viking Penguin,
a member of Penguin Putnam Inc.

1   3   5   7   9   10   8   6   4   2

PUBLISHER'S NOTE
This is a work of fiction. Names, characters, places, and incidents either
are the product of the author's imagination or are used fictitiously, and any
resemblance to actual persons, living or dead, business establishments,
events, or locales is entirely coincidental.

LIBRARY OF CONGRESS CATALOGING-IN-PUBLICATION DATA
Fforde, Jasper.
Lost in a good book : a novel / Jasper Fforde.
p. cm.
ISBN 0-670-03190-9
I. Title: Lost in a good book. II. Title.
PR6106.F67 T48 2002
823'.92—dc21
2002071304

This book is printed on acid-free paper. ♾

Printed in the United States of America
Set in Berkeley Book
Designed by Francesca Belanger

## This Book

is dedicated to assistants everywhere.
*You* make it happen for them.
*They* couldn't do it without you.
*Your* contribution is everything.

# Contents

# Lost
## in a
# Good Book

"It's a grammasite," explained Miss Havisham, "a parasitic life form that lives inside books."

# 1.

## *The Adrian Lush Show*

Sample viewing figures for major TV networks in England, September 1985

NETWORKTOAD

*The Adrian Lush Show* (Wednesday) (Chat show) 16,428,316
*The Adrian Lush Show* (Monday) (Chat show) 16,034,921
*Bonzo the Wonder Hound* (Canine thriller) 15,975,462

MOLETV

*Name That Fruit!* (Answer questions for cash prizes) 15,320,340
*65 Walrus Street* (Soap opera; Episode 3,352) 14,315,902
*Dangerously Dysfunctional People Argue Live on TV* (Chat show) 11,065,611

OWLVISION

*Will Marlowe or Kit Shakespeare?* (Literary quiz show) 13,591,203
*One More Chance to See!* (Reverse extinction show) 2,321,820

GOLIATH CABLE CHANNEL (1 TO 32)

*Whose Lie Is It Anyway?* (Corporate comedy quiz show) 428
*Cots to Coffins: Goliath. All you'll ever need.* (Docuganda) 9 (disputed)

NEANDERTHAL CABLE NETWORK 4

*Powertool Club Live* (Routers and power planers edition) 9,032
*Jackanory Gold* ( *Jane Eyre* edition) 7,219

WARWICK FRIDGE,
*The Ratings War*

**I** DIDN'T ASK to be a celebrity. I never wanted to appear on
*The Adrian Lush Show.* And let's get one thing straight right
now—the world would have to be hurtling toward imminent

destruction before I'd agree to anything as dopey as *The Thursday Next Workout Video.*

The publicity surrounding the successful rebookment of Jane Eyre was fun to begin with but rapidly grew wearisome. I happily posed for photocalls, agreed to newspaper interviews, hesitantly appeared on *Desert Island Smells* and was thankfully excused the embarrassment of *Celebrity Name That Fruit.* The public, ever fascinated by celebrity, had wanted to know *everything* about me following my excursion within the pages of *Jane Eyre,* and since the Special Operations Network have a PR record on par with that of Vlad the Impaler, the Top Brass thought it would be a good wheeze to use me to boost their flagging popularity. I dutifully toured all points of the globe doing signings, library openings, talks and interviews. The same questions, the same SpecOps-approved answers. Supermarket openings, literary dinners, offers of book deals. I even met the actress Lola Vavoom, who said that she would simply *adore* to play me if there was a film. It was tiring, but more than that—*it was dull.* For the first time in my career at the Literary Detectives I actually missed authenticating Milton.

I'd taken a week's leave as soon my tour ended so Landen and I could devote some time to married life. I moved all my stuff to his house, rearranged his furniture, added my books to his and introduced my dodo, Pickwick, to his new home. Landen and I ceremoniously partitioned the bedroom closet space, decided to *share* the sock drawer, then had an argument over who was to sleep on the wall side of the bed. We had long and wonderfully pointless conversations about nothing in particular, walked Pickwick in the park, went out to dinner, stayed in for dinner, stared at each other a lot and slept in late every morning. It was *wonderful.*

On the fourth day of my leave, just between lunch with Landen's mum and Pickwick's notable first fight with the neighbor's cat, I got a call from Cordelia Flakk. She was the senior SpecOps PR agent here in Swindon and she told me that Adrian Lush wanted me on his show. I wasn't mad keen on the idea—or the show. But there was an upside. *The Adrian Lush Show* went out live, and Flakk assured me that this would be a "no holds barred" interview, something that held a great deal of appeal. Despite my many appearances, the true story about *Jane Eyre* was yet to be told—and I had been wanting to drop the Goliath Corporation in it for quite a while. Flakk's assurance that this would finally be the end of the press junket clinched my decision. Adrian Lush it would be.

I traveled up to the NetworkToad studios a few days later on my own; Landen had a deadline looming and needed to get his head down. But I wasn't alone for long. As soon as I stepped into the large entrance lobby a milk-curdling shade of green strode purposefully towards me.

"Thursday, *darling!*" cried Cordelia, beads rattling. "*So* glad you could make it!"

The SpecOps dress code stated that our apparel should be "dignified," but in Cordelia's case they had obviously stretched a point. She looked about as far from a serving officer as one could get. Looks, in her case, were highly deceptive. She was SpecOps all the way from her high heels to the pink-and-yellow scarf tied in her hair.

She air-kissed me affectionately. "How's married life treating you?"

"Very well."

"Excellent, my dear, I wish you and . . . er . . ."

"Landen?"

"Yes; I wish you and Landen both the best. *Love* what you've done with your hair!"

"My hair? I haven't done anything with my hair!"

"Exactly!" replied Flakk quickly. "It's so incredibly *you*. What do you think of the outfit?"

"One's attention is drawn straight to it," I replied ambiguously.

"This *is* 1985," she explained. "Bright colors are the future. See this top? Half price in the sales. I'll let you loose in my wardrobe one day."

"I think I've got some pink socks of my own somewhere."

She smiled.

"It's a start, my dear. Listen, you've been a shining star about all this publicity work; I'm very grateful—and so is SpecOps."

"Grateful enough to post me somewhere other than the Literary Detectives?" I asked hopefully.

"Well," murmured Cordelia reflectively, "first things first. As soon as you've done the Lush interview your transfer application will be aggressively considered, you have my word on *that*."

I sighed. "Aggressively considered" had the ring of "definitely perhaps" about it and wasn't as promising as I could have wished. Despite the successes at work, I still wanted to move up within the Network. Cordelia, reading my disappointment, took my arm in a friendly gesture and steered me towards the waiting area.

"Coffee?"

"Thanks."

"Spot of bother in Auckland?"

"Brontë Federation offshoot caused a bit of trouble," I explained. "They didn't like the new ending of *Jane Eyre*."

"There'll always be a few malcontents," observed Flakk with a smile. "Milk?"

"Just a tad."

"Oh," she said, staring at the milk jug, "this milk's off. No matter. Listen," she said quietly, "I'd love to stay and watch, but some SpecOps-17 clot in Penzance staked a Goth by mistake; it's going to be PR hell on earth down there."

SO-17 were the Vampire and Werewolf Disposal Operation. Despite a new three-point confirmation procedure, a jumpy cadet with a sharpened stake could still spell *big* trouble.

"Everything is all absolutely hunky-dory here. I've spoken to Adrian Lush and the others so there won't be any embarrassments."

"No holds barred, eh?" I grimaced, but Flakk was unapologetic.

"Needs must, Thursday. SpecOps requires your support in these difficult times. President Formby *himself* has called for an inquiry into whether SpecOps are value-for-money—or even necessary at all."

"Okay," I agreed, quite against my better judgment, "but this is the *very last interview,* yes?"

"Of course!" agreed Flakk hastily, then added in an over-dramatic manner: "Oh my goodness is that the time? I have to catch the airship to Barnstaple in an hour. This is Adie; she'll be looking after you and . . . and—" here Cordelia leaned just a little bit closer—"remember you're SpecOps, darling!"

She air-kissed me again, glanced at her watch and took to her heels in a cloud of expensive scent.

"How could I forget?" I muttered as a bouncy girl clutching a clipboard appeared from where she had been waiting respectfully out of earshot.

"Hi!" squeaked the girl. "I'm Adie. I'm *so* pleased to meet you!"

She grasped my hand and told me repeatedly what a *fantastic* honor it was.

"I don't want to bug you or anything," she asked shyly, "but was Edward Rochester *really* drop-dead-gorgeous-to-die-for?"

"Not handsome," I answered as I watched Flakk slink off down the corridor, "but certainly attractive. Tall, deep voice and glowering looks, if you know the type."

Adie turned a deep shade of pink.

"Gosh!"

I was taken into makeup, where I was puffed and primped, talked at mercilessly and made to sign copies of the *FeMole* I had appeared in. I was very relieved when Adie came to rescue me thirty minutes later. She announced into her wireless that we were "walking" and then, after leading me down a corridor and through some swing doors, asked:

"What's it like working in SpecOps? Do you chase bad guys, clamber around on the outside of airships, defuse bombs with three seconds to go, that sort of stuff?"

"I wish I did," I replied good-humoredly, "but in truth it's 70% form filling, 27% mind-numbing tedium and 2% sheer terror."

"And the remaining 1%?"

I smiled. "That's what keeps us going."

We walked the seemingly endless corridors, past large grinning photographs of Adrian Lush and assorted other Network-Toad celebrities.

"You'll like Adrian," she told me happily, "and he'll like you. Just don't try to be funnier than him; it doesn't suit the format of the show."

"What does *that* mean?"

She shrugged.

"I don't know. I'm meant to tell all his guests that."

"Even the comedians?"

"*Especially* the comedians."

I assured her being funny was furthest from my mind, and pretty soon she directed me onto the studio floor. Feeling unusually nervous and wishing that Landen was with me, I walked across the familiar front-room set of *The Adrian Lush Show.* But Mr. Lush was nowhere to be seen—and neither were the "Live Studio Audience" a Lush show usually boasted. Instead, a small group of officials were waiting—the "others" Flakk had told me about. My heart fell when I saw who they were.

"Ah, there you are, Next!" boomed Commander Braxton Hicks with forced bonhomie. "You're looking well, healthy, and, er, vigorous." He was my divisional chief back at Swindon, and despite being head of the Literary Detectives, was not that good with words.

"What are you doing here, sir?" I asked him, straining not to show my disappointment. "Cordelia told me the Lush interview would be uncensored in every way."

"Oh it *is*, dear girl—up to a point," he said, stroking his large mustache. "Without benign intervention things can get very confused in the public mind. We thought we would listen to the interview and perhaps—if the need arose—offer *practical advice* as to how the proceedings should—er—proceed."

I sighed. My untold story looked set to remain exactly that. Adrian Lush, supposed champion of free speech, the man who had dared to air the grievances felt by the neanderthal, the first to suggest publicly that the Goliath Corporation "had short-comings," was about to have his nails well and truly clipped.

"Colonel Flanker you've already met," went on Braxton without drawing breath.

I eyed the man suspiciously. I knew him well enough. He was at SpecOps-1, the division that polices SpecOps itself. He had interviewed me about the night I had first tried to tackle master criminal Acheron Hades—the night Snood and Tamworth died. He tried to smile several times but eventually gave up and offered his hand for me to shake instead.

"This is Colonel Rabone," carried on Braxton. "She is head of Combined Forces Liaison." I shook hands with the colonel.

"Always honored to meet a holder of the Crimean Cross," she said, smiling.

"And over here," continued Braxton in a jocular tone that was obviously designed to put me at ease—a ploy that failed spectacularly—"is Mr. Schitt-Hawse of the Goliath Corporation."

Schitt-Hawse was a tall, thin man whose pinched features seemed to compete for position in the center of his face. His head tilted to the left in a manner that reminded me of an inquisitive budgerigar, and his dark hair was fastidiously combed back from his forehead. He put out his hand.

"Would it upset you if I didn't shake it?" I asked him.

"Well, yes," he replied, trying to be affable.

"Good."

The Goliath Corporation's pernicious hold over the nation was not universally appreciated, and I had a far greater reason to dislike them—the last Goliath employee I had dealt with was an odious character by the name of Jack Schitt. We had tricked him into a copy of Edgar Allan Poe's "The Raven," a place in which I hoped he could do no harm.

"Schitt-Hawse, eh?" I said. "Any relation to Jack?"

"He was—is—my half brother," said Schitt-Hawse slowly, "and believe me, Ms. Next, he wasn't working for us when he planned to prolong the Crimean War in order to create demand for Goliath weaponry."

"And you never knew he had sided with Hades either, I suppose?"

"Of course not!" replied Schitt-Hawse in an offended tone.

"If you had known, would you admit it?"

Schitt-Hawse scowled and said nothing. Braxton coughed politely and continued:

"And this is Mr. Chesterman of the Brontë Federation."

Chesterman blinked at me uncertainly. The changes I had

wrought upon *Jane Eyre* had split the federation. I hoped he was one of the ones who preferred the happier ending.

"Back there is Captain Marat of the ChronoGuard," continued Braxton. Marat, at this moment in *his* time, was a schoolboy of about twelve. He looked at me with interest. The ChronoGuard were the SpecOps division that took care of Anomalous Time Ripplation—my father *had been* one or *was* one or *would* be one, depending on how you looked at it.

"Have we met before?" I asked him.

"Not yet," he replied cheerfully, returning to his copy of *The Beano.*

"Well!" said Braxton, clapping his hands together. "I think that's everyone. Next, I want you to pretend *we're just not here.*"

"*Observers,* yes?"

"Absolutely. I—"

Braxton was interrupted by a slight disturbance offstage.

"The *bastards!*" yelled a high voice. "If the network dares to replace my Monday slot with reruns of *Bonzo the Wonder Hound* I'll sue them for every penny they have!"

A tall man of perhaps fifty-five had walked into the studio accompanied by a small group of assistants. He had handsome chiseled features and a luxuriant swirl of white hair that looked as though it had been carved from polystyrene. He wore an immaculately tailored suit and his fingers were heavily weighed down with gold jewelry. He stopped short when he saw us.

"Ah!" said Adrian Lush disdainfully. "SpecOps!"

His entourage flustered around him with lots of energy but very little purpose. They seemed to hang on his every word and action, and I suddenly felt a great sense of relief that I wasn't in the entertainments business.

"I've had a lot to do with you people in the past," explained Lush as he made himself comfortable on his trademark green sofa, something he clearly regarded as a territorial safe retreat. "It was I that coined the phrase 'SpecOops' whenever you make a mistake—sorry, 'Operational unexpectation'—isn't that what you like to call them?"

But Hicks ignored Lush's inquiries and introduced me as though I were his only daughter being offered up for marriage.

"Mr. Lush, this is Special Operative Thursday Next."

Lush jumped up and bounded over to shake me by the hand in an effusive and energetic manner. Flanker and the others sat down; they looked very small in the middle of the empty studio. They weren't going to leave and Lush wasn't going to ask them to—I knew that Goliath owned NetworkToad and was beginning to doubt whether Lush had any control over this interview at all.

"Hello, Thursday!" said Lush excitedly. "Welcome to my Monday show. It's the second-highest-rated show in England— my Wednesday show is the first!"

He laughed infectiously and I smiled uneasily.

"Then this will be your *Thursday* show," I replied, eager to lighten the situation.

There was dead silence.

"Will you be doing that a lot?" asked Lush in a subdued tone.

"Doing what?"

"Making jokes. You see . . . have a seat, darling. You see, I *generally* make the jokes on this show and although it's *perfectly* okay for you to make jokes, then I'm going to have to pay someone to write funnier ones, and our budget, like Goliath's scruples, is on the small side of Leptonic."

"Can I say something?" said a voice from the small audience. It was Flanker, who carried on talking without waiting for a reply. "SpecOps is a serious business and should be reflected so in your interview. Next, I think you should let Mr. Lush tell the jokes."

"Is that all right?" asked Lush, beaming.

"Sure," I replied. "Is there anything else I shouldn't do?"

Lush looked at me and then looked at the panel in the front row.

"Is there?"

They all mumbled among themselves for a few seconds.

"I think," said Flanker again, "that we—sorry, *you*—should just do the interview and then we can discuss it later. Miss Next can say whatever she wants as long as it doesn't contravene any SpecOps or Goliath Corporate guidelines."

"—or military," added Colonel Rabone, anxious not to be left out.

"Is that okay?" asked Lush.

"Whatever," I returned, eager to get on with it.

"Excellent! I'll do your intro, although you'll be off camera for that. The floor manager will cue you and you'll enter. Wave to where the audience might have been and when you are comfy, I'll ask you some questions. I may offer you some toast at some point as our sponsors, the Toast Marketing Board, like to get a plug in now and again. Is there any part of that you don't understand?"

"No."

"Good. Here we go."

There was a flurry of activity as Lush had his hair adjusted, his makeup checked and his costume tweaked. After a cursory glance at me I was ushered offstage and after what seemed like an epoch of inaction, Lush was counted in by a floor manager. On cue he turned to camera one and switched on his best and brightest smile.

"Tonight is a very special occasion with a very special guest.

She is a decorated war heroine, a literary detective whose personal intervention not only restored the novel of *Jane Eyre* but actually improved the ending. She single-handedly defeated Acheron Hades, ended the Crimean War and boldly hoodwinked the Goliath Corporation. Ladies and gentlemen, in an unprecedented interview from a serving SpecOps officer, please give a warm welcome to Thursday Next of the Swindon Literary Detective office!"

A bright light swung onto my entrance doorway, and Adie smiled and tapped my arm. I walked out to meet Lush, who rose to greet me enthusiastically.

"Excuse me," came a voice from the small group sitting in the front row of the empty auditorium. It was Schitt-Hawse, the Goliath representative.

"Yes?" asked Lush in an icy tone.

"You're going to have to drop the reference to the Goliath Corporation," said Schitt-Hawse in the sort of tone that brooks no argument. "It serves no purpose other than to needlessly embarrass a large company that is doing its very best to improve everyone's lives."

"I agree," said Flanker. "And all references to Hades will have to be avoided. He is still listed as 'Missing, fervently hoped dead,' so any unauthorized speculation might have dangerous consequences."

"Okay," murmured Lush, scribbling a note. "Anything else?"

"Any reference to the Crimean War and the Plasma Rifle," said the colonel, "might be considered *inappropriate*. The peace talks at Budapest are still at a delicate stage; the Russians will make any excuse to leave the table. We know that your show is very popular in Moscow."

"The Brontë Federation is not keen for you to say the new ending is *improved*," put in the small and bespectacled Chesterman, "and talking about any of the characters you met within *Jane Eyre* might cause some viewers to suffer Xplkqul-kiccasia."

The condition was unknown before my jump into *Eyre*. It was so serious that the Medical Council were compelled to make up an *especially* unpronounceable word to describe it.

Lush looked at them, looked at me and then looked at his script.

"How about if I just said her name?"

"That would be admirable," intoned Flanker, "except you might also want to assure the viewers that this interview is uncensored. Everyone else agree?"

They all enthusiastically added their assent to Flanker's suggestion. I could see this was going to be a very long and tedious afternoon.

Lush's entourage came back on and made the tiniest adjustments, I was repositioned, and after waiting what seemed like another decade, Lush began again.

"Ladies and gentlemen, in a frank and open interview tonight, Thursday Next talks unhindered about her work at SpecOps."

No one said anything, so I entered, shook Lush's hand and took a seat on his sofa.

"Welcome to the show, Thursday."

"Thank you."

"We'll get on to your career in the Crimea in a moment, but I'd like to kick off by asking—"

With a magician's flourish he pulled a serviette off the table in front of us, revealing a platter of toast with assorted toppings.

"—if you would care for some toast?"

"No, thanks."

"Tasty and nutritious!" He smiled, facing the camera.

"Perfect as a snack or even a light meal—good with eggs, sardines or even—"

"No, thank you."

Lush's smile froze on his face as he muttered through clenched teeth:

"Have . . . some . . . toast."

But it was too late. The floor manager came on the set and announced that the unseen director of the show had called *cut*. Lush's face dropped its permanent smile and his small army of beauticians came on and fussed over him once more. The floor manager had a one-way conversation into his headphones before turning to me with a concerned expression on his face.

"The Director of Placements wants to know if you would take a small bite of toast when offered."

"I've eaten already."

The floor manager turned and spoke into his headphones again.

*"She says she's eaten already!* . . . I know. . . . Yes. . . . What if . . . Yes. . . . Ah-ha. . . . *What do you want me to do? Sit on her and force it down her throat!?!* . . . Yesss. . . . Ah-ha. . . . I know. . . . Yes. . . . Yes. . . . Okay."

He turned back to me.

"How about jam instead of marmalade?"

"I don't *really* like toast," I told him—which was partly true, although to be honest I think I was just feeling a bit troublesome because of Braxton and his entourage.

"What?"

"I said I don't—"

"She says she doesn't like toast!" said the floor manager in an exasperated tone. *"What in hell's name are we going to do!?!"*

Flanker stood up.

"Next, eat the sodding toast will you? I've got a meeting in two hours."

*14*

"And I've a golf tournament," added Braxton.

I sighed. I thought perhaps I had a small amount of control on the show, but even that had vanished.

"Does marmalade fit in with your plans, sir?" I asked Braxton, who grunted in the affirmative and sat down again.

"Okay. Make it granary with marmalade, go easy on the butter."

The floor manager smiled as though I had just saved his job—which I probably had—and everything started over once again.

"Would you like some toast?" asked Lush.

"Thanks."

I took a small bite. Everyone was watching me, so I decided to make it easy for them.

"Very good indeed."

I saw the floor manager giving me an enthusiastic thumbs-up as he dabbed his brow with a handkerchief.

"Right," sighed Lush. "Let's get on with it. First I would like to ask the question that everyone wants to know: How did you actually get into the book of *Jane Eyre* in the first place?"

"That's easily explained," I began. "You see, my uncle Mycroft invented a device called a Prose Portal—"

Flanker coughed. I could sense what he was going to say and I cursed myself for being so foolish as to believe *The Adrian Lush Show* would be uncensored. I *was* SpecOps, after all.

"Ms. Next," began Flanker, "perhaps you don't know it but your uncle is still the subject of a secrecy certificate dating back to 1934. It might be prudent if you didn't mention him—or the Prose Portal."

The floor manager yelled, "We've cut!" again and Lush thought for a moment.

"Can we talk about how Hades stole the manuscript of *Martin Chuzzlewit*?"

"Let me think," replied Flanker, then after a tiny pause, said: "No."

"It's not something we want the citizenry to think is—" said Marat so suddenly that quite a few people jumped. Up until that moment he hadn't said a word.

"Sorry?" asked Flanker.

"Nothing," said the ChronoGuard operative, who was now in his mid-sixties. "I'm just getting a touch proleptic in my old age."

"Can we talk about the successful return of Jane to her book?" I asked wearily.

"I refer you to my previous answer," growled Flanker.

"How about the time my partner Bowden and I drove through a patch of bad time on the motorway?"

"It's not something we want the citizenry to think is easy," said Marat—who was now in his early twenties—with renewed enthusiasm. "If the public think that ChronoGuard work is straightforward, confidence might well be shaken."

"Quite correct," asserted Flanker.

"Perhaps you'd like to do this interview?" I asked him.

"Hey!" said Flanker, standing up and jabbing a finger in my direction. "There's no need to get snippy with us, Next. You're here to do a job in your capacity as a serving SpecOps officer. You are *not* here to tell the truth as you see it!"

Lush looked uneasily at me; I raised my eyebrows and shrugged.

"Now look here," said Lush in a strident tone, "if I'm going to interview Ms. Next I must ask questions that the public want to hear!"

"Oh, you can!" said Flanker agreeably. "You can ask whatever you want. Free speech is enshrined in statute, and neither SpecOps nor Goliath have any business to coerce you in any way. We are just here to observe, comment, and *enlighten.*"

Lush knew what Flanker meant and Flanker knew that Lush knew. I knew that Flanker and Lush knew it and they both knew I knew it too. Lush looked nervous and fidgeted slightly. Flanker's assertion of Lush's independence was anything but. A word To NetworkToad from Goliath and Lush would end up presenting *SheepWorld* on Lerwick TV, and he didn't want that. Not one little bit.

We fell silent for a moment as Lush and I tried to figure out a topic that *was* outside their broad parameters.

"How about commenting on the ludicrously high tax on cheese?" I asked. It was a joke, but Flanker and Co. weren't terribly expert when it came to jokes.

"I have no objection," murmured Flanker. "Anyone else?"

"Not me," said Schitt-Hawse.

"Or me," added Rabone.

"*I* have an objection," said a woman who had been sitting quietly at the side of the studio. She spoke with a clipped home counties accent and was dressed in a tweed skirt, twinset and pearls.

"Allow me to introduce myself," she said in a loud and strident voice. "Mrs. Jolly Hilly, Governmental Representative to the Television Networks." She took a deep breath and carried on: "The so-called 'unfair cheese duty burden' is a very contentious subject at present. Any reference to it might be construed as an inflammatory act."

"587% duty on hard cheeses and 620% on smelly?" I asked. "Cheddar Classic Gold Original at £9.32 a pound—Bodmin Molecular Unstable Brie at almost £10! What's going on?"

The others, suddenly interested, all looked to Mrs. Hilly for an explanation. For a brief moment and probably the only moment ever, we were in agreement.

"I understand your concern," replied the trained apologist, "but I think you'll find that the price of cheese has, once adjusted for positive spin, actually gone *down* measured against the retail price index in recent years. Here, have a look at this."

She passed me a picture of a sweet little old lady on crutches.

"Old ladies who are not dissimilar to the actress in this picture will have to go without their hip replacements and suffer crippling pain if you selfishly demand cut-price cheese."

She paused to let this sink in.

"The Master of the Sums feels that it is not for the public to dictate economic policy, but he is willing to make concessions for those who suffer particular hardship in the form of area-tactical needs-related cheese coupons."

"So," said Lush with a smile, "*wheyving* cheese tax is out of the question?"

"Or he could raise the custard duty," added Mrs. Hilly, missing the pun. "The pudding lobby is less—well—how should I put it—*militant*."

"*Wheyving*," said Lush again, for the benefit of anyone who had missed it. "*Wheyve*—oh, never mind. I've never heard a bigger load of crap in all my life. I aim to make the ludicrous price of cheese the subject of an Adrian Lush Special Report."

Mrs. Hilly flushed slightly and chose her words carefully.

"If there were another cheese riot following your Special Report we might look very carefully as to where to place responsibility."

She looked at the Goliath representative as she said this. The implication wasn't lost on Schitt-Hawse or Lush. I had heard enough.

"So I won't talk about cheese either," I sighed. "What *can* I talk about?"

The small group all looked at one another with perplexed expressions. Flanker clicked his fingers as an idea struck him.

"Don't you own a dodo?"

# 2.

## The Special Operations Network

The Special Operations Network was initiated to handle policing duties considered either too unusual or too specialized to be tackled by the regular force. There were thirty-two departments in all, starting at the more mundane Horticultural Enforcement Agency (SO-32) and going on to Literary Detectives (SO-27) and Transport Authority (SO-21). Anything below SO-20 was restricted information, although it was common knowledge that the Chrono-Guard were SO-12 and SO-1 were the department that polices the SpecOps themselves. Quite what the others do is anyone's guess. What *is* known is that the individual operatives themselves are mostly ex-military or ex-police. Operatives rarely leave the service after the probationary period has ended. There is a saying: "A SpecOps job isn't for probation—it's for life."

MILLON DE FLOSS,
*A Short History of the Special Operations Network* (revised)

**I**t was the morning after the transmission of *The Adrian Lush Show*. I had watched for five minutes, cringed, then fled upstairs to rearrange our sock drawer. I managed to file all the socks by color, shape and how much I liked them before Landen told me it was all over and I could come back downstairs. It was the last public interview I'd agreed to give, but Cordelia didn't seem to remember this part of our conversation. She had continued to besiege me with requests to speak at literary festivals, appear as a guest on *65 Walrus Street* and even attend one of President Formby's informal song-and-ukulele evenings. Job offers arrived daily. Numerous libraries and private security firms asked for my services as either "Active Associate" or "Security Consultant." The sweetest letter I got was from the local library asking me to come in and read to the elderly—something I delighted in doing. But SpecOps itself, the body to which I had committed much of my adult life, energy and resources, hadn't even *spoken* to me about advancement. As far as they were concerned I was SO-27 and would remain so until they decided otherwise.

"Mail for you!" announced Landen, dumping a large pile of post onto the kitchen table. Most of my mail these days was fan mail—and pretty strange it was, too. I opened an envelope at random.

"Anyone I should be jealous of?" he asked.

"I should keep the divorce lawyer on hold for a few more minutes—it's another request for underwear."

"I'll send him a pair of mine," grinned Landen.

"What's in the parcel?"

"Late wedding present. It's a—"

He looked at the strange knitted object curiously.

"It's a . . . *thing.*"

"Good," I replied, "I always wanted one of those. What are you doing?"

"I'm trying to teach Pickwick to stand on one leg."

"Dodos don't do tricks," I told him.

"For a marshmallow I think I can make him do anything. Up, Pickwick, come on, one leg, up!"

Landen was a writer. We first met when he, my brother Anton and I fought in the Crimea. Landen came home minus a leg but alive—my brother was still out there, making his way through eternity from the comfort of a military cemetery near Sevastopol. I opened another letter and read aloud:

"Dear Miss Next, I am one of your biggest fans. I thought you should know that I believe David Copperfield, far from being the doe-eyed innocent, actually murdered his first wife, Dora Spenlow, in order to marry Agnes Wickfield. I suggest an exhumation of Miss Spenlow's remains and a test for botulism and/or arsenic. While we are on the subject, have you ever stopped to wonder why Homer changed his mind about dogs somewhere between the Iliad and the Odyssey? Was he, perhaps, given a puppy between the two? Another thing: Do you find Joyce's Ulysses as boring and as unintelligible as I do? And why don't Hemingway's works have any smells in them?"

"Seems everyone wants you to investigate their favorite book," observed Landen, sliding his arms around my neck and looking over my shoulder so closely our cheeks touched and I shivered. He put his mouth close to my ear and whispered:

"While you're about it can you try and get Tess acquitted and Max de Winter convicted?"

"Not you as well!"

I took the marshmallow from his hand and ate it, much to Pickwick's shock and dismay. Landen took another marshmallow from the jar and tried again.

"Up, Pickwick, come on, *up, up,* one leg!"

Pickwick stared at Landen blankly, eyes fixed on the marshmallow and not at all interested in learning tricks.

"You'll need a truckload of them, Land."

I refolded the letter, finished my coffee, got up and put on my jacket.

"Have a good day," said Landen, seeing me to the door. "Be nice to the other children. No scratching or biting."

"I'll behave myself. I promise."

I wrapped my arms round his neck and kissed him.

"Mmm," I whispered softly. "That was nice."

"I've been practicing," he told me, "on that pretty young thing at number 56. You don't mind, do you?"

"Not at all," I replied, kissing him again, "so long as you want to keep your other leg."

"O-kay. I think I'll stick to you for practice from now on."

"I'm depending on it. Oh, and Land?"

"Yuh?"

"Don't forget it's Mycroft's retirement party this evening."

"I won't."

We bade each other goodbye and I walked down the garden path, shouting a greeting to Mrs. Arturo, who had been watching us.

It was late autumn or early winter—I wasn't sure which. It had been mild and windless; the leaves were still brown on the trees and on some days it was hardly cold at all. It had to *really* get chilly to put the top up on my Speedster, so I drove into the SpecOps divisional HQ with the wind in my hair and WESSEX-FM blaring on the wireless. The upcoming election was the talk of the airwaves; the controversial cheese duty had suddenly become an issue in the way things do just before an election. There was a snippet about Goliath declaring themselves to be "the world's favorite conglomerate" for the tenth year running whilst in the Crimean peace talks Russia had demanded Kent County as war reparations. In sport, Aubrey Jambe had led the Swindon Mallets croquet team into SuperHoop '85 by thrashing the Reading Whackers.

I drove through the morning traffic in Swindon and parked the Speedster at the rear of the SpecOps HQ. The building was of a brusque no-nonsense Germanic design; hastily erected during the occupation, the facade still bore battle scars from Swindon's liberation in 1949. It housed most of the SpecOps divisions but not all. Our Vampire and Werewolf Disposal Operation also encompassed Reading and Salisbury, and in return

Salisbury's Art Theft division looked after our area as well. It all seemed to work quite well.

"Hullo!" I said to a young man who was taking a cardboard box out of the boot of his car. "New SpecOps?"

"Er, yes," he replied, putting down his box for a moment to offer me his hand.

"John Smith—Weeds & Seeds."

"Unusual name," I said, shaking his hand, "I'm Thursday Next."

"Oh!" he said, looking at me with interest. Sadly my anonymity had, it seemed, departed for good.

"Yes," I replied, picking up several large box files for him, "*that* Thursday Next. Weeds & Seeds?"

"Domestic Horticulture Enforcement Agency," explained John as we walked towards the SpecOps building. "SO-32. I'm starting an office here. There's been a rise in the number of hackers just recently. The Pampas Grass Vigilante Squad are becoming more brazen in their activities; pampas grass might well be an eyesore, but there's nothing illegal in it."

We showed our ID cards to the desk sergeant and walked up the stairs to the second floor.

"I heard something about that," I murmured. "Any links to the Anti-Leylandii Association?"

"Nothing positive," replied Smith, "but I'm following all leads."

"How many in your squad?"

"Including me, one," grinned Smith. "Thought you were the most underfunded department in SpecOps? Think again. I've got six months to sort out the hackers, get the Japanese knotweed under control and find an acceptable plural form of *narcissus.*"

We reached the upstairs corridor and a small office that had once been home to SO-31, the Good Taste Education

Authority. The division had been disbanded a month ago when the proposed legislation against stone cladding, pictures of crying clowns, and floral-patterned carpets failed in the upper house. I placed the box files on the table, told him *narcissi* was my favorite, wished him well and left him to unpack.

I was just walking past the office of SO-14 when I heard a shrill voice.

"Thursday! Thursday, yoo-hoo! Over here!"

I sighed. It was Cordelia Flakk. She quickly caught up with me and gave me an affectionate hug.

"The Lush show was a disaster!" I told her. "You said it was no-holds-barred! I ended up talking about dodos, my car and anything but *Jane Eyre*!"

"You were *terrific!*" she enthused. "I've got you lined up for another set of interviews the day after tomorrow."

"No more, Cordelia."

She looked crestfallen.

"I don't understand."

"What part of *no more* don't you understand?"

"Don't be like that, Thursday," she replied, smiling broadly. "You're good PR, and believe me, in an institution that routinely leaves the public perforated, confused, old before their time or, if they're lucky, dead, we need every bit of good PR we can muster."

"Do we do *that* much damage to the public?" I asked.

Flakk smiled modestly.

"Perhaps my PR is not so bad after all," she conceded, then added quickly: "But every Joe that gets trounced in a crossfire is one too many."

"That's as may be," I retorted, "but the fact remains you told me the Lush show would be the last."

"Ah! But I *also* told you the Lush show would be no-holds-barred, didn't I?" observed Cordelia brightly, displaying staggering reverse logic.

"However you want to spin it, Cordelia, the answer is still *no*."

As I watched with a certain detached amusement, Flakk went through a bizarre routine that included hopping up and down for a bit, pulling pleading expressions, wringing her hands, puffing out her cheeks and staring at the ceiling.

"Okay," I sighed, "you've got my attention. What do you want me to do?"

"Well," said Cordelia excitedly, "we ran a competition!"

"Oh yes?" I asked suspiciously, wondering whether it could be any more daft than her "win a mammoth" idea the week before. "What sort of competition?"

"Well, we thought it would be a good idea if you met a few members of the public on a one-to-one basis."

"Did we? Now listen, Cordelia—"

"Dilly, Thursday, since we're pals."

She sensed my reticence and added:

"Cords, then. Or Delia. How about Flakky? I used to be called Flik-flak at school. Can I call you Thurs?"

"*Cordelia!*" I said in a harsher tone, before she ingratiated herself to death. "*I'm not going to do this!* You said the Lush interview would be the last, and it is."

I started to walk away, but when God was handing out insistence, Cordelia Flakk was right at the front of the queue.

"Thursday, this hurts me *really* personally when you're like this. It attacks me right—right—er—here."

She made a wild guess at where her heart might be and looked at me with a pained expression that she probably learnt off a springer spaniel.

"I've got them waiting right here, *now*, in the canteen. It won't take a moment, ten minutes *tops*. Pleasepleasepleasepleaseplease. I've only asked two dozen journalists and news crews—the room will be practically empty."

I looked at my watch.

"Ten minutes,[1] whoa!—Who's that?"

"Who's what?"

"Someone calling my name. Didn't you hear it?"

"No," replied Cordelia, looking at me oddly.

I tapped my ears and looked around to see if there was anyone close by. Apart from Cordelia, we were alone in the corridor. It had sounded so real it was disconcerting.[2]

"There it goes again!"

"There goes what again?"

"A man's voice! Speaking *here* inside my head!"

I pointed to my temple to demonstrate. Cordelia took a step backwards, her look turning to one of consternation.

"Are you okay, Thursday? Can I call someone?"

"Oh. No no, I'm fine. I just realized I—ah—left a receiver in my ear. It must be my partner; there's a 12-14 or a 10-30 or . . . *something* numerological in progress. Tell your competition winners another time. Goodbye!"

I dashed off down the corridor toward the Literary Detectives offices. There wasn't a receiver, of course, but I wasn't having Flakk tell the quacks I was hearing voices.[3] I stopped and looked around. The corridor was empty.

"I can *hear* you," I said, "but where are you?"[4]

"Her name's Flakk. Works over at SpecOps PR."[5]

"What is this? SpecOps Blind Date? *What's going on?*"[6]

1. "Thursday Next!"
2. "Miss Next—hello? Testing testing. One, two, three."
3. "If you're busy, Ms. Next, we can talk later."
4. "The name is Snell, Akrid Snell. Who was that disturbingly attractive woman in the tight pink—"
5. "Really? Is she married?"
6. "Sorry. Should have said. I'm the defense attorney assigned to your case."

"Case? What case? I haven't done anything!"[7]

My indignation was real. For someone who had spent her life enforcing law and order, it seemed a grave injustice that I should be accused of something—especially something I knew nothing about.

"For God's sake, Snell, what *is* the charge?"

"Are you okay, Next?"

It was Commander Braxton Hicks. He had just turned the corner and was staring at me with curiosity.

"Nothing, sir," I said, thinking fast. "The SpecOps tensionologist said I should vocalize any stress regarding past experiences. Listen: *'Get away from me, Hades, go!'* See? I feel better already."

"Oh!" said Hicks doubtfully. "Well, the quacks know best, I suppose. That Lush fellow's interview was a cracker, don't you think?"

Thankfully he didn't give me time to answer and carried on talking.

"Listen here, Next, did you sign that picture for my godson Max?"

"On your desk, sir."

"Really? Jolly good. What else? Oh yes. That PR girlie—"

"Miss Flakk?"

"That's the chap. She ran a competition or something. Would you liaise with her over it?"

"I'll make it my top priority, sir."

"Good. Well, carry on vocalizing then."

"Thank you, sir."

But he didn't leave. He just stood there, watching me.

"Sir?"

---

7. "Of course not! That's our defense strategy in a nutshell. You are *completely* innocent. If we can convince the examining magistrate we can probably get a postponement."

"Don't mind me," replied Hicks, "I just want to see how this stress vocalizing works. My tensionologist told me to arrange pebbles as a hobby—or count blue cars."

So I vocalized my stress there in the corridor for five minutes, reciting every Shakespearean insult I could think of while my boss watched me. I felt a complete twit but rather that than the quacks, I suppose.

"Jolly good," he said finally and walked off.

After checking I was alone in the corridor I spoke out loud: *"Snell!"*

Silence.

"Mr. Snell, can you hear me?"

More silence.

I sat down on a convenient bench and put my head between my knees. I felt sick and hot; both the SpecOps resident tensionologist and stresspert had said I might have some sort of traumatic aftershock from tackling Acheron Hades, but I hadn't expected anything so vivid as voices in my head. I waited until my head cleared and then made my way not towards Flakk and her competition winners but towards Bowden and the LiteraTec's office.[8]

I stopped.

"Prepared for what? I haven't done anything!"[9]

"No, no!" I exclaimed. "I *really* don't know what I've done. *Where are you!?!*"[10]

---

8. "Miss Next, I'm *so* sorry, I had to take a call. Portia again; she wanted to discuss the timing of her 'drop of blood' defense. Bit of a feisty one, that. Your hearing is next Thursday—so be prepared!"

9. "That's good, Thursday. Can I call you Thursday? Keep up that sort of wide-eyed innocent babe-in-the-woods stuff and we'll have you off the hook quicker than you can say verruca."

10. "I'll explain it all when we meet. Sorry to have to communicate with you in footnotes but I'm due in court in ten minutes. Don't speak *to anyone at all* about the case and I'll see you on Thursday, Thursday. That's

"Wait! Shouldn't I see you *before* the hearing?"

There was no answer. I was about to yell again, but several people came out of the elevator, so I kept quiet. I waited for a moment but Mr. Snell didn't seem to have anything more to add, so I made my way into the LiteraTec office, which closely resembled a large library in a country home somewhere. There weren't many books we *didn't* have—the result of bootleg seizures of literary works collected over the years. My partner, Bowden Cable, was already at his desk, which was as fastidiously neat as ever. He was dressed conservatively and was a few years younger than me although he had been in SpecOps a lot longer. Officially he was a higher rank, but we never let it get in the way—we worked as equals but in different ways: Bowden's quiet and studious approach contrasted strongly with my own directness. It seemed to work well.

"Morning, Bowden."

"Hello Thursday. Saw you on the telly last night."

I took off my coat, sat down and started to rummage through telephone messages.

"How did I look?"

"Fine. They didn't let you talk about *Jane Eyre* much, did they?"

"Press freedom was on holiday that day."

He understood and smiled softly.

"Never fear—someday the full story will be told. Are you okay? You look a little flushed."

"I'm okay," I told him, giving up on the telephone messages. "Actually, I'm not. I've been hearing voices."

"Stress, Thursday. It's not unusual. Anyone specific?"

---

quite funny, that. 'Thursday . . . Thursday.' Hmm. Maybe not. Got to go. Remember: Speak to *no one* about the case, and if you have a moment, see if you can find out anything about that Flakk girl's domestic arrangements. Well, chin-chin and toodle-pip."

I got up to fetch some coffee, and Bowden followed me.

"A lawyer named Akrid Snell. Said he was representing me. Refill?"

"No, thanks. On what charge?"

"He wouldn't say."

I poured myself a large coffee as Bowden thought for a moment.

"Sounds like an inner guilt conflict, Thursday. In policing we have to sometimes—"

He stopped as two other LiteraTec agents walked close by, discussing the merits of a recently discovered seventy-eight-word palindrome *that made sense*. We waited until they were out of earshot before continuing:

"—we have to sometimes close off our emotions. Could you have killed Hades if you were thinking clearly?"

"I don't think I would have been able to kill him if I *wasn't*," I replied, sniffing at the milk. "I've not lost a single night's sleep over Hades, but poor Bertha Rochester bothers me a bit."

We went and sat down at our desks.

"Maybe that's it," replied Bowden, idly filling in the *Owl* crossword. "Perhaps you secretly *want* to be held accountable for her death. I heard Crometty talking to me for weeks after his murder—I thought I should have been there to back him up—but I wasn't."

"How are you getting along with the crossword?"

He passed it over and I scanned the answers.

"What's a 'RILK'?" I asked him.

"It's a—"

"Ah, there you are!" said a booming voice. We turned to see Victor Analogy striding across from his office. Head of the Swindon LiteraTecs since who knows when, he was a sprightly seventy-something with a receding hairline and a figure that *guaranteed* the part of Santa Claus at the SpecOps Christmas party. Despite his jocular nature he could be as hard as nails on occasion and was a good buffer between SO-27 and Braxton Hicks, who was strictly a company man. Analogy guarded our independence closely and regarded all his staff as family, and we thought the world of him. We all said our good mornings and Victor sat on my desk.

"How's the PR stuff going, Thursday?"

"More tedious than Spenser, sir."

"That bad, eh? Saw you on the telly last night. Rigged, was it?"

"Just a little."

"I hate to be a bore, but it's all important stuff. Have a look at this fax."

He handed me a sheet of paper, and Bowden read over my shoulder.

"Ludicrous," I said, handing the fax back. "What possible benefit could the Toast Marketing Board get from sponsoring us?"

Victor shrugged.

"Not a clue. But if they have cash to give away we could certainly do with some of it."

"What are you going to do?"

"Braxton's speaking to them this afternoon. He's very big on the idea."

"I bet he is."

Braxton Hicks's life revolved around his precious SpecOps budget. If any of us even *thought* of doing any sort of overtime, you could bet that Braxton would have something to say about it—and something in his case meant "no." Rumor had it that he had spoken to the canteen about giving out smaller helpings for dinner. He had been known as "Small Portions" in the office ever since—but never to his face.

"Did you find out who's been forging and trying to sell the missing ending to Byron's *Don Juan*?" asked Victor.

Bowden showed him a black-and-white photo of a dashing figure climbing into a parked car somewhere near the airship field. He was extravagantly dressed according to "the Byron Look"—it was quite popular, even amongst non-Byrons.

"Our prime suspect is a fellow named Byron$_2$."

Victor looked at the picture carefully, first through his spectacles, then over the top of them.

"Byron number two, eh? How many Byrons are there now?"

"Byron$_{2620}$ was registered last week," I told him. "We've been following Byron$_2$ for a month, but he's smart. None of the forged scraps of *Heaven and Earth* can be traced back to him."

"Wiretap?"

"We tried, but the judge said that even though Byron$_2$'s surgery to *make* his foot clubbed in an attempt to emulate his hero was undeniably strange, and then getting his half sister pregnant was plainly disgusting, those acts only showed a fevered Byronic mind, and not *necessarily* one of intent to forge. We have to catch him inky-fingered, but at the moment he's off on a tour of the Mediterranean. We're going to attempt to get a search warrant while he's away."

"So you're not that busy, then?"

"What had you in mind?"

"Well," began Victor, "it seems there have been a couple more attempts to forge *Cardenio*. I know it's small beer for you two but it helps Braxton with his damnable statistics. Would you go and have a look?"

"Sure," replied Bowden, knowing full well I would concur. "Got the addresses?"

He handed over a sheet of paper and bade us luck. We rose to leave, Bowden studying the list carefully.

"We'll go to Roseberry Street first," he muttered. "It's closer."

# 3.

## *Cardenio* Unbound

*Cardenio* was performed at court in 1613. It was entered in the stationer's register in 1653 as "by Mr. Fletcher and Shakespeare" and in 1728 Theobald Lewis published his play *Double Falsehood*, which he claimed to have written using an old prompt copy of *Cardenio*. Given the uneven Shakespearean value of his play and his refusal to produce the original manuscript, this claim seems doubtful. Cardenio was the name of the Ragged Knight in Cervantes' *Don Quixote* who falls in love with Lucinda, and it is assumed Shakespeare's play followed the same story. But we will never know. Not one single scrap of the play has survived.

MILLON DE FLOSS,
*"Cardenio": Easy Come, Easy Go*

A FEW MINUTES LATER we were turning into a street of terraced houses close by the new thirty-thousand-seat croquet stadium. *Cardenio* scams were the three-card trick of the literary world; the bread and butter for literary lowlife. Since there were only five signatures, three pages of revisions to *Sir Thomas More* and a fragment of *King Lear,* anything that might conceivably have been near Shakespeare in his lifetime had big money attached to it. The rediscovery of *Cardenio* was the Holy Grail of the small-time antiquarians, the greatest lottery win there might ever be.

We rang on the doorbell of number 216. After a few moments a large middle-aged woman of ruddy complexion opened the door. Her hair looked newly coiffured and she was dressed in a lurid Prospero-patterned dress that might have been *her* Sunday best, but not anyone else's.

"Mrs. Hathaway$_{34}$?"

"Yes?"

We held up our badges.

"Cable and Next, Swindon Literary Detectives. You called the office this morning?"

Mrs. Hathaway$_{34}$ beamed and ushered us in enthusiastically. As we stepped in we noticed that on every available wall space were hung pictures of Shakespeare, framed playbills, engravings and commemorative plates. The bookshelves were packed with numerous Shakespeare studies and volumes, the coffee table was carefully arrayed with rare back issues of the Shakespeare Federation's weekly magazine, *We Love Willy,* and in the corner of the room was a beautifully restored Will-Speak machine from the thirties. It was clear she was a serious fan. Not quite rabid enough to speak only in lines from the plays, but close enough.

"Would you like a cup of tea?" asked Hathaway$_{34}$, proudly putting on an ancient 78 of Sir Henry Irving playing *Hamlet* that was so bad it sounded as if he had recited it with a sock in his mouth.

"No, thank you, ma'am. You said you had a copy of *Cardenio*?"

"Of course!" she enthused, then added with a wink: "Will's lost play popping up like a jack-in-a-box must come as quite a surprise to you, I imagine?"

I didn't tell her that a *Cardenio* scam was almost a weekly event.

"We spend our days surprised, Mrs. Hathaway$_{34}$."

"Call me Anne$_{34}$!" she said as she opened a desk and gently withdrew a book wrapped in pink tissue paper. She placed it in front of us with great reverence.

"I bought it in a garage sale last week," she confided. "I don't think the owner knew that he had a copy of a long-lost Shakespeare play in amongst unread Daphne Farquitt novels and back issues of *Vintage Toaster Monthly*."

She leaned forward.

"I bought it for a song, you know."

And she giggled.

"I think this is the most important find since the *King Lear* fragment," she went on happily, clasping her hands to her bosom and staring adoringly at the engraving of the Bard above the mantelpiece. "*That* fragment was in Will's hand and covers only two lines of dialogue between Lear and Cordelia. It sold at auction for one point eight million! Just think how much *Cardenio* would be worth!"

"A genuine *Cardenio* would be almost priceless, ma'am," said Bowden politely, emphasizing the "genuine."

I closed the cover. I had read enough.

"I'm sorry to disappoint you, Mrs. Hathaway$_{34}$—"

"Anne$_{34}$. Call me Anne$_{34}$."

"—Anne$_{34}$. I'm afraid to say I believe this to be a forgery."

She didn't seem very put out.

"Are you sure, my dear? You didn't read very much of it."

"I'm afraid so. The rhyme, meter and grammar don't really match any of Shakespeare's known works."

There was silence for a moment as Hathaway$_{34}$ digested my words, frowned to herself and bit her lip. I could almost see common sense and denial fighting away at each other within her. In the end, denial won, as it so often does, and she retorted belligerently:

"Will was adaptable to the nth degree, Miss Next—I hardly think that any *slight* deviation from the norm is of any great relevance!"

"You misunderstand me," I replied, trying to be as tactful as possible. "It's not even a *good* forgery."

"Well!" said Anne, putting on an air of aggrieved indignation and switching off Henry Irving as though to somehow punish us. "Such authentication is notoriously difficult. I may have to seek a second opinion!"

"You are more than welcome to do that, ma'am," I replied slowly, "but they will say the same as I. It's not just the text. You see, Shakespeare never wrote on lined paper with a ballpoint, and even if he did, I doubt he would have had Cardenio seeking Lucinda in the Sierra Morena mountains driving an open-top Range Rover whilst playing 'It's the Same Old Song' by the Four Tops."

"Goodness!" said Bowden, amazed by the effrontery of the forger. "Is that what it says?"

I passed him the manuscript to have a look at, and he chuckled to himself. But Hathaway$_{34}$ was having none of it.

"And what of that?" returned Hathaway$_{34}$ angrily. "In *Julius Caesar* there are plenty of clocks striking the hour, yet they weren't invented until much later. I think Shakespeare introduced the Range Rover in much the same way; a literary anachronism, that's all!"

I smiled agreeably and backed towards the door.

"We'd like you to come in and file a report. Let you look at some mug shots; see if we can find out who pulled this."

"Nonsense!" said the woman loftily. "I will seek a second opinion, and if necessary, a third and a fourth—or as many as it takes. Good day, officers!"

And she opened the door, shooed us out and slammed it behind us.

"One born every minute," muttered Bowden as we walked to the car.

"I'd say. Well—that's *interesting*."

"What?"

"Don't look now, but up the road there is a black Pontiac. It was parked outside the SpecOps building when we left."

Bowden had a quick glance in their direction as we got into the car.

"What do you think?" I asked when we were inside.

"Goliath?"

"Could be. They're probably still pissed off about losing Jack Schitt into 'The Raven.' "

"I refuse to lose any sleep over him," replied Bowden, pulling into the main road.

"Me too."

I looked in the vanity mirror at the black automobile four vehicles behind.

"Still with us?" asked Bowden.

"Yup. Let's find out what they want. Take a left here, then left again and drop me off. Carry on for a hundred yards and then pull up."

Bowden turned off the main road and into another narrow residential road, dropped me off as instructed, sped on past the next corner and stopped, blocking the street. I ducked behind a parked car, and sure enough, the large black Pontiac swept past me. It drove round the next corner and stopped abruptly when it saw Bowden and started to reverse. I tapped on the smoked glass window and waved my badge. The driver stopped and wound down the window.

"Thursday Next, SO-27. Why are you following us?" I demanded.

The driver and passenger were both dressed in dark suits and were clean-shaven. Only Goliath looked like this. Goliath—

or SpecOps. The driver looked blankly at me for a moment and then launched into a well-practiced excuse.

"We seem to have taken a wrong turning, miss. Can you tell us the way to Pete and Dave's Dodo Emporium?"

I was unimpressed by their drab cover story, but I smiled anyway. They were SpecOps as much as I was.

"Why don't you just tell me who you are? We'll all get along a lot better, believe me."

The two men looked at one another, sighed resignedly and then held up their badges for me to see. They were SO-5, the same search & containment that hunted down Hades.

"SO-5?" I queried. "Tamworth's old outfit?"

"I'm Phodder," said the driver. "My associate here is Kannon. SpecOps-5 has been reassigned."

"Reassigned? Does that mean Acheron Hades is officially dead?"

"No SO-5 case is ever *completely* closed. Acheron was only the *third* most evil criminal mind on the planet, Miss Next."

"Then who—or *what*—are you after this time?"

It seemed that they preferred asking questions to answering them.

"Your name came up in preliminary inquiries. Tell me, has anything odd happened to you recently?"

"What do you mean, odd?"

"Unusual. Deviating from the customary. Something outside the usual parameters of normalcy. An occurrence of unprecedented *weird*."

I thought for a moment.

"No."

"Well," announced Phodder with an air of finality, "if it does, would you call me at this number?"

I took the card, bade them goodbye and returned to Bowden.

\* \* \*

We were soon heading north on the Cirencester road, the Pontiac nowhere in sight. I explained who they were to Bowden, who raised his eyebrows and said:

"Sounds ominous. Someone worse than Hades? That'll take some doing."

"Hard to believe, isn't it? Where are we heading now?"

"Vole Towers."

"Really?" I replied in some surprise. "Why would someone as eminent and respectable as Lord Volescamper get embroiled in a *Cardenio* scam?"

"Search me. He's a golfing buddy of Braxton's, so this could be political. Better not dismiss it out of hand and make him look an idiot—we'll only be clobbered by the chief."

We swung in through the battered and rusty gates of Vole Towers and motored up the long drive, which was more weed than gravel. We pulled up outside the imposing Gothic Revival house that was clearly in need of repair, and Lord Volescamper came out to meet us. Volescamper was a tall thin man with gray hair and a ponderous air. He was wearing an old pair of herringbone tweeds and brandished a pair of secateurs like a cavalry saber.

"Blasted brambles!" he muttered as he shook our hands. "Look here, they can grow two inches a day, you know; inexorable little blighters that threaten to engulf all that we know and love—a bit like anarchists, really. You're that Next girl, aren't you? I think we met at my niece Gloria's wedding—who did she marry again?"

"My cousin Wilbur."

"Now I remember. Who was that sad old fart who made a nuisance of himself on the dance floor?"

"I think that was you, sir."

Lord Volescamper thought for a moment and stared at his feet.

"Goodness. It was, wasn't it? Saw you on the telly last night. Look here, it was a rum business about that Brontë book, eh?"

"*Very* rum," I assured him. "This is Bowden Cable, my partner."

"How do you do, Mr. Cable? Bought one of the new Griffin Sportinas, I see. How do you find it?"

"Usually where I left it, sir."

"Indeed? You must come inside. Victor sent you, yes?"

We followed Volescamper as he shambled into the decrepit mansion. We passed into the main hall, which was heavily decorated with the heads of various antelope, stuffed and placed on wooden shields.

"In years gone by the family were prodigious hunters," explained Volescamper. "But look here, I don't carry on that way myself. Father was heavily into killing and stuffing things. When he died he insisted on being stuffed himself. That's him over there."

We stopped on the landing and Bowden and I looked at the deceased earl with interest. With his favorite gun in the crook of his arm and his faithful dog at his feet, he stared blankly out of the glass case. I thought perhaps his head and shoulders should also be mounted on a wooden shield but I didn't think it would be polite to say so. Instead I said:

"He looks very young."

"But look here, he was. Forty-three and eight days. Trampled to death by antelope."

"In Africa?"

"No," sighed Volescamper wistfully, "on the A30 near Chard one night in '34. He stopped the car because there was a stag with the most magnificent antlers lying in the road. Father got out to have a peek and, well look here, he didn't stand a chance. The herd came from nowhere."

"I'm sorry."

"Sort of ironic, really," he rambled on as Bowden looked at his watch, "but do you know the *really* odd thing was, when the herd of antelope ran off, the magnificent stag had *also* gone."

"It must have just been stunned," suggested Bowden.

"Yes, yes, I suppose so," replied Volescamper absently, "I suppose so. But look here, you don't want to know about Father. Come on!"

And so saying he strutted off down the corridor that led to the library. We had to trot to catch up with him and soon arrived at a pair of steel vault doors—clearly, Volescamper had no doubts as to the value of his collection. I touched the blued steel of the doors thoughtfully.

"Oh, yes," said Volescamper, divining my thoughts, "look here, the old library is worth quite a few pennies—I like to take precautions; don't be fooled by the oak paneling inside—the library is essentially a vast steel safe."

It wasn't unusual. The Bodleian these days was like Fort Knox—and Fort Knox itself had been converted to take the Library of Congress's more valuable works. We entered, and if I was prepared to see an immaculate collection, I was to be disappointed—the library looked more like a box room than a depository of knowledge; the books were piled up on tables, in boxes, arranged haphazardly and in many cases just stacked on the floor ten or twelve high. *But what books!* I picked up a volume at random which turned out to be a second-impression copy of *Gulliver's Travels*. I showed it to Bowden, who responded by holding up a signed first edition of *Decline and Fall*.

"You didn't just buy *Cardenio* recently or something, then?" I asked, suddenly feeling that perhaps my early dismissal of the find might have been too hasty.

"Goodness me, no. Look here, we found it only the other

day when we were cataloguing part of my great-grandfather Bartholomew Volescamper's private library. Didn't even know I had it. Ah!—this is Mr. Swaike, my security consultant."

A thickset man with a humorless look and jowls like bananas had entered the library. He eyed us suspiciously as Volescamper made the introductions, then laid a sheaf of roughly cut pages bound into a leather book on the table.

"What sort of security matters do you consult on, Mr. Swaike?" asked Bowden.

"Personal and insurance, Mr. Cable," replied Swaike in a drab monotone. "This library is uncatalogued and uninsured; criminal gangs would regard it as a valuable target, despite the security arrangements. *Cardenio* is only one of a dozen books I am currently keeping in a secure safe *within* the locked library."

"I can't fault you there, Mr. Swaike," replied Bowden.

I looked at the manuscript. At first glance, things looked good, so I quickly donned a pair of cotton gloves, something I hadn't even considered with Mrs. Hathaway$_{34}$'s *Cardenio*. I pulled up a chair and studied the first page. The handwriting was very similar to Shakespeare's with loops at the top of the L's and W's and spirited backward-facing extensions to the top of the D's; and the spelling was erratic, too—always a good sign. It all *looked* real, but I had seen some good copies in my time. There were a lot of scholars who were versed well enough in Shakespeare, Elizabethan history, grammar and spelling to *attempt* a forgery but none of them ever had the wit and charm of the Bard himself. Victor used to say that Shakespeare forgery was inherently impossible because the act of copying overrode the act of inspired creation—the heart being squeezed out by the mind, so to speak. But as I turned the first page and read the *dramatis personae,* butterflies stirred within me. I'd read fifty or sixty *Cardenios* before, but—I turned the page and read Cardenio's opening soliloquy:

*"Know'st thou, O love, the pangs which I sustain—"*

"It's a sort of Spanish thirty-something *Romeo and Juliet* but with a few laughs and a happy ending," explained Volescamper helpfully. "Look here, would you care for some tea?"

"What? Yes—thank you."

Volescamper told us that he would lock us in for security reasons but we could press the bell if we needed anything.

The steel door clanged shut and we read with increased interest as the knight Cardenio told the audience of his lost love Lucinda and how he had fled to the mountains after her marriage to the deceitful Ferdinand and become a ragged, destitute wretch.

"Good Lord," murmured Bowden over my shoulder, a sentiment that I agreed with wholeheartedly. The play, forgery or not, was *excellent*. After the opening soliloquy we soon went into a flashback where Cardenio and Lucinda write a series of passionate love letters in an Elizabethan version of a Rock Hudson/Doris Day split screen, Lucinda on one side reacting to Cardenio writing them on the other and then vice versa. It was funny, too. We read on and learned of Cardenio's plans to marry Lucinda, then the Duke's demand for him to be a companion to his son Ferdinand, Ferdinand's hopeless infatuation for Dorothea, the trip to Lucinda's town, how Ferdinand's love transfers to Lucinda—

"What do you think?" I asked Bowden as we reached the end of the second act.

"Amazing! I've not seen anything like this, *ever*."

"Real?"

"I think so—but mistakes have been made before. I'll copy out the passage where Cardenio finds he has been duped and Ferdinand is planning to wed Lucinda. We can run it through the Verse Meter Analyzer back at the office."

We eagerly read on. The sentences, the meter, the style—it

was all pure Shakespeare. *Cardenio* had been missing for over four hundred years, but for it to surface now and quite out of the blue gave me mixed feelings. Yes, it would throw the literary world off kilter and send every single Shakespeare fan and scholar into paroxysms of litjoy, but on the other hand it worried me, too. My father always used to say that whenever something is too fantastic to be true, it generally is. I voiced my concerns to Bowden, who pointed out less pessimistically that the original manuscript of Marlowe's *Edward II* surfaced only in the thirties. So unearthing new plays wasn't unprecedented— but I still felt uneasy.

The tea was apparently forgotten, and while Bowden copied out the five-page scene for the VMA I looked around the library, wondering just what other treasures might be hidden here. The large safe-within-a-safe stood at the side of the room and contained, Swaike had said, another dozen or so rare books. I tried the safe door but it was locked, so I made a few notes for Victor in case he thought we should apply for a Compulsory Literary Disclosure Order. I then ambled round the old library, looking at books that caught my eye. I was thumbing through a collection of first-edition Evelyn Waugh novels when a key turned in the heavy steel door. I hurriedly replaced the volume as Lord Volescamper popped his head in and announced in an excited manner that due to "prior engagements" we would have to resume our work the following day. Swaike walked in to lock *Cardenio* back in the safe, and we followed Volescamper out through the shabby building to the entrance, just as a pair of large Bentley limousines rolled up. Volescamper bade us a hasty goodbye before striding forward to greet the passenger in the first car.

"Well well," said Bowden. "Look who it is."

A young man flanked by two large bodyguards got out and shook hands with the enthusiastic Volescamper. I recognized him from his numerous TV appearances. It was Yorrick Kaine, the charismatic young leader of the marginal Whig party. He and Volescamper walked up the steps talking animatedly and then vanished inside Vole Towers.

We drove away from the moldering house with mixed feelings about the treasure we had been studying.

"What do you think?"

"Fishy," said Bowden. "Very fishy. How could something like *Cardenio* turn up out of the blue?"

"How fishy on the fishiness scale?" I asked him. "Ten is a stickleback and one is a whale shark."

"A whale isn't a fish, Thursday."

"A whale shark is—sort of."

"All right, it's as fishy as a crayfish."

"A crayfish isn't a fish," I told him.

"A starfish, then."

"*Still* not a fish."

"A silverfish?"

"Try again."

"This is a very odd conversation, Thursday."

"I'm pulling your leg, Bowden."

"Oh I see," he replied as the penny dropped. "Tomfoolery."

Bowden's lack of humor wasn't necessarily a bad thing. After all, none of us *really* had much of a sense of humor in SpecOps. But he thought it socially desirable to have one, so I did what I could to help. The trouble was, he could read *Three Men in a Boat* without a single smirk and viewed P. G. Wodehouse as "infantile," so I had a suspicion the affliction was long-lasting and permanent.

"My tensionologist suggested I should try stand-up comedy," said Bowden, watching me closely for my reaction.

"Well, 'How do you find the Sportina? / Where I left it' was a good start," I told him.

He stared at me blankly. It hadn't been a joke.

"I've booked myself in at the *Happy Squid* talent night on Monday. Do you want to hear my routine?"

"I'm all ears."

He cleared his throat.

"There are these three anteaters, see, and they go into a—"

There was a sharp crack, the car swerved, and we heard a fast flapping noise. I tensed as we fishtailed for a moment before Bowden brought the car under control.

"Damn!" he muttered. "Blowout."

There was another concussion like the first, but we weren't going so fast by now and Bowden eased the car in towards the car park at the South Cerney stop of the Skyrail.

"*Two* blowouts?" muttered Bowden as we got out. We looked at the remnants of the car tire still on the rim, then at each other—and then at the busy road to see if anyone else was having problems. They weren't. The traffic zoomed up and down the road quite happily.

"How is it possible for *both* tires to go within ten seconds of each other?"

I shrugged. I didn't have an answer for this. It was a new car, after all, and I'd been driving all my life and never had a single blowout, much less two. With only one spare wheel we were stuck here for a while. I suggested he call SpecOps and get them to send a tow truck.

"Wireless seems to be dead," he announced, keying the mike and turning the knob. "That's odd."

Something, I felt, wasn't quite right.

"No more odd than a double blowout," I told him, walking a few paces to a handy phone booth. I lifted the receiver and said: "Do you have any change—"

I stopped because I'd just noticed a ticket on top of the

phone. As I picked it up a Skyrail shuttle approached high up on the steel tracks, as if on cue.

"What have you found?" asked Bowden.

"A Skyrail day pass," I replied slowly, replacing the receiver. Broken images of something half forgotten or not yet remembered started to form in my head. It was confusing, but I knew what I had to do. "I'm going to take the Skyrail and see what happens."

"Why?"

"There's a neanderthal in trouble."

"How do you know?"

I frowned, trying to make sense of what I was feeling.

"I'm not sure. What's the opposite of *déjà vu,* when you see something that hasn't happened yet?"

"I don't know—*avant verrais?*"

"That's it. Something's going to happen—and I'm part of it."

"I'll come with you."

"No, Bowden; if you were meant to come I would have found *two* tickets."

I left my partner looking confused and walked briskly up to the station, showed my ticket to the inspector and climbed the steel steps to the platform fifty feet above ground. I was alone apart from a young woman sitting by herself on a bench, checking her makeup in a mirror. She looked up at me for a moment before the doors of the shuttle hissed open and I stepped inside, wondering what events were about to unfold.

# 4.

## Five Coincidences,
## Seven Irma Cohens and
## One Confused Neanderthal

*The neanderthal experiment* was conceived in order to create the euphemistically entitled "medical test vessels," living creatures that were as close as possible to humans without actually *being* human within the context of the law. Using cells reengineered from DNA discovered in a *Homo Llysternef* forearm preserved in a peat bog near Llysternef in Wales, the experiment was an unparalleled success. Sadly for Goliath, even the hardiest of medical technicians balked at experiments conducted upon intelligent and speaking entities, so the first batch of neanderthals were trained instead as "expendable combat units," a project that was shelved as soon as the lack of aggressive instincts in the neanderthal was noted. They were subsequently released into the community as cheap labor and became a celebrated tax write-off. Infertile males and an expected life span of fifty years meant they would soon be relegated to the reengineerment industries' ever-growing list of "failures."

GERHARD VON SQUID,
*Neanderthals: Back After a Short Absence*

OINCIDENCES ARE strange things. I like the one about Sir Edmund Godfrey, who was found murdered in 1678 and left in a ditch on Greenberry Hill in London. Three men were arrested and hanged for the crime—Mr. *Green*, Mr. *Berry* and Mr. *Hill*. My father told me that for the most part coincidences could be safely ignored: They were merely the chance discovery of one pertinent fact from a million or so possible daily interconnections. "Stop a stranger in the street," he would say, "and delve into each other's past. Pretty soon an *astounding-too-amazing-to-be-chance* coincidence will appear."

I suppose he's right, but that didn't explain how a twin puncture outside the station, a broken wireless which led *directly* to the discovery of a valid Skyrail ticket and the Skyrail itself approaching at that precise moment can all happen out of the blue. Some things happen for a reason, and I was inclined to think that this was one of those times.

I stepped into the single Skyrail car, which was the same as every other I had been in. It was clean, had about forty seats and room for standing if required. I took a seat at the front as the doors sighed shut and, accompanied by the hum of electric motors, we were soon gliding effortlessly above the Cerney lakes. Since I was here for a purpose, I looked around carefully to see what that might be. The Skyrail operator was neanderthal; he had his hand on the throttle and gazed absently at the view. His eyebrows twitched and he sniffed the air occasionally. The car was almost empty; seven people, all of them women and no one familiar.

"Three down," exclaimed a squat woman who was staring at a folded-up newspaper, half to herself and half to the rest of us. "*Well decorated for prying, perhaps?* Ten letters."

No one answered as we sailed past Cricklade Station without stopping, much to the annoyance of a large, expensively dressed lady who huffed loudly and pointed at the operator with her umbrella.

"You there!" she boomed like a captain before the storm. "What are you doing? I wanted to get off at Cricklade, damn you!"

The operator seemed unperturbed at the insult and muttered an apology. This obviously wasn't good enough for the loud and objectionable woman, who jabbed the small neanderthal violently in the ribs with her umbrella. He didn't yell out in pain, he just flinched, pulled the driver's door closed behind him and locked it. I stood up and snatched the umbrella from the woman.

"What the—!" she said indignantly.

"Don't do that," I told her. "It's not nice."

"Poppycock!" she guffawed loudly. "Why, he's only neanderthal!"

"*Meddlesome*," said one of the other passengers sitting near the back with an air of finality, staring at an advert for the Gravitube.

The objectionable lady and I stared at her, wondering who she was referring to. She looked at us both, flushed, and said:

"No, no. Ten letters, three down. *Well decorated for prying. Meddlesome.*"

"Very good," muttered the lady with the crossword as she scribbled in the answer.

I handed the umbrella back to the well-heeled woman, who eyed me malevolently; we were barely two feet apart but she wasn't going to sit down first, and neither was I.

"Jab the neanderthal again and I'll arrest you for assault," I told her.

"I happen to know," announced the woman tartly, "that neanderthals are legally classed as *animals*. You cannot assault a neanderthal any more than you can a mouse!"

My temper began to rise—always a bad sign. I would probably end up doing something stupid.

"Perhaps," I replied, "but I *can* arrest you for cruelty, bruising the calm and anything else I can think of."

But the woman wasn't the least bit intimidated.

"My husband is a justice of the peace," she announced like a hidden trump. "I can make things *very* tricky for you. What is your name?"

"Next," I told her without hesitation. "Thursday Next. SO-27."

Her eyelids flickered slightly and she stopped rummaging in her bag for a pencil and paper.

"The *Jane Eyre* Thursday Next?" she asked, her mood changing abruptly.

"I saw you on the telly," chirped the woman with the crossword. "You seem a bit obsessed with your dodo, I must say. Why couldn't you talk about *Jane Eyre*, Goliath, or ending the Crimean War?"

"Believe me, I tried."

The well-heeled woman decided that this was a good moment to withdraw, so she sat back in her seat two rows behind me and stared out of the window as the Skyrail swept on past Broad Blunsdon Station; the passengers variously sighed, made tut-tut noises and shrugged to one another.

"I am going to complain to the Skyrail management about *this*," said a heavyset woman with makeup like builder's plaster. She carried a disgruntled-looking Pekinese. "A good cure for insubordination is—"

Her speech came to an abrupt end as the neanderthal suddenly increased the speed of the car.

I knocked on the acrylic door and said: "What's going on, pal?"

The neanderthal had taken about as much umbrella jabbing as he could that day, or any day, come to that.

"We are going home now," he said simply, staring straight ahead.

"We?" echoed the woman with the umbrella. "No, we're not. I live at Cricklade—"

"He means *I*," I told her. "Neanderthals don't use the personal pronoun."

"Damn stupid!" she replied. I glared at her and she got the

message and lapsed into sulky silence. I leaned closer to the driver.

"What's your name?"

"Kaylieu," he replied.

"Good. Now Kaylieu, I want you to tell me what the problem is."

He paused for a moment as the Swindon Airship stop came and went. I saw another shuttle that had been diverted to a siding and several Skyrail officials waving at us, so it was only a matter of time before the authorities knew what was going on.

"We want to be *real*."

"*Day's hurt?*" murmured the squat woman at the back, sucking the end of her pencil and staring at the crossword.

"What did you say?" I said.

"*Day's hurt?*" she repeated, oblivious to the situation. "Nine down; eight letters—I think it's an anagram."

"I have no idea," I replied before returning my attention to Kaylieu. "What do you mean, *real?*"

"We are *not* animals," announced the once extinct cousin of mankind. "We want to be a protected species—like dodo, mammoth—and *you*. We want to speak to head man at Goliath *and* someone from Toad News."

"I'll see what I can do."

I walked to the back of the shuttle and picked up the emergency phone.

"Hello?" I said to the operator. "This is Thursday Next, SO-27. We have a situation in shuttle number—ah—6174."

When I told the operator what was going on she took a sharp intake of breath and asked how many people were with me and whether anyone was hurt.

"Seven females, myself and the driver; we are all fine."

"Don't forget Pixie Frou-Frou," said the large woman with the overdone makeup.

"And one Pekinese."

The operator told me they were clearing all the tracks ahead, we would have to keep calm and she would call back. I tried to tell her that it wasn't a *bad* situation, but she had rung off.

I sat down close to the neanderthal again. Jaw fixed, he was staring intently ahead, knuckles white on the throttle lever. We approached the Wanborough junction, crossed the M4 and were diverted west. The passenger directly behind me, a shy-looking girl in her late teens and dressed in a De La Mare label sweatshirt, caught my eye; she looked frightened.

I smiled to try to put her at ease.

"What's your name?" I asked her.

"Irma," she replied in a small voice. "Irma Cohen."

"Poppycock!" said the umbrella woman. "*I'm* Irma Cohen!"

"So am I," said the woman with the Peke.

"And me!" exclaimed the thin woman at the back. It seemed after a short period of frenzied cries of "Ooh fancy that!" and "Well I never!" that *everyone* in the Skyrail except me and Kaylieu and Pixie Frou-Frou was called Irma Cohen. Some of them were even vaguely related. It was an unnerving coincidence—for today, the best yet.

"*Thursday*," announced the squat woman.

"Yes?"

But she wasn't talking to me; she was writing in the answer: *Day's hurt—Thursday*—it *was* an anagram.

The emergency phone rang.

"This is Diana Thuntress, trained negotiator for SpecOps-9," said a businesslike voice. "Who is this?"

"Di, it's me, Thursday."

There was a pause.

"Hello Thursday. Saw you on the telly last night. Trouble seems to follow you around, doesn't it? What's it like in there?"

I looked at the small and unconcerned crowd of commuters

who were showing each other pictures of their children. Pixie Frou-Frou had fallen asleep and the Irma Cohen with the crossword had announced the clue for six across: *The parting bargain?*

"They're fine. A little bored, but not hurt."

"What does the perp want?"

"He wants to talk to someone at Goliath about species self-ownership."

"Wait—he's *neanderthal?*"

"Yes."

"It's not possible! A neanderthal being violent?"

"There's no violence up here, Di—just desperation."

*"Shit,"* muttered Thuntress. "What do I know about dealing with thals? We'll have to get one of the SpecOps neanderthals in."

"He also wants to see a reporter from Toad News."

There was silence on the other end of the phone.

"Di?"

"Yes?"

"What can I tell Kaylieu?"

"Tell him that—er—Toad News are supplying a car to take him to the Goliath Genetic Labs in the Preselli Mountains where Goliath's governor, chief geneticist and a team of lawyers will be waiting to agree to terms."

As lies go, it was a real corker.

"But is that right?" I asked.

"There is no 'right,' Thursday," snapped Diana, "not since he took control of the Skyrail. There are eight lives in there. It doesn't take the winner of *Name That Fruit!* to figure out what we have to do. Pacifist neanderthal or not, there is a chance he *could* harm the passengers."

"Don't be ridiculous! No neanderthal has ever harmed anyone. What is this," I added, outraged by the crude approach, "staff training day for the trigger-happy clots at SO-14?"

"It's not unusual for hostages to start to empathize with their captors, Thursday. Let us handle this."

"Di," I said in a clear voice, "listen to me: *No one is either threatened or in danger!*"

"Yet, Thursday. *Yet.* Listen, we're not going to take that risk. This is how it's going to be: We're going to divert you back up along the Cirencester line. We'll have SO-14 agents in position at Cricklade. As soon as he stops I'm afraid we will have no alternative but to take him out. I want you to make sure the passengers are all in the back of the car."

"Diana, that's crazy! You'd kill him because he took a few lamebrained commuters for a merry trip round the Swindon loop?"

"You don't kill neanderthals; they are *destroyed.* There's a big difference—and besides, the law is very strict on hijackers."

"He's nothing of the sort, Di. He's just a confused extinctee!"

"Sorry, Thursday—this is out of my hands."

I hung up the phone angrily as the shuttle was diverted back up towards Cirencester. We flew through Shaw Station, much to the surprise of the waiting commuters, and were soon heading north again. I returned to the driver.

"Kaylieu, you *must* stop at Purton."

He grunted in reply but showed little sign of being happy or sad—the subtleties of neanderthal facial expressions were mostly lost on us. He stared at me for a moment and then asked:

"You have childer?"

I hastily changed the subject. Being sequenced infertile was the neanderthals' biggest cause of complaint against their sapien masters. Within thirty years or so the last of the experimental neanderthals would die of old age. Unless Goliath sequenced some more, that would be it. Extinct again—it was unlikely even *we* would manage that.

"No, no, I don't," I replied hastily.

"Nor us," returned Kaylieu, "but you have a *choice*. We don't. We should *never* have been brought back. Not to this. Not to carry bags for sapien, no childer and umbrellas jab-jab."

He stared bleakly into the middle distance—perhaps to a better life thirty thousand years ago when he was free to hunt large herbivores from the relative safety of a drafty cave. Home for Kaylieu was extinction again—at least for him. He didn't want to hurt any of us and would never do so. He couldn't hurt himself either, so he would rely on SpecOps to do the job for him.

*"Goodbye."*

I jumped at the finality of the pronouncement but upon turning found that it was merely the crossword Mrs. Cohen filling in the last clue.

*"The parting bargain,"* she muttered happily. "Good buy. *Goodbye*. Finished!"

I didn't like this; not at all. The three clues of the crossword had been "Meddlesome," "Thursday" and "Goodbye." *More* co-incidences. Without the dual blowout and the fortuitous day ticket, I wouldn't be here at all. Everyone was called Cohen and now the crossword. But *goodbye?* If all went according to SpecOps, the only person worthy of *that* interjection would be Kaylieu. Still, I had other things to worry about as we passed Purton without stopping. I asked everyone to move to the back of the car and once done, joined Kaylieu at the front.

"Listen to me, Kaylieu. If you don't make any threatening movements they may not open fire."

"We thought of that," said the neanderthal as he pulled an imitation automatic from his tunic.

"They will fire," he said as Cricklade Station hove into view a half mile up the line. "We carved it from soap—*Dove* soap," he added. "We thought it ironic."

We approached Cricklade at full speed; I could see SpecOps-14 vehicles parked on the road and black uniformed SWAT teams waiting on the platform. With a hundred yards to run, the power to the Skyrail abruptly cut out and the shuttle skidded, power off, towards the station. The door to the driver's compartment swung open and I squeezed in. I grabbed his soapy gun and threw it to the floor. Kaylieu wasn't going to die, at least not if I could help it. We rumbled into the station. The doors were opened by SO-14 operatives and all the Irma Cohens rapidly evacuated. I put my arm round Kaylieu. It was the first time I had done so to any neanderthal and I was surprised by how hard the muscles were—and how warm to the touch.

"Move away from the thal!" said a voice from a bullhorn.

"So you can shoot him?" I yelled back.

"He threatened the lives of commuters, Next. He is a danger to civilized society!"

"Civilized?" I shouted angrily. "Look at you!"

"Next!" said the voice. "Move aside. That is a *direct* order!"

"You *must* do as they say," said the neanderthal.

"Over my dead body."

As if in reply there was a gentle *POK* sound and a single bullet hole appeared in the windshield of the shuttle. Someone had decided he could take out Kaylieu anyway. My temper flared and I tried to yell out in anger but no sound came from my lips. My legs felt weak and I fell to the floor in a heap, the world turning gray about me. I couldn't even feel my legs. I heard someone yell: *Medic!* and the last thing I saw before the darkness overtook me was Kaylieu's broad face looking down at me. He had tears in his eyes and was mouthing the words *We're so sorry. So very, very, sorry.*

# 5.

## Vanishing Hitchhikers

Urban legends are older than congress gaiters but far more interesting. I'd heard most of them, from the dog in the microwave to ball lightning chasing a housewife in Preston, to the fried dodo leg found in a Smiley Fried Chicken, to the carnivorous *Diatryma* supposedly reengineered and now living in the New Forest. I'd read all about the alien spaceship that crash-landed near Lambourn in 1952, the story that Charles Dickens was a woman and that the president of the Goliath Corporation was actually a 142-year-old man kept alive in a bottle by medical science. Stories about SpecOps abound, the favorite at present relating to "something odd" dug up in the Quantock Hills. Yes, I'd heard them all. Never believed any of them. Then one day, I *was* one. . . .

THURSDAY NEXT,
*A Life in SpecOps*

I OPENED ONE EYE, then the other. It was a warm summer's day on the Marlborough downs. A light zephyr brought with it the delicate scent of honeysuckle and wild thyme. The air was warm and small puffy clouds were tinged red from the setting sun. I was standing by the side of a road in open country. In one direction I could just see a lone cyclist moving towards where I stood and in the other the road wound away into the distance past fields in which sheep grazed peacefully. If this was life after death, then a lot of people had not much to worry about and the Church had delivered the goods after all.

"*Psssst!*" hissed a voice close at hand. I turned to see a figure crouched behind a large Goliath Corporation billboard advertising buy-two-get-one-free grand pianos.

"Dad—?"

He pulled me behind the billboard with him.

"Don't stand there like a tourist, Thursday!" he snapped crossly. "Anyone would think you *wanted* to be seen!"

"Hi, Dad!" I said fondly, giving him a hug.

"Hello, hello," he said absently, glancing up and down the road and consulting the chronograph on his wrist and muttering: "fundamental things apply as time goes by. . . ."

I regarded my father as a sort of time-traveling knight errant, but to the ChronoGuard he was nothing less than a criminal. He threw in his badge and went rogue seventeen years ago when his "historical and moral" differences brought him into conflict with the ChronoGuard High Chamber. The downside of this was that he didn't really exist at all in any accepted terms of the definition; the ChronoGuard had interrupted his conception in 1917 by a well-timed knock on his parents' front door. But despite all this Dad *was* still around and I and my brothers *had* been born. "Things," Dad used to say, "are a whole lot weirder than we *can* know."

He thought for a moment and made a few notes on the back of an envelope with a pencil stub.

"How are you, by the way?" he asked.

"I think I was just accidentally shot dead by a SpecOps marksman."

He burst out laughing but suddenly stopped when he saw I was serious.

"Goodness!" he said. "You *do* live an exciting life. But never fear. You can't die until you've lived, and you've barely started *that* at all. What's the news from home?"

"A ChronoGuard officer turned up at my wedding bash wanting to know where you were."

"Lavoisier?"

"Yes; do you know him?"

"I should think so," sighed my father. "We were partners for nearly seven centuries."

"He said you were very dangerous."

"No more dangerous than anyone else who dares speak the truth. How's your mother?"

"She's fine, although you might try and clear up that misunderstanding about Emma Hamilton."

"Emma and I—I mean *Lady Hamilton* and I—are simply 'good friends.' There's nothing to it, I swear."

"Tell *her* that."

"I try, but you know what a temper she has. I only have to mention I've been anywhere *near* the turn of the nineteenth century and she gets in a frightful strop."

I looked around.

"Where are we?"

"Summer of '72," he replied. "All well at work?"

"We found a thirty-third play by Shakespeare."

"Thirty-three?" echoed my father. "That's odd. When I took the entire works back to the actor Shakespeare to distribute there were only *eighteen*."

"Perhaps the actor Shakespeare started writing them himself?" I suggested.

"By thunder you could be right!" he exclaimed. "He looked a bright spark. Tell me, how many comedies are there now?"

"Fifteen."

"But I only gave him *three*. They must have been so popular he started writing new ones himself!"

"It would explain why all the comedies are pretty much the same," I added. "Spells, identical twins, shipwrecks—"

"—usurped Dukes, men dressed as women," continued my father. "You could be right."

"Wait a moment—!" I began. But my father, sensing my disquiet over the many seemingly impossible paradoxes in his work in the timestream, silenced me with his hand.

"One day you'll understand and everything will be more different than you can, at present, possibly hope to imagine."

I must have looked blank, for he checked the road again, leaned against the back of the billboard and continued:

"Remember, Thursday, that scientific thought, indeed, *any* mode of thought whether it be religious or philosophical or anything else, is just like the fashions that we wear—only much longer-lived. It's a little like a boy band."

"Scientific thought a boy band? How do you figure *that*?"

"Well, every now and then a boy band comes along. We like it, buy the records, posters, parade them on TV, idolize them right up until—"

"—the next boy band?" I suggested.

"Precisely. Aristotle was a boy band. A very good one, but only number six or seven. He was the best boy band until Isaac Newton, but even Newton was transplanted by an even *newer* boy band. Same haircuts—but different moves."

"Einstein, right?"

"Right. Do you see what I'm saying?"

"That the way we think is nothing more than a passing fad?"

"Exactly. Hard to visualize a new way of thinking? Try this. Go thirty or forty boy bands *past* Einstein. Where we would regard Einstein as someone who *glimpsed* a truth, played one good chord in seven forgettable albums."

"Where is this going, Dad?"

"I'm nearly there. Imagine a boy band so good that you

never needed another boy band ever again—*or even any more music*. Can you imagine that?"

"It's hard. But yes, okay."

He let this sink in for a moment.

"When we reach *that* boy band, my dear, *everything* we have ever puzzled about becomes crystal clear—and we will kick ourselves that we hadn't thought of it earlier!"

"We will?"

"Sure. And you know the best thing about it? It's so devilishly *simple*."

"I see," I replied, slightly dubiously. "And when is this amazing Boy Band discovered?"

Dad suddenly turned serious.

"That's why I'm here. Perhaps never—which would be frightfully awkward in the grand scheme of things, believe me. Did you see a cyclist on the road?"

"Yes?"

"Well," he said, consulting the large chronograph on his wrist, "in ten seconds that cyclist will be knocked over and killed."

"And—?" I asked, sensing that I was missing something.

He looked around furtively and lowered his voice.

"Well, it seems that right here and now is the key event whereby we can avert whatever it is that *destroys every single speck of life on this planet!*"

I looked into his earnest eyes.

"You're not kidding, are you?"

He shook his head.

"In December 1985, *your* 1985, for some unaccountable reason, all the planet's organic matter turns to . . . *this*."

He withdrew a plastic specimen bag from his pocket. It contained a thick pinkish opaque slime. I took the bag and shook it curiously as we heard a loud screech of tires and a sickly thud. A moment later a broken body and twisted bicycle landed close by.

"On the 12th December at 20:23, give or take a second or two, all organic material—every plant, insect, fish, bird, mammal and the three billion human inhabitants of this planet—will start turning to *that*. End of all of us. End of Life—and there won't be that boy band I was telling you about. The problem is—" he went on as a car door slammed and we heard feet running towards us—"that we don't know *why*. The ChronoGuard are not doing any upstreaming work at present."

"Why is that?"

"Labor dispute. They're on strike for shorter hours. Not actually *less* hours, you understand, just the hours that they do work they want to be—er—shorter."

"So while the upstreamers are on strike the world could end and everyone will die, including them? But that's crazy!"

"From an industrial action viewpoint," said my father, furrowing his brow and going silent for a moment, "I think it's a very good strategy indeed. I hope they can thrash out a new agreement in time."

"And we'll know if they don't because the world ends?" I remarked sarcastically.

"Oh, they'll come to some arrangement," explained my father, smiling. "The dispute regarding *under*time rates lasted almost two decades—time's easy to waste when you've got lots of it."

"Okay," I sighed, unwilling to get too embroiled in SO-12 labor disputes, "what can we do about averting this crisis?"

"Global disasters are like ripples in a pond, Sweetpea. There is *always* an epicenter—a place in time and space where it all begins, however innocuously."

I began to understand. I looked around at the summer's evening. The birds were twittering happily and barely a soul could be seen in any direction.

"This is the epicenter?"

"Exactly so. Doesn't look like much, does it? I've run trillions of timestream models and the outcome is the same—whatever happens here and now somehow relates to the averting of the crisis. And since the cyclist's death is the only event of any significance for hours in either direction, it *has* to be the key event. The cyclist *must* live to ensure the continued health of the planet!"

We stepped out from behind the billboard to confront the driver, a youngish man who was dressed in flares and black leather jacket. He was visibly panicking.

"Oh my God!" he said as he stared at the broken body at our feet. "Oh my God! Is he—?"

"At the moment, yes," replied my father in a matter-of-fact sort of way as he filled his pipe.

"I must call an ambulance!" stammered the man. "He could still be alive!"

"Anyway," continued my father, ignoring the motorist completely, "the cyclist obviously *does* something or *doesn't* do something, and that's the key to this whole stupid mess."

"I wasn't speeding, you know," said the motorist quickly. "The engine might have been revving, but it was stuck in second . . ."

"Hang on!" I said, slightly confused. "You've been beyond 1985, Dad—you told me so yourself!"

"I know that," replied my father grimly, "so we'd better get this *absolutely* right."

"There was a low sun," continued the driver as he thought hard, "and he swerved in front of me!"

"Male guilt avoidance syndrome," explained my father. "It's a recognized medical condition by 2054."

Dad held me by the arm and there was a series of rapid flashes and an intense burst of noise, and we were about a half mile and five minutes in the direction the cyclist had come. He rode past and waved cheerily.

We returned the wave and watched him pedal off.

"Don't you stop him?"

"Tried. Doesn't work. Stole his bike—he borrowed a friend's. Diversion signs he ignored and the pools win didn't stop him either. I've tried everything. Time is the glue of the cosmos, Thursday, and it has to be *eased* apart—try to force events and they end up whacking you on the frontal lobes like a cabbage from six paces. I thought you might have better luck. Lavoisier will have locked on to me by now. The car is due in thirty-eight seconds. Hitch a ride and do your best."

"Wait!" I said. "What about me?"

"I'll take you out again after the cyclist is safe."

"Back to where?" I asked suddenly. I had *no* desire to return the moment I'd left. "The SpecOps marksman, Dad, remember? Can't you put me back, say, thirty minutes earlier?"

He smiled and gave me a wink.

"Give my love to your mother. Thanks for helping out. Well, *Time waits for no man,* as we—"

But he was gone, melted into the air about me. I paused for a moment and put out a thumb to hail the approaching Jaguar. The car slowed and stopped and the motorist, oblivious to the impending accident, smiled and asked me to hop aboard.

I said nothing, jumped in, and we roared off.

"Just picked the old girl up this morning," mused the driver, more to himself than me. "Three point eight liters with triple DCOE Webers. Six cylinders of big cat—lovely!"

"Mind the cyclist," I said as we rounded the corner. The driver stamped on the brake and swerved past the man on the bike.

"Bloody cyclists!" he exclaimed. "A danger to themselves and everyone else. Where are you bound, little lady?"

"I'm, ah . . . visiting my father," I explained, truthfully enough.

"Where does he live?"

"Everywhere," I replied—

"Wireless seems to be dead," Bowden announced, keying the mike and turning the knob. "That's odd."

"No more odd than a double blowout," I told him, walking a few paces to the handy phone booth and picking up the Skyrail ticket.

"What have you found?" asked Bowden.

"A Skyrail day pass," I replied slowly, the broken images in my head that much clearer. "I'm going to take the Skyrail—there's a neanderthal in trouble."

"How do you know?"

"Call it *déjà vu* this time. Something's going to happen—and I'm part of it."

I left my partner and walked briskly up to the station, showed my ticket to the inspector and climbed the steel steps to the platform. The doors of the shuttle hissed open and I stepped inside, this time knowing *exactly* what I had to do.

# 4a.

## Five Coincidences,
## Seven Irma Cohens and
## One Confused Thursday Next

*The neanderthal experiment* was simultaneously the high and low point of the genetic revolution. Successful in that a long-dead cousin of *Homo sapien* was brought back from extinction, yet a failure in that the scientists, so happy to gaze upon their experiments from their ever lofty ivory towers, had not seen so far as to consider the social implications that a new species of man might command in a world unvisited by their like for over thirty millennia. It was little surprise that so many neanderthals felt confused and unprepared for the pressures of modern life. It was *Homo sapien* at his least sapient.

GERHARD VON SQUID,
*Neanderthals: Back After a Short Absence*

COINCIDENCES ARE strange things. I like the one about the poker player named Fallon, shot dead for cheating in San Francisco in 1858. It was considered unlucky to split the dead man's $600 winnings, so they gave the money to a passerby, hoping to win it back. The stranger converted the $600 to $2,200 and when the police arrived, was asked to hand over the original $600, as it was to be given to the dead gambler's next of kin. After a brief investigation, the money was returned to the passerby, as he turned out to be Fallon's son, who hadn't seen his father for seven years.

My father told me that for the most part coincidences could be safely ignored. "It would be *much* more remarkable," he would say, "if there *weren't* any coincidences."

I stepped into the Skyrail car and pulled the emergency lever. The neanderthal operator looked at me curiously as I jammed a foot in the open door of his driver's cubicle. I hauled him out and thumped him on the jaw before handcuffing him. A few days in the cooler and he would be back to Mrs. Kaylieu. The group of women in the Skyrail sat silent and shocked as I searched him and found—nothing. I looked in the cab and his sandwich box but the carved-soap gun wasn't there either.

The well-heeled woman who had earlier been so keen to jab the driver with her umbrella was now full of self-righteous indignation:

"Disgraceful! Attacking a poor defenseless neanderthal in this manner! I shall speak to my husband about this!"

One of the other women had called SpecOps-21 and a third had given the neanderthal a handkerchief to dab his bleeding mouth. I uncuffed Kaylieu and apologized, then sat down and put my head in my hands, wondering what had gone wrong. All the women were called Irma Cohen, but none of them would ever know it; Dad said this sort of thing happens all the time.

"You did *what?*" asked Victor, a few hours later at the LiteraTec office.

"I punched a neanderthal."

"Why?"

"I thought he had a gun on him."

"A neanderthal? With a gun? Don't be ridiculous!"

I was in Victor's office with the door closed—a rarity for him. I had been arrested, charged, processed—and delivered under guard to Victor, who vouched for me before I was released.

I would have been indignant had I not been so confused. And I was sorry for Kaylieu, too—I had knocked out one of his teeth.

"If the gun *had* been there it would have been carved from soap," I continued. "He wanted SO-14 to kill him. But that's not the half of it. The intended victim was *me*. If I had journeyed on the Skyrail it would have been Thursday in the body bag, not Kaylieu. I was set up, Victor. Someone manipulated events to try and bump me off with a stray SpecOps bullet—maybe that was their idea of a joke. If it hadn't been for Dad taking me out I'd be playing a harp by now."

Victor had been staring out of the window, his back to me.

"And there were the crossword clues—!"

Victor turned and walked back to his desk, picked up the paper and read the answers outlined in green.

*"Meddlesome, Thursday, Goodbye."*

He shrugged.

"Coincidence. I could make any sentence I wanted from any other clues just as easily. Look here."

He scanned the answers for a moment.

*"Planet, Destroyed, Soonest.* What does that mean? The world's about to end?"

"Well—"

He dumped my arrest report in his out tray and sat down.

"Thursday," he said quietly, staring at me soberly, "I've been in law enforcement for most of my life and I will tell you right now there is no such offense as 'attempted murder by coincidence in an alternative future by person or persons unknown.' "

I sighed and rubbed my face with my hands. He was right, of course.

"O-kay," he sighed. "Take my advice, Thursday. Tell them you thought the neanderthal was a felon, that he reminded you of the bogeyman—*anything*. Mention any unauthorized ChronoGuard shenanigans and Flanker will have your badge as a paperweight. I'll write a good report to SO-1 about your work and conduct so far. With a bit of luck and some serious lying on your behalf, maybe you can get away with a reprimand. For goodness sake, didn't you learn *anything* from that bad time junket on the M1?"

He got up and rubbed his legs. His body was failing him. The hip he'd had replaced four years ago needed to be replaced. Bowden joined us from where he had been running the copied pages of *Cardenio* through the Verse Meter Analyzer. Unusually for him he seemed to be showing some form of outward excitement. Bouncing, almost.

"How does it look?" I asked.

"Astounding!" replied Bowden as he waved a printed report. "94% probability of Will being the author—not even the best fake *Cardenio* managed higher than a 76. The VMA detected slight traces of collaboration, too."

"Did it say who?"

"73% likelihood of Fletcher—something that would seem to bear out against historical evidence. Forging Shakespeare is one thing, forging a collaborated work is *quite* another."

We all fell silent. Victor rubbed his forehead in contemplation and chose his words carefully.

"Okay, strange and impossible as it might seem, we may have to accept that this is the real thing. This could turn out to be the biggest literary event in history, *ever*. We keep this quiet and I'll get Professor Spoon to look it over. We will have to be 100% sure. I'm not going to suffer the same embarrassment we had over that *Tempest* fiasco."

"Since it isn't in the public domain," observed Bowden, "Volescamper will have the sole copyright for the next seventy-six years."

"Every playhouse on the planet will want to put it on," I added. "And think of the movie rights."

"Exactly," replied Victor. "He's sitting on not only the most fantastic literary discovery for three centuries but also a keg of purest gold. The question is, how did it languish in his library undiscovered all this time? Scholars have studied there since 1709. How on earth was it overlooked? Ideas, anyone?"

"Retrosnatch?" I suggested. "If a rogue ChronoGuard operative decided to go back to 1613 and steal a copy he could have a tidy little nest egg on his hands."

"SO-12 take retrosnatch very seriously and they assure me that it is *always* detected, sooner or later or both—and dealt with severely. But it's possible. Bowden, give SO-12 a call, will you?"

Bowden put out his hand to pick up the phone just as it started to ring.

"Hello? . . . It's not, you say? Okay, thanks."

He put the phone down.

"The ChronoGuard say not."

"How much do you think it's worth?" I asked.

"Hundred million," replied Victor. "Two hundred. Who knows. I'll call Volescamper and tell him to keep quiet about it. People would kill to even read it. No one else is to know about it, do you hear?"

We nodded our agreement.

"Good. Thursday, the network takes internal affairs very seriously. SO-1 will want to speak to you here tomorrow at four about the Skyrail thing. They asked me to suspend you, but I told them bollocks. Just take some leave until tomorrow. Good work, the two of you. Remember, *not a word to anyone!*"

We thanked him and he left. Bowden stared at the wall for a moment before saying: "The crossword clues bother me, though. If I wasn't of the opinion that coincidences are merely chance or an overused Dickensian plot device, I might conclude that an old enemy of yours wants to get even."

"One with a sense of humor, obviously," I murmured in agreement.

"That rules out Goliath, I suppose," mused Bowden. "Who are you calling?"

"SO-5."

I dug Agent Phodder's card out of my pocket and rang the number. He had told me to call him if "an occurrence of unprecedented *weird*" took place, so I was doing precisely that.

"Hello?" said a brusque voice after the telephone had rung for a long time.

"Thursday Next, SO-27," I announced. "I have some information for Agent Phodder."

There was a long pause.

"Agent Phodder has been reassigned."

"Agent Kannon, then."

"Both Phodder *and* Kannon have been reassigned," replied the man sharply. "Freak accident laying linoleum. The funeral's on Friday."

This was unexpected news. I couldn't think of anything intelligent to say, so I mumbled: "I'm sorry to hear that."

"Quite," said the brusque man, and put the phone down.

"What happened?" asked Bowden.

"Both dead," I said quietly.

"Hades?"

"Linoleum."

We sat in silence for a moment, unnerved by the news.

"Does Hades have the sort of powers that might be necessary to manipulate coincidences?" asked Bowden.

I shrugged.

"Perhaps," said Bowden thoughtfully, "it *was* a coincidence after all."

"Perhaps," I said, wishing I could believe it. "Oh—I almost forgot. The world's going to end on the 12th December at 20:23."

"Really?" replied Bowden in a disinterested tone. Apocalyptic pronouncements were nothing new to any of us. The world had been predicted as about to be destroyed almost every year since the dawn of man.

"Which one is it this time?" asked Bowden. "Plague of mice or the wrath of God?"

"I'm not sure. I've got to be somewhere at five. Do us a favor, would you?"

I reached into my pocket and retrieved the small evidence bag my father had given to me. Bowden took the bag from my outstretched arm and looked at it curiously.

I checked the time and rose to leave.

"What is it?" he asked, staring at the pink goo.

"That's what I need to know. Will you have the labs analyze it?"

We bade each other goodbye and I trotted out of the building, bumping into John Smith, who was maneuvering a wheelbarrow with a carrot the size of a vacuum cleaner in it. There was a big label attached to the oversized vegetable that read *evidence,* and I held the door open for him.

"Thanks," he panted.

I jumped in my car and pulled out of the car park. My appointment at five was at the doctor's, and I wasn't going to miss it for anything.

# 6.

## Family

Landen Parke-Laine had been with me in the Crimea in '72. He lost a leg to a land mine and his best friend to a military blunder. His best friend was my brother, Anton—and Landen testified against him at the hearing that followed the disastrous "charge of the light armored brigade." My brother was blamed for the debacle, Landen was honorably discharged, I was awarded the Crimea Star for gallantry, I didn't speak to him for ten years and now we're married. It's funny how things turn out.

THURSDAY NEXT,
*Crimean Reminiscences*

**H**ONEY, I'M HOME!" I yelled out. There was a scrabbling noise from the kitchen as Pickwick's feet struggled to get a purchase on the tiles in his eagerness to greet me. I had engineered him myself when you could still buy home cloning kits over the counter. He was an early version 1.2, which explained his lack of wings—they didn't complete the sequence for two more years. He made excited *plock plock* noises and bobbed his head in greeting, rummaged in the wastebasket for a gift and eventually brought me a discarded junk mail flyer for *Lorna Doone* merchandising. I tickled him under the chin, and he ran to the kitchen, stopped, looked at me and bobbed his head some more.

"Hell-ooo!" yelled Landen from his study. "Do you like surprises?"

"When they're nice ones!" I yelled back.

Pickwick returned to my side, plock-plocked some more and tugged the leg of my jeans. He scuttled off into the kitchen again and waited for me at his basket. Intrigued, I followed. I could see the reason for his excitement. In the middle of the basket, amongst a large heap of shredded paper, was an egg.

"Pickwick!" I cried excitedly. *"You're a girl!"*

Pickwick bobbed some more and nuzzled me affectionately. After a while she stopped and delicately stepped into her basket, ruffled her feathers, tapped the egg with her beak and then walked round it several times before gently placing herself over it. A hand rested on my shoulder. I touched Landen's fingers and stood up. He kissed me on the neck and I wrapped my arms round his chest.

"I thought Pickwick was a boy?" he asked.

"So did I."

"Is it a sign?"

"Pickers laying an egg and turning out to be a girl?" I replied. "What do you mean—you're going to have a baby, Land?"

"No, silly, you *know* what I mean."

"I do?" I asked, looking up at him with carefully engineered innocence.

*"Well?"*

"Well what?" I stared into his bright concerned face with what I thought was a blank expression. But I couldn't hold it for long and was soon a bundle of girlish giggles and salty tears. He hugged me tightly and placed his hand gently on my tum.

"In there? A baby?"

"Yes. Small pink thing that makes a noise. Seven weeks. Probably appear July-ish."

"How are you feeling?"

"All right," I told him. "I felt a bit sick yesterday, but that might have had nothing to do with it. I'll work until I start waddling and then take leave. How are *you* feeling?"

"Odd," said Landen, hugging me again, "in a very nice kind of *elated* sort of way. . . . Who can I tell?"

"No one quite yet. Probably just as well—your mum would knit herself to death!"

"And what's wrong with my mother's knitting?" asked Landen, feigning indignation.

"Nothing," I giggled, "but there is a limit to storage space."

"At least the things she knits are recognizable," he replied. "That jumper your mum gave me for my birthday—what does she think I am, a squid?"

I buried my face in his collar and held him close. He rubbed my back gently and we stood together for several minutes without talking.

"Did you have a good day?" he asked at last.

"Well," I began, "we found *Cardenio*, I was shot dead by an SO-14 marksman, became a vanishing hitchhiker, saw Yorrick Kaine, suffered a few too many coincidences and knocked a neanderthal unconscious."

"No puncture this time?"

"Two, actually—at the same time."

"What was Kaine like?"

"Difficult to say. He arrived at Volescamper's as we were leaving. Aren't you even *curious* about the marksman?"

"Yorrick Kaine is giving a talk tonight about the economical realities of a Welsh free trade agreement—"

"Landen," I said, "it's my uncle's party tonight. I promised Mum we'd be there."

"Yeah, I know."

"Are you going to ask me about the incident with SO-14 now?"

"All right," sighed Landen. "What was it like?"

"Don't ask."

My uncle Mycroft had announced his retirement. He was seventy-seven, and following the events of the Prose Portal and Polly's imprisonment in "I wandered lonely as a cloud," they had both decided that enough was enough. The Goliath Corporation had been offering Mycroft not one but *two* blank checks for him to resume work on a new Prose Portal, but Mycroft had steadfastly refused, maintaining that the Portal could not be replicated even if he had wanted to. We took my car up to Mum's house and parked a little way up the road.

"I never thought of Mycroft retiring," I said as we walked down the street.

"Me neither," he replied. "What do you suppose he'll do?"

"Watch *Name That Fruit!* most likely. He says that soaps and quiz shows are the ideal way to fade out."

"He's not far wrong," added Landen. "After a few years of *65 Walrus Street,* death might become something of a welcome distraction."

We heaved open the garden gate and greeted the dodos, who all had a bright pink ribbon tied round their necks for the occasion. I offered them a few marshmallows and they pecked and plocked greedily at the proffered gifts. The front door was opened by Wilbur, who was one of Mycroft's sons and had reached middle age well before his time. Landen thought he did it on purpose, as though he could somehow accelerate through the days of work and get to retirement and golf just that little bit sooner.

"Hello, Thursday!" he enthused, ushering us inside.

"Hi, Wilbers. All well?"

"I'm *very* well," replied Wilbur, smiling benignly. "Hello,

Landen—I read your latest book. It was a big improvement on the last one, I must say."

"You're very kind," replied Landen dryly.

"Drink?"

He offered us both a glass, and I took mine eagerly. I had just got it to my lips when Landen took it out of my hands. I looked at him and he mouthed, "Baby." Blast. Hadn't thought of that.

"I was *promoted*, you know," continued Wilbur, walking through the hall and towards the living room.

He paused to allow us to murmur a congratulatory sound before continuing: "Consolidated Useful Stuff always promote those within the company that show particular promise, and after ten years in pension fund management ConStuff felt I was ready to branch into something new and dynamic. I'm now Services Director at a subsidiary of theirs named MycroTech Developments."

"But my goodness *what* a coincidence!" said Landen sarcastically. "Isn't that Mycroft's company?"

"Coincidental," replied Wilbur forcefully, "as you say. Mr. Perkup—the CEO of MycroTech—told me it was solely due to my diligence; I—"

"Thursday, *darling!*" interrupted Gloria, Wilbur's wife. Formerly a Volescamper, she had married Wilbur under the accidental misapprehension that A: he would be coming into a fortune and B: he was as intelligent as his father. She had been wrong—in a spectacular fashion—on both counts.

"Darling, you are looking simply divine—have you lost weight?"

"I have no idea, Gloria, but . . . you're looking different."

And she was. Habitually dressed to the nines in expensive clothes, hats, makeup and lashings of what-have-you, tonight Gloria was dressed in chinos and a shirt. She hardly wore any makeup and her hair, usually perfectly coiffured, was tied up in a ponytail with a black scrunchie.

"What do you think?" she asked, doing a twirl for us both.

"What happened to the £500 dresses?" asked Landen. "Bailiffs been in?"

"No, this is all the rage—and you should know, Thursday. *FeMole* is promoting the Thursday Next look. This is very much 'in' at present."

"Ridiculous," I told her, wondering if there was an end to the ludicrous media spin-offs from the whole *Eyre* thing. Cordelia had gone so far as to license jigsaw puzzles and action figures before I had a chance to stop her. I wondered if she'd had a hand in this, too.

"If Bonzo the Wonder Hound had rescued Jane Eyre," I asked, trying to keep a straight face, "would you all be wearing studded collars and smelling each other's bottoms?"

"There is no need to be offensive," replied Gloria haughtily as she looked me up and down. "You should be *honored*. Mind you, the December issue of *FeMole* thinks that a brown leather flier's jacket is more in keeping with 'the look.' Your black leather is a little bit passé, I'm afraid. And those shoes—hell's teeth!"

"Wait a moment!" I returned. "How can you tell me that I don't have the Thursday Next look? I *am* Thursday Next!"

"Fashions evolve, Thursday—I've heard that next month's fashions will be marine invertebrates. You should enjoy it while you can."

"Marine invertebrates?" echoed Landen. "What happened to that squidlike jumper of your mum's? We could be sitting on a fortune!"

"Can neither of you be serious?" asked Gloria disdainfully. "If you're not in you're out, and where would you be then?"

"Out, I guess," I replied. "Land, what do you think?"

"Totally out, Thurs."

We stared at her half smiling, and she laughed. Gloria was a good sort once you broke down the barriers. Wilbur, seizing the chance to tell us more about his fascinating new job, carried on as soon as his wife stopped talking.

"I'm now on £20K *plus* car and a good pension package. I could take voluntary retirement at fifty-five and still draw two-thirds of my wage. What is the SpecOps retirement fund like?"

"Crap, Wilbur—but you know that."

A slightly smaller and more follicularly challenged version of Wilbur walked up.

"Hello, Thursday."

"Hello, Orville. How's the ear?"

"Just the same. What was that you were saying about retiring at fifty-five, Will?"

In all the excitement of pension plans I was forgotten. Charlotte, who was Orville's wife, also had the Thursday Next look; she and Gloria fell eagerly into untaxing conversation about whether leather shoes in "the look" should be worn above or below the ankle and whether a small amount of eyeliner was acceptable. As usual, Charlotte tended to agree with Gloria; in fact, she tended to agree with everybody about everything. She was as hospitable as the day was long; just don't get caught in an elevator with her—she could agree you to death.

We left them to their conversation, and I walked into the living room, deftly catching the wrist of my elder brother Joffy, who had been hoping to give me a resounding slap on the back of my head as was his thirty-five-year-old custom. I twisted his arm into a half nelson and had his face pressed against the door before he knew what had happened.

"Hello, Joff," I said. "Slowing up in your old age?"

I let him go, he laughed energetically, straightened his jaw and dog collar and hugged me tightly while proffering a hand for Landen to shake. Landen, after checking for the almost mandatory hand buzzer, shook it heartily.

"How's Mr. and Mrs. Doofus, then?"

"We're fine, Joff. You?"

"Not that good, Thurs. The Church of the Global Standard Deity has undergone a split."

"No!" I said with as much surprise and concern in my voice as I could muster.

"I'm afraid so. The new Global Standard *Clockwise* Deity have broken away due to unresolvable differences over the direction in which the collection plate is passed round."

"*Another* split? That's the third this week!"

"Fourth," replied Joffy dourly, "and it's only Tuesday. The Standardized pro-Baptist conjoined Methodarian-Lutheran sisters of something-or-other split into two subgroups yesterday. Soon," he added grimly, "there won't be enough ministers to man the splits. As it is I have to attend two dozen different breakaway church groups every week. I often forget which one I'm at, and as you can imagine, preaching to the Idolatry Friends of St. Zvlkx the Consumer the sermon that I should have been reading to the Church of the Misrepresented Promise of Eternal Life can be highly embarrassing. Mum's in the kitchen. Do you think Dad will turn up?"

I didn't know and told him so. He looked crestfallen for a moment and then said: "Will you come and do a professional mingle at my Les Artes Modernes de Swindon show next week?"

"Why me?"

"Because you're vaguely famous and you're my sister. Yes?"

"Okay."

He tugged my ear affectionately and we walked into the kitchen.

"Hello, Mum!"

My mother was bustling around some chicken vol-au-vent. By some bizarre twist of fate the pastry had turned out not at all burned and actually quite tasty—it had thrown her into a bit of a panic. Most of her cooking ended up as the culinary equivalent of the Tunguska event.

"Hello, Thursday, hello, Landen, can you pass me that bowl, please?"

Landen passed it over, trying to guess the contents.

"Hello, Mrs. Next," said Landen.

"Call me Wednesday, Landen—you're family now, you know." She smiled and giggled to herself.

"Dad said to say hello," I put in quickly before Mum cooed herself into a frenzy. "I saw him today."

My mother stopped her random method of cooking and recalled for a moment, I imagine, fond embraces with her eradicated husband. It must have been quite a shock, waking up one morning and finding your husband never existed. Then, quite out of the blue, she yelled: "DH-82, *down!*"

Her anger was directed at a small Tasmanian tiger that had been nosing the remains of some chicken on the table edge.

"Bad boy!" she added in a scolding tone. The Tastiger looked crestfallen, sat on its blanket by the Aga and stared down at its paws.

"Rescue Thylacine," explained my mother. "Used to be a lab animal. He smoked forty a day until his escape. It's costing me a fortune in nicotine patches. Isn't it, DH-82?"

The small reengineered native of Tasmania looked up and shook his head. Despite being vaguely dog-shaped, this species was more closely related to a kangaroo than a Labrador. You always expected one to wag its tail, bark or fetch a stick, but they never did. The closest behavioral similarities were a propensity to steal food and an almost fanatical devotion to tail chasing.

"I miss your dad a lot, you know," said my mother wistfully. "How—"

There was a loud explosion, the lights flickered, and something shot past the kitchen window.

"What was that?" said my mother.

"I think," replied Landen soberly, "it was Aunt Polly."

We found her in the vegetable patch dressed in a deflating rubber suit that was meant to break her fall but obviously hadn't—she was holding a handkerchief to a bloodied nose.

"My goodness!" exclaimed my mother. "Are you okay?"

"Never been better!" she replied, looking at a stake in the ground and then yelling: "Seventy-five yards!"

"Righty-oh!" said a distant voice from the other end of the garden. We turned to see Uncle Mycroft, who was consulting a clipboard next to a smoking Volkswagen convertible.

"Car seat ejection devices in case of road accidents," explained Polly, "with a self-inflating rubber suit to cushion the fall. Pull on a toggle and *bang*—out you go. Prototype, of course."

"Of course."

We helped her to her feet and she trotted off, seemingly none the worse for her experience.

"Mycroft still inventing, then?" I said as we walked back inside to discover that DH-82 had eaten all the vol-au-vent, main course *and* the trifle for pudding.

"DH!" she said crossly to the guilty-looking and very bloated Tastiger. "That was *very* bad! What am I going to feed everybody on now?"

"How about thylacine cutlets?" suggested Landen.

I elbowed him in the ribs and Mum pretended not to hear.

Landen rolled up his sleeves and searched through the kitchen for something he could cook quickly and easily. It was going to be hard—all of the cupboards were full of tinned pears.

"Have you anything apart from canned fruit, Mrs.—I mean, Wednesday?"

Mum stopped trying to chastise DH-82, who, soporific through gluttony, had settled down for a long nap.

"No," she admitted. "The man in the shop said there would be a shortage, so I bought his entire stock."

I walked down to Mycroft's laboratory, knocked and, when there was no reply, entered. Usually, the lab presented an Aladdin's cave of inventive genius, the haphazard and eclectic mix of machines, papers, blackboards and bubbling retorts a shrine to disarray; an antidote to order. But today it was different: All his machines had been dismantled and now lay about the room, tagged and carefully stacked. Mycroft himself, having obviously finished testing the ejection system, was now tweaking a small bronze object. He was startled when I spoke his name but relaxed as soon as he saw it was me.

"Hello, love!" he said kindly.

"Hello, Uncle. How have you been?"

"Good. I'm off on retirement in—*don't touch that!*—in one hour and nine minutes. You looked good on the telly last night."

"Thank you. What are you up to, Uncle?"

He handed me a large book.

"*Enhanced* indexing. In a Nextian dictionary, godliness *can* be next to cleanliness—or anything else for that matter."

I opened the book to look up "trout" and found it on the first page I opened.

"Saves time, eh?"

"Yes; but—"

Mycroft had moved on.

"Over here is a Lego filter for vacuum cleaners. Did you

know that over a million pounds' worth of Lego is hoovered up every year, and a total of ten thousand man-hours are wasted sorting through the dust bags?"

"I didn't know that, no."

"This device will sort any sucked-up bits of Lego into colors or shapes, according to how you set this knob here."

"Very impressive."

"This is just hobby stuff. Come and look at some *real* innovation."

He beckoned me across to a blackboard, the surface covered with a jumbled mass of complicated algebraic functions.

"This is Polly's hobby, really. It's a new form of mathematical theory that makes Euclid's work seem like little more than long division. We have called it Nextian geometry. I won't bother you with the details, but watch this."

Mycroft rolled up his shirtsleeves and placed a large ball of dough on the workbench and rolled it out into a flat ovoid with a rolling pin.

"Scone dough," he explained. "I've left out the raisins for purposes of clarity. Using *conventional* geometry, a round scone cutter always leaves waste behind, agreed?"

"Agreed."

"Not with *Nextian* geometry! You see this pastry cutter? Circular, wouldn't you say?"

"Perfectly circular, yes."

"Well," carried on Mycroft in an excited voice, "it isn't. It *appears* circular but actually it's a square. A *Nextian* square. Watch."

And so saying he deftly cut the dough into twelve perfectly circular shapes with no waste. I frowned and stared at the small pile of disks, not quite believing what I had just seen.

"How—?"

"Clever, isn't it?" he chuckled. "Admittedly it only works with Nextian dough, which doesn't rise so well and tastes like denture paste, but we're working on that."

"It *seems* impossible, Uncle."

"We didn't know the nature of lightning or rainbows for three and a half million years, pet. Don't reject it just because it *seems* impossible. If we closed our minds, there would never be the Gravitube, antimatter, Prose Portals, thermos flasks—"

"Wait!" I interrupted. "How does a *thermos* fit in with that little lot?"

"Because, my dear girl," replied Mycroft, cleaning the blackboard and drawing a crude picture of a thermos with a question mark, "no one has the least idea *why* they work." He stared at me for a moment and continued: "You will agree that a vacuum flask keeps hot things hot in the winter and cold things cold in the summer?"

"Yes—?"

"Well, *how does it know?* I've studied vacuum flasks for many years and *not one* of them gave any clues as to their inherent seasonal cognitive ability. It's a mystery to me, I can tell you."

"Okay, okay, Uncle—how about applications for Nextian geometry?"

"Hundreds. Packaging and space management will be revolutionized overnight. I can pack Ping-Pong balls in a cardboard box without any gaps, punch steel bottle tops with no waste, drill a square hole, tunnel to the moon, divide cake more efficiently and also—and this is the most exciting part—*collapse matter.*"

"Isn't that dangerous?"

"Not at all," replied Mycroft airily. "You accept that all matter is mostly empty space? The gaps between the nucleus and the electrons? Well, by applying Nextian geometry to the subatomic level I can collapse matter to a fraction of its former size. I will be able to reduce almost anything to the microscopic!"

He stopped for a moment and regathered his thoughts.

"Miniaturization is a technology that *needs* to be utilized," explained Mycroft. "Can you imagine tiny nanomachines barely bigger than a cell, building, say, food protein out of nothing more than garbage? Banoffee pie from landfills, ships from scrap iron—! It's a fantastic notion. Consolidated Useful Stuff are financing some R&D with me as we speak."

"At MycroTech Developments?"

"Yes," he said sharply. "How did you know?"

"Wilbur said he had got a job there—by coincidence, of course."

"Of course," affirmed Mycroft, who never supported, or admitted to, any sort of nepotism.

"On the subject of coincidences, Uncle, any thoughts on what they are and how they come about?"

Mycroft fell silent for a moment as his huge brain clicked over the facts as he understood them.

"Well," he said thoughtfully, "it is my considered opinion that most coincidences are simply quirks of chance—if you extrapolate the bell curve of probability you will find statistical abnormalities that seem unusual but are, in actual fact, quite likely, given the amount of people on the planet and the amount of different things we do in our lives."

"I see," I replied slowly. "That explains things on a minor coincidental level, but what about the *bigger* coincidences? How high would you rate seven people in a Skyrail shuttle all called Irma Cohen and the clues of a crossword reading out 'Meddlesome Thursday goodbye' just before someone tried to kill me?"

Mycroft raised an eyebrow.

"That's quite a coincidence. More than a coincidence, I

think." He took a deep breath. "Thursday, think for a moment about the fact that the universe always moves from an ordered state to a disordered one; that a glass may fall to the ground and shatter yet you *never* see a broken glass reassemble itself and then jump back onto the table."

"I accept that."

"But why doesn't it?"

"Search me."

"Every atom of the glass that shattered would contravene no laws of physics if it were to rejoin—on a subatomic level all particle interactions are reversible. Down *there* we can't tell which event precedes which. It's only out *here* that we can see things age and define a strict direction in which time travels."

"So what are you saying, Uncle?"

"That these things *don't* happen is because of the second law of thermodynamics, which states that disorder in the universe *always* increases; the amount of this disorder is a quantity known as entropy."

"So how does this relate to coincidences?"

"I'm getting to that," muttered Mycroft, gradually warming up to his explanation and becoming more and more animated each second. "Imagine a box with a partition—the left side is filled with gas, the right a vacuum. Remove the partition and the gas will expand into the other side of the box—yes?"

I nodded.

"And you wouldn't expect the gas to cramp itself up in the left-hand side again, would you?"

"No."

"Ah!" replied Mycroft with a knowing smile. "Not *quite* right. You see, since every interaction of gas atom is reversible, sometime, sooner or later, the gas *must* cramp itself back into the left-hand side!"

"It must?"

"Yes; the key here is *how much later.* Since even a small box of gas might contain $10^{20}$ atoms, the time taken for them to try all *possible* combinations would take far longer than the age of the universe; a decrease in entropy strong enough to allow gas to separate, a shattered glass to re-form or the statue of St. Zvlkx outside to get down and walk to the pub is not, I think, against any physical laws but just fantastically unlikely."

"So," I said slowly, "what you are saying is that really *really* weird coincidences are caused by a drop in entropy?"

"Exactly so. But it's only a theory. As to why entropy might spontaneously decrease and how one might conduct experiments into localized entropic field decreasement, I have only a few untried notions that I won't trouble you with here, but look, take this—it could save your life."

He picked up a jam jar from one of the many worktops and passed it to me. It seemed the contents were half rice and half lentils.

"I'm not hungry, thanks," I told him.

"No, no. I call this device an entroposcope. Shake it for me."

I shook the jam jar and the rice and lentils settled together in that sort of random clumping way that chance usually dictates.

"So?" I asked.

"Entirely usual," replied Mycroft. "Standard clumping, entropy levels normal. Shake it every now and then. You'll know when a decrease in entropy occurs as the rice and lentils will separate out into more ordered patterns—and *that's* the time to watch out for ludicrously unlikely coincidences."

Polly entered the workshop and gave her husband a hug.

"Hello, you two," she said. "Having fun?"

"I'm showing Thursday what I've been up to, my dear," replied Mycroft graciously.

"Did you show her your memory erasure device, Crofty?"

"No, he didn't," I said.

"Yes, I *did*," replied Mycroft with a smile, adding: "You're going to have to leave me, pet—I've work to do. I retire in fifty-six minutes precisely."

My father didn't turn up that evening, much to my mother's disappointment. At five minutes to ten, Mycroft, true to his word and with Polly behind him, emerged from his laboratory to join us for dinner.

Next family dinners are always noisy affairs, and tonight was no different. Landen sat next to Orville and did a very good impression of someone who was trying not to be bored. Joffy, who was next to Wilbur, thought his new job was utter crap, and Wilbur, who had been needled by Joffy for at least three decades, replied that he thought the Global Standard Deity Faith was the biggest load of phony codswallop he had ever come across.

"Ah," replied Joffy loftily, "wait until you meet the Brotherhood of Unconstrained Verbosity."

Gloria and Charlotte always sat next to each other, Gloria to talk about something trivial—such as buttons—and Charlotte to agree with her. Mum and Polly talked about the Women's Federation and I sat next to Mycroft.

"What will you do in your retirement, Uncle?"

"I don't know, pet. I have some books I've been wanting to write for some time."

"About your work?"

"Much too dull. Can I try an idea out on you?"

"Sure."

He smiled, looked around, lowered his voice and leaned closer.

"Okay, here it is. Brilliant young surgeon Dexter Colt starts work at the highly efficient yet underfunded children's hospital doing pioneering work on relieving the suffering of orphaned amputees. The chief nurse is the headstrong yet beautiful Tiffany Lampe. Tiffany has only recently recovered from her shattered love affair with anesthetist Dr. Burns, and—"

"—they fall in love?" I ventured.

Mycroft's face fell.

"You've heard it then?"

"The bit about the orphaned amputees is good," I said, trying not to dishearten him. "What are you going to call it?"

"I thought of *Love Among the Orphans*. What do you think?"

By the end of the meal Mycroft had outlined several of his books to me, each one with a plot more lurid than the last. At the same time Joffy and Wilbur had come to blows in the garden, discussing the sanctity of peace and forgiveness amidst the thud of fists and the crunch of broken noses.

At midnight Mycroft took Polly in his arms and thanked us all for coming.

"I have spent my entire life in pursuit of scientific truth and enlightenment," he announced grandly, "of answers to conundrums and unifying theories of everything. Perhaps I should have spent the time going out more. In fifty-four years neither Polly nor I have ever taken a holiday, so that is where we're off to now."

We walked into the garden, the family wishing Mycroft and Polly well on their travels. Outside the door of the workshop they stopped and looked at each other, then at all of us.

"Well, thanks for the party," said Mycroft. "Pear soup followed by pear stew with pear sauce and finishing with *bombe surprise*—which was pear—was quite a treat. Unusual, but quite a treat. Look after MycroTech while I'm away, Wilbur, and thanks for all the meals, Wednesday. Right, that's it," concluded Mycroft. "We're off. Toodle-oo."

"Enjoy yourselves," I said.

"Oh, we will!" he said, bidding us all goodbye again and disappearing into the workshop. Polly kissed us all, waved farewell and followed him, closing the door behind her.

"It won't be the same without him and his daft projects, will it?" said Landen.

"No," I replied. "It's—"

There was a tingling sensation like an electrical storm in summer as a noiseless white light erupted from within the workshop and shone in pencil-thin beams from every crack and rivet hole, each speck of grime showing up on the dirty windows, every crack in the glass suddenly alive with a rainbow of colors. We winced and shielded our eyes, but no sooner had the light started than it had gone again, faded to nothing in a crackle of electricity. Landen and I exchanged looks and stepped forward. The door opened easily and we stood there, staring into the large and now very empty workshop. Every single piece of equipment had gone. Not a screw, not a bolt, not a washer.

"He isn't just going to write romantic novels in his retirement," observed Joffy, putting his head round the door.

"No," I replied, "he most probably took it all so no one else would carry on with his work. Mycroft's scruples were the equal of his intellect."

My mother was sitting on an upturned wheelbarrow, her dodos clustered around her on the off chance of a marshmallow.

"They're not coming back," said my mother sadly. "You know that, don't you?"

"Yes," I said, giving her a hug, "I know."

# 7.

## White Horse, Uffington, Picnics, for the Use of

We decided that "Parke-Laine-Next" was a bit of a mouthful, so I kept my surname and he kept his. I called myself "Ms." instead of "Miss," but nothing else changed. I liked being called his wife in the same way I liked calling Landen my husband. It felt sort of *tingly*. I had the same feeling when I stared at my wedding ring. They say you get used to it but I hoped that they were wrong. Marriage, like spinach and opera, was something I had never thought I would like. I changed my mind about opera when I was nine years old. My father took me to the first night of *Madama Butterfly* at Brescia in 1904. After the performance Dad cooked while Puccini regaled me with hilarious stories and signed my autograph book—from that day on I was a devoted fan. In the same way, it took being in love with Landen to make me change my mind about marriage. I found it exciting and exhilarating; two people, together, as one. It was where I was meant to be. I was happy; I was contented; I was fulfilled.

And spinach? Well, I'm still waiting.

THURSDAY NEXT,
*Private Diaries*

**W**HAT DO YOU THINK they'll do?" asked Landen as we lay in bed, he with one hand resting gently on my stomach and the other wrapped tightly around me. The bedclothes had been thrown off and we had only just regained our breath.

"Who?"

"SO-1 this afternoon. About you punching the neanderthal."

"Oh, *that*. I don't know. Technically speaking, I really haven't done anything wrong at all—I think they'll let me off, considering all the good PR work I've done. Look a bit daft to arrest their star operative, don't you think?"

"That's always assuming they think logically like you or me."

"It is, isn't it?"

I sighed.

"People *have* been busted for less. SO-1 like to make an example from time to time."

"You don't *have* to work, you know."

I looked across at him, but he was too close to focus on, which was sort of nice, in its way.

"I know," I replied, "but I'd like to keep it up. I don't really see myself as a mummsy sort of person."

"Your cooking might tend to support that fact."

"Mother's cooking is terrible, too—I think it's hereditary. My SO-1 hearing is at four. Want to go and see the mammoth migration?"

"Sure."

The doorbell rang.

"Who could that be?"

"It's a little early to tell," quipped Landen. "I understand the 'go and see' technique sometimes works."

"Very funny."

I pulled on some clothes and went downstairs. There was a gaunt man with lugubrious features standing on the doorstep. He looked as close to a bloodhound as one can get without actually having a tail and barking.

"Yes?"

He raised his hat and gave me a somnambulant smile.

"The name is Hopkins," he explained. "I'm a reporter for

*The Owl*. I was wondering if I could interview you about your time within the pages of *Jane Eyre*."

"You'll have to go through Cordelia Flakk at SpecOps, I'm afraid. I'm not really at liberty—"

"I know you were inside the book. In the first and original ending, Jane goes to India, yet in *your* ending she stays and marries Rochester. How did you engineer this?"

"You really have to get clearance from Flakk, Mr. Hopkins."

He sighed.

"Okay, I will. Just one thing. Did you prefer the new ending, *your* new ending?"

"Of course. Didn't you?"

Mr. Hopkins scribbled in a notepad and smiled again.

"Thank you, Miss Next. I'm very much in your debt. Good day!"

He raised his hat again and was gone.

"What was all that about?" asked Landen as he handed me a cup of coffee.

"Pressman."

"What did you tell him?"

"Nothing. He has to go through Flakk."

The grassy escarpment at Uffington was busy that morning. The mammoth population in England, Wales and Scotland amounted to 249 individuals in nine groups, all of whom migrated north to south around late autumn and back again in the spring. The routes followed the same pattern every year with staggering accuracy. Inhabited areas were mostly avoided—except Devizes, where the High Street was shuttered up and deserted twice a year as the plodding elephantines crashed and trumpeted their way through the center of the town, cheerfully following the ancient call of their forebears. No one in Devizes could get any sleep or Proboscidea damage insurance cover, but the extra cash from tourism generally made up for it.

But there weren't just mammoth twitchers, walkers, druids and a neanderthal "right to hunt" protest up the hill that morning. A dark blue automobile was waiting for us, and when somebody is waiting for you in a place you hadn't planned on being, then you take notice. There were three of them standing next to the car, all dressed in dark suits with blue enameled Goliath badges on their lapels. The only one I recognized was Schitt-Hawse; they all hastily hid their ice creams as we approached.

"Mr. Schitt-Hawse," I said, "what a surprise! Have you met my husband?"

Schitt-Hawse offered his hand, but Landen didn't take it. The Goliath agent grimaced for a moment, then gave a bemused grin.

"Saw you on the telly, Ms. Next. It was a *fascinating* talk about dodos, I must say."

"I'd like to expand my subjects next time," I replied evenly. "Might even try and include something about Goliath's malignant stranglehold on the nation."

Schitt-Hawse shook his head sadly.

"Unwise, Next, unwise. What you singularly fail to grasp is that Goliath is all you'll ever need. All *anyone* will ever need. We manufacture everything from cots to coffins and employ over eight million people in our six thousand or so subsidiary companies. Everything from the womb to the wooden overcoat."

"And how much profit do you expect to scavenge as you massage us from hatched to dispatched?"

"You can't put a price on human happiness, Next. Political and economic uncertainty are the two biggest forms of stress. You'll be pleased to know that the Goliath Cheerfulness Index has reached a four-year high this morning at nine point one three."

"Out of a hundred?" asked Landen sarcastically.

"Out of *ten*, Mr. Parke-Laine," he replied testily. "The nation has grown beyond all measure under our guidance."

"Growth purely for its own sake is the philosophy of cancer, Schitt-Hawse."

His face dropped and he stared at us for a moment, doubtless wondering how best to continue.

"So," I said politely, "out to watch the mammoths?"

"Goliath don't watch mammoths, Next. There's no profit in it. Have you met my associates Mr. Chalk and Mr. Cheese?"

I looked at his two gorillalike lackeys. They were immaculately dressed, had impeccably trimmed goatees, and stared at me through impenetrable dark glasses.

"Which is which?" I asked.

"I'm Cheese," said Cheese.

"I'm Chalk," said Chalk.

"When is he going to ask you about Jack Schitt?" asked Landen in an unsubtly loud whisper.

"Pretty soon," I replied.

Schitt-Hawse shook his head sadly. He opened the briefcase Mr. Chalk was holding, and inside, nestled in the carefully cut foam innards, lay a copy of *The Poems of Edgar Allan Poe.*

"You left Jack imprisoned in this copy of 'The Raven.' Goliath need him out to face a disciplinary board on charges of embezzlement, Goliath contractual irregularities, misuse of the corporation's leisure facilities, missing stationery—and crimes against humanity."

"Oh yes?" I asked. "Why not just leave him in?"

Schitt-Hawse sighed and stared at me.

"Listen, Next. We need Jack out of here, and believe me, we'll manage it."

"Not with my help."

Schitt-Hawse stared silently at me for a moment.

"Goliath are not used to being refused. We asked your uncle to build another Prose Portal. He told us to come back in a month's time. We understand he left on retirement last night. Destination?"

"Not a clue."

Mycroft had retired, it seemed, not out of choice but out of necessity. I smiled to myself. Goliath had been hoodwinked and they didn't like it.

"Without the Portal," I told him, "I can't jump into books any more than Mr. Chalk can."

Chalk shuffled slightly as I mentioned his name.

"You're lying," replied Schitt-Hawse. "The ineptness card doesn't work on us. You defeated Hades, Jack Schitt and the Goliath Corporation. We have a great deal of admiration for you. Goliath has been more than fair given the circumstances, and we would hate for you to become a victim of *corporate impatience.*"

"Corporate impatience?" I repeated, staring Schitt-Hawse straight in the eye. "What's that, some sort of threat?"

"This unhelpful attitude of yours might make me vindictive— and you wouldn't like me when I get vindictive."

"I don't like you when you're *not* vindictive."

Schitt-Hawse shut the briefcase with a snap. His left eye twitched and the color drained out of his face. He looked at us both and started to say something, stopped, got ahold of his temper and managed to squeeze out a half-smile before he climbed back into his car with Chalk and Cheese and was gone.

Landen was still chuckling as we spread a groundsheet and blanket on the well-nibbled grass just above the White Horse. Below us at the bottom of the escarpment a herd of mammoths were quietly browsing, and on the horizon we could see several airships on the approach to Oxford. It was a pleasant day, and since airships don't fly in poor weather, they were all making the best use of it.

"You don't have much fear of Goliath, do you, darling?" he asked.

I shrugged.

"Goliath are nothing more than a bully, Land. Stand up to them and they'll soon scurry away. All that large car and henchman stuff—it's for frighteners. But I'm kind of puzzled as to how they knew we would be here."

Landen shrugged.

"Cheese or ham?"[1]

"What?"

"I said: 'Cheese or ham."

"Not *you*."

Landen looked around. We were about the only ones within a hundred-yard radius.

"Who then?"

"Snell."

"Who?"

"Snell!" I yelled out loud. "Is that you?"[2]

"I didn't!"[3]

"Prosecution? Who?"[4]

"Thursday," said Landen, now looking worried, "what the hell's going on?"

"I'm talking to my lawyer."

1. "Thursday, for heaven's sake what have you done?!"
2. "I told you not to talk to anyone about your case!"
3. "How can I be expected to help you if you go and blab everything to the prosecution?"
4. "Why Hopkins, you idiot! You pretty much confessed there and then on your own doorstep. This is going to really screw things up for us. Don't speak to *anyone* about *anything,* for Christ's sake—do you want to spend the next thousand readings imprisoned in *Castle Doubting* or something?"

"What have you done wrong?"

"I'm not sure."

Landen threw his hands up in the air and I addressed Snell again.

"Can you tell me the charge I'm facing *at the very least*?"[5]

I sighed.

"She's not married, apparently."[6]

"Snell! Wait! Snell? Snell—!"

But he had gone. Landen was staring at me.

"How long have you been like this, darling?"

"I'm fine, Land. But something weird is going on. Can we drop it for the moment?"

Landen looked at me, then at the clear blue sky and then at the cheese he was still holding.

"Cheese or ham?" he said at last.

"Both—but go easy on the cheese; this is a very limited supply."

"Where did you find it?" asked Landen, looking at the anonymously wrapped block suspiciously.

"From Joe Martlet at the Cheese Squad. They intercept about twelve tons a week coming over the Welsh border. It seems a shame to burn it, so everyone at SpecOps gets a pound or two. You know what they say: 'Cops have the best cheese.' "

"Goodbye, Thursday," muttered Landen, looking at the ham.

"Are you going somewhere?" I replied, unsure of what he meant.

"Me? No. Why?"

"You just said 'Goodbye.' "

5. "No time. I'll speak to you before we go in to court. Remember: Don't talk to *anyone at all* about the case. By the way, did you manage to find anything out about that delightfully odd Flakk girlie?"

6. "Really? That is interesting news. Well, must dash. Pip pip."

"No," he laughed, "I was commenting on the ham. It's a *good buy*."

"Oh."

He cut me a slice and put it with the cheese in a sandwich, then made one for himself. There was a distant trumpet of a mammoth as it made heavy weather of the escarpment and I took a bite.

"It's farewell and so long, Thursday."

"Are you doing this on purpose?"

"Doing what? Isn't that Major Tony *Fairwelle* and your old school chum *Sue Long* over there?"

I turned to where Landen was pointing. It *was* Tony and Sue, and they waved cheerily before walking across to say hello.

"Goodness!" said Tony when they had seated themselves. "Looks like the regimental get-together is early this year! Remember Sarah Nara, who lost an ear at Bilohirsk? I just met her in the car park; quite a *coincidence*."

As he said the word my heart missed a beat. I rummaged in my jacket pocket for the entroposcope Mycroft had given me.

"What's the matter, Thurs?" asked Landen. "You're looking kind of . . . odd."

"I'm checking for coincidences," I muttered, shaking the jam jar of mixed lentils and rice. "It's not as stupid as it sounds."

The two pulses had gathered in a sort of swirly pattern. Entropy was decreasing by the second.

"We're out of here," I said to Landen, who looked at me quizzically. "Let's go. Leave the things."

"What's the problem, Thurs?"

"I've just spotted my old croquet captain, *Alf Widdershaine*. This is *Sue Long* and Tony *Fairwelle*; they just saw *Sarah Nara*—see a pattern emerging?"

"Thursday—!" sighed Landen. "Aren't you being a little—"

"Want me to prove it? Excuse me!" I said, shouting to a passerby. "What's your name?"

"Bonnie," she said. "Bonnie Voige. Why?"

"See?"

"Voige is *not* a rare name, Thurs. There are probably *hundreds* of them up here."

"All right, smarty-pants, *you* try."

"I will," replied Landen indignantly, heaving himself to his feet. "Excuse me!"

A young woman stopped, and Landen asked her name.

"Violet," she replied.

"You see?" said Landen. "There's nothing—"

"Violet *De'ath*," continued the woman. I shook the entroposcope again—the lentils and rice had separated almost entirely.

I clapped my hands impatiently. Tony and Sue looked perturbed but got to their feet nonetheless.

"Everybody! Let's *go!*" I shouted.

"But the cheese—!"

"Bugger the cheese, Landen, trust me—*please!*"

They all grudgingly joined me, confused and annoyed at my strange behavior. Their minds changed when, following a short *whooshing* noise, a large and very heavy Hispano-Suiza motorcar landed on the freshly vacated picnic blanket with a teeth-jarring *thump* that shook the ground and knocked us to our knees. We were showered with soil, pebbles, and a grassy sod or two as the vast phaeton-bodied automobile sank itself into the soft earth, the fine bespoke body bursting at the seams as the massive chassis twisted with the impact. One of the spoked wheels broke free and whistled past my head as the heavy engine, torn from its rubber mounting blocks, ripped through the polished bonnet and landed at our feet with a heavy thud. There was silence for a moment as we all stood up, brushed ourselves off and checked for any damage. Landen had cut his hand on a piece of twisted wing mirror, but apart from that—miraculously, it seemed—no one had been hurt. The huge motorcar had landed so perfectly on the picnic that the blanket, thermos, basket, food—everything, in fact—had disappeared from sight. In the deathly hush that followed, everyone in the small group was staring—not at the twisted wreck of the car, but at me, their mouths open. I stared back, then looked slowly upwards to where a large airship freighter was still flying, minus a couple of tons of freight, on to the north and—one presumes—a lengthy stop for an accident inquiry. I shook the entroposcope and the random clumping pattern returned.

"Danger's passed," I announced.

"You haven't changed, Thursday Next!" said Sue angrily. "Whenever you're about, something dangerously *other* walks with you. There's a reason I didn't keep in contact after school, you know—*weirdbird!* Tony, we're leaving."

Landen and I stood and watched them go. He put his arm round me.

*"Weirdbird?"* he asked.

"They used to call me that at school," I told him. "It's the price for being different."

"You got a bargain. I would have paid *double* that to be different. Come on, let's skedaddle."

We slipped quietly away as a crowd gathered around the twisted automobile, the incident generating all manner of "instant experts" who all had theories on why an airship should jettison a car. So to a background chorus of "needed more lift" and "golly, that was close" we crept away and sat in my car.

"That's not something you see very often," murmured Landen after a pause. "What's going on?"

"I don't know, Land. There are a few too many coincidences around at present—I think someone's trying to kill me."

"I love it when you're being weird, darling, but don't you

think you are taking this a little too far? Even if you *could* drop a car from a freighter, no one could hope to hit a picnic blanket from five thousand feet. Think about it, Thurs—it makes no sense at all. Who would *do* something like this anyway?"

"Hades," I whispered.

"Hades is *dead,* Thursday. You killed him yourself. It was a coincidence, pure and simple. They mean nothing—you might as well rail against your dreams or bark at shadows on the wall."

We drove in silence to the SpecOps building and my disciplinary hearing. I switched off the engine and Landen held my hand tightly.

"You'll be fine," he assured me. "They'd be nuts to take any action against you. If things get bad, just remember what Flanker rhymes with."

I smiled at the thought. He said he'd wait for me in the café across the road, kissed me again and limped off.

# 8.

## Mr. Stiggins and SO-1

Contrary to popular belief, neanderthals are not stupid. Poor reading and writing skills are due to fundamental differences in visual
acuity—in humans it is called dyslexia. Facial acuity in neanderthals, however, is highly developed—the same silence might
have thirty or more different meanings depending on how you
looked. "Neanderthal English" has a richness and meaning that is
lost on the relatively facially blind human. Because of this highly
developed facial grammar, neanderthals instinctively know when
someone is lying—hence their total disinterest in plays, films or
politicians. They like stories read out loud and speak of the
weather a great deal—another area in which they are expert. They
never throw anything away and love tools, especially power tools.
Of the three cable channels allocated to neanderthals, two of them
show nothing but woodworking programs.

GERHARD VON SQUID,
*Neanderthals: Back After a Short Absence*

**T**HURSDAY NEXT?" inquired a tall man with a gravelly voice
as soon as I stepped into the SpecOps building.

"Yes?"

He flashed a badge.

"Agent Walken, SO-5; this is my associate, James Dedmen."

Dedmen tipped his hat politely and I shook their hands.

"Can we talk somewhere privately?" asked Walken.

I took them down the corridor and we found an empty interview room.

"I'm sorry about Phodder and Kannon," I told them as soon as we had sat down.

"They were careless," intoned Dedmen gravely. "Contact adhesive should always be used in a well-ventilated room—it says so on the tin."

"We were wondering," asked Walken in a slightly embarrassed manner, "whether you could fill us in on what they were up to; they both died before submitting a report."

"What happened to their case notes?"

Dedmen and Walken exchanged looks.

"They were eaten by rabbits."

"How could *that* happen?"

"Classified," announced Dedmen. "We analyzed the remains but everything was pretty well digested—except these."

He placed three small scraps of tattered and stained paper wrapped in cellophane on the desk. I leaned closer. I could just read out part of my name on the first one, the second was a fragment of a credit card statement, and the third had a single name on it that gave me a shiver: *Hades*.

"Hades?" I queried. "Do you think he's still alive?"

"You killed him, Next—what do you think?"

I had seen him die up there on the roof at Thornfield and even found his charred remains when we searched the blackened ruins. But Hades had died before—or so he had made us believe.

"As sure as I can be. What does the credit card statement mean?"

"Again," replied Walken, "we're not sure. The card was stolen. Most of these purchases are of women's clothes, shoes, hats, bags and so forth—we've got Dorothy Perkins and Camp

Hopson under twenty-four-hour observation. Does any of this ring any bells?"

I shook my head.

"Then tell us about your meeting with Phodder."

I told them as much as I could about our short meeting while they made copious notes.

"So they wanted to know if anything odd had happened to you recently?" asked Walken. "Had it?"

I told them about the Skyrail and the Hispano-Suiza and they made even more notes. Finally, after asking me several times whether there was anything more I could add, they got up and Walken handed me his card.

"If you discover anything at all—?"

"No problem," I replied. "I hope you catch them."

They grunted in reply and left.

I sighed, got up and walked back into the lobby to await Flanker and SO-1. I watched the busy station around me and then suddenly felt very hot as the room started to swim. The sides of my vision started to fade and if I hadn't put my head between my knees I would have passed out there and then. The buzz from the room became a dull rumble and I closed my eyes, temples thumping. I stayed there for several moments until the nausea lessened. I opened my eyes and stared at the flecks of mica in the concrete floor.

"Lost something, Next?" came Flanker's familiar voice.

I very gently raised my head. He was reading some notes and spoke without looking at me.

"I'm running late—someone's misappropriated an entire cheese seizure. Fifteen minutes, interview room three—be there."

He strode off without waiting for a reply and I stared at the floor again. Somehow Flanker and SpecOps seemed insignificant given that this time next year I could be a mother. Landen had enough money for us both and it wasn't as though I needed to actually resign—I could go on the SpecOps reservist list and do the odd job when necessary. I was just starting to ponder on whether I was really cut out for motherhood when I felt a hand on my shoulder and someone pushed a glass of water into my line of vision. I gratefully took the glass and drank half of it before looking up at my rescuer. It was a neanderthal dressed in a neat double-breasted suit with an SO-13 badge clipped to its top pocket.

"Hello, Mr. Stiggins," I said, recognizing him.

"Hello, Ms. Next—the nausea will pass."

There was a shudder and the world whirled backwards in time a couple of seconds so suddenly it made me jump. Stiggins spoke again but this time made less sense:

"*Helto, our m Ms. Next—the nauplea will knoass.*"

"What the hell—" I muttered as the lobby snapped backwards again and the mauve-painted walls switched to green. I looked at Stiggins, who said:

"*Hatto, is our am Mss Next—bue nauplea will kno you.*"

The people in the lobby were now wearing hats. Stiggins jumped back again and said:

"*Thato is our ame Miss Next—bue howplea kno you?*"

My feet felt strange as the world rippled again and I looked down and saw that I was wearing trainers instead of boots. It was clear now that time was flexing slightly, and I expected my father to appear, but he didn't. Stiggins flicked back to the beginning of his sentence yet again and said, this time in a voice I could make out clearly:

"That is our name, Miss Next, but how know you?"

"Did you feel anything odd just then?"

"No. Drink the water. You are very pale."

I had another sip, leaned back and took a deep breath.

"This wall used to be mauve," I mused as Stiggins looked at me.

"How you know our name, Miss Next?"

"You turned up at my wedding party," I told him. "You said you had a job for me."

He stared at me for almost half a minute through his deep-set eyes. His large nose sniffed the air occasionally. Neander-thals thought a great deal about what they said before they said it—if they said anything at all.

"You speak the truth," he said at last. It was almost impossible to lie to a neanderthal, and I wasn't going to try. "We are to represent you on this case, Miss Next."

I sighed. Flanker was taking no chances; I had nothing against neanderthals, but they wouldn't have been my first choice to defend me, particularly against an attack on one of their own.

"If you have a problem you should tell us," said Stiggins, eyeing me carefully.

"I have no problem with you representing me."

"Your face does not match your words. You think we have been placed here to hurt your case. It is our belief too. But as to whether it *will* hurt your case, we shall see. Are you well enough to walk?"

I said I was, and we went and sat down in the interview room. Stiggins opened his case and drew out a buff file. It was a large-print version made out in underlined capitals. He brought out a wooden ruler and placed it across the page to help him read.

"Why you hit Kaylieu, the Skyrail operator?"

"I thought he had a gun."

"Why would you think that?"

I stared into Mr. Stiggins's unblinking brown eyes. If I lied he would know. If I told him the truth he might feel it his duty to tell SO-1 that I had been involved in my father's work. With the world due to end and the trust in my father implicit, it was a sticky moment, to say the least.

"*They* will ask you, Miss Next. Your evasion will not be appreciated."

"I'll have to take that chance."

Stiggins tilted his head to one side and regarded me for a moment.

"They know about your father, Miss Next. We advise you to be careful."

I didn't say anything, but to Stiggins I probably spoke volumes. Half the thal language is about body movements. It's possible to conjugate verbs with facial muscles; dancing is conversation.

We didn't have a chance to say anything else as the door opened and Flanker and two other agents trooped in.

"You know my name," he told me. "These are Agents King and Nosmo."

The two officers stared at me unnervingly.

"This is a preliminary interview," announced Flanker, who now fixed me with a steely gaze. "There will be time enough for a full inquiry—if we so decide. Anything you say and do can affect the outcome of the hearing. It's really up to you, Next."

He wasn't kidding. SO-1 were not within the law—they *made* the law. If they really meant business I wouldn't be here at all—I'd be spirited away to SpecOps Grand Central, wherever the hell that was. It was at times like this that I suddenly realized quite why my father had rebelled against SpecOps in the first place.

Flanker placed two tapes into the recorder and idented it with the date, time and all our names. Once done, he asked in a voice made more menacing by its softness: "You know why you are here?"

"For hitting a Skyrail operator?"

"Striking a neanderthal is hardly a crime worthy of SO-1's valuable time, Miss Next. In fact, technically speaking, it's not a crime at all."

"What then?"

"When did you last see your father?"

The other SpecOps agents leaned forward imperceptibly to hear my answer. I wasn't going to make it easy for them.

"I don't have a father, Flanker—you know that. He was eradicated by your buddies in the ChronoGuard seventeen years ago."

"Don't play me for a fool, Next," warned Flanker. "This is not something I care to joke about. *Despite* Colonel Next's non-actualization he continues to be a thorn in our side. Again: When did you last see your father?"

"At my wedding."

Flanker frowned and looked at his notes.

"You married? When?"

I told him, and he squiggled a note in the margin.

"And what did he say when he turned up at your wedding?"

"Congratulations."

He stared at me for a few moments, then changed tack.

"This incident with the Skyrail operator," he began. "You were convinced that he had a *soap* gun hidden about his person. According to a witness you thumped him on the chin, handcuffed and searched him. They said you seemed very surprised when you didn't find anything."

I shrugged and remained silent.

"We don't give a sod about the thal, Next. Your father's deputizing you is something we could overlook—replacing you out-of-time is something we most definitely will *not*. Is this what happened?"

"Is that the charge? Is that why I'm here?"

"Answer the question."

"No sir."

"You're lying. He brought you back early but your father's control of the timestream is not that good. Mr. Kaylieu decided *not* to threaten the Skyrail that morning. You were *sideslipped*, Next. Joggled slightly in the timestream. Things happened the same way but not *exactly* in the same order. Not a big one either—barely a Class IX. Sideslips are an occupational hazard in ChronoGuard work."

"That's preposterous," I scoffed. Stiggins would know I was lying, but perhaps I could fool Flanker.

"I don't think you understand, Miss Next. This is more important than just you or your father. Two days ago we lost all communications beyond the 12th December. We know there is industrial action, but even the freelancers we've sent upstream haven't reported back. We think it's *the Big One.* If your father was willing to risk using you, we reckon he thinks so too. Despite our animosity for your father, he knows his business—if he didn't we'd have had him years from now. *What's going on?*"

"I just thought he had a gun," I repeated.

Flanker stared at me silently for a few moments.

"Let's start again, Miss Next. You search a neanderthal for a fake gun he carries the following day, you apologize to him using his name, and the arresting officer at the Skyrail station tells me she saw you resetting your watch. A bit *out of time,* were you?"

"What do you mean, 'for a fake gun he carries the following day'?"

Flanker answered without the merest trace of emotion. "Kaylieu was shot dead this morning. I think you should talk and talk fast. I've enough to loop you for twenty years. Fancy that?"

I glared back at him, at a loss to know what to do or say. "Looping" was a slang term for Closed Loop Temporal Field Containment. They popped the criminal in an eight-minute repetitive time loop for five, ten, twenty years. Usually it was a Laundromat, doctor's waiting room or bus stop, and your presence often caused time to slow down for others near the loop. Your body aged but never needed sustenance. It was cruel and unnatural—yet cheap and required no bars, guards or food.

I opened my mouth and shut it again, gaping like a fish.

"Or you can tell us about your father and walk out a free woman."

I felt a prickly sweat break out on my forehead. I stared at Flanker and he stared at me, until, mercifully, Stiggins came to my rescue.

"Miss Next was working for us at SO-13 that morning, Commander," he said in a low monotone. "Kaylieu had been implicated in neanderthal sedition. It was a secret operation. Thank you, Miss Next, but we will have to tell SO-1 the truth."

Flanker shot an angry glance at the neanderthal, who stared back at him impassively.

"Why the hell didn't you tell me this, Stiggins?"

"You never asked."

All Flanker had on me now was a slow watch. He lowered his voice to a growl.

"I'll see you looped behind the Crunch if your father is up to no good and you didn't tell us."

He paused for a moment and jabbed a finger in the direction of Stiggins.

"If you've been bearing false witness I'll have you too. You're running the thal end of SO-13 for one reason and one reason only—window dressing."

"How you managed to become the dominant species we will never know," Stiggins said at last. "So full of hate, anger and vanity."

"It's our evolutionary edge, Stiggins. Change and adapt to a hostile environment. We did, you didn't. QED."

"Darwin won't mask your sins, Flanker," replied Stiggins. "*You* made our environment hostile. You will fall too. But you won't fall because of a more dominant life form. You will fall over *yourselves.*"

"Garbage, Stiggins. You lot had your chance and blew it."

"We have right to health, freedom and pursuit of happiness, too."

"Legally speaking you don't," replied Flanker evenly. "Those rights belong only to *humans.* If you want equality, speak to Goliath. They sequenced you. They *own* you. If you get lucky, perhaps you can be *at risk.* Beg and we might make you *endangered.*"

Flanker shut my file with a snap, grabbed his hat, removed both interview tapes and was gone without another word.

As soon as the door closed I breathed a sigh of relief. My heart was going like a trip-hammer but I still had my liberty.

"I'm sorry about Mr. Kaylieu."

Stiggins shrugged.

"He was not happy, Miss Next. He did not ask to come back."

"You *lied* for me," I added in a disbelieving tone. "I thought neanderthals couldn't lie."

He stared at me for a moment or two.

"It's not that we can't," he said at last. "We just have no reason to. We helped because you are a good person. You have sapien aggression, but you have compassion, too. If you need help again, we will be there."

Stiggins's normally placid and unmoving face curled up into a grimace that showed two rows of widely gapped teeth. I was fearful for a moment until I realized that what I was witnessing was a neanderthal *smile.*

"Miss Next—"

"Yes?"

"Our friends call us Stig."

"Mine call me Thursday."

He put out a large hand and I shook it gratefully.

"You're a good man, Stig."

"Yes," he replied slowly, "we were sequenced that way."

He gathered up his notes and left the room.

I left the SpecOps building ten minutes later and looked for Landen in the café opposite. He wasn't there, so I ordered a coffee and waited twenty minutes. He didn't turn up, so I left a message with the café owner and drove home, musing that with death-by-coincidence, the world ending in a fortnight, charges in a court for I didn't know what and a lost play by Shakespeare, things couldn't get much stranger. But I was wrong. I was *very* wrong.

# 9.

## The More Things Stay
## the Same

Minor changes to soft furnishings are the first indications of a sideslip. Curtains, cushion covers and lampshades are all good litmus indicators for a slight diversion in the timestream—the same way as canaries are used down the mines or goldfishes to predict earthquakes. Carpet and wallpaper patterns and changes in paint hues can also be used, but this requires a more practiced eye. If you are within the sideslip then you will notice nothing, but if your pelmets change color for no good reason, your curtains switch from festoon to swish or your antimacassars have a new pattern on them, I should be worried; and if you're the only one who notices, then worry some more. A great deal more . . .

BENDIX SCINTILLA,
*Timestream Navigation for CG Cadets Module IV*

**L**ANDEN'S ABSENCE made me feel unsettled. All sorts of reasons as to why he wasn't waiting for me ran through my head as I pushed open the gate and walked up to our front door. He could have lost track of time, gone to pick up his running leg from the menders or dropped in to see his mum. But I was fooling myself. Landen said he would be there and he wasn't. And that wasn't like him. Not at all.

I stopped abruptly halfway up the garden path. For some reason Landen had taken the opportunity to change all the curtains. I walked on more slowly, a feeling of unease rising within me. I stopped at the front door. The footscraper had gone. But it hadn't been taken recently—the hole had been concreted over long ago. There were other changes, too. A tub of withered *Tickia orologica* had appeared in the porch next to a rusty pogo stick and a broken bicycle. The dustbins were all plastic rather than steel, and a copy of Landen's least favorite paper, *The Mole,* was resting in the newspaper holder. I felt a hot flush rise in my cheeks as I fumbled in vain to find my door key—not that it would have mattered if I *had* found it, because the lock I used that morning had been painted over years ago.

I must have been making a fair amount of noise, because all of a sudden the door opened to reveal an elderly version of Landen complete with paunch, bifocals and a shiny bald pate.

"Yes?" he inquired in a slow Parke-Laine sort of baritone.

Filbert Snood's time aggregation sprang instantly—and unpleasantly—to mind.

"Oh my God. Landen? *Is that you?*"

The elderly man seemed almost as stunned as I was.

"Me? Good heavens, no!" he snapped and started to close the door. "No one of that name lives here!"

I jammed my foot against the closing door. I'd seen it done in cop movies but the reality is somewhat different. I had forgotten I was wearing trainers and the weatherboard squashed my big toe. I yelped in pain, withdrew my foot and the door slammed shut.

"Buggeration!" I yelled as I hopped up and down. I pressed the doorbell long and hard but received only a muffled "Clear off!" for my troubles. I was just about to bang on the door when I heard a familiar voice ring out behind. I turned to find Landen's mum staring at me.

"Houson!" I cried. "Thank goodness! There's someone in our house and they won't answer, and . . . Houson?"

She was looking at me without a flicker of recognition.

"Houson?" I said again, taking a step towards her. "It's me, Thursday!"

She hurriedly took a pace backwards and corrected me sharply: "That's Mrs. Parke-Laine to you. What do you want?"

I heard the door open behind me. The elderly Landen-that-wasn't had returned.

"She's been ringing the doorbell," explained the man to Landen's mother. "She won't go away." He thought for a moment and then added in a quieter voice, "She's been asking about *Landen.*"

"Landen?" replied Houson sharply, her glare becoming more baleful by the second. "How is Landen any business of *yours?*"

"He's my husband."

There was a pause as she mulled this over.

"Your sense of humor is severely lacking, Miss whoever-you-are," she retorted angrily, pointing towards the garden gate. "I suggest you leave."

"Wait a minute!" I exclaimed, almost wanting to laugh at the situation. "If I *didn't* marry Landen, then who gave me this wedding ring?"

I held up my left hand for them to see, but it didn't seem to have much effect. A quick glance told me why. I didn't *have* a wedding ring.

"Shit—!" I mumbled, looking around in a perplexed manner. "I must have dropped it somewhere—"

"You're very confused," said Houson more with pity than anger. She could see I wasn't dangerous—just positively, and irretrievably, insane. "Is there anyone we can call?"

"I'm *not* crazy," I declared, trying to get a grip on the situation. "This morning, no, less than *two hours ago,* Landen and I lived in this very house—"

I stopped. Houson had moved to the side of the man at the door. As they stood together in a manner bred of long association, I knew exactly who he was; it was Landen's father. Landen's *dead* father.

"You're *Billden*," I murmured. "You died when you tried to rescue . . ."

My voice trailed off. Landen had never known his father. Billden Parke-Laine had died saving the two-year-old Landen from a submerged car thirty-eight years ago. My heart froze as the true meaning of this bizarre confrontation began to dawn. *Someone had eradicated Landen.*

I put out a hand to steady myself, then sat quickly on the garden wall and closed my eyes as a dull thumping started up in my head. Not Landen, not now of all times—

"Billden," announced Houson, "you had better call the police—"

"NO!" I shouted, opening my eyes and glaring at him.

"You didn't go back, did you?" I said slowly, my voice cracking. "You didn't rescue him that night. You lived, and he—"

I braced myself for his anger, but it never came. Instead, Billden just stared at me with a mixture of pity and confusion on his face.

"I wanted to," he said in a quiet voice.

I swallowed my emotion.

"Where's Landen now?"

"If we tell you," asked Houson in a slow and patronizing tone, "will you promise to go away and never come back?"

She took my silence for assent and continued: "Swindon Municipal Cemetery—and you're right, our son drowned thirty-eight years ago."

"*Shit!*" I cried, my mind racing as I tried to figure out who might be responsible. Houson and Billden took a fearful step backwards. "Not *you*," I added hastily. "Goddammit, I'm being *blackmailed.*"

"You should report that to SpecOps."

"They wouldn't believe me any more than you—"

I paused and thought for a moment.

"Houson, I know you have a good memory, because when Landen *did* exist, you and I were the best of pals. Someone has taken your son, my husband, and believe me, I'll get him back. But listen to me, I'm not crazy, and here's how I can prove it: He's allergic to bananas, has a mole on his neck—and a birthmark the shape of a lobster on his bum. How could I know that unless—?"

"Oh yes?" said Houson slowly, staring at me with growing interest. "This birthmark. Which cheek?"

"The left."

"Looking from the front, or looking from the back?"

"Looking from the back," I said without hesitating.

There was silence for a moment. They looked at each other, then at me, and in that instant, they *knew*. When Houson spoke it was in a quiet voice, her temper transplanted with a sadness all her own.

"How—how would he have turned out?"

She started to cry, large tears that rolled uninhibited down her cheeks; tears of loss, tears for what might have been.

"He was *wonderful!*" I returned gratefully. "Witty and generous and tall and clever—you would have been *so* proud!"

"What did he become?"

"A novelist," I explained. "Last year he won the Armitage Shanks Fiction Award for *Bad Sofa*. He lost a leg in the Crimea. We were married two months ago."

"Were we there?"

I looked at them both and said nothing. Houson had been there, of course, shedding tears of joy for us both—but Billden, well, Billden had swapped his life for Landen's when he returned to the submerged car and ended up in the Swindon Municipal Cemetery instead. We stood for a moment or two, the three of us lamenting the loss of Landen. Houson broke the silence.

"I think it would really be better for all concerned if you left now," she said quietly, "and please don't come back."

"Wait!" I said. "Was there someone there, someone who stopped you from rescuing him?"

"More than one," replied Billden. "Five or six—one woman; I was sat upon—"

"Was one a Frenchman? Tall, distinguished-looking? Named *Lavoisier*, perhaps?"

"I don't know," answered Billden sadly. "It was a long time ago."

"You really *have* to leave now," repeated Houson in a forth-right tone.

I sighed, thanked them, and they shuffled back inside and closed the door.

I walked out of the garden gate and sat in my car, trying to contain the emotion within me so I could think straight. I was breathing heavily and my hands were clenched so tightly on the steering wheel my knuckles showed white. How could SpecOps do this to me? Was this Flanker's way of compelling me to talk about my father? I shook my head. Futzing with the timestream was a crime punishable by almost unimaginable brutality. I couldn't imagine Flanker would have risked his career—and his life—on a move so rash.

I took a deep breath and leaned forward to press the starter button. As I did so I glanced into my wing mirror and saw a Packard parked on the other side of the road. There was a well-dressed figure leaning on the wing, nonchalantly smoking a cigarette and looking in my direction. It was Schitt-Hawse. He appeared to be smiling. Suddenly, the whole plan came into sharp focus. Jack Schitt. What had Schitt-Hawse threatened me with? *Corporate impatience?* My anger reestablished itself.

Muttering *Bastard!* under my breath I jumped out of the car and walked briskly and purposefully towards Schitt-Hawse, who stiffened slightly as I approached. I ignored a car that screeched to a halt inches from me and as Schitt-Hawse took a pace forward I put out both hands and pushed him hard against the car. He lost his footing and fell heavily to the ground; I was quickly upon him, grabbed his shirt lapels and raised a fist to punch him. But the blow never fell. In my blind anger I had failed to see that his associates Chalk and Cheese were close by, and they did their job admirably, efficiently and yes, painfully, too. I fought like hell and was gratified that in the confusion I managed to kick Schitt-Hawse hard on the kneecap—he yelped in pain. But my victory, such as it was, was short-lived. I must have been a tenth of their combined weight, and my struggles were soon in vain. They held me tightly, and Schitt-Hawse approached with an unpleasant smile etched upon his pinched features.

I did the first thing I could think of. I spat in his face. I'd never tried it before, but it turned out delightfully; I got him right in the eye.

He raised the back of his hand to strike me, but I didn't flinch—I just stared at him, anger burning in my eyes. He stopped, lowered his hand and wiped his face with a crisply laundered pocket handkerchief.

"You are going to have to control that temper of yours, Next."

"That's Mrs. Parke-Laine to you."

"Not anymore. If you'd stop struggling, perhaps we could talk sensibly, like adults. You and I need to come to an *arrangement*."

I gave up squirming, and the two men relaxed their grip. I straightened my clothes and glared at Schitt-Hawse, who rubbed his knee.

"What sort of arrangement?" I demanded.

"A trade," he answered. "Jack Schitt for Landen."

"Oh yes?" I retorted. "And how do I know I can trust you?"

"You can't and you don't," replied Schitt-Hawse simply, "but it's the best offer you're going to get."

"My father will help me."

Schitt-Hawse laughed.

"Your father is a washed-out clock jockey. I think you over-estimate his chances—and his talents. Besides, we've got the summer of 1947 locked down so tight not even a transtemporal gnat could get back there without us knowing about it. Retrieve Jack from 'The Raven' and you can have your own dear hubby back."

"And how do you propose I do that?"

"You're a resourceful and intelligent woman—I'm sure you'll think of something. Do we have a deal?"

I stared hard at him, shaking with fury. Then, almost without thinking, I had my automatic pressed against Schitt-Hawse's forehead. I heard two safety catches click off behind me. Associates Chalk and Cheese were fast, too.

Schitt-Hawse seemed unperturbed; he smiled at me in a supercilious manner and ignored the weapon.

"You won't kill me, Next," he said slowly. "It's not the way you do things. It might make you feel better, but believe me, it won't get your Landen back, and Mr. Chalk and Mr. Cheese would make quite sure you were dead long before you hit the asphalt."

Schitt-Hawse was good. He'd done his homework and he hadn't underestimated me one little bit. I'd do all I could to get Landen back, and he knew it. I reholstered my pistol.

"Splendid!" he enthused. "We'll be hearing from you in due course, I trust, hmm?"

# 10.

## A Lack of Differences

Landen Parke-Laine's eradication was the best I'd seen since Veronica Golightly's. They plucked him out and left everything else *exactly* as it was. Not a crude hatchet job like Churchill or Victor Borge—we got those sorted out eventually. What I never figured out was how they took him out and left her memories of him completely intact. Agreed, there would be no point to the eradication *without* her knowing what she had missed, but it still intrigued me over four centuries later. Eradication was never an exact art.

COLONEL NEXT, QT CG (nonexist.),
*Upstream/Downstream* (unpublished)

**I** STARED AFTER their departing car, trying to figure out what to do. Finding a way into "The Raven" to release Jack Schitt would be my first priority. It wasn't going to be hard—it was going to be impossible. It wouldn't deter me. I'd done impossible things several times in the past, and the prospect didn't scare me as much as it used to. I thought of Landen and the last time I saw him, limping across to the café just opposite the SpecOps building. It was going to be his birthday in two weeks—we planned to take the airship to Spain, or somewhere hot for a break; we knew we wouldn't be able to go on holiday so easily once there was a baby—

The baby. With all that had happened, I didn't know whether I was still pregnant. I jumped into my car and screeched off into town, startling a few great auks who were picking their way through a nearby garbage can.

I was heading for the doctor's surgery on Shelley Street. Every shop I passed seemed to either stock prams or high chairs, toys or something else baby-related, and all the toddlers and infants, heavily pregnant women and prams in Swindon seemed to be crowding the route—and all staring at me. I skidded to a halt outside the surgery. It was a double yellow line and a traffic warden looked at me greedily.

"Hey!" I said, pointing a finger at her. "Expectant mother. Don't even *think* about it."

I dashed in and found the nurse I'd seen the day before.

"I was in here yesterday," I blurted out. "Was I pregnant?"

She looked at me without even the least vestige of surprise. I guess she was used to this sort of thing.

"Of course!" she replied. "Confirmation is in the post. Are you okay?"

I sat down heavily on a chair and burst into tears. The sense of relief was overwhelming. I had more than just Landen's memories—I had his child, too. I rubbed my face with my hands. I'd been in a lot of difficult and dangerous life-or-death situations both in the military and law enforcement—but nothing even comes *close* to the tribulations of emotion. I'd face Hades again twice rather than go through that little charade again.

"Yes, yes," I assured her happily. "I really couldn't be better!"

"Good," beamed the nurse. "Is there anything else you'd like to know?"

"Yes, actually," I replied. "Tell me, where do I live?"

The shabby block of flats in the old town didn't look like my sort of place, but who knows where I might be living without

Landen. I trotted briskly up the stairs to the top landing and flat six. I took a deep breath, unlocked and opened the door. There was a brief scrabble of activity from the kitchen and Pickwick was there to greet me as usual, bearing a gift that turned out to be the torn cover off last month's *SpecOps-27 Gazette*. I closed the door with my foot as I tickled her under the chin and looked cautiously about. I was relieved to discover that despite the shabby exterior my apartment was south-facing, warm and quite comfortable. I couldn't remember a thing about any of it, of course, but I was glad to see that Pickwick's egg was still in residence. I walked softly around the flat, exploring my new surroundings. It seemed I painted a lot more without Landen about, and the walls were covered with half-finished canvases. There were several of Pickwick and the family which I could remember painting, and a few others that I couldn't—but none, sadly, of Landen. I looked at the other canvases and wondered why several included images of amphibious aircraft. I sat on the sofa, and when Pickwick came up to nuzzle me I put my hand on her head.

"Oh, Pickers," I murmured, "what shall we do?"

I sighed, tried to get Pickwick to stand on one leg with the promise of a marshmallow, failed, then made a cup of tea and something to eat before searching the rest of the apartment in an inquisitive sort of way. Most things were where I would expect to find them; there were more dresses in the closet than usual and I even found a few copies of *FeMole* stashed under the sofa. The fridge was well stocked with food, and it seemed that in this non-Landen world I was a vegetarian. There were a lot of things that I couldn't remember ever having acquired, including a table light shaped like a pineapple, a large enamel sign advertising Dr. Spongg's footcare remedies and—slightly more worryingly—a size twelve pair of socks in the laundry and some boxer shorts. I rummaged further and found two toothbrushes in the bathroom, a large Swindon Mallets jacket on the hook and several XXL-size T-shirts with *SpecOps-14 Swindon* written on them. I called Bowden straightaway.

"Hello, Thursday," he said. "Have you heard? Professor Spoon has given his 100% backing to *Cardenio*—I've never heard him actually laugh before!"

"That's good, that's good," I said absently. "Listen, this might seem an odd question, but do I have a boyfriend?"

"A what?"

"A boyfriend. You know. A male friend I see on a regular basis for dinner and picnics and . . . *thingy*, y'know?"

"Thursday, are you okay?"

I took a deep breath and rubbed my neck.

"No, no, I'm not," I gabbled. "You see, my husband was eradicated this afternoon. I went to see SO-1 and just before I went in the walls changed color and Stig talked funny and Flanker didn't know I was married—which I'm not, I suppose—and then Houson didn't know me and Billden *wasn't* in the cemetery but Landen *was* and Goliath said they'd bring him back if I got Jack Schitt out and I thought I'd lost Landen's baby which I haven't so everything was fine and now it's not fine anymore because *I've found an extra toothbrush and some men's clothes in my flat!*"

"Okay, okay," said Bowden in a soothing voice. "Slow down a bit and just let me think."

There was a pause as Bowden mulled all this over. When he answered his voice was tinged with urgency—and concern. I knew he was a good friend, but until now I never knew *how* good.

"Thursday. Calm down and listen to me. Firstly, *we keep this to ourselves.* Eradication can *never* be proved—mention this to anyone at SpecOps and the quacks will enforce your retirement on a Form D4. We don't want that. I'll try and fill you in with any lost memories I might have that you don't. What was the name of your husband, again?"

"Landen."

I found strength in his approach. You could always rely on Bowden to be analytical about a problem—no matter how strange it might seem. He made me go over the day again in more detail, something that I found very calming. I asked him again about a possible boyfriend.

"I'm not sure," he replied. "You're kind of a private person."

"Come on—office rumors, SpecOps gossip—there must be *something*."

"There *is* some talk, but I don't hear a lot of it, since I'm your partner. Your love life is a matter of some quiet speculation. They call you—"

He went quiet.

"What do they call me, Bowden?"

"You don't want to know."

"Tell me."

"All right," sighed Bowden. "It's—they call you the Ice Maiden."

"The Ice Maiden?"

"It's not as bad as my nickname," continued Bowden. "I'm known as Dead Dog."

"Dead dog?" I repeated, trying to sound as though I'd not heard it before. "Ice Maiden, eh? It's kind of, well, *corny*. Couldn't they think of something better? Anyway, did I have a boyfriend or not?"

"There was a rumor of someone over at SO-14—"

I held up the croquet jacket, trying to figure out how tall this unnamed beau might be.

"Do we have a positive ID?"

"I think it's only a rumor, Thursday."

"Tell me, Bowden."

"Miles," he said at last. "His name's Miles Hawke."

"Is it serious?"

"I have no idea. You don't talk about these things to me."

I thanked him and put the phone down nervously, butterflies dancing in my stomach. I knew I was still pregnant, but the trouble was: *who was the father?* If I had a casual boyfriend named Miles, then perhaps it *wasn't* Landen's after all. I called my mother, who seemed more interested in putting out a fire on the kitchen stove than in talking to me. I asked her when she last met one of my boyfriends and she said that if memory served, not for at least six years, and if I didn't hurry up and get married she was going to have to adopt some grandchildren— or steal some from outside Tesco's, whichever was easier. I told her I would go out and look for one as soon as possible and put the phone down.

I paced the room in a flurry of nerves. If I *hadn't* introduced this Miles bloke to Mum, then it was quite likely he wasn't that serious; yet if he *did* leave his gear here then it undoubtedly *was*. I had an idea and rummaged in the bedside table and found a packet of unopened condoms which were three years out of date. I breathed a sigh of relief. This *did* sound more like me—unless Miles brought his own, of course—but then if I *had* a bun in the oven, then finding them was immaterial, as we didn't use them. Or perhaps the clothes weren't Miles's at all? And what about my memories? If they had survived, then surely Landen's share in Junior-to-be had *also* survived. I sat down on the bed and pulled out my hair tie. I ran my fingers through my hair, flopped backwards, covered my face and groaned—long and loud.

# 11.

## Granny Next

Young Thursday came that morning, as I knew she would. She had just lost Landen, as I had lost my own husband all those years ago. She had youth and hope on her side, and although she did not yet know it, she had plenty of what we call *the Other Stuff*. She would, I hoped, use it wisely. At the time not even her own father knew quite how important she was. More than Landen's life would depend on her. *All* life would depend on her, from the lowliest paramecium to the most complex life form that would ever exist.

*From papers discovered in ex–SpecOps agent Next's effects*

I TOOK PICKWICK to the park first thing in the morning. Perhaps it would be better to say that she took me—she was the one who knew the way. She played coyly with a few other dodos while I sat on a park bench. A crotchety old woman sat next to me and turned out to be Mrs. Scroggins, who lived directly below. She told me not to make so much noise in future, and then, without drawing breath, gave me a few extremely useful tips about smuggling pets in and out of the building. I picked up a copy of *The Owl* on the way home and was just crossing the road back to my apartment when a patrol car drew up beside me and the driver rolled down his window. It was Officer "Spike" Stoker of SpecOps-17—the Vampire and Werewolf Disposal Operation, or Suckers and Biters as they preferred to call themselves. I helped him out once on a vampire stakeout; dealing with the undead is not a huge barrel of fun, but I liked Spike a great deal.

"Hey, Thursday, word is you lipped Flanker."

"Good news travels fast, doesn't it? But he got the last laugh—I'm suspended."

He switched off the engine and thought about this for a moment.

"If the shit hits the fan I can offer you some freelance staking for cash at Suckers and Biters; the minimum entry requirements have been reduced to 'anyone mad enough to join me.' "

I sighed.

"Sorry, Spike. I can't. Not right now. I've got husband troubles."

"You're married? When?"

"Exactly," I said, showing him my empty ring finger. "Someone eradicated my husband."

Spike hit the steering wheel with the flat of his hand.

"Bastards. I'm sorry to hear that, but listen, it's not the end of the world. A few years back my uncle Bart was eradicated. Someone goofed and left some memories of him with my aunt. She lodged an appeal and had him reactualized a year later. Thing is, I never knew I had an uncle after he left, and never knew he had gone when he came back—I've only my aunt's word that it ever happened at all. Does any of this make any sense to you?"

"Twenty-four hours ago it would have sounded insane. Right now it seems—stop that, Pickwick!—as clear as day."

"Hmm," murmured Spike. "You'll get him back, don't worry. Listen: I wish they'd sideslip all this vampire and werewolf crap so I could go and work at SommeWorld™ or something."

I leaned against his car, SpecOps gossip a welcome distraction.

"Got a new partner yet?" I asked him.

"For this shit? You must be kidding. But there is *some* good news. Look at this."

He pulled a photo from his breast pocket. It was of himself standing next to a petite blond girl who barely came up to his elbow.

"Her name's Cindy," he murmured affectionately. "A cracker—and smart, too."

"I wish you both the best. How does she feel about all this vampire and werewolf stuff?"

"Oh, she's *fine* with all that—or at least she will be, when I tell her." His face fell. "Oh, craps. How can I tell her that I thrust sharpened stakes through the undead and hunt down werewolves like some sort of dogcatcher?" He stopped and sighed, then asked, in a brighter tone, "You're a woman, aren't you?"

"Last time I looked."

"Well, can't you figure out some sort of a—I don't know—strategy for me? I'd hate to lose this one as well."

"How long do they last when you tell them?"

"Oh, they're usually peachy about it," said Spike, laughing. "They hang about for, well, five, six, maybe more—"

"Weeks?" I asked. "Months?"

"Seconds," replied Spike mournfully, "and those were the ones that *really* liked me."

He sighed deeply.

"I think you should tell her the truth. Girls don't like being lied to—unless it's about surprise holidays and rings and stuff like that."

"I thought you'd say something like that," replied Spike, rubbing his chin thoughtfully. "But the shock—!"

"You don't have to tell her outright. You could always scatter a few copies of *Van Helsing's Gazette* around the house."

"Oh, I get it!" replied Spike, thinking hard. "Sort of build her up to it—stakes and crucifixes in the garage—"

"And you could drop werewolves into the conversation every now and then."

"It's a great plan, Thurs," replied Spike happily. "Hang on."

The wireless had started to report an occurrence of unspeakable nastiness up near Banbury. He started the engine.

"I've got to go. Think about my offer. Always some work if you need it!"

And he was gone in a screech of tires.

I smuggled Pickwick back to my apartment and read the paper—I was glad to see the discovery of *Cardenio* had not yet broken in the press, but I was distracted. I stared out of the window for a moment, trying to formulate some sort of plan to get Landen back. Get into books? I didn't know where to even *begin.* On reflection, that wasn't quite right. It was time to go and visit the closest thing to the Delphic Oracle I would ever know: Granny Next.

Gran was playing Ping-Pong at the SpecOps Twilight Homes when I found her. She was thrashing her opponent, who was at least twenty years her junior—but still about eighty. Nervous nurses looked on, trying to stop her before she fell over and broke a bone or two. Granny Next was old. *Really* old. Her pink skin looked more wrinkled than the most wrinkled prune I had ever seen, and her face and hands were livid with dark liver spots. She was dressed in her usual blue gingham dress and hailed me from the other side of the room as I walked in.

"Ah!" she said. "Thursday! Fancy a game?"

"Don't you think you've played enough today?"

"Nonsense! Grab a paddle and we'll play to the first point."

I picked up a paddle as a ball careened past me.

"Wasn't ready!" I protested as another ball came over the net. I swiped at it and missed.

"Ready is as ready does, Thursday. I'd have thought you knew that more than most!"

I grunted and returned the next ball, which was deftly deflected back to me.

"How are you, Gran?"

"Old," she replied, behaving quite the opposite as she skipped nimbly sideways and whacked the ball towards me with savage backspin. "Old and tired, and I need looking after. The grim reaper is lurking close by—I can almost smell him!"

"Gran!"

She missed my shot and declared, "No ball," before pausing for a moment.

"Do you want to know a secret, young Thursday?" she asked, leaning on the table.

"Go on then," I replied, taking the opportunity to retrieve some balls.

"*I am cursed to eternal life!*"

"Perhaps it just *seems* like it, Gran."

"Insolent pup," she replied as she returned my serve. "I didn't attain one hundred and eight years on physical fortitude or a statistical quirk alone. Your point."

I served again and missed her return. She paused for a moment.

"I got mixed up with some oddness in my youth, and the long and short of it is that I can't shuffle off this mortal coil until I have read the ten most boring classics."

I looked into her bright eyes. She wasn't kidding.

"How far have you got?" I replied, returning another ball that flew wide.

"Well, that's the trouble, isn't it?" she replied, serving again.

"I read what I think is the dullest book on God's own earth, finish the last page, go to sleep with a smile on my face and wake up the following morning feeling better than ever!"

"Have you tried Edmund Spenser's *Faerie Queene*?" I asked. "Six volumes of boring Spenserian stanza, the only saving grace of which is that he *didn't* write the twelve volumes he had planned."

"Read them all," replied Gran. "And his other poems, too, just in case."

I put down my paddle. The balls kept plinking past me.

"You win, Gran. I need to talk to you."

She reluctantly agreed, and I helped her to her bedroom, a small chintzily decorated cell she darkly referred to as her "departure lounge." It was sparsely furnished; there was a picture of me, Anton, Joffy and my mother alongside a couple of empty frames.

As soon as she was seated I said: "They . . . they sideslipped my husband, Gran."

"When did they take him?" she asked, looking at me over her glasses in the way that grannies do; she never questioned what I said, and I explained everything to her as quickly as I could—except for the bit about the baby.

"Hmm," said Granny Next when I had finished. "They took my husband too—I know how you feel."

"Why did they do it?"

"The same reason they did it to you. Love is a wonderful thing, my dear, but it leaves you wide open for blackmail. Give way to tyranny and others will suffer just as badly as you— perhaps worse."

"Are you saying I shouldn't try to get Landen back?"

"Not at all; just think carefully before you help them. They don't care about you or Landen; all they want is Jack Schitt. Is Anton still dead?"

"I'm afraid so."

"What a shame. I hoped to see your brother before I popped myself. Do you know what the worst bit about dying is?"

"Tell me, Gran."

"You never get to see how it all turns out."

"Did you get your husband back, Gran?"

Instead of answering she unexpectedly placed her hand on my midriff and smiled that small and all-knowing smile that grandmothers seem to learn at granny school, along with crochet, January sales battle tactics and wondering what you are doing upstairs.

"June?" she asked.

You never argue with Granny Next, nor seek to know how she knows such things.

"July. But Gran, I don't know if it's Landen's, or Miles Hawke's, or whose!"

"You should call this Hawke fellow and ask him."

"I can't do that!"

"Worry yourself woolly then," she retorted. "Mind you, my money is on Landen as the father—as you say, the memories avoided the sideslip, so why not the baby? Believe me, everything will turn out fine. Perhaps not in the way that you imagine, but fine nonetheless."

I wished I could share her optimism. She took her hand off my stomach and lay back on the bed, the energy expended during the Ping-Pong having taken its toll.

"I need to find a way to get back into books without the Prose Portal, Gran."

She opened her eyes and looked at me with a keenness that belied her old age.

"Humph!" she said, then added: "I was SpecOps for seventy-seven years in eighteen different departments. I jumped backwards and forwards and even sideways on occasion. I've chased bad guys who make Hades look like St. Zvlkx and saved the world from annihilation eight times. I've seen such weird shit you can't even *begin* to comprehend, but for all of that I have *absolutely no idea* how Mycroft managed to jump you into *Jane Eyre*."

"Ah."

"Sorry, Thursday—but that's the way it is. If I were you I'd work the problem out *backwards*. Who was the last person you met who could bookjump?"

"Mrs. Nakajima."

"And how did she manage it?"

"She just read herself in, I suppose."

"Have you tried it?"

I shook my head.

"Perhaps you should," she replied with deadly seriousness. "The first time you went into *Jane Eyre*—wasn't that a bookjump?"

"I guess."

"Perhaps," she said as she picked a book at random off the shelf above her bed and tossed it across to me, "you had better *try*."

I picked the book up.

"*The Tale of the Flopsy Bunnies*?"

"Well, you've got to start somewhere, haven't you?" replied Gran with a chuckle. I helped her take off her blue gingham shoes and made her more comfortable.

"One hundred and eight!" she muttered. "I feel like the bunny in that Fusioncell ad, you know, the one that has to run on brand X?"

"You're Fusioncell all the way to me, Gran."

She gave a faint smile and leaned back on the pillows.

"Read the book to me, my dear."

I sat down and opened the small Beatrix Potter volume. I glanced up at Gran, who had closed her eyes.

"Read!"

So I did, right from the front to the back.

"Anything?"

"No," I replied sadly, "nothing."

"Not even the whiff of garden refuse or the distant buzz of a lawn mower?"

"Not a thing."

"Hah!" said Gran. "Read it to me again."

So I read it again, and again after that.

"Still nothing?"

"No, Gran," I replied, beginning to get bored.

"How do you see the character of Mrs. Tittlemouse?"

"Resourceful and intelligent," I replied. "Probably a gossip and likes to name-drop. Leagues ahead of Benjamin in the brain department."

"How do you figure that?" queried Gran.

"Well, by allowing his children to sleep so vulnerably in the open air, Benjamin clearly shows minimal parenting skills, yet he has enough *self*-preservation to cover his own face. It was Flopsy who had to come and look for him, as this sort of thing has obviously happened before—it is clear that Benjamin can't be trusted with the children. Once again the mother has to show restraint and wisdom."

"Maybe so," replied Gran, "but where's the wisdom in watching from the window while Mr. and Mrs. McGregor discovered they had been duped with the rotten vegetables?"

She had a point.

"A narrative necessity," I declared. "I think there is more high drama if you follow the outcome of the rabbit's subterfuge, don't you? I think Flopsy, had she been making all the decisions, would have just returned to the burrow but was, on this occasion, overruled by Beatrix Potter."

"It's an interesting theory," commented Gran, stretching her toes out on the counterpane and wriggling them to keep the circulation going. "Mr. McGregor's a nasty piece of work, isn't he? Quite the Darth Vader of children's literature."

"Misunderstood," I told her. "I see *Mrs.* McGregor as the villain of the piece. A sort of Lady Macbeth. His labored counting and inane chuckling might indicate a certain degree of dementia that allows him to be easily dominated by Mrs. McGregor's more aggressive personality. I think their marriage is in trouble, too. She describes him as a 'silly old man' and 'a doddering old fool' and claims the rotten vegetables in the sack are just a pointless prank to annoy her."

"Anything else?"

"Not really. I think that's about it. Good stuff, isn't it?"

But Gran didn't answer; she just chuckled softly to herself.

"So you're still here then," she asked, "you didn't jump into Mr. and Mrs. McGregor's cottage?"

"No."

"In that case," began Gran with a mischievous air, "how did you know she called him a 'doddering old fool'?"

"It's in the text."

"Better check, young Thursday."

I flicked to the correct page and found, indeed, that Mrs. McGregor had said no such thing.

"How odd!" I said. "I must have made it up."

"Maybe," replied Gran, "or perhaps you *overheard* it. Close your eyes and describe the kitchen in Mr. McGregor's cottage."

"Lilac-washed walls," I muttered, "a large range with a kettle singing merrily above a coal fire. There is a dresser against one wall with floral-patterned crocks upon it and atop the scrubbed kitchen table there is a jug with flowers—"

I lapsed into silence.

"And how would you have known that," asked Gran triumphantly, *"unless you had actually been there?"*

I quickly skimmed the book, surprised and impressed by the tantalizing glimmer of another world beyond the attractive watercolors and simple prose. I concentrated hard but nothing similar happened. Perhaps I wanted it too much; I don't know. After the tenth reading I was just looking at the words and ink and nothing else.

"It's a start," said Gran encouragingly. "Try another book when you get home, but don't expect too much too soon—and I'd strongly recommend you go and look for Mrs. Nakajima. Where does she live?"

"She took retirement in *Jane Eyre*."

*"Before* that?"

"Osaka."

"Then perhaps you should seek her there—and for heaven's sake, relax!"

I told her I would, kissed her on the forehead and quietly left the room.

# 12.

## At Home with My
## Memories

ToadNewsNetwork was the top news station, Lydia Startright their
top reporter. If there was a top event, you could bet your top dollar
that Toad would make it their top story. When Tunbridge Wells
was given to the Russians as war reparations there was no topper
story—except, that is, the mammoth migrations, speculation on
Bonzo the Wonder Hound's next movie or whether Lola Vavoom
shaved her armpits or not. My father said that it was a delightfully
odd—and dangerously self-destructive—quirk of humans that we
were far more interested in pointless trivia than in genuine news
stories.

THURSDAY NEXT,
*A Life in SpecOps*

Since I was still on official leave pending the outcome of
the SO-1 hearing, I went home and let myself into my apartment, kicked off my shoes and poured some pistachios into
Pickwick's dish. I made some coffee and called Bowden for a
long chat, trying to find out what else had changed since Landen's eradication. As it turned out, not much. Anton had still
been blamed for the charge of the light armored brigade, I had
still lived in London for ten years, still arrived back in Swindon
at the same time, still been up at Uffington picnicking the day
before. Dad had once said the past has an astonishing resilience

to change; he wasn't kidding. I thanked Bowden, hung up and painted for a while, trying to relax. When that failed I went up for a walk at Uffington, joining the sightseers who had gathered to watch the smashed Hispano-Suiza being loaded onto a trailer. The Leviathan Airship Company had begun an inquiry and volunteered one of their directors to accept charges of corporate manslaughter. The hapless executive had begun his seven-year term already, thus hoping to avoid an expensive and damaging lawsuit for his company.

I returned home to find a dangerous-looking man was standing on my doorstep. I'd never seen him before but he knew me well enough.

"Next!" he bellowed. "I want three months' rent in advance or I'll throw all your stuff in the skip!"

"In advance?" I replied as I unlocked my door, hoping to sneak inside and close it as soon as possible. "You can't do that!"

"I *can*," he said holding up a dog-eared lease agreement. "Pets are strictly against the terms of the lease. Clause 7 subsection B, under 'Pets—special conditions.' Now pay up."

"There's no pet in here," I explained innocently.

"What's that, then?"

Pickwick had made a quiet *plock-plock* noise and poked her head round the door to see what was going on. It was a badly timed move.

"Oh *that*. I'm looking after her for a friend."

My landlord's eyes suddenly lit up as he looked closer at Pickwick, who shrank back nervously. She was a rare Version 1.2 and my landlord seemed to know this.

He eyed Pickwick greedily. "Hand over the dodo," he said, "and I'll give you four months' free rent."

"She's not for trade," I said firmly. I could feel Pickwick quivering behind me.

"Ah," said my landlord. "Then you have two days to pay all your bills or you're out on your sweet little SpecOps arse. Capishe?"

"You say the nicest things."

He glared at me, handed me a bill and disappeared off down the corridor to harass someone else.

I didn't have three months' advance rent, and he knew it. After a search I eventually found a lease agreement, and he was right—the clause was there in case of something much bigger and more dangerous, such as a saber-tooth, but he was within his rights. My cards had reached their limit and my overdraft was nearly full. SpecOps wages were just about enough to keep you fed and a roof over your head, but buying the Speedster had all but cleared me out and I hadn't even *seen* the garage repair bills yet. There was a nervous *plock-plock* from the kitchen.

"I'd sooner sell myself," I told Pickwick, who was standing expectantly with collar and lead in her beak.

I stashed the bank statements back into the shoebox, fixed myself some supper and then flopped in front of the telly, switching to ToadNewsNetwork.

"—the czar's chief negotiator has accepted the foreign minister's offer of Tunbridge Wells as war reparations," intoned the anchorman gravely. "The small town and two-thousand-acre environs would become a Russian-owned enclave named Botchkamos Istochnik within England and all citizens of the new Russian colony would be offered dual nationality. On the spot for TNN is Lydia Startright. Lydia, how are things down there?"

The screen changed to ToadNewsNetwork's preeminent reporter in the main street of Tunbridge Wells.

"There is a mixture of disbelief and astonishment amongst the residents of this sleepy Kent town," responded Startright soberly, surrounded by an assortment of retired gentlefolk carrying shopping and looking vaguely bemused. "Panic warm-clothing shopping has given way to anger that the foreign secretary could make such a decision without mentioning some sort of generous compensation package. I have with me retired cavalry officer Colonel Prongg. Tell me, Colonel, what is your reaction to the news that you might be Colonel Pronski this time next month?"

"Well," said the colonel in an aggrieved tone, "I would like to say that I am disgusted and appalled at the decision. Appalled and disgusted in the strongest possible terms. I didn't fight the Russkies for forty years only to become one in my retirement. Myself and Mrs. Prongg will be moving, obviously!"

"Since Imperial Russia is the second-wealthiest nation on the planet," replied Lydia, "Tunbridge Wells may find itself, like the island of Fetlar, to be an important offshore banking institution for Russia's wealthy nobility."

"Obviously," replied the colonel, thinking hard, "I would have to wait to see how things went before coming to any final decision. But if the takeover means colder winters, we'll move back to Brighton. Chilblains, y'know."

"There you have it, Carl. This is Lydia Startright reporting for ToadNewsNetwork, Tunbridge Wells."

The camera switched back to the studio.

"Trouble at MoleTV," continued the anchorman, "and a bitter blow for the producers of *Surviving Cortes*, the channel's popular Aztec conquering reenactment series when, instead of being simply voted out of the sealed set of Tenochtitlán, a contestant was sacrificed live to the Sun God. The show has been canceled and an inquiry has been launched. MoleTV were said to be 'sorry and dismayed about the incident' but pointed out that the show was 'the highest-rated on TV, even *after* the blood sacrifice.' Brett?"

The camera switched to the other newsreader.

"Thank you, Carl. Henry, a two-and-a-half-ton male juvenile from the Kirkbride herd, was the first mammoth to reach the winter pastures of Redruth at 6:07 p.m. this evening. Clarence Oldspot was there. Clarence?"

The scene changed to a field in Cornwall where a bored-looking mammoth had almost vanished inside a scrum of TV news reporters and crowds of well-wishers. Clarence Oldspot was still wearing his flak jacket and looked bitterly disappointed that he was reporting on hairy once extinct herbivores and not at the Crimean front line.

"Thank you, Brett. Well, the migration season is truly upon us, and Henry, a two-hundred-to-one outsider, wrongfooted the bookies when—"

I flicked the channel. It was *Name That Fruit!*, the nauseating quiz show. I flicked again to a documentary about the Whig political party's links to Radical Baconian groups in the seventies. I switched through several other channels before returning to the ToadNewsNetwork.

The phone rang and I picked it up.

"It's Miles," said a voice that sounded like one hundred push-ups in under three minutes.

"Who?"

"Miles."

*"Ah!"* I said in shock. Miles. Miles Hawke, the owner of the boxer shorts and the tasteless sports jacket.

"Thursday? You okay?"

"Me? Fine. Fine. Completely fine. Couldn't be finer. Finer than a— How are *you*?"

"Do you want me to come round? You sound kinda odd."

*"No!"* I answered a little too sharply. "I mean, no, thanks—I mean, we saw each other only—um—"

"Two weeks ago?"

"Yes. And I'm very busy. God how busy I am. Never been busier. That's me. Busy as a busy thing—"

"I heard you went up against Flanker. I was concerned."

"Tell me, did you and I ever—"

I couldn't say it but I needed to know.

"Did you and I ever what?"

"Did you and I—"

Think, think.

"Did you and I ever . . . visit the mammoth migrations?"

*Damn and blast!*

"The migrations? No. Should we have? Thursday, are you *sure* you're okay?"

I started to panic—and that was daft, given the circumstances. When facing people like Hades I didn't panic at all.

"Yes—I mean no. Oops, there's the doorbell. Must be my cab."

"A cab? What happened to your car?"

"A pizza. A cab *delivering* a pizza. Got to go!"

And before he could protest I had put the phone down.

I slapped my forehead with the palm of my hand and muttered:

"Idiot . . . idiot . . . *idiot!*"

I then ran around the flat like a lunatic, closing all the curtains and switching off the lights in case Miles decided to pop round to see me. I sat in the dark listening to Pickwick walking into the furniture for a bit before deciding I was being a twit and elected to go to bed with a copy of *Robinson Crusoe*.

I fetched a flashlight from the kitchen, undressed in the dark and climbed into bed, rolled around a bit on the unfamiliar mattress and then started to read the book, somehow hoping to repeat the sort of semisuccess I had enjoyed with *The Flopsy Bunnies*. I read of Crusoe's shipwreck and his arrival on the island and skipped the dull religious philosophizing. I stopped for a moment and looked around my bedroom to see whether anything was happening. It wasn't; the only changes in the room were the lights of cars sweeping around my bedroom as they turned out of the road opposite. I heard Pickwick plock-plocking to herself, and returned to my book. I was more tired than I thought and as I read, I lapsed into slumber.

I dreamt I was on an island somewhere, hot and dry, the palms languid in the slight breeze, the sky a deep blue, the sunlight pure and clear. I trod barefoot in the surf, the water cooling my feet as I walked. There was a wrecked ship, all broken masts and tangled rigging, resting on the reef a hundred yards from the shore. As I watched I could see a naked man climb aboard the ship, rummage on the deck, pull on a pair of trousers and disappear below. After waiting a moment or two and not seeing him again I walked further along the beach, where I found Landen sitting under a palm tree gazing at me with a smile on his face.

"What are you looking at?" I asked him, returning his smile and raising my hand to shield my eyes from the sun.

"I'd forgotten how beautiful you are."

"Oh *stop!*"

"I'm not kidding," he replied as he jumped to his feet and hugged me tightly. "I'm really missing you."

"I'm missing you, too," I told him, "but where are you?"

"I'm not exactly sure," he replied with a confused look. "Strictly speaking I don't think I'm anywhere—just here, alive in your memories."

"This is my memory? What's it like?"

"Well," replied Landen, "there are some really *outstanding* parts but some pretty dreadful ones too—in that respect it's a little like Majorca. Would you care for some tea?"

I looked around for the tea but Landen simply smiled.

"I've not been here long but I've learnt a trick or two. Remember that place in Winchester where we had scones that were fresh warm from the oven? You remember, on the second floor, when it was raining outside and the man with the umbrella—"

"Darjeeling or Assam?" asked the waitress.

"Darjeeling," I replied, "and two cream teas. Strawberry for me and quince for my friend."

The island had gone. In its place was the tearoom in Winchester. The waitress scribbled a note, smiled and departed. The rooms were packed with amiable-looking middle-aged couples dressed in tweed. It was, not surprisingly, just as I remembered it.

"That was a neat trick!" I exclaimed.

"Naught to do with me!" replied Landen grinning. "This is all yours. Every last bit of it. The smells, the sounds—*everything.*"

I looked around in silent wonderment.

"I can remember all this?"

"Not *quite,* Thurs. Look at our fellow tea drinkers again."

I turned in my chair and scanned the room. All the couples were more or less identical. Each was a middle-aged couple dressed in tweed and twittering in a home counties twang. They weren't really eating or talking coherently; they were just moving and mumbling to give the *impression* of a packed tearoom.

"Fascinating, isn't it?" said Landen excitedly. "Since you can't actually remember anything about who was here, your mind has just filled in the room with an amalgam of who you might *expect* to see in a teashop in Winchester. Mnemonic wallpaper, so to speak. There is nothing in this room that won't be familiar. The cutlery is your mother's and the pictures on the walls are all odd mixes of the ones we had up in the house. The waitress is a compound of Lottie from your lunch with Bowden and the woman in the chip shop. Every blank space in your memory has been filled with something that you *do* remember—a sort of shuffling of facts to fill in the gaps."

I looked back at our fellow tea-takers, who now seemed faceless.

I had a sudden—and worrying—thought.

"Landen, you haven't been around my late teenage years, have you?"

"Of course not. That's like opening private mail."

I was glad of this. My wholly unlikely infatuation for a boy named Darren and my clumsy introduction to being a woman in the back of a stolen Morris 8 was not something I wanted Landen to witness in all its ignominious glory. For once I was kind of wishing I had a bad memory—or that Uncle Mycroft had perfected his memory erasure device.

Landen poured the tea and asked: "How are things in the real world?"

"I have to figure out a way into books," I told him. "I'm going to take the Gravitube to Osaka tomorrow and see if I can track down anyone who knew Mrs. Nakajima. It's a long shot, but who knows."

"Take care won't y—"

Landen stopped short as something over my shoulder caught his eye. I turned to see probably the last person I wanted to be there. I quickly stood up, knocked my chair over backwards with a clatter and aimed my automatic at the tall figure who had just entered the tearoom.

"No call for *that!*" grinned Acheron Hades. "The way to kill me here is to forget about me, and there is about as much chance of doing that as forgetting little hubbles here."

I looked at Landen, who rolled his eyes heavenward.

"Sorry, Thurs. I meant to tell you about *him*. He's quite alive here in your memories—but harmless, I assure you."

Hades told the couple next to us to scram if they knew what was good for them and then sat down, tucking into their unfinished seed cake. He was exactly as I last saw him on the roof at

Thornfield—his clothes were even smoking slightly. I could smell the dry heat of the blaze at Rochester's old house, almost hear the crackle of the fire and the unearthly scream of Bertha as Hades threw her to her death. Hades smiled a supercilious grin. He was relatively safe in my memories, and he knew it—the worst I could do was to wake up.

I reholstered my gun.

"Hello, Hades," I said, sitting back down again. "Tea?"

"Would you? Frightfully kind."

I poured him a cup. He stirred in four sugars and observed Landen for a bit with an inquisitorial eye before asking: "So you're Parke-Laine, eh?"

"What's left of him."

"And you and Next are in love?"

"Yes."

I took Landen's hand as though to reinforce the statement.

"I was in love once, you know," murmured Hades with a sad and distant smile. "I was quite besotted, in my own sort of way. We used to plan heinous deeds together, and for our first anniversary we set fire to a large public building. We then sat on a nearby hill together to watch the fire light up the sky, the screams of the terrified citizens a symphony to our ears."

He sighed again, only this time more deeply.

"But it didn't work out. The course of true love rarely runs smooth. I had to kill her."

"You *had* to kill her?"

"Yes," he sighed, "but I spared her any pain—and said I was sorry."

"That's a very heartwarming story," murmured Landen.

"You and I have something in common, Mr. Parke-Laine."

"I sincerely hope not."

"We live only in Thursday's memories. She'll never be rid of me until she dies, and the same goes for you—sort of ironic, isn't it? The man she loves, the man she hates—!"

"He'll be returning," I replied confidently, "when Jack Schitt is out of 'The Raven.' "

Acheron laughed.

"I think you overestimate Goliath's commitment to their promises. Landen is as dead as I am, perhaps more so—at least I survived childhood."

"I beat you fair and square, Hades," I said, handing him a jam pot and a knife as he helped himself to a scone, "and I'll take on Goliath and win, too."

"We'll see," replied Acheron thoughtfully, "we'll see."

I thought of the Skyrail and the falling Hispano-Suiza.

"Did you try and kill me the other day, Hades?"

"If only!" he answered, waving the jam spoon in our direction and laughing. "But then again I *might* have done—after all, I'm here only as your *memory* of me. I sincerely hope that I am, perhaps, not dead and out there somewhere for real, plotting, plotting . . . !"

Landen stood up.

"C'mon, Thurs. Let's leave this clown to our scones. Do you remember when we first kissed?"

The tearoom was suddenly gone and in its place was a warm night in the Crimea. We were back at Camp Aardvark watching the shelling of Sevastopol on the horizon, the finest fireworks show on the planet if only you could forget what it was doing. The sound of the barrage was softened almost into a lullaby by the distance. We were both in battle dress and standing together but not touching—and by God how much we wanted to.

"Where's this?" asked Landen.

"It's where we kissed for the first time," I replied.

"No—!" replied Landen. "I remember watching the shelling with you, but we only *talked* that evening. I didn't actually kiss you until the night you drove me out to forward CP and we got stuck in the minefield."

I laughed out loud.

"Men have such crap memories when it comes to things like this! We were standing apart like this and desperately wanting to just *touch* each other. You put your hand on my shoulder to pretend to point something out and I slid my hand into the small of your back like . . . *so*. We didn't say anything but when we held each other it was like, like *electricity!*"

We did. It was. The shivers went all the way to my feet, bounced back, returned in a spiral up my body and exited my neck as a light sweat.

"Well," replied Landen in a quiet voice a few minutes later. "I think I prefer *your* version. So if we kissed *here*, then the night in the minefield was—"

"Yes," I told him, "yes, yes it was."

And there we were, sitting outside an armored personnel carrier in the dead of night two weeks later, marooned in the middle of probably the best-signposted minefield in the area.

"People will think you did this on purpose," I told him as unseen bombers droned overhead, off on a mission to bomb someone to pulp.

"I got away only with a reprimand, as I recall," he replied. "And anyway, who's to say that I didn't?"

"You drove *deliberately* into a minefield just for a legover?" I asked, laughing.

"Not any old legover," he replied. "Besides, there was no risk involved."

He pulled a hastily drawn map out of his battle-dress pocket.

"Captain Bird drew this for me."

"You scheming little shitbag!" I told him, throwing an empty K-ration tin at him. "I was terrified!"

"Ah!" replied Landen with a grin. "So it was terror and not passion that drove you into my arms?"

"Well"—I shrugged—"maybe a bit of both."

Landen leaned forward, but I had a thought and pressed a fingertip to his mouth.

"But this wasn't the *best*, was it?"

He stopped, smiled and whispered in my ear: "At the furniture store?"

"In your dreams, Land. I'll give you a clue. You still had a leg and we both had a week's leave—by lucky coincidence at the same time."

"No coincidence," said Landen with a smile.

"Captain Bird again?"

"Two hundred bars of chocolate but worth every packet."

"You're a bit of a rake, y'know, Land—but in the nicest kind of way. Anyhow," I continued, "we elected to go cycling in the Republic of Wales."

As I spoke the APC vanished, the night rolled back and we were walking hand in hand through a small wood to the side of a stream. It was summer and the water babbled excitedly among the rocks, the springy moss a warm carpet to our bare feet. The blue sky was devoid of clouds and the sunlight trickled in amongst the verdant foliage above our heads. We pushed aside low branches and followed the sound of a waterfall. We came across two bicycles leaning up against a tree, the panniers open and the tent half pegged out on the ground. My heart quickened as the memories of that particular summer's day flooded back. We had started to put the tent up but stopped for a moment, the passion overcoming us. I squeezed Landen's hand and he curled his hands round my waist. He smiled at me with his funny half-smile.

"When I was alive I came to this memory a lot," he confided to me. "It's one of my favorites, and amazingly, your memory seems to have got most things correct."

"Is that a fact?" I asked him as he kissed me gently on my neck. I shivered slightly and ran my fingers down his naked back.

"Most—*plock*—definitely."

"What did you say?"

"Nothing—*plock plock*—why?"

"Oh *no!* Not now of all times!"

"What?" asked Landen.

"I think I'm about to—"


"—wake up."

But I was talking to myself. I was back in my bedroom in Swindon, my memory excursion annoyingly cut short by Pickwick, who was staring at me from the rug, leash in beak and making quiet plock-plock noises. I gave her a baleful stare.

"Pickers, you are *such* a pest. Just when I was getting to the good bit."

She stared at me, little comprehending what she had done.

"I'm going to drop you round at Mum's," I told her as I sat up and stretched. "I'm going to Osaka for a couple of days."

She cocked her head on one side and stared at me curiously.

"You and Junior will be in good hands, I promise."

I got out of bed and trod on something hard and whiskery. I looked at the object and smiled to myself. It was a good sign. Lying on the carpet was an old coconut husk—and better than that, there was still some sand stuck to my feet. My reading of *Robinson Crusoe* hadn't been a total failure after all.

# 14.

## The Gravitube™

By the time this decade is out, we aim to construct a transport system that can take a man or a woman from New York to Tokyo and back again in two *hours*. . . .

—U.S. PRESIDENT JOHN F. KENNEDY

For mass transport over the globe there were primarily the railroads and the airship. Rail was fast and convenient but stopped short of crossing the oceans. Airships could cover greater distances—but were slow and fraught with delays due to weather. In the fifties the journey time to Australia or New Zealand was typically ten days. In 1960, a new form of transportation system was begun—the Gravitube. It promised delay-free travel to anywhere on the planet. Any destination, whether Auckland, Rome or Los Angeles, would take exactly the same: a little over forty minutes. It was, quite possibly, the greatest feat of engineering that mankind would ever undertake.

VINCENT DOTT,
*The Gravitube: Tenth Wonder of the World*

**P**ICKWICK INSISTED on sitting on her egg all the way to Mum's house and plocked nervously whenever I went over twenty miles per hour. I made her a nest in the airing cupboard and left her fussing over her egg while the other dodos strained at the window, trying to figure out what was going on. I rang Bowden while Mum fixed me a sandwich.

"Are you okay?" he inquired. "Your phone's been off the hook!"

"I'm okay, Bowd. What's happening at the office?"

"The news is out."

"About Landen?"

"About *Cardenio*. Someone blabbed to the press. Vole Towers is besieged by news channels as we speak. Lord Volescamper has been yelling at Victor about one of us talking."

"Wasn't me."

"Nor me. Volescamper has turned down fifty million quid for it already—every impresario on the planet wants to buy the rights for first performance. And get this—you've been cleared by SO-1 of any wrongdoing. They thought that since Kaylieu was shot by SO-14 marksmen yesterday morning you might have been right after all."

"Big of them. Does this mean my leave is over?"

"Victor wants to see you as soon as possible."

"Tell him I'm ill, would you? I have to go to Osaka."

"Why?"

"Best not to know. I'll call you."

I replaced the receiver and Mum gave me some cheese on toast and a cup of tea. She sat down at the other side of the table and flicked through a well-thumbed copy of last month's *FeMole*—the one with me in it.

"Any news from Mycroft and Polly, Mum?"

"I got a card from London saying they were fit and well," she replied, "but they said they needed a jar of piccalilli and a torque wrench. I left them in Mycroft's study and they'd vanished by the afternoon."

"Mum?"

"Yes?"

"How often do you see Dad?"

She smiled. "Most mornings. He drops by to say hello. Sometimes I even make him a packed lunch—"

She was interrupted by a roar that sounded like a thousand tubas in unison. The sound reverberated through the house and set the teacups in the corner cupboard rattling.

"Oh Lordy!" she exclaimed. "Not mammoths *again!*" And was out of the door in a flash.

And a mammoth it was, in name and stature. Covered with thick brown hair and as big as a tank, it had walked through the garden wall and now sniffed suspiciously at the wisteria.

"Get away from there!" yelled my mother, searching around for a weapon of some sort. Wisely, the dodos had all run away and hid behind the potting shed. Rejecting the wisteria, the mammoth delicately scraped through the vegetable patch with a long curved tusk and then picked the vegetables up with its trunk, stuffed them into its mouth and munched slowly and deliberately. My mother was wide-eyed and almost apoplectic with rage.

"Second time this has happened!" she yelled defiantly. "Get off my hydrangeas, you . . . you . . . *thing!*" The mammoth ignored her, sucked up the entire contents of the ornamental pond in one go and clumsily trampled the garden furniture to matchwood.

"A weapon," announced my mother. "I need a weapon. I've sweated blood over this garden and no reactivated herbivore is going to have it for dinner!"

She disappeared into the shed and reappeared a moment later brandishing a yard broom. But the mammoth had little to fear, even from my mother. It did, after all, weigh almost five tons. It was used to doing *exactly* what it pleased. The only good news about the invasion was that it wasn't the whole herd.

"Giddout!" yelled my mother, raising the broom to whack the mammoth on the hindquarters.

"Hold it right there!" said a loud voice. We turned. A man

dressed in a safari suit had hopped over the wall and was running towards us.

"Agent Durrell, SO-13," he announced breathlessly, showing my mother an ID. "Spank the mammoth and you're under arrest."

My mother's fury switched to the SpecOps agent.

"So he eats my garden and I'm supposed to do *nothing?*"

"*Her* name is Buttercup," corrected Durrell. "The rest of the herd went to the west of Swindon as planned, but Buttercup here is a bit of a dreamer. And yes, you do *nothing*. Mammoths are a protected species."

"Well!" said my mother indignantly. "If you did your job properly then ordinary law-abiding citizens like me would still have gardens!"

The once verdant garden looked as though it had been the target of an artillery bombardment. Buttercup, her voluminous tum now full of Mum's vegetable patch, stepped over the wall and scratched herself against an iron streetlamp, snapping it like a twig. The lamp standard dropped heavily on the roof of a car and popped the windscreen. Buttercup let out another almighty trumpeting, which set off a few car alarms, and in the distance there was an answer. She stopped, listened for a bit and then happily lumbered off down the road.

"I've got to go!" said Durrell, handing Mum a card. "Compensation can be claimed if you call this number. You might like to ask for our free leaflet 'How to Make Your Garden Less Palatable to Proboscidea.' Good morning!"

He tipped his hat and jumped over the wall to where his partner had pulled up in an SO-13 Land Rover. Buttercup gave out another call and the Land Rover screeched off, leaving my mother and me staring at her wrecked garden. The dodos, sensing the danger had passed, crept out from behind the potting shed and plock-plocked quietly to themselves as they pecked and scratched at the scoured earth.

"Perhaps it's time for a Japanese garden," sighed my mother, throwing down the broom handle. "Reverse engineering! Where will it all end? They say there's a *Diatryma* living wild in the New Forest!"

"Urban legend," I assured her as she started to tidy up the garden. I looked at my watch. I would have to run if I was to get to Osaka that evening.

I took the train to the busy Saknussum International Gravitube Terminus, located just to the west of London. I made my way into the departures terminal and studied the board. The next DeepDrop to Sydney would be in an hour. I bought a ticket, hurried to the check-in and spent ten minutes listening to a litany of pointless antiterrorist questions.

"I don't have a bag," I explained. She looked at me oddly, so I added: "Well, I *did,* but you lost it the last time I traveled. In fact, I don't think I've *ever* had a bag returned to me after tubing."

She thought about this for a moment and then said: "*If* you had a bag and *if* you had packed it yourself, and *if* you had not left it unattended, might it contain any of the following?"

She showed me a list of prohibited items and I shook my head.

"Would you like an in-drop meal?"

"What are my choices?"

"Yes or no."

"No."

She looked at the next question on her sheet.

"Who would you prefer to sit next to?"

"Nun or a knitting granny, if that's possible."

"Hmm," mused the check-in girl, studying the passenger manifest carefully. "All the nuns, grannies and intelligent non-amorous males are taken. It's technobore, lawyer, self-pitying drunk or copiously vomiting baby, I'm afraid."

"Technobore and lawyer, then."

She marked me down on the seating plan and then announced: "There will be slight delay in receiving the excuse for the lateness of the DeepDrop to Sydney, Miss Next. The reason for the delay in the excuse has yet to be established."

Another check-in girl whispered something in her ear.

"I've just been informed that the reason for the excuse for the delay has been delayed itself. As soon as we find out why the reason for the excuse has been delayed we will tell you—in line with government guidelines. If you are at all unhappy with the speed at which the excuse has been delivered, you might be eligible for a 1% refund. Have a nice drop."

I was handed my boarding card and told to go to the gate when the drop was announced. I thanked her, bought some coffee and biscuits and sat down to wait. The Gravitube seemed to be plagued with delays. There were a lot of travelers sitting around looking bored as they waited for their trip. In theory every drop took under an hour irrespective of destination; but even if they developed a twenty-minute accelerated DeepDrop to the other side of the planet, you'd still spend four hours at either end waiting for baggage or customs or something.

The PA barked into life again.

"Attention, please. Passengers for the 11:04 DeepDrop to Sydney will be glad to know that the delay was due to too many excuses being created by the Gravitube's Excuse Manufacturing Facility. Consequently we are happy to announce that since the excess excuses have now been used, the 11:04 DeepDrop to Sydney is ready for boarding at gate six."

I finished my coffee and made my way with the throng to where the shuttle was waiting to receive us. I had ridden on the Gravitube several times before, but never the DeepDrop. My recent tour of the world had all been by overmantles, which are more like trains. I carried on through passport control, boarded the shuttle and was shown to my seat by a stewardess whose fixed smile reminded me of a synchronized swimmer's. I sat next to a man with a shock of untidy black hair who was reading a copy of *Astounding Tales*.

"Hello," he said in a subdued monotone. "Ever Deep-Dropped before?"

"Never," I replied.

"Better than any roller coaster," he announced with finality and returned to his magazine.

I strapped myself in as a tall man in a large check suit sat down next to me. He was about forty, had a luxuriant red mustache and wore a carnation in his buttonhole.

"Hello, Thursday!" he said in a friendly voice as he proffered his hand. "Allow me to introduce myself—Akrid Snell."

I stared at him in surprise, and he laughed.

"We needed some time to talk, and I've never been on one of these before. How does it work?"

"The Gravitube? It's a tunnel running through the center of the earth. We freefall all the way to Sydney. But . . . but . . . how on earth did you find me?"

"Jurisfiction has eyes and ears everywhere, Miss Next."

"Plain English, Snell—or I could turn out to be the most difficult client you've ever had."

Snell looked at me with interest for a few moments as a stewardess gave a monotonous safety announcement, culminating with the warning that there were no toilet facilities until gravity returned to 40%.

"You work in SpecOps, don't you?" asked Snell as soon as we were comfortable and all loose possessions had been placed in zippered bags.

I nodded.

"Jurisfiction is the service we run *inside* novels to maintain the integrity of popular fiction. The printed word might look solid to you, but where I come from, 'movable type' has a much deeper meaning."

"The ending of *Jane Eyre*," I murmured, suddenly realizing what all the fuss was about. "I changed it, didn't I?"

"I'm afraid so," agreed Snell, "but don't admit that to anyone but me. It was the biggest Fiction Infraction to a major work since someone futzed so badly with Thackeray's *Giant Despair* we had to delete it completely."

"Drop is D minus two minutes," said the announcer. "Would all passengers please take their seats, check their straps and make sure all infants are secured."

"So what's happening now?" asked Snell.

"Do you really not know anything about the Gravitube?"

Snell looked around and lowered his voice.

"All of your world is a bit strange to me, Next. I come from a land of trench coats and deep shadows, complex plot lines, frightened witnesses, underground bosses, gangster's molls, seedy bars and startling six-pages-from-the-end denouements."

I must have looked confused, for he lowered his voice further and hissed: "I'm *fictional*, Miss Next. Co-lead in the Perkins & Snell series of crime books. I expect you've read me?"

"I'm afraid not," I admitted.

"Limited print run," sighed Snell, "but we had a good review in *CrimeBooks Digest*. I was described as 'a well rounded and amusing character . . . with quite a few memorable lines.' *The Mole* placed us on their 'Read of the Week' list but *The Toad* were less enthusiastic—but listen, who takes any notice of the critics?"

"You're *fictional?*" I said at last.

"Keep it to yourself though, won't you?" he urged. "Now, about the Gravitube?"

"Well," I replied, gathering my thoughts, "in a few minutes

the shuttle will have entered the airlock and depressurization will commence—"

"Depressurization? Why?"

"For a frictionless drop. No air resistance—and we are kept from touching the sides by a powerful magnetic field. We then simply free-fall the eight thousand miles to Sydney."

"So all cities have a DeepDrop to every other city, then?"

"Only London and New York connecting to Sydney and Tokyo. If you wanted to get from Buenos Aires to Auckland, you'd first take the overmantle to Miami, then to New York, DeepDrop to Sydney, and finally another overmantle to Auckland."

"How fast does it go?" asked Snell, slightly nervously.

"Peaks at fourteen thousand miles per hour," said my neighbor from behind his magazine, "give or take. We'll fall with increasing velocity but *decreasing* acceleration until we reach the center of the earth, at which point we will have attained our maximum velocity. Once past the center our velocity will *decrease* until we reach Sydney, when our velocity will have decreased to zero."

"Is it safe?"

"Of course!" I assured him.

"What if there's another shuttle coming the other way?"

"There can't be," I assured him. "There's only one shuttle per tube."

"What you say is true," said my boring neighbor. "The only thing we have to worry about is a failure of the magnetic containment system that keeps the ceramic tube and us from melting in the liquid core of the earth."

"Don't listen to this, Snell."

"Is that likely?" he asked.

"Never happened before," replied the man somberly, "but then if it had, they wouldn't tell us about it, now would they?"

Snell thought about this for a few moments.

"Drop is D minus ten seconds," said the announcer.

The cabin went quiet and everyone tensed, subconsciously counting down. The drop, when it came, was a bit like going over a very large humpback bridge at a great deal of speed, but the initial unpleasantness—which was accompanied by grunts from the passengers—gave way to the strange and curiously enjoyable feeling of weightlessness. Many people do the drop for this reason only. I turned to Snell.

"You okay?"

He nodded and managed a wan smile.

"It's a bit . . . strange," he said at last, watching as his tie floated in front of him.

"So I'm charged with a Fiction Infraction, yes?"

"Fiction Infraction *Class II*," corrected Snell, swallowing hard. "It's not as though you did it on purpose. Even though we could argue convincingly that you *improved* the narrative of *Jane Eyre*, we still have to prosecute; after all, we can't have people blundering around in *Little Women* trying to stop Beth from dying, can we?"

"Can't you?"

"Of course not. Not that people don't try. When you get before the magistrate, just deny everything and play dumb. I'm trying to get the case postponed on the grounds of *strong reader approval*."

"Will that work?"

"It worked when Falstaff made his illegal jump to *The Merry Wives of Windsor* and proceeded to dominate and alter the story. We thought he'd be sent packing back to *Henry IV*, Part 2. But no, his move was approved. The judge was an opera fan, so maybe that had something to do with it. You haven't had any operas written about you by Verdi or Vaughan Williams, have you?"

"No."

"Pity."

The feeling of weightlessness didn't last long. The increasing deceleration once more gently returned weight to us all. At 40% normal gravity the cabin warning lights went out and we could move around if we wanted.

The technobore on my right started up again.

"—but the *real* beauty of the Gravitube is its simplicity," he continued. "Since the force of gravity is the same irrespective of the declination of the tunnel, the trip to Tokyo will take *exactly* the same time as the trip to New York—and it would be the same again to Carlisle if it didn't make more sense to use a conventional railway. Mind you," he went on, "if you could use a wave induction system to keep us accelerating all the way to the surface at the other end, the speed could be well in excess of the seven miles per second needed to achieve escape velocity."

"You'll be telling me that we'll fly to the moon next," I said.

"We already have," returned my technobore neighbor in a conspiratorial whisper. "Secret government experiments have already constructed a base on the far side of the moon where transmitters control our thoughts and actions from atop the Empire State Building using interstellar communications from extraterrestrial life forms intent on world domination with the express agreement of the Goliath Corporation and a secret cabal of world leaders known as *SPORK*."

"And don't tell me," I added, "there's a *Diatryma* living in the New Forest."

"How did you know?"

I ignored him, and only thirty-eight minutes after leaving London we came in for a delicate dock in Sydney, the faintest *click* being heard as the magnetic locks held on to the shuttle to stop it falling back down again. After the safety light had extinguished and the airlock had been pressurized we made our way to the exit, avoiding the technobore, who was trying to tell anyone who would listen that the Goliath Corporation were responsible for smallpox.

Snell, who genuinely seemed to enjoy the DeepDrop, walked with me until baggage retrieval, looked at his watch and announced: "Well, that's me. Thanks for the chat. I've got to go and defend Tess for the umpteenth time. As Hardy originally wrote it she gets off. Listen, try and figure some extenuating circumstances as to your actions. If you can't, then try and think up some stonking great lies. The bigger the better."

"That's your best advice? Perjure myself?"

Snell coughed politely.

"The astute lawyer has many strings to his bow, Miss Next. They've got Mrs. Fairfax and Grace Poole to testify against you. It doesn't look great, but no case is lost until it's lost. They said I couldn't get Henry V off the war crimes rap when he ordered the French POWs murdered, but I managed it—the same as Max de Winter's murder charge. No one figured he'd get off *that* in a million years. By the by, can you give this letter to that gorgeous Flakky girl? I'd be eternally grateful."

He handed me a crumpled letter from his pocket and made to move off.

"Wait!" I said. "Where and when is the hearing?"

"Didn't I say? Sorry. The prosecution has chosen the Examining Magistrate from Kafka's *The Trial*. Not my choice, believe me. Tomorrow at 9:25. Do you speak German?"

"No."

"Then we'll make sure it's an English translation—drop in at the end of Chapter Two; we're on after Herr K. Remember what I said. So long!"

And before I could ask him how I might even *begin* to enter Kafka's masterpiece of frustrating circuitous bureaucracy, he was gone.

*　　*　　*

I caught the overmantle to Tokyo a half hour later. It was almost deserted, and I hopped on board a Skyrail to Osaka and alighted in the business district at one in the morning, four hours after leaving Saknussum. I took a hotel room and sat up all night, staring out at the blinking lights and thinking about Landen.

# 15.

## Curiouser & Curiouser
## in Osaka

I first learned of my strange bookjumping skills as a little girl in the English school where my father taught in Osaka. I had been instructed to stand up and read to the class a passage from *Winnie-the-Pooh*. I began with Chapter Nine—"It rained and it rained and it rained . . . "—but then had to stop abruptly as I felt the hundred-acre wood move rapidly in all around me. I snapped the book shut and returned, damp and bewildered, to my classroom. Later on I visited the hundred-acre wood from the safety of my own bedroom and enjoyed wonderful adventures there. But I was always careful, even at that tender age, never to alter the visible story lines. Except, that is, to teach Christopher Robin how to read and write.

O. NAKAJIMA,
*Adventures in the Book Trade*

**O**SAKA WAS LESS FLASHY than Tokyo but no less industrious. In the morning I took breakfast at the hotel, bought a copy of the *Far Eastern Toad* and read the home news but from a Far Eastern viewpoint—which makes for a good take on the whole Russian thing. During breakfast I pondered just how I might find one woman in a city of a million. Apart from her surname and perfect English, there was little to go on. As a first step I asked the concierge to photocopy all the Nakajima entries from the telephone directory. I was dismayed to discover that Naka-jima was quite a common name—there were 2,729 of them. I called one at random and a very pleasant Mrs. Nakajima spoke to me for about ten minutes. I thanked her profusely and put the phone down, having not understood a single word. I sighed, ordered a large jug of coffee from room service, and began.

It was 351 non-bookjumper Nakajimas later that, tired and annoyed, I started telling myself that what I was doing was useless—if Mrs. Nakajima *had* retired to the distant backstory of *Jane Eyre*, was she really going to be anywhere near a telephone?

I sighed, stretched one of those groany-clicky stretches, drank the rest of my cold coffee and decided to go for a brief stroll to loosen up. I was staring at the photocopied pages as I strolled along, trying to think of something to narrow the search, when a young man's jacket caught my eye.

As is popular in the Far East, many T-shirts and jackets have English writing upon them—some of them making sense, but others just collections of words that must appear as fashionable to the Japanese youth as kanji appear elegant to us. I had seen jackets with the strange legend *100% Chevrolet OK Fly-boy* and later one with *Pratt & Whitney squadron movie,* so I should have been ready for anything. But this one was different. It was a smart leather jacket with the following message embroidered on the back:

*Follow me, Next Girl!*

So I did. I followed the young man for two blocks before I noticed a *second* jacket much like the first. By the time I had crossed the canal I had seen another jacket with *SpecOps this way* emblazoned on the back, then *Jane Eyre forever!* followed quickly by *Bad Boy Goliath*. But that wasn't all—like some bizarre homing call, all the people wearing these jackets, hats and T-shirts seemed to be heading *in the same direction*. Thoughts of falling Hispano-Suizas and ambushed Skyrails suddenly filled my head, so I dug the entroposcope from my bag, shook it and noticed a slight separation between the rice and lentils. Entropy was decreasing. I rapidly turned and started walking in the opposite direction. I took three paces and stopped as a daring notion filled my head. Of course—why not make the entropic failure do the work for me? I followed the logos to a nearby market square, where I noticed the rice and lentils in the entroposcope had settled—despite repeated shakings—into curved bands. Coincidence had increased to the point where everyone I saw was wearing something with a relevant logo. *MycroTech Developments, Charlotte Brontë, Hispano-Suiza, Goliath* and *Skyrail* were all sewn or stuck to hats, jackets, umbrellas, shirts, bags. I looked around, desperately trying to find the coincidental epicenter. Then I found it. In an inexplicably vacant gap within the busy market, an old man was seated in front of a small table. He was as brown as a nut and quite bald, and opposite him the other chair had just been vacated by a young woman. A piece of battered card leaning against his small valise declared, in eight languages, the fortune-teller's trade and pledge. The English part of the sign read: "I have the answer you seek!" And I was in no doubt that whatever he said would be so—but, given the unlikely modes of death already meted out by my unseen assailant, probably, yet very *improbably* in its undertaking, would result in my demise. I took two paces closer to the fortune-teller and shook the entroposcope again. The patterns were more defined but not the clean half-and-half separation I needed. The little man had seen me dither and beckoned me closer.

"Please!" he said. "Please come. Tell you *everything!*"

I paused and looked around for any sign of jeopardy. There was nothing. I was in a perfectly peaceful square in a prosperous area of a large city in Japan. Whatever my anonymous foe had in store for me, it was something that I would least expect.

I stayed back, unsure of the wisdom of what I was doing. It was the appearance of a T-shirt that had *nothing* to do with me that clinched it. If I let this opportunity slide I would never find Mrs. Nakajima this side of a month. I took out my ballpoint, clicked it open and marched purposefully towards the small man, who grinned at me.

"You come!" he said in poor English. "You learn everything. Good buy, from me!"

But I didn't stop. As I walked towards the fortune-teller I thrust my hand in my bag and pulled out a sheet of the Nakajima pages at random, then, just as I passed the little nut-brown man, I stabbed arbitrarily on the page with my pen and broke into a run. There was a horrified gasp from the onlookers as a bolt of lightning came to earth in the small square and struck the clearly not very talented fortune-teller with a bright flash. I didn't stop until I was away from that place, back to plain polo shirts, ordinary designer labels and my entroposcope to random clumping. I sat on a bench to get my breath back, felt nauseous again and almost threw up in a nearby trash can, much to the consternation of a little old lady who was sitting next to me. I recovered slightly and looked at the Nakajima that the fall of my ballpoint had decreed. If coincidences were running as high as I had hoped, then this Nakajima *had* to be the one I sought. I turned to ask the little old lady next to me the way, but she had gone. I stopped a passerby and asked for directions. It seemed that a small amount of negative entropy still lingered—I was barely two minutes' walk from my quarry.

The apartment block I was directed to was not in a very good state of repair. The plaster that was covering the cracks had cracks, and the grime on the peeling paint was itself starting to peel. Inside there was a small lobby where an elderly doorman was watching a dubbed version of *65 Walrus Street*. He directed me to the fourth floor, where I found Mrs. Nakajima's apartment at the end of the corridor. The varnish on the door had lost its shine and the brass doorknob was tarnished, dusty and dull; no one had been in here for some time. I knocked despite this, and when silence was all that answered me, grasped the knob and turned it slowly. To my surprise it turned easily and the door creaked open. I paused to look about me, and, seeing no one, pushed open the door and stepped in.

Mrs. Nakajima's apartment was ordinary in the extreme. Three bedrooms, bathroom and kitchen. The walls and ceiling were plainly painted, the flooring a light-colored wood. It seemed as though she had moved out a few months ago and taken almost everything with her. The only notable exception to this was a small table near the window of the living room, upon which I found four slim leather-bound volumes lying next to a brass reading lamp. I picked up the uppermost book. It had *Jurisfiction* embossed on the cover, above a name I didn't recognize. I tried to open the book, but the covers were stuck fast. I tried the second book with no better luck, but paused for a moment when I saw the third book. I gently touched the slim volume and ran my fingertips across the thin layer of dust that had accumulated on the spine. The hair bristled on my neck and I shivered. But it wasn't a fearful feeling. It was the light tingle of apprehension; this book, I knew, would open. *The name on the cover was my own.* I had been expected. I opened the book. On the title page was a handwritten note from Mrs. Nakajima that was short and to the point:

*For Thursday Next, in grateful anticipation of good work and fine times ahead with Jurisfiction. I jackanoried you into a book when you were nine but now you must do it for yourself—and you can, and you shall. I also suggest that you be quick; Mr. Schitt-Hawse is walking along the corridor outside as you read this and he isn't out collecting for ChronoGuard orphans.*

*Mrs. Nakajima*

I ran to the door and slid the bolt just as the door handle rattled. There was a pause and then a loud thump on the door.

"Next!" went Schitt-Hawse's unmistakable voice. "I know you're in there! Let me in and we can fetch Jack together!"

I had been followed, obviously. It suddenly struck me that perhaps Goliath were more interested in how to get into books than in Jack Schitt himself. There was a billion-pound hole in the budget for their advanced weapons division, and a Prose Portal, *any* Prose Portal, would be just the thing to fill it.

"Go to hell!" I shouted as I returned to my book. On the first page, under a large heading that read READ ME FIRST!, there was a description of a library somewhere. I needed no second bidding; the door flexed under a heavy blow and I saw the paint crack near the lock. If it were Chalk and Cheese they wouldn't take long to gain entry.

I relaxed, took a deep breath, cleared my throat and read in a clear, strong and confident voice, expressive and expansive. I added pauses and inflections and raised the tone of my voice where the text required it. I read like I had never read before.

"I was in a long, dark, wood-paneled corridor," I began, "lined with bookshelves that reached from the richly carpeted floor to the vaulted ceiling—"

The sound of thumping increased, and as I spoke the door-frame splintered near the hinges and collapsed inwards with

Chalk, who fell with a heavy thump onto the floor, closely followed by Cheese, who landed on top of him.

"The carpet was elegantly patterned with geometric designs and the ceiling was decorated with sculpted reliefs that depicted scenes from the classics—"

"Next!" yelled Schitt-Hawse, putting his head round the door as Chalk and Cheese struggled to get up. "Coming to Osaka was *not* part of the deal! I told you to keep me informed. Nothing will happen to you—"

But something *was* happening. Something new, something *other*. My utter loathing of Goliath, the urge to get away, the knowledge that without entry to books I would never see Landen again—all of these things gave me the will to soften the barriers that had hardened since the day I first entered *Jane Eyre* in 1958.

"—High above me, spaced at regular intervals, were finely decorated circular apertures through which light gained entry—"

I could see Schitt-Hawse move towards me, but he had started to become less tangible; although I could see his lips move, the sound arrived at my ears a full second later. I continued to read, and as I did so the room about me began to *fworp* from view.

"Next!" yelled Schitt-Hawse. "You'll regret this, I swear—!"

I carried on reading.

" '—reinforcing the serious mood of the library—' "

"Bitch!" I heard Schitt-Hawse cry. "Grab her—!"

But his words were as a zephyr; the room took on the appearance of morning mist and darkened. I felt a gentle tingling sensation on my skin—and in the next instant, I had gone.

I blinked twice, but Osaka was far behind. I closed the book, carefully placed it in my pocket and looked around. I was in a long, dark, wood-paneled corridor lined with bookshelves that reached from the richly carpeted floor to the vaulted ceiling. The carpet was elegantly patterned with geometric designs and the ceiling was decorated with sculpted reliefs that depicted scenes from the classics, each cornice supporting the marble bust of an author. High above me, spaced at regular intervals, were finely decorated circular apertures through which light gained entry and reflected off the polished wood, reinforcing the serious mood of the library. Running down the center of the corridor was a long row of reading tables, each with a green-shaded brass lamp. The library appeared endless; in both directions the corridor vanished into darkness with no definable end. But this wasn't important. Describing the library would be like going to see a Turner and commenting on the frame. On all of the walls, end after end, shelf after shelf, were *books*. Hundreds, thousands, millions of books. Hardbacks, paperbacks, leather-bound, uncorrected proofs, handwritten manuscripts, *everything*. I stepped closer and rested my fingertips lightly against the pristine volumes. They felt warm to the touch, so I leaned closer and pressed my ear to the spines. I could hear a distant hum, the rumble of machinery, people talking, traffic, seagulls, laughter, waves on rocks, wind in the winter branches of trees, distant thunder, heavy rain, children playing, a blacksmith's hammer— a million sounds all happening together. And then, in a revelatory moment, the clouds slid back from my mind and a crystal-clear understanding of the very nature of books shone upon me. They weren't just collections of words arranged neatly on a page to give the *impression* of reality—each of these volumes *was* reality. The similarity of these books to the copies I had read back home was no more than the similarity a photograph has to its subject. These books *were alive!*

I walked slowly down the corridor, running my fingers along the spines and listening to the comfortable pat-pat-pat sound they made, every now and then recognizing a familiar title. After a couple of hundred yards I came across a junction where a second corridor crossed the first. In the middle of the crossways was a large circular void with a wrought-iron rail and a spiral staircase bolted securely to one side. I peered cautiously down. Not more than thirty feet below me I could see another floor, exactly like this one. But in the middle of *that* floor was another circular void through which I could see another floor, and another and another and so on to the depths of the library. I looked up. It was the same above me, more circular light wells and the spiral staircase reaching up into the dizzy heights above. I leaned on the balcony and looked about me at the vast library once again.

"Well," I said to no one in particular, "I don't think I'm in Osaka anymore."

# 16.

## Interview with the Cat

The Cheshire Cat was the first character I met at Jurisfiction, and his sporadic appearances enlivened the time I spent there. He gave me much advice. Some was good, some was bad and some was so nonsensically nonsequitous that it confuses me even now to think about it. And yet, during all that time, I never learnt his age, where he came from or where he went when he vanished. It was one of Jurisfiction's lesser mysteries.

THURSDAY NEXT,
*The Jurisfiction Chronicles*

VISITOR!" exclaimed a voice behind me. "What a *delight-ful* surprise!"

I turned and was astonished to see a large and luxuriant tabby cat sitting precariously on the uppermost bookshelf. He was staring at me with a curious mixture of insanity and benevolence and remained quite still except for the tip of his tail, which twitched occasionally from side to side. I had never come across a talking cat before, but good manners, as my father used to say, cost nothing.

"Good afternoon, Mr. Cat."

The Cat's eyes opened wide and the grin fell from his face. He looked up and down the corridor for a few moments and then inquired:

"Me?"

I stifled a laugh.

"I don't see any others."

"Ah!" replied the Cat, giving me another broad grin. "That's because you have a temporary form of *cat blindness.*"

"I'm not sure I've heard of that."

"It's quite common," he replied airily, licking a paw and stroking his whiskers. "I suppose you *have* heard of knight blindness, when you can't see any knights?"

"It's *night,* not knight," I corrected him.

"It all sounds the same to *me.*"

"Suppose I *do* have cat blindness," I ventured. "Then how is it I can see you?"

"Suppose we change the subject?" retorted the Cat, waving a paw at the surroundings. "What do you think of the library?"

"It's pretty big," I murmured, looking all around me.

"Two hundred miles in every direction," said the Cat off-handedly and beginning to purr. "Twenty-six floors above ground, twenty-six below."

"You must have a copy of every book that's been written," I observed.

"Every book that will *ever* be written," corrected the Cat, "and a few others besides."

"How many?"

"Well, I've never counted them myself, but certainly more than twelve."

As the Cat grinned and blinked at me with his large green eyes I suddenly realized where I had seen him before.

"You're the Cheshire Cat, aren't you?" I asked.

"I *was* the Cheshire Cat," he replied with a slightly aggrieved air. "But they moved the county boundaries, so technically speaking I'm now the Unitary Authority of Warrington

Cat, but it doesn't have the same ring to it. Oh, and welcome to Jurisfiction. You'll like it here; everyone is *quite* mad."

"But I don't want to go among mad people," I replied indignantly.

"Oh, you can't help that," said the Cat. "We're all mad here. I'm mad. You're mad."

I snapped my fingers.

"Wait a moment!" I exclaimed. "This is the conversation you had in *Alice in Wonderland*, just after the baby turned into a pig!"

"Ah!" returned the Cat with an annoyed flick of his tail. "Fancy you can write your own dialogue, do you? I've seen people try; it's never a pretty sight. But have it your own way. And what's more, the baby turned into a fig, not a pig."

"It was a pig, actually."

"Fig," said the Cat stubbornly. "Who was in the book, me or you?"

"It was a pig," I insisted.

"Well!" exclaimed the Cat. "I'll go and check. *Then* you'll look pretty stupid, I can tell you!"

And so saying, he vanished.

I stood there for a moment or two wondering if things could get much odder. By the time I had thought that, no, they probably couldn't, the Cat's tail started to appear, then his body and finally his head and mouth.

"Well?" I asked.

"All right," grumbled the Cat, "so it *was* a pig. My hearing is not so good; I think it's all that pepper. By the by, I almost forgot. You're apprenticed to Miss Havisham."

"Miss Havisham? *Great Expectations'* Miss Havisham?"

"Is there any other? You'll be fine—just don't mention the wedding."

"I'll try not to. Wait a moment—apprenticed?"

"Of course. Getting here is only half the adventure. If you want to join us you'll have to learn the ropes. Right now all you can do is journey. With a bit of practice on your own you *might* learn to be page-accurate when you jump. But if you want to delve deep into the backstory or take an excursion beyond the sleeve notes, you're going to have to take instruction. Why, by the time Miss Havisham has finished with you, you'll think nothing of being able to visit early drafts, deleted characters or long-discarded chapters that make little or no sense at all. Who knows, you may even glimpse the core of the book, the central nub of energy that binds a novel together."

"You mean the spine?" I asked, not quite up to speed yet.

The Cat lashed its tail in exasperation.

"No, stupid, the idea, the notion, the *spark*. Once you've laid your eyes on the raw concept of a book, everything you've ever seen or felt will seem about as interesting as a stair carpet. Try and imagine this: You are sitting on soft grass on a warm summer's evening in front of a dazzling sunset; the air is full of truly inspiring music and you have in your hands a wonderful book. Are you there?"

"I think so."

"Okay, now imagine a simply *vast* saucer of warm cream in front of you and consider lapping it *really* slowly until your whiskers are completely drenched."

The Cheshire Cat shivered deliriously.

"If you do all of that and multiply it by a thousand, then perhaps, just *perhaps,* you will have some idea of what I'm talking about."

"Can I pass on the cream?"

"Whatever you want. It's your daydream, after all."

And with a flick of his tail, the Cat vanished. I turned to explore my surroundings and was surprised to find that the

Cheshire Cat was sitting on another shelf on the other side of the corridor.

"You seem a bit old to be an apprentice," continued the Cat, folding its paws and staring at me with an unnerving intensity. "We've been expecting you for almost twenty years. Where on earth have you been?"

"I . . . I . . . didn't know I could do this."

"What you mean is that you *did* know that you *couldn't*—it's quite a different thing. The point is, do you think you have what it takes to help us here at Jurisfiction?"

"I really don't know," I replied, truthfully enough—although I hung to the hope that this was the only way I even had a *chance* to get Landen back. But since I didn't see why he should ask all the questions, I asked: "What do *you* do?"

"I," said the Cat proudly, "am the librarian."

"You look after all these books?"

"Certainly. Ask me any question you want."

"*Jane Eyre*," I asked, intending only to ask its location but realizing when the Cat answered that a librarian *here* was far removed from the sort I knew at home.

"Ranked the 728th favorite fictional book ever written," the Cat replied, parrot-fashion. "Total readings to date: 82,581,430. Current reading figure: 829,321—1,421 of whom are reading it as we speak. It's a good figure; quite possibly because it has been in the news recently."

"So what's the most-read book?"

"Up until now or forever and all time?"

"For all time."

The Cat thought for a moment.

"In fiction, the most-read book ever is *To Kill a Mockingbird*. Not just because it is a cracking good read for us, but because of all the Vertebrate überclassics it was the only one that really translated well into Arthropod. And if you can crack the Lobster market—if you'll pardon the pun—a billion years from now, you're really going to flog some copies. The Arthropod title is *tlkĭltlĭlkĭxlkilkĭxlklĭ*, or, literally translated, *The Past Nonexistent State of the Angelfish*. Atticus Finch is a lobster called Tklĭkĭ, and he defends a horseshoe crab named Klikĭflik."

"How does it compare?"

"Not too bad, although the scene with the prawns is a little harrowing. It's the crustacean readership that makes Daphne Farquitt such a major player, too."

"Daphne Farquitt?" I echoed with some surprise. "But her books are *frightful!*"

"Only to us. To the highly evolved Arthropods, Farquitt's work is considered sacred and religious to the point of lunacy. Listen, I'm no fan of Farquitt's, but her bodice-ripping pot-boiler *The Squire of High Potternews* sparked one of the biggest, bloodiest, shellbrokenist wars the planet has ever witnessed."

I was getting off the point.

"So all these books are your responsibility?"

"Indeed," replied the Cat airily.

"If I wanted to go into a book I could just pick it up and read it?"

"It's not quite *that* easy," replied the Cat. "You can only get into a book if someone has already found a way in and then exited through the library. Every book, you will observe, is bound in either red or green. Green for go, red for no-go. It's quite easy, really—you're not color-blind, are you?"

"No. So if I wanted to go into—oh, I don't know, let's pull a title out of the air—'The Raven,' then—"

But the Cat flinched as I said the title.

"There are some places you *should not go!*" he muttered in a reproachful tone, lashing his tail from side to side. "Edgar Allan Poe is one of them. His books are not fixed; there is a certain *otherness* that goes with them. Most of Macabre Gothic fiction tends to be like that—Sade is the same; also Webster, Wheatley and King. Go into those and you may *never* come out—they have a way of *weaving* you in the story, and before you know it you're stuck there. Let me show you something."

And all of a sudden we were in a large and hollow-sounding vestibule where huge Doric columns rose to support a high vaulted ceiling. The floor and walls were all dark red marble and reminded me of the entrance lobby of an old hotel—only about forty times as big. You could have parked an airship in here and *still* had room to hold an air race. There was a red carpet leading up from the high front doors, and all the brasswork shone like gold.

"This is where we honor the Boojummed," said the Cat in a quiet voice. He waved a paw in the direction of a large granite memorial about the size of two upended cars. The edifice was shaped like a large book, open in the center and splayed wide with the depiction of a person walking into the left-hand page, the person's form covered by text as he entered. On the opposite page were row upon row of names. A mason was delicately working on a new name with a mallet and chisel. He tipped his hat respectfully and resumed his work.

"Prose Resource Operatives deleted or lost in the line of duty," explained the Cat from where he was perched on top of the statue. "We call it the Boojumorial."

I pointed to a name on the memorial.

"Ambrose Bierce was a Jurisfiction agent?"

"One of the best. Dear, sweet Ambrose! A master of prose, but *quite* impetuous. He went—alone—into 'The Literary Life of Thingum Bob'—a Poe short story that one would've thought held no terrors."

The Cat sighed before continuing.

"He was trying to find a back door into Poe's poems. We know you can get from 'Thingum Bob' into 'The Black Cat' by way of an unstable verb in the third paragraph, and from 'Black Cat' into 'The Fall of the House of Usher' by the simple expedient of hiring a horse from the Nicaean stables; from there he was hoping to use the poem within 'Usher,' 'The Haunted Palace,' to springboard him into the rest of the Poe poetical canon."

"What happened?"

"Never heard from him again. Two fellow booksplorers went in after him. One lost his breath, and the other, well, poor Ahab went completely bonkers—thought he was being chased by a white whale. We suspect that Ambrose was either walled up with a cask of Amontillado or buried alive or suffered some other unspeakable fate. It was decided that Poe was out of bounds."

"So Antoine de St. Exupéry, he disappeared on assignment too?"

"Not at all; he crashed on a reconnaissance sortie."

"It was tragic."

"It certainly was," replied the Cat. "He owed me forty francs *and* had promised to teach me to play Debussy on the piano using only oranges."

"Oranges?"

"Oranges. Well, I'm off now. Miss Havisham will explain everything. Go through those doors into the library, take the elevator to the fourth floor, first right, and the books are about a hundred yards on your left. *Great Expectations* is green-bound, so you should have no trouble."

"Thanks."

"Oh, it's nothing," said the Cat, and with a wave of his paw he started to fade, very slowly, from the tip of his tail. He just had time to ask me to get some tuna-flavored Moggilicious for him the next time I was home before he vanished completely and I was alone in front of the granite Boojumorial, the quiet tapping of the mason's hammer echoing around the lofty heights of the library vestibule.

I took the marble stairs into the library and ascended by one of the wrought-iron lifts, walked down the corridor until I came across several shelves of Dickens novels. There were, I noted, twenty-nine different editions of *Great Expectations* from early draft to the last of Dickens's own revised editions. I picked up the newest tome, opened it at the first chapter and heard the gentle sound of wind in the trees. I flipped through the pages, the sounds changing as I moved from scene to scene, page to page. I located the first mention of Miss Havisham, found a good place to start and then read loudly to myself, *willing* the words to live. And live they did.

# 17.

## Miss Havisham

*Great Expectations* was written in 1860–61 to reverse flagging sales of *All the Year Round*, the weekly periodical founded by Dickens himself. The novel was regarded as a great success. The tale of Pip the blacksmith's apprentice and his rise to the position of young gentleman through an anonymous benefactor introduced readers to many new and varied characters: Joe Gargery, the simple and honorable blacksmith; Abel Magwitch, the convict Pip helps in the first chapter; Jaggers, the lawyer; Herbert Pocket, who befriends him and teaches him how to behave in London society. But it is Miss Havisham, abandoned at the altar and living her life in dreary isolation dressed in her tattered wedding robes, that steals the show. She remains one of the book's most memorable fixtures.

MILLON DE FLOSS,
*"Great Expectations": A Study*

I FOUND MYSELF in a large and dark hall which smelt of musty decay. The windows were tightly shuttered, the only light from a few candles scattered around the room; they added little to the room except to heighten the gloominess. In the center of the room a long table was covered with what had once been a wedding banquet but was now a sad arrangement of tarnished silver and dusty crockery. In the bowls and meat platters dried remnants of food were visible, and in the middle of the table a large wedding cake bedecked with cobwebs had begun to collapse like a dilapidated building. I had read the scene many times, but it was somehow different when you saw it for real—for a start, it was more colorful—and there was also a smell of mustiness that rarely comes out in the readings. I was on the other side of the room from Miss Havisham, Estella and Pip. I stood silently and watched.

A game of cards had just ended between Pip and Estella, and Miss Havisham, resplendently shabby in her rotting wedding dress and veil, seemed to be trying to come to a decision.

"When shall I have you here again?" said Miss Havisham in a low growl. "Let me think."

"Today is Wednesday, ma'am—" began Pip, but he was silenced by Miss Havisham.

"There, there! I know nothing of days of the week; I know nothing of weeks of the year. Come again after six days. You hear?"

"Yes, ma'am."

Miss Havisham sighed deeply and addressed the young woman, who seemed to spend most of her time glaring at Pip; his discomfort in the strange surroundings seemed to fill her with inner mirth.

"Estella, take him down. Let him have something to eat, and let him roam and look about him while he eats. Go, Pip."

They left the darkened room, and I watched as Miss Havisham stared at the floor, then at the half-filled trunks of old and yellowed clothes that might have accompanied her on her honeymoon. I watched her as she pulled off her veil, ran her fingers through her graying hair and kicked off her shoes. She looked about her, checked the door was closed and then opened a bureau that I could see was full, not of the trappings of her wretched life, but of small luxuries that must, I presumed, make her existence here that much more bearable. Amongst other things I saw a Sony Walkman, a stack of *National Geographics*, a few Daphne Farquitt novels, and one of those bats that has a rubber ball attached to a piece of elastic. She rummaged some more and took out a pair of trainers and pulled them on, with a great deal of relief. She was just about to tie the laces when I shifted my weight and knocked against a small table. Havisham, her senses heightened by her long incarceration in silent intro-spection, gazed in my direction, her sharp eyes piercing the gloom.

"Who is there?" she asked sharply. "Estella, is that you?"

Hiding didn't seem to be a worthwhile option, so I stepped from the shadows. She looked me up and down with a criti-cal eye.

"What is your name, child?" she asked sternly.

"Thursday Next, ma'am."

"Ah!" she said again. "The *Next* girl. Took you long enough to find your way in here, didn't it?"

"Sorry—?"

"*Never* be sorry, girl—it's a waste of time, believe me. If only you had seriously attempted to come to Jurisfiction after Mrs. Nakajima showed you how up at Haworth—well, I'm wasting my breath, I have no doubt."

"I had no idea—!"

"I don't often take apprentices," she carried on, disregarding me completely, "but they were going to allocate you to the Red Queen. The Red Queen and I don't get along, I suppose you've heard that?"

"No, I've—"

"Half of all she says is nonsense and the other half is irrele-vant. Mrs. Nakajima recommended you most highly, but she has been wrong before; cause any trouble and I'll bounce you out of Jurisfiction quicker than you can say ketchup. How are you at tying shoelaces?"

So I tied Miss Havisham's trainers for her, there in Satis

House amongst the rotted trappings of her abandoned marriage. It seemed churlish to refuse, and I really didn't mind. If Havisham was my teacher, I would do whatever she reasonably expected of me. I'd not get into "The Raven" without her help, that much was obvious.

"There are three simple rules if you want to stay with me," continued Miss Havisham in the sort of voice that seeks no argument. "Rule One: You do *exactly* as I tell you. Rule Two: You don't patronize me with your pity. I have no desire to be helped in any way. What I do to myself and others is my business and my business alone. Do you understand?"

"What about Rule Three?"

"All in good time. I shall call you Thursday and you may call me Miss Havisham when we are together; in company I shall expect you to call me ma'am. I may summon you at any time and you will come running. Only funerals, childbirth or Vivaldi concerts take precedence. Is that clear?"

"Yes, Miss Havisham."

I stood up and she thrust a candle nearer to my face and regarded me closely. It gave me a chance to look at her too—despite her pallid demeanor, her eyes sparkled brightly and she was not nearly as old as I supposed; all she needed was a fortnight of good meals and some fresh air. I was tempted to say something to enliven the dismal surroundings but her iron personality stopped me; I felt as though I were facing my teacher at school for the first time.

"Intelligent eyes," muttered Havisham. "Committed and honest. Quite, quite sickeningly self-righteous. Are you married?"

"Yes—" I mumbled. "That is to say—no."

"Come, come!" said Havisham angrily. "It is a simple enough question."

"I *was* married," I answered.

"Died?"

"No—" I mumbled. "That is to say—yes."

"I'll try harder questions in future," announced Havisham, "for you are obviously not adept at the easy ones. Have you met the Jurisfiction staff?"

"I've met Mr. Snell—and the Cheshire Cat."

"As useless as each other," she announced shortly. "Everyone at Jurisfiction is either a charlatan or an imbecile—except the Red Queen, who is both. We'll go to Norland Park and meet them all, I suppose."

"Norland? Jane Austen? The house of the Dashwoods? *Sense and Sensibility*?"

But Havisham had moved on. She held my wrist to look at my watch and took me by the elbow, and before I knew what had happened we had joggled out of Satis House to the library. Before I could recover from this sudden change of surroundings, Miss Havisham was reading from a book she had drawn from a shelf. There was another strange joggle and we were in a small kitchen parlor somewhere.

"What was that?" I asked in alarm; I wasn't at all accustomed to the sudden move from book to book, but Havisham, well used to such maneuvers, thought little of it.

"That," replied Miss Havisham, "was a standard book-to-book transfer. When you're jumping solo you can sometimes make it through without going to the library—so much the better; the Cat's banal musings can make one's head ache. But since I am taking you with me, a short visit is sadly necessary. We're now in the backstory of Kafka's *The Trial*. Next door is Josef K's hearing; you're up after him."

"Oh," I remarked, "is that all?"

Miss Havisham missed the sarcasm, which was probably just as well, and I looked around. The room was sparsely furnished. A washing tub sat in the middle of the room, and next door, from the sound of it at least, a political meeting seemed to be in progress. A woman entered from the courtroom, smoothed her skirts, curtsied and returned to her washing.

"Good morning, Miss Havisham," she said politely.

"Good morning, Esther," replied Miss Havisham. "I brought you something." Havisham handed her a box of Pontefract cakes and then asked: "Are we on time?"

There was a roar of laughter from behind the door which quickly subsided into excited talking.

"Won't be long," replied the washerwoman. "Snell and Hopkins have both gone in already. Would you like to take a seat?"

Miss Havisham sat, but I remained standing.

"I hope Snell knows what he's doing," muttered Havisham darkly. "The Examining Magistrate is something of an unknown quantity."

The applause and laughter suddenly dropped to silence in the room next door and we heard the door handle grasped. Behind the door a deep voice said: "I only wanted to point out to you, since you may not have realized it yet, that today you have thrown away all the advantage that a hearing affords an arrested man in every case."

I looked at Havisham with some consternation, but she shook her head, as though to tell me not to worry.

"You scoundrels!" shouted a second voice, still from behind the door. "You can keep all your hearings!"

The door opened and a young man with a red face and dressed in a dark suit ran out, fairly shaking with rage. As he left, the man who had spoken—I assumed this to be the Examining Magistrate—shook his head sadly and the courtroom started to chatter about Josef K's outburst. The Magistrate, a small fat man who breathed heavily, looked at me and said: "Thursday N?"

"Yes sir?"

"You're late."

And he shut the door.

"Don't worry," said Miss Havisham kindly, "he always says that. It's to make you ill at ease."

"It works. Aren't you coming in with me?"

She shook her head and placed her hand on mine. "Have you read *The Trial*?"

I nodded.

"Then you will know what to expect. Good luck, my dear."

I thanked her, took a deep breath, grasped the door handle and with heavily beating heart, entered.

# 18.

## The Trial of Fräulein N

*The Trial,* Franz Kafka's enigmatic masterpiece of bureaucratic paranoia, was unpublished in the writer's lifetime. Indeed, Kafka lived out his short life in relative obscurity as an insurance clerk and bequeathed his manuscripts to his best friend on the understanding that they would be destroyed. How many other great writers, one wonders, penned masterworks which actually *were* destroyed upon their death? For the answer, you will have to look in amongst the subbasements of the Great Library, twenty-six floors of unpublished manuscripts. Amongst a lot of self-indulgent rubbish and valiant yet failed attempts at prose you will find works of pure genius. For the greatest nonwork of non-nonfiction, go to subbasement thirteen, Category MCML, Shelf 2919/B12, where a rare and wonderful treat awaits you—*Bunyan's Footscraper* by John McSquurd. But be warned. No trip to the *Well of Lost Plots* should be undertaken alone. . . .

UNITARY AUTHORITY OF WARRINGTON CAT,
*The Jurisfiction Guide to the Great Library*

**T**HE COURTROOM was packed full of men all dressed in dark suits and chattering and gesticulating constantly. There was a gallery running around just below the ceiling where more people stood, also talking and laughing, and the room was hot and airless to the point of suffocation. There was a narrow path between the men, and I slowly advanced, the crowd merging behind me and almost propelling me forward. As I walked the spectators chattered about the weather, the previous case, what I was wearing and the finer points of my case—of which, it seemed, they knew nothing. At the other end of the hall was a low dais upon which was seated, just behind a low table, the Examining Magistrate. He was on a high chair to make himself seem bigger and was shiny with perspiration. Behind him were court officials and clerks talking with the crowd and each other. To one side of the dais was the lugubrious man who had knocked on my door and tricked me into confessing back in Swindon. He was holding an impressive array of official-looking papers. This, I assumed, was Mathew Hopkins, the prosecution lawyer. Snell was standing next to him but joined me as soon as I approached and whispered in my ear:

"This is only a formal hearing to see if there is a case to answer. With a bit of luck we can get your case postponed to a more friendly court. Ignore the onlookers—they are simply here as a narrative device to heighten paranoia and have no bearing on your case. We will deny all charges.

"Herr Magistrate," said Snell as we took the last few paces to the dais, "my name is Akrid S, defending Thursday N in *Jurisfiction v. The Law,* case number 142857."

The Magistrate looked at me, took out his watch and said:

"You should have been here an hour and five minutes ago."

There was an excited murmur from the crowd. Snell opened his mouth to say something, but it was I that answered.

"I know," I said, having read a bit of Kafka in my youth and attempting a radical approach to the proceedings, "*I am to blame.* I beg the court's pardon."

At first the Magistrate didn't hear me and he began to repeat himself for the benefit of the crowd: "You should have been here an hour and— What did you say?"

"I said I was sorry and begged your pardon, sir," I repeated.

"Oh," said the Examining Magistrate as a hush fell upon the room. "In *that* case, would you like to go away and come back in, say, an hour and five minutes' time, when you *will* be late through no fault of your own?"

The crowd applauded at this, although I couldn't see why.

"At your honor's pleasure," I replied. "If it is the court's ruling that I do so, then I will comply."

"Very good," whispered Snell.

"Oh!" said the Magistrate again. He briefly conferred with his clerks behind him, seemed rattled for a moment, stared at me again and said: "It is the court's decision that you be one hour and five minutes late!"

"I am *already* one hour and five minutes late!" I announced to scattered applause from the room.

"Then," said the Magistrate simply, "you have complied with the court's ruling and we may proceed."

"Objection!" said Hopkins.

"Overruled," replied the Magistrate as he picked up a tatty notebook that lay on the table in front of him. He opened it, read something and passed the book to one of his clerks.

"Your name is Thursday N. You are a housepainter?"

"No, she—" said Snell.

"Yes," I interrupted, "I have *been* a housepainter, your honor."

There was a stunned silence from the crowd, punctuated by someone at the back who yelled "Bravo!" before another spectator thumped him. The Examining Magistrate peered closer at me.

"Is this relevant?" demanded Hopkins, addressing the bench.

"Silence!" yelled the Magistrate, continuing slowly and with very real gravity: "You mean to tell me that you have, at one time, been a housepainter?"

"Indeed, your honor. After I left school and before college I painted houses for two months. I think it might be safe to say that I was indeed—although not permanently—a housepainter."

There was another burst of applause and excited murmuring.

"Herr S?" said the Magistrate. "Is this true?"

"We have several witnesses to attest to it, your honor," answered Snell, getting into the swing of the strange proceedings.

The room fell silent again.

"Herr H," said the magistrate, taking out a handkerchief and mopping his brow carefully and addressing Hopkins directly, "I thought you told me the defendant was *not* a housepainter?"

Hopkins looked flustered.

"I didn't say she *wasn't* a housepainter, your honor, I merely said she *was* an operative for SpecOps-27."

"To the exclusion of all other professions?" asked the Magistrate.

"Well, no," stammered Hopkins, now thoroughly confused.

"Yet you did not state she was *not* a housepainter in your affidavit, did you?"

"No sir."

"Well then!" said the Magistrate, leaning back on his chair as another peal of laughter and spontaneous applause broke out for no reason. "If you bring a case to my court, Herr H, I expect it to be brought with all the details intact. First she apologizes for being late, then she readily agrees to a past profession as a housepainter. Court procedure will *not* be compromised—your prosecution is badly flawed."

Hopkins bit his lip and turned a dark shade of crimson.

"I beg the court's pardon, your honor," he replied through gritted teeth, "but my prosecution *is* sound. May we proceed with the charge?"

"Bravo!" said the man at the back again.

The Magistrate thought for a moment and handed me his dirty notebook and a fountain pen.

"We will prove the veracity of prosecution counsel by a simple test," he announced. "Fräulein N, would you please write the most popular color that houses were painted in, when you were—" and here he turned to Hopkins and spat the words out—"a housepainter!"

The room erupted into cheers and shouts as I wrote the answer in the back of the exercise book and returned it.

"Silence!" announced the Magistrate. "Herr H?"

"What?" he replied sulkily.

"Perhaps you would be good enough to tell the court the color that Fräulein N has written in my book?"

"Your honor," began Hopkins in an exasperated tone, "what has this to do with the case in hand? I arrived here in good faith to arraign Fräulein N on a charge of a Class II Fiction Infraction and instead I find myself embroiled in some lunatic rubbish about housepainters. I do not believe this court represents justice—"

"You do *not* understand," said the Magistrate, rising to his feet and raising his short arms to illustrate the point, "the manner in which this court works. It is the responsibility of the prosecution council to not only bring a clear and concise case before the bench, but also to fully verse himself in the procedures that he must undertake to achieve that goal."

The Magistrate sat down amidst applause.

"Now," continued the Magistrate in a quieter voice, "either you tell me what Fräulein N has written in this book or I will be forced to arrest you for wasting the court's time."

Two guards had pushed their way through the throng and now stood behind Hopkins, ready to seize him. The Magistrate waved the book and fixed the lawyer with an imperious stare.

"Well?" he inquired. "What was the most popular color?"

"Blue," said Hopkins in a miserable voice.

"What's that you say?"

"Blue," repeated Hopkins in a louder voice.

"Blue, he said!" bellowed the Magistrate. The crowd were silent and pushed and shoved to get closer to the action. Slowly and with high drama, the Magistrate opened the book to reveal the word *green* written across the page. The crowd burst into an excited cry, several cheers went up, and hats rained down upon our heads.

"Not blue, *green*," said the Magistrate, shaking his head sadly and signaling to the guards to take hold of Hopkins. "You have brought shame upon your profession, Herr H. You are under arrest!"

"On what charge?" replied Hopkins arrogantly.

"I am not authorized to tell you," said the Magistrate triumphantly. "Proceedings have been started and you will be informed in due course."

"But this is preposterous!" shouted Hopkins as he was dragged away.

"No," replied the Magistrate, "this is Kafka."

When Hopkins had gone and the crowd had stopped chattering, the Magistrate turned back to me and said: "You are Thursday N, age thirty-six, one hour and five minutes late and occupation housepainter?"

"Yes?"

"You are brought before this court on a charge of—what is the charge?"

There was silence.

"Where," asked the magistrate, "is the prosecution counsel?"

One of his clerks whispered in his ear as the crowd spontaneously burst into laughter.

"Indeed," said the Magistrate grimly. "Most remiss of him. I am afraid, in the absence of prosecuting counsel, this court has no alternative but to grant a postponement."

And so saying he pulled a large rubber stamp from his pocket and brought it down with a crash on some papers that Snell, quick as a flash, managed to place beneath it.

"Thank you, your honor," I managed to say before Snell grasped me by the arm, whispered in my ear, "Let's get the hell out of here!" and steered me ahead of him past the throng of dark suits to the door.

"Bravo!" yelled a man from the gallery. "Bravo! . . . and bravo again!"

We walked out to find Miss Havisham deep in conversation with Esther about the perfidious nature of men in general and Esther's husband in particular. They were not the only ones in the room. A bronzed Greek was sitting sullenly next to a Cyclops who had a bloodied bandage round his head. The lawyers who were accompanying them were discussing the case quietly in the corner.

"How did it go?" asked Havisham.

"Postponement," said Snell, mopping his brow and shaking me by the hand. "Well done, Thursday. Caught me unawares with your housepainter defense. Very good indeed!"

"But only a postponement?"

"Oh yes. I've never known a single acquittal from this court. But next time we'll be up before a proper judge—one of *my* choosing!"

"And what will become of Hopkins?"

"He," laughed Snell, "will have to get a *very* good lawyer!"

"Good!" said Havisham, getting to her feet. "It's time we were at the sales. Come along!"

As we made for the door, the Magistrate called into the kitchen parlor: "Odysseus? Charge of Grievous Bodily Harm against Polyphemus the Cyclops?"

"He devoured my comrades—!" growled Odysseus angrily.

"That's tomorrow's case. We will not hear about that today. You're next up—and you're late."

And the Examining Magistrate shut the door again.

# 19.

## Bargain Books

Jurisfiction was the fastest learning curve I had ever experienced. I think they were all expecting me to arrive a lot earlier than I did. Miss Havisham tested my bookjumping prowess soon after I arrived and I was marked up a dismal 38 out of a hundred. Mrs. Nakajima was 93 and Havisham a 99. I would always need a book to read from to make a jump, no matter how well I had memorized the text. It had its disadvantages but it wasn't all bad news. At least I could read a book without vanishing off inside it. . . .

THURSDAY NEXT,
*The Jurisfiction Chronicles*

OUTSIDE THE ROOM, Snell tipped his hat and vanished off to represent a client currently languishing in debtor's prison. The day was overcast yet mild. I leaned on the balcony and looked down into the yard below at the children playing.

"So!" said Havisham. "On with your training now *that* hurdle is over. The Swindon Booktastic closing-down sale begins at midday and I'm in the mood for a bit of bargain-hunting. Take me there."

"How?"

"Use your head, girl!" replied Havisham sternly as she grabbed her walking stick and thrashed it through the air a few times. "Come, come! If you can't jump me straight there, then take me to your apartment and we'll drive—but hurry. The Red Queen is ahead of us and there is a boxed set of novels that she is particularly keen to get her hands on—we *must* get there first!"

"I'm sorry—" I stammered. "I can't—"

"No such word as *can't!*" exploded Miss Havisham. "Use the book, girl, use *the book!*"

Suddenly, I understood. I took the leather-bound Jurisfiction book from my pocket and opened it. The first page, the one I had read already, was of the Great Library. On the second page there was a passage from Austen's *Sense and Sensibility* and on the third a detailed description of my apartment back at Swindon—it was good, too, right down to the water stains on the kitchen ceiling and the magazines stuffed under the sofa. The rest of the pages were covered with closely printed rules and regulations, hints and tips, advice and places to avoid. There were illustrations, too, and maps quite unlike any I had seen before. There were, in fact, far *more* pages in the book than could possibly be fitted within the covers.

"Well?" said Havisham impatiently. "Are we going?"

I flicked to the page that held the short description of my apartment in Swindon. I started to read and felt Havisham's bony hand hang on to my elbow as the Prague rooftops and aging tenement buildings faded out and my own apartment hove into view.

"Ah!" said Havisham, looking around at the small kitchen with a contemptuous air. "And this is what you call home?"

"At the moment. My husband—"

"The one who you're not sure is alive or dead or married to you or not?"

"Yes," I said firmly, "*that* one."

She smiled at this and added with a baleful stare: "You wouldn't have an ulterior motive for joining me, would you?"

"No," I lied.

"Didn't come to do something else?"

"Absolutely not."

"Not some sort of *book privateer* or something, out for riches and adventure?"

I shook my head. Doing what I was doing for Landen might not have sat too well with Havisham, so I decided to keep myself to myself.

"You're lying about something," she announced slowly, "but about *what* I'm not so sure. Children are such consummate liars. Have your servants recently left you?"

She was staring at the dirty dishes.

"Yes," I lied again, not so keen on her disparagement anymore. "Domestic service is a tricky issue in 1985."

"It's no bed of roses in the nineteenth century either," Miss Havisham replied, leaning on the kitchen table to steady herself. "I find a good servant but they never stay. It's the lure of *them,* you know—the liars, the *evil ones.*"

"Evil ones?"

"*Men!*" hissed Havisham contemptuously. "The lying sex. Mark my words, child, for no good will ever come of you if you succumb to their charms—and they have the charms of a snake, believe me!"

"I'll try to keep on my toes," I told her.

"And your chastity *firmly* guarded," she told me sternly.

"Goes without saying."

"Good. Can I borrow that jacket?"

She was pointing at Miles Hawke's Swindon Mallets jacket. Without waiting for a reply she put it on and replaced her veil with a SpecOps cap. Satisfied, she asked: "Is this the way out?"

"No, that's the broom cupboard. This is the way out over here."

We opened the door to find my landlord with his fist raised ready to knock.

"Ah!" he said in a low growl. "Next!"

"You said I had until Friday," I told him.

"I'm turning off the water. The gas, too."

"You can't do that!"

"If you've got six hundred quid or a V1.2 dodo on you," he leered, "perhaps I can be convinced not to."

But his smirk changed to fear as the point of Miss Havisham's stick shot out and caught him in the throat. She pushed him heavily against the wall in the corridor. He choked and made to move the stick, but Miss Havisham knew just how much pressure was needed—she pushed the stick harder and he stayed his hand.

"Listen to me!" she snapped. "Annoy Miss Next once more and you'll have me to answer to. She'll pay you on time, you worthless wretch—you have Miss Havisham's word on *that!*"

He gasped in short breaths, the tip of Miss Havisham's stick stuck fast against his windpipe. His eyes were clouded with the panic of suffocation; all he could do was breathe fitfully and try to nod.

"Good!" replied Miss Havisham, releasing the man, who fell into a heap on the floor.

"The evil ones," announced Miss Havisham. "You see what men are like?"

"They're not *all* like that," I tried to explain.

"Nonsense!" replied Miss Havisham as we walked downstairs. "He was one of the better ones. At least he didn't attempt to lie his way into your favors. In fact, I would go as far as to say that this one was barely repulsive at all. Do you have a car?"

Miss Havisham's eyebrows rose slightly as she saw the curious paintwork on my Porsche.

"It was painted this way when I bought it," I explained.

"I see," replied Miss Havisham in a disapproving tone. "Keys?"

"I don't think—"

"The *keys*, girl! What was Rule One again?"

"Do exactly as you say."

"Disobedient perhaps," she replied with a thin smile, "but not forgetful!"

I reluctantly handed over the keys. Havisham grasped them with a gleam in her eye and jumped in the driver's seat.

"Is it the four-cam engine?" she asked excitedly.

"No," I replied, "standard 1.6 unit."

"Oh well!" snorted Havisham, pumping the accelerator twice before turning the key. "It'll have to do, I suppose."

The engine burst into life. Havisham gave me a smile and a wink as she revved the engine up to the redline before briskly snapping the gearshift into first gear and dropping the clutch. There was a screech of rubber as we careered off up the road, the rear of the car swinging from side to side as the spinning wheels sought to find traction on the asphalt.

I have not been frightened many times in my life. Charging into the massed artillery of the Imperial Russian Army had a surreal detachment that I had found eerie rather than fearsome. Tackling Hades first in London and then on the roof of Thornfield Hall had been quite unpleasant. So had leading an armed police raid, and the two occasions I had stared at close quarters down the barrel of a gun hadn't been a bundle of joy either.

None of those, however, *even came close* to the feeling of almost certain death that I experienced during Miss Havisham's driving. We must have violated every road traffic regulation that had ever been written. We narrowly missed pedestrians, other cars and traffic bollards and ran three traffic lights at red before Miss Havisham had to stop at a junction to let a juggernaut go past. She was smiling to herself, and although erratic and bordering on homicidal, her driving had a sort of *idiot savant* skill about it. Just when I thought it was impossible to avoid a postbox she tweaked the brakes, flicked down a gear— and missed the unyielding iron lump by the width of a hair.

"The carburetors seem slightly unbalanced!" she bellowed above the terrified screams of pedestrians. "Let's have a look, shall we?" She hauled on the handbrake and we slid sideways up a dropped curbstone and stopped next to an open-air café, causing a group of nuns to run for cover. Havisham climbed out of the car and opened the engine cover.

"Rev the car for me, girl!" she shouted. I did as I was told. I offered a weak smile to one of the customers at the café, who eyed me malevolently.

"She doesn't get out often," I explained as Havisham returned to the driver's seat, revved the engine loudly and left the customers at the café in a cloud of foul-smelling rubber smoke.

"That's better!" yelled Miss Havisham. "Can't you hear it? *Much* better!"

All I could hear was the wail of a police siren that had started up.

"Oh, Christ!" I muttered; Miss Havisham punched me painfully on the arm.

"What was that for?"

"Blaspheming! If there is one thing I hate more than men, it's blaspheming— Get out of my way, you godless heathens!"

A group of people at a pedestrian crossing scattered in confused panic as Havisham shot past, angrily waving her fist. I looked behind us as a police car came into view, blue lights flashing, sirens blaring. I could see the occupants bracing themselves as they took the corner; Miss Havisham dropped a gear and we took a tight left bend, ran the wheels on the curb, swerved to avoid a mother with a pram and found ourselves in a car park. We accelerated between the rows of parked cars, but the only way out was blocked by a delivery van. Miss Havisham stamped on the brakes, flicked the car into reverse and negotiated a neat reverse slide that took us off in the opposite direction.

"Don't you think we'd better stop?" I asked.

"Nonsense, girl!" snapped Havisham, looking for a way out while the police car nosed up to our rear bumper. "Not with the sales about to open. Here we go! Hold on!"

There was only one way out of the car park that didn't involve capture: a path between two concrete bollards that looked *way* too narrow for my car. But Miss Havisham's eyes were sharper than mine and we shot through the gap, bounced across a grass bank, skidded past the statue of Brunel, drove the wrong way down a one-way street, through a back alley, past the Carer's Monument and across the pedestrianized precinct to screech to a halt in front of a large queue that had gathered for the Swindon Booktastic closing-down sale—just as the town clock struck twelve.

"You nearly killed eight people!" I managed to gasp out loud.

"My count was closer to twelve," returned Havisham as she opened the door. "And anyhow, you can't *nearly* kill someone. Either they are dead or they are not; and not one of them was so much as scratched!"

The police car slid to a halt behind us; both sides of the car had deep gouges down the side—the bollards, I presumed.

"I'm more used to my Bugatti than this," said Miss Havisham as she handed me the keys, got out and slammed the door, "but it's not so very bad, now is it? I like the gearbox especially."

I knew both of the officers and they didn't look very amused. The local PD didn't much care for SpecOps and we didn't much care for them. They would be overjoyed to pin something on any of us. They peered at Miss Havisham closely, unsure of how to put their outrage at her flagrant disregard for the Road Traffic Act into words.

"You," said one of the officers in a barely controlled voice, "you, madam, are in a lot of trouble."

She looked at the young officer with an imperious glare.

"Young man, you have no idea of the word!"

"Listen, Rawlings," I interrupted, "can we—"

"Miss Next," replied the officer firmly but positively, "your turn will come, okay?"

I got out of the car.

"Name?"

"Miss *Dame-rouge*," announced Havisham, lying spectacularly, "and don't bother asking me for my license or insurance—I haven't either!"

The officer pondered this for a moment.

"I'd like you to get in my car, madam. I'm going to have to take you in for questioning."

"Am I under arrest?"

"If you refuse to come with me."

Havisham glanced at me and mouthed, "After three." She then sighed deeply and walked over to the police car in a very overdramatic manner, shaking with muscle tremors and generally behaving like the ancient person she wasn't. I looked at her hand as she signaled to me—out of sight of the officers—a single finger, then two, then finally, as she rested for a moment against the front wing of their car, the third and final finger.

*"Look out!"* I yelled, pointing up.

The officers, mindful of the Hispano-Suiza accident two days before, dutifully looked up as Havisham and I bolted to the head of the queue, pretending we knew someone. The two officers wasted no time and leapt after us, only to lose us in the crowd as the doors to Swindon Booktastic opened and a sea of keen bibliophiles of all different ages and reading tastes moved forward, knocking both officers off their feet and sweeping Miss Havisham and me into the bowels of the bookstore.

Inside there was a near riot in progress, and I was soon separated from Miss Havisham; ahead of me a pair of middle-aged men were arguing over a signed copy of Kerouac's *On the Road* which eventually ripped down the middle. I fought my way round the ground floor past Cartography, Travel and Self-Help and was just giving up the idea of ever seeing Havisham again when I noticed a red flowing robe poking out from beneath a fawn macintosh. I watched the crimson hem cross the floor and go into the elevator. I ran across and put my foot in the door just before it shut. The neanderthal lift operator looked at me curiously, opened the doors to let me in and then closed them again. The Red Queen stared at me loftily and shuffled slightly to achieve a more regal position. She was quite heavily built; her hair was a bright auburn shade tied up in a neat bun under her crown, which had been hastily concealed under the hood of her cloak. She was dressed completely in red, and I suspected that under her makeup her skin might be red, too.

"Good morning, your majesty," I said, as politely as I could.

"Humph!" replied the red queen, then after a pause, added: "Are you that tawdry Havisham woman's new apprentice?"

"Since this morning, ma'am."

"A morning wasted, I shouldn't wonder. Do you have a name?"

"Thursday Next, ma'am."

"You may curtsy if you so wish."

So I did.

"You will regret not learning with me, my dear—but you are, of course, merely a child, and right and wrong are *so* difficult to spot at your tender age."

"Which floor, your majesty?" asked the neanderthal.

The Red Queen beamed at him, told him that if he played his cards right she would make him a duke and then added, "Three," as an afterthought.

There was one of those funny empty pauses that seem to exist only in elevators and dentist waiting rooms. We stared at the floor indicator as it moved slowly upwards and stopped on the second floor.

"Second floor," announced the neanderthal. "Historical, Allegorical, Historical-Allegorical, Poetry, Plays, Theology, Critical Analysis and Pencils."

Someone tried to get on. The Red Queen barked "Taken!" in such a fearful tone that the person backed out again.

"And how is Havisham these days?" asked the Red Queen with a diffident air as the lift moved upwards again.

"Well, I think," I replied.

"You must ask her about her wedding."

"I don't think that's very wise," I returned.

"Decidedly not!" said the Red Queen, guffawing like a sea lion. "But it will elicit an amusing effect. Like Vesuvius, as I recall!"

"Third floor," announced the neanderthal. "Fiction, Popular, authors A–J."

The doors opened to reveal a mass of book fans, fighting in a most unseemly fashion over what even I had to admit were some very good bargains. I had heard about these Fiction Frenzies before—but never witnessed one.

"Come, this is more like it!" announced the Red Queen

happily, rubbing her hands together and knocking a little old lady flying as she hopped out of the elevator.

"Where are you, Havisham?" she yelled, looking to left and right. "She has to be . . . Yes! Yes! Ahoy there, Stella, you old trollop!"

Miss Havisham stopped in mid-stride and stared in the Queen's direction. In a single swift movement she drew a small pistol from the folds of her tattered wedding dress and loosed off a shot in our direction. The Red Queen ducked as the bullet knocked a corner off a plaster cornice.

"Temper, temper!" shouted the Red Queen, but Havisham was no longer there.

"Hah!" said the Red Queen, hopping into the fray. "The devil take her—she's heading towards Romantic Fiction!"

"Romantic Fiction?" I echoed, thinking of Havisham's hatred of men. "I don't think that's very likely!"

The Red Queen ignored me and made a detour through Fantasy to avoid a scrum near the Agatha Christie counter. I knew the store a little better and nipped in between Haggard and Hergé, where I was just in time to see Miss Havisham make her first mistake. In her haste she had pushed past a little old lady sizing up a "buy two get one free" offer on contemporary fiction. The little old lady—no stranger to department store sales battle tactics—parried Havisham's blow expertly and hooked her bamboo-handled umbrella around her ankle. Havisham came down with a heavy thud and lay still, the breath knocked out of her. I kneeled beside her as the Red Queen hopped past, laughing loudly and making "nyah, nyah" noises.

"Thursday!" panted Miss Havisham as several stockinged feet ran across her. "A complete set of Daphne Farquitt novels in a walnut display case—*run!*"

And run I did. Farquitt was so prolific and popular she had

a bookshelf all to herself, and her recent boxed sets were fast becoming collector's items—it was not surprising that there was a fight in progress. I entered the scrum behind the Red Queen and was instantly punched on the nose. I reeled with the shock and was pushed heavily from behind while someone else—an accomplice, I assumed—thrust a walking stick between my shins. I lost my footing and fell with a thud on the hard wooden floor. This was not a safe place to be. I crawled out of the battle and joined Miss Havisham where she had taken cover behind a display of generously discounted Du Maurier novels.

"Not so easy as it looks, eh, girl?" asked Havisham with a rare smile, holding a lacy white handkerchief to my bleeding nose. "How close is the Royal Harridan to the Farquitt shelves?"

"I last saw her fighting somewhere between Ervine and Euripides."

"Blast!" replied Havisham with a grunt. "Listen, girl, I'm done for. My ankle's twisted and I think I've had it. But you—you might be able to make it."

I looked out at the squabbling masses as a pocket derringer fell to the ground not far from us.

"I thought this might happen," she continued, "so I drew a map."

She unfolded a piece of Satis House notepaper and pointed out where she thought we were.

"You won't make it across the main floor alive. You're going to have to climb over the Police Procedurals bookcase, make your way past the cash register and stock returns, crawl under the Chicklit and then fight the last six feet to the Farquitt boxed set. It's a limited edition of one hundred—I will *never* get another chance like this!"

"This is lunacy, Miss Havisham!" I replied indignantly. "I will *not* fight over a set of Daphne Farquitt novels!"

Miss Havisham looked sharply at me as the muffled crack of a small-caliber firearm sounded and there was the thud of a body falling.

"I thought as much!" she sneered. "A streak of yellow a mile wide all the way down your back! How did you think you were going to handle the *otherness* at Jurisfiction if you can't handle a few crazed fiction-fanciers hell bent on finding bargains? Your apprenticeship is at an end. Good day, Miss Next!"

"Wait! This is a *test?*"

"What did you think it was? Think someone like me with all the money I have *enjoys* spending my time fighting for books I can read for free in the library?"

I resisted the temptation to say "Well, yes" and answered instead: "Will you be okay here, ma'am?"

"I'll be fine," she replied, tripping up a man near us for no reason I could see. "Now go!"

I turned and crawled rapidly across the carpet, climbed over the Police Procedurals to just beyond the registers, where the sales assistants rang in the bargains with a fervor bordering on messianic. I crept past them, through the empty returns department, and dived under the Chicklit table to emerge a scant two yards from the Daphne Farquitt special editions display; by a miracle no one had yet grabbed the boxed set. And it was *very* discounted—down from £300 to only £50. I looked to my left and could see the Red Queen fighting her way through the crowd. She caught my eye and dared me to try and beat her. I took a deep breath and waded into the swirling maelstrom of popular-prose-induced violence. Almost instantly I was punched on the jaw and thumped in the kidneys; I cried out in pain and quickly withdrew. I met a woman next to the J. G. Farrell section who had a nasty cut above her eye; she told me in a concussed manner that the Major Archer character appeared in both *Troubles* and *The Singapore Grip*. I glanced to where the Red Queen was cutting a swath through the crowd, knocking people aside in her bid to beat me. She smiled triumphantly as she head-butted a woman who had tried to poke her in the eye with a silver-plated bookmark. I took a step forward to join the fray, then stopped, considered my condition for a moment and decided that perhaps pregnant women shouldn't get involved in bookshop brawls.

So instead I took a deep breath and yelled: *"Ms. Farquitt is signing copies of her books in the basement!"*

There was a moment's silence, then a mass exodus towards the stairs and escalators. The Red Queen, caught up in the crowd, was dragged unceremoniously away with them; in a few seconds the room was empty. Daphne Farquitt was notoriously private—I didn't think there was a fan of hers anywhere who wouldn't jump at the chance of actually meeting her. I walked calmly up to the boxed set, picked it up and took it to the counter, paid and rejoined Miss Havisham behind the discounted Du Mauriers, where she was idly flicking through a copy of *Rebecca*. I showed her the books.

"Not bad," she said grudgingly. "Did you get a receipt?"

"Yes, ma'am."

"And the Red Queen?"

"Lost somewhere between here and the basement."

A thin smile crossed Miss Havisham's lips, and I helped her to her feet. Together we walked slowly past the mass of squabbling book-bargainers and made for the exit.

"How did you manage it?" asked Miss Havisham.

"I told them Daphne Farquitt was signing in the basement."

"She is?" exclaimed Miss Havisham, turning to head off downstairs.

"No, no, no," I added, taking her by the arm and steering her to the exit. "That's just what I *told* them."

"Oh, I get it!" replied Havisham. "Very good indeed. Resourceful and intelligent. Mrs. Nakajima was quite right—I think you'll do as an apprentice after all."

She regarded me for a moment, making up her mind about something. Eventually she nodded, gave another rare smile and handed me a simple gold ring that slipped easily over my little finger.

"Here—this is for you. *Never take it off.* Do you understand?"

"Thank you, Miss Havisham, it's very pretty."

"Pretty nothing, Next. Save your gratitude for *real* favors, not baubles, my girl. Come along. I know of a very good bun shop in *Little Dorrit*—and I'm buying!"

Outside, paramedics were dealing with the casualties, many of them still clutching the remnants of the bargains for which they had fought so bravely. My car was gone—towed away, most likely—and we trotted as fast as we could on Miss Havisham's twisted ankle, round the corner of the building until—

"Not so fast!"

The officers who had chased us earlier were blocking our path.

"Looking for something? *This,* I suppose?"

My car was on the back of a low loader being taken away.

"We'll take the bus," I stammered.

"You'll take the car," corrected the police officer. "*My* car— Hey! Where do you think *you're* going?"

He was talking to Miss Havisham, who had taken the Farquitt boxed set and walked into a small group of women to disguise her bookjump—back to *Great Expectations* or the bun shop in *Little Dorrit* or somewhere. I wished I could join her but my skills in these matters were not really up to scratch. I sighed.

"We want some answers, Next," said the policeman in a grim tone.

"Listen, Rawlings, I don't know the lady very well. What did she say her name was? Dame-rouge?"

"It's *Havisham,* Next—but you know that, don't you? That 'lady' is *extremely* well known to the police—she's racked up seventy-four outrageously *serious* driving offenses in the past twenty-two years."

"Really?"

"Yes, really. In June she was clocked driving a chain-driven Liberty-engined Higham Special automobile at 171.5 MPH down the M4. It's not only irresponsible, it's— Why are you laughing?"

"No reason."

The officer stared at me.

"You seem to know her quite well, Next. Why does she do these things?"

"Probably," I replied, "because they don't have motorways where she comes from—or 27-liter Higham Specials."

"And where would that be, Next?"

"I have no idea."

"I could arrest you for helping the escape of an individual in custody."

"She wasn't arrested, Rawlings, you said so yourself."

"Perhaps not, but you are. In the car."

# 20.

## Yorrick Kaine

In 1983 the youthful Yorrick Kaine was elected leader of the Whigs, at that time a small and largely inconsequential party whose desire to put the aristocracy back in power and limit voting rights to homeowners had placed it on the outer edges of the political arena. A pro-Crimean stance coupled with a wish for British unification helped build nationalist support, and by 1985 the Whigs had three MPs in Parliament. They built their manifesto on populist tactics such as reducing the cheese duty and offering dukedoms as prizes on the National Lottery. A shrewd politician and clever tactician, Kaine was ambitious for power—in whatever way he could get it.

A.J.P. MILLINER,
*The New Whigs: From Humble*
*Beginnings to Fourth Reich*

IT TOOK TWO HOURS for me to convince the police I wasn't going to tell them anything about Miss Havisham other than her address. Undeterred, they thumbed through a yellowed statute book and eventually charged me with a little-known 1621 law about *permissioning a horse and carte to be driven by personn of low moral turpithtude,* but with the "horse and carte" bit crossed out and "car" written in instead—so you can see how desperate they were. I would have to go before the magistrate the following week. I started to sneak out of the building to go home, but—

"So there you are!"

I turned and hoped my groan wasn't audible.

"Hello, Cordelia."

"Thursday, are you okay? You look a bit bruised!"

"I got caught in a Fiction Frenzy."

"No more nonsense, now—I need you to meet the couple who won my competition."

"Do I have to?"

Flakk looked at me sternly.

"It's *very* advisable."

"Okay," I replied. "Where are they?"

"I'm—um—not sure," said Cordelia, biting her lip and looking at her watch. "They said they'd be here half an hour ago. Can you wait a few minutes?"

So we stood around for a bit, Cordelia looking at her watch and staring at the front door. After ten minutes of waiting and without her guests turning up, I made my excuses and nipped up to the LiteraTec's office.

"Thursday!" said Bowden as I entered. "I told Victor you had the flu. How did you get on in Osaka?"

"Pretty well, I think. I've been inside books *without* a Prose Portal. I can do it on my own—more or less."

"You're kidding."

"No," I told him, "Landen's almost as good as back. I've seen *The Trial* from the inside and have just been at the Swindon Booktastic closing-down sale with Miss Havisham."

"What's she like?" asked Bowden with interest.

"Odd—and don't ever let her drive. It seems there is something very like SpecOps-27 *inside* books—I've yet to figure it all out. How have things been out here?"

He showed me a copy of *The Owl*. The headline read: *New Play by Will Found in Swindon. The Mole* had the headline *Cardenio Sensation!* and *The Toad*, predictably enough, led with *Swindon Croquet Supremo Aubrey Jambe Found in Bath with Chimp.*

"So Professor Spoon authenticated it?"

"He did indeed," replied Bowden. "One of us should take the report up to Volescamper this afternoon. This is for you."

He handed me the bag of pinkish goo attached to a report from the SpecOps forensic labs. I thanked him and read the analysis of the slime Dad had given me with interest and confusion in equal measures.

"Sugar, fatty animal protein, calcium, sodium, maltodextrin, carboxy-methyl-cellulose, phenylalanine, complex hydrocarbon compounds and traces of chlorophyll."

I flicked to the back of the report but was none the wiser. Forensics had faithfully responded to my request for analysis— but it told me nothing new.

"What does it mean, Bowd?"

"Search me, Thursday. They're trying to match the profile to known chemical compounds, but so far, nothing. Perhaps if you told us where you got it?"

"I don't think that would be safe. I'll drop the *Cardenio* report in to Volescamper—I'm keen to avoid Cordelia. Tell forensics that the future of the planet depends on them—that should help. I *have* to know what this pink stuff is."

I saw Cordelia waiting for me in the lobby with her two guests, who had finally, it seemed, turned up. Unluckily for them, Spike Stoker had been passing and Cordelia, eager to do *something* to amuse her competition winners, had obviously asked him to say a few words. The look of frozen jaw-dropping horror on her guests' faces said it all. I hid my face behind the *Cardenio* report and left Cordelia to it.

I blagged a ride in a squad car up to the crumbling but now far busier Vole Towers. The mansion was besieged by the news stations, all keen to report any details regarding the discovery of *Cardenio*. Two dozen outside broadcast trucks were parked on the weed-infested gravel, all humming with activity. Dishes were trained into the afternoon sky, transmitting the pictures to an airship repeater station that had been routed in to bounce the stories live to the world's eager viewers. For security, SpecOps-14 had been drafted in and stood languidly about, idly chatting to one another. Mostly, it seemed, about Aubrey Jambe's apparent indiscretion with the chimp.

"Hello, Thursday!" said a handsome young SO-14 agent at the front door. It was annoying; I didn't recognize him. People I didn't know hailing me as friends was something that had happened a lot since Landen's eradication; I supposed I would get used to it.

"Hello!" I replied to the stranger in an equally friendly tone. "What's going on?"

"Yorrick Kaine is heading a press conference."

"Really?" I asked, suddenly suspicious. "What's *Cardenio* got to do with him?"

"Hadn't you heard? Lord Volescamper has *given* the play to Yorrick Kaine and the Whig party!"

"Why would," I asked slowly, smelling a political rat of epic proportions, "Lord Volescamper have anything to do with a minor right-wing pro-Crimean Welsh-hater like Kaine?"

The SpecOps-14 agent shrugged. "Because he's a lord and wants to reclaim some lost power?"

At that moment two other SpecOps agents walked past, and one of them nodded to the young agent at the door and said: "All well, Miles?"

The dashing young SO-14 agent said that all was well, but he was wrong. All was *not* well—at least it wasn't for me. I'd thought I might bump into Miles Hawke eventually, but not unprepared, like this. I stared at him, hoping my shock and surprise wouldn't show. He had spent time in my flat and knew me a lot better than I knew him. My heart thumped inside my chest and I tried to say something intelligent and witty, but it came out more like:

"Asterfobulongus?"

He looked confused and leaned forward slightly.

"I'm sorry, what was that?"

"Nothing."

"You seemed a bit upset when I called, Thursday. Is there a problem with our *arrangement?*"

I stared at him for a few seconds in numbed silence before mumbling: "No—no, not at all."

"Good!" he said. "We must fix a date or two."

"Yes," I said, running on auto-fear, "yes we must. *Gottogo*—bye."

I trotted off before he could say anything else. I paused for breath outside the door to the library. Sooner or later I was going to have to ask him straight out. I decided on the face of it that later suited me better than sooner, so I walked through the heavy steel doors and into the library. Yorrick Kaine and Lord Volescamper were sitting behind a table, and beyond them was Mr. Swaike and two security guards who were standing on either side of the play itself, proudly displayed behind a sheet of bulletproof glass. The press conference was halfway through, and I tapped Lydia Startright—who happened to be standing quite near—on the arm.

"Hey, Lyds!" I said in a low whisper.

"Hey, Thursday," replied the reporter. "I heard you did the initial authentication. How good is it?"

"Very good," I replied. "Somewhere on par with *The Tempest*. What's happening here?"

"Volescamper has just officially announced he is *giving* the play to Yorrick Kaine and the Whigs."

"Why?"

"Who knows? Hang on, I want to ask a question."

Lydia stood up and raised her hand. Kaine pointed at her.

"What do you propose to do with the play, Mr. Kaine? We understand that there has been talk of offers in the region of a hundred million pounds."

"Good question," replied Yorrick Kaine, getting to his feet. "We in the Whig party thank Lord Volescamper for his kind generosity. I am of the opinion that *Cardenio* is not for one person or group to exploit, so we at the Whig party propose offering free licenses to perform the play to anyone who wishes to do so."

There was an excited babbling from the attendant journalists as they took this in. It was an act of unprecedented generosity, especially from Kaine, but more than that, it was the *right* thing to do, and the press suddenly warmed towards Yorrick. It was as if Kaine had never suggested the invasion of Wales two years ago or the reduction of the right to vote the year before; I was instantly suspicious.

There were several more questions about the play and a lot of well-practiced answers from Kaine, who seemed to have reinvented himself as a caring and sharing patriarch and not the extremist of yore. After the press conference had ended, I made my way to the front and approached Volescamper, who looked at me oddly for a moment.

"The Spoon report," I told him, handing him the buff-colored file, "about the authentication . . . we thought you might want to see it."

"What? Of course!"

Volescamper took the report and glanced at it in a cursory manner before passing it to Kaine, who seemed to show more interest. Kaine didn't even look at me, but since I obviously wasn't going to leave like some message girl, Volescamper introduced me.

"Oh yes! Mr. Kaine, this is Thursday Next, SpecOps-27."

Kaine looked up from the report, his manner abruptly changed to one of charm and gushing friendship.

"Ms. Next, delighted!" he enthused. "I read of your exploits with great interest, and believe me, your intervention improved the narrative of *Jane Eyre* considerably!"

I wasn't impressed by him or his faux charm.

"Think you can change the Whig party's fortunes, Mr. Kaine?"

"The party is undergoing something of a restructuring at present," replied Kaine, fixing me with a serious stare. "Old ideology has been retired and the party now looks forward to a fresh look at England's political future. Rule by informed patriarch and voting restricted to responsible property owners is the future, Miss Next—ruling by committee has been the death of common sense for far too long."

"And Wales?" I asked. "Where do you stand on Wales these days?"

"Wales is historically part of greater Britain," announced Kaine in a slightly more guarded manner. "The Welsh have been flooding the English market with cheap goods, and this has to stop—but I have no plans *whatsoever* for forced unification."

I stared at him for a moment.

"You have to get in power first, Mr. Kaine."

The smile dropped from his face.

"Thank you for delivering the report, Miss Next," put in Volescamper hurriedly. "Can I offer you a drink or something before you go?"

I took the hint and made my way to the front door. I stood and looked at the outside broadcast units thoughtfully. Yorrick Kaine was playing his hand well.

# 21.

## Les Artes Modernes
## de Swindon '85

The very Irreverent Joffy Next was the minister for the Global
Standard Deity's first church in England. The GSD had a little bit
of all religions, arguing that if there *was* one God, then He would
really have very little to do with all the fluff and muddle down
here on the material plane, and a streamlining of the faiths might
very well be in His interest. Worshipers came and went as they
pleased, prayed according to how they felt most happy, and min-
gled freely with other GSD members. It enjoyed moderate success,
but what God actually thought of it no one ever really knew.

PROFESSOR M. BLESSINGTON, PR (ret.),
*The Global Standard Deity*

I PAID TO HAVE my car released with a check that I felt sure
would bounce, then drove home and had a snack and a shower
before driving over to Wanborough and Joffy's first Les Artes
Modernes de Swindon exhibition. Joffy had asked me for a list
of my colleagues to boost the numbers, so I fully expected to
see some work people there. I had even asked Cordelia, who I
had to admit was great fun when not in PR mode. The art exhibition was being held in the Global Standard Deity church at
Wanborough and had been opened by Frankie Saveloy a half
hour before I arrived. It seemed quite busy as I stepped inside.
All the pews had been moved out, and artists, critics, press and

potential purchasers milled amongst the eclectic collection of art. I grabbed a glass of wine from a passing waiter, suddenly remembered I shouldn't be drinking, sniffed at it longingly and put it down again. Joffy, looking very smart indeed in a dinner jacket and dog collar, leapt forward when he saw me, grinning wildly.

"Hello, Doofus!" he said, hugging me affectionately. "Glad you could make it. Have you met Mr. Saveloy?"

Without waiting for an answer, he propelled me towards a puffy man who stood quite alone at the side of the room. He introduced me as quickly as he could and then legged it. Frankie Saveloy was the compère of *Name That Fruit!* and looked more like a toad in real life than he did on TV. I half expected a long sticky tongue to shoot out and capture a wayward fly, but I smiled politely nonetheless.

"Mr. Saveloy?" I said, offering my hand. He took it in his clammy mitt and held on to it tightly.

"Delighted!" grunted Saveloy, his eyes flicking to my cleavage. "I'm sorry we couldn't get you to appear on my show—but you're probably feeling quite honored to meet me, just the same."

"*Quite* the reverse," I assured him, retrieving my hand forcibly.

"Ah!" said Saveloy, grinning so much the sides of his mouth almost met his ears and I feared the top of his head might fall off. "I have my Rolls-Royce outside—perhaps you might like to join me for a ride?"

"I think," I replied, "that I would sooner eat rusty nails."

He didn't seem in the least put out. He grinned some more and said: "Shame to put such magnificent hooters to waste, Miss Next."

I raised my hand to slap him but my wrist was caught by Cordelia Flakk, who had decided to intervene.

"Up to your old tricks, Frankie?"

Saveloy grimaced at Cordelia.

"Damn you, Dilly—out to spoil my fun!"

"Come on, Thursday, there are plenty of bigger fools to waste your time on than this one."

Flakk had dropped the bright pink outfit for a more reserved shade but was still able to fog film at forty yards. She took me by the hand and steered me towards some of the art on display.

"You have been leading me around the houses a bit, Thursday," she said testily. "I only need ten minutes of your time with those guests of mine!"

"Sorry, Dilly. Things have been a bit hectic. Where are they?"

"Well," she replied, "they were *meant* to be both performing in *Richard III* at the Ritz."

"Meant to be?"

"They were late and missed curtain up. Can you *please* make time for them both tomorrow?"

"I'll try."

"Good."

We approached a small scrum where one of the featured artists was presenting his latest work to an attentive audience composed mostly of art critics who all wore collarless black suits and were scribbling notes in their catalogues.

"So," said one of the critics, gazing at the piece through his half-moon spectacles, "tell us all about it, Mr. Duchamp$_{2924}$."

"I call it *The Id Within*," said the young artist in a quiet voice, avoiding everyone's gaze and pressing his fingertips together. He was dressed in a long black cloak and had sideburns cut so sharp that if he turned abruptly he would have had someone's eye out. He continued: "Like life, my piece reflects the many different layers that cocoon and restrict us in society today. The outer layer—reflecting yet counterpoising the harsh exoskeleton we all display—is hard, thin, yet somehow brittle—but beneath this a softer layer awaits, yet of the same shape and almost the same size. As one delves deeper one finds many different shells, each smaller yet no softer than the one before. The journey is a tearful one, and when one reaches the center there is almost nothing there at all, and the similarity to the outer crust is, in a sense, illusory."

"It's an onion," I said in a loud voice.

There was a stunned silence. Several of the art critics looked at me, then at Duchamp$_{2924}$, then at the onion.

I was sort of hoping the critics would say something like "I'd like to thank you for bringing this to our attention. We nearly made complete dopes of ourselves," but they didn't. They just said: "Is this true?"

To which Duchamp$_{2924}$ replied that this *was* true in *fact,* but untrue *representationally,* and as if to reinforce the fact he drew a bunch of shallots from within his jacket and added: "I have *here* another piece I'd like you to see. It's called *The Id Within II (Grouped)* and is a collection of concentric three-dimensional shapes locked around a central core . . ."

Cordelia pulled me away as the critics craned forward with renewed interest.

"You seem very troublesome tonight, Thursday," smiled Cordelia. "Come on, I want you to meet someone."

She introduced me to a young man with a well-tailored suit and well-tailored hair.

"This is Harold Flex," announced Cordelia. "Harry is Lola Vavoom's agent and a big cheese in the film industry."

Flex shook my hand gratefully and told me how *fantastically* humbled he was to be in my presence.

"Your story *needs* to be told, Miss Next," enthused Flex, "and Lola is *very* enthusiastic."

"Oh no," I said hurriedly, realizing what was coming. "No, no. Not in a million years."

"You should hear Harry out, Thursday," pleaded Cordelia.

"He's the sort of agent who could cut a *really* good financial deal for you, do a fantastic PR job for SpecOps *and* make sure your wishes and opinions in the whole story were rigorously listened to."

"A movie?" I asked incredulously. "Are you nuts? Didn't you see *The Adrian Lush Show*? SpecOps and Goliath would pare the story to the bone!"

"We'd present it as *fiction,* Miss Next," explained Flex. "We've even got a title: *The Eyre Affair.* What do you think?"

"I think you're both out of your tiny minds. Excuse me."

I left Cordelia and Mr. Flex plotting their next move in low voices and went to find Bowden, who was staring at a dustbin full of paper cups.

"How can they present this as art?" he asked. "It looks just like a rubbish bin!"

"It *is* a rubbish bin," I replied. "That's why it's next to the refreshments table."

"Oh!" he said, then asked me how the press conference went.

"Kaine is fishing for votes," he told me when I had finished. "Got to be. A hundred million might buy you some serious airtime for advertising, but putting *Cardenio* in the public domain could sway the Shakespeare vote—that's one group of voters you can't buy."

I hadn't thought of this.

"Anything else?"

Bowden unfolded a piece of paper.

"Yes. I'm trying to figure out the running order for my stand-up comedy routine tomorrow night."

"How long is your slot?"

"Ten minutes."

"Let me see."

He had been trying out his routine on me, although I

protested that I probably wasn't the best person to ask. Bowden himself didn't find any of the jokes funny, although he understood the technical process involved.

"I'd start off with the penguins on the ice floe," I suggested, looking at the list as Bowden made notes, "then move on to the pet centipede. Try the white horse in the pub next, and if that works well do the tortoise that gets mugged by the snails—but don't forget the voice. Then move on to the dogs in the waiting room at the vet's and finish with the one about meeting the gorilla."

"What about the lion and the baboon?"

"Good point. Use that instead of the white horse if the centipede goes flat."

Bowden made a note.

"Centipede . . . goes . . . flat. Got it. What about the man going bear hunting? I told that to Victor and he sprayed Earl Grey out of both nostrils at once."

"Keep it for an encore. It's three minutes long on its own—but don't hurry; let it build. Then again, if your audience is middle-aged and a bit fuddy-duddy I'd drop the bear, baboon and the dogs and use the greyhound and the racehorses instead—or the one about the two Rolls-Royces."

"Canapés, darling?" said Mum, offering me a plate.

"Got any more of those prawny ones?"

"I'll go and see."

I followed her into the vestry, where she and several other members of the Women's Federation were getting food ready.

"Mum, Mum," I said, following her to where the profoundly deaf Mrs. Higgins was laying doilies on plates, "I must talk to you."

"I'm busy, sweetness."

"It's *very* important."

She stopped doing what she was doing, put everything

down and steered me to the corner of the vestry, just next to a worn stone effigy, reputedly a follower of St. Zvlkx.

"What's the problem that's more important than canapés, oh daughter-my-daughter?"

"Well," I began, unsure of how to put it, "remember you said how you wanted to be a grandmother?"

"Oh *that*," she said, laughing and moving to get up. "I've known you had a bun in there for a while—I was just wondering when you were going to tell me."

"Wait a minute!" I said, feeling suddenly cheated. "You're meant to be all surprised and tearful."

"Done that, darling. Can I be so indelicate as to ask who the father is?"

"My husband's, I hope—and before you ask, the Chrono-Guard eradicated him."

She pulled me into her arms and gave me a long hug.

"Now *that* I can understand. Do you ever see him in the sort of way I see your father?"

"No," I replied a bit miserably. "He's only in my memories."

"Poor little duck!" exclaimed my mother, giving me another hug. "But thank the Lord for small mercies—at least you got to remember him. Many of us never do—just vague feelings of something that might have been. You must come along to Eradications Anonymous with me one evening. Believe me, there are more Lost Ones than you might imagine."

I'd never really talked about Dad's eradication with my mother. All her friends had assumed my brothers and I had been fathered by youthful indiscretions. To my highly principled mother this had been almost as painful as Dad's eradication. I'm not really one for any organization with "anonymous" in the title, so I decided to backtrack slightly.

"How did you know I was pregnant?" I asked as she rested her hand on mine and smiled kindly.

"Spot it a mile off. You've been eating like a horse and staring at babies a lot. When Mrs. Pilchard's little cousin Henry came round last week you could hardly keep your hands off him."

"Aren't I like that usually?"

"Not even remotely. You're filling out along the bustline too—that dress has never looked so good on you. When's sprogging time? July?"

I paused as a wave of despondency washed over me, brought about by the sheer inevitability of motherhood. When I first knew about it Landen had been with me and everything seemed that much easier.

"Mum, what if I'm no good at it? I don't know the first thing about babies. I've spent my working life chasing after bad guys. I can field-strip an M-16 blindfold, replace an engine in an APC and hit a twopence piece from thirty yards eight times out of ten. I'm not sure a cot by the fireside is really my sort of thing."

"It wasn't mine either," confided my mother, smiling kindly. "It's no accident that I'm a dreadful cook. Before I met your father and had you and your brothers I worked at SO-3. Still do, on occasions."

"You didn't meet him on a day trip to Portsmouth then?" I asked slowly, wondering whether I really wanted to hear what I was hearing.

"Not at all. It was in another place *entirely.*"

"SO-3?"

"You'd never believe me if I told you, so I'm not going to. But the point is, I was very happy to have children when the time came. Despite all your ceaseless bickering when you were kids and teenage grumpiness, it's been a wonderful adventure. Losing Anton was a storm cloud for a bit, but on balance it's been good—better than SpecOps any day." She paused for a moment. "But I was the same as you, worrying about not being ready, about being a bad mother. How did I do?"

She stared at me and smiled kindly.

"You did good, Mum."

I hugged her tightly.

"I'll do what I can to help, sweetness, but strictly no nappies or potty training, and Tuesday and Thursday evenings are *right out.*"

"SO-3?"

"No," she replied, "bridge and skittles."

She handed me a handkerchief and I dabbed at my eyes.

"You'll be fine, sweetness."

"Thanks, Mum."

She bustled off, muttering something about having a million mouths to feed. I watched her leave, smiling to myself. I thought I knew my mother but I didn't. Children rarely know their parents at all.


"Thursday!" said Joffy as I reappeared from the vestry. "What use are you if you don't mingle? Will you take that wealthy Flex fellow to meet Zorf, the neanderthal artist? I'd be ever so grateful. Oh my goodness!" he muttered, staring at the church door. "It's Aubrey Jambe!"

And so it was. Mr. Jambe, Swindon's croquet captain, *despite* his recent indiscretion with the chimp, was still attending functions as though nothing had happened.

"I wonder if he's brought the chimp?" I said, but Joffy flashed me an angry look and rushed off to press flesh. I found Cordelia and Mr. Flex discussing the merits of a minimalist painting by Welsh artist Tegwyn Wedimedr that was *so* minimalist it wasn't there at all. They were staring at a blank wall with a picture hook on it.

"What does it say to you, Harry?"

"It says . . . *nothing,* Cords—but in a very different way. How much is it?"

Cordelia bent forward to look at the price tag.

"It's called *Beyond Satire* and it's twelve hundred pounds; quite a snip. Hello, Thursday! Changed your mind about the book-flick?"

"Nope. Have you met Zorf, the neanderthal artist?"

I guided them over to where Zorf was exhibiting. Some of his friends were with him, one of whom I recognized—it was Stiggins of SpecOps-13.

"Good evening, Stig."

He nodded his head politely and introduced me to a younger neanderthal who was dressed in a boiler suit that was almost completely covered in different-colored blobs of paint.

"Good evening, Thursday," returned Stig. "This is our friend Zorf." The younger neanderthal shook my hand as I explained who Harry and Cordelia were.

"Well, this is a *very* interesting painting, Mr. Zorf," said Harry, staring at a mass of green, yellow and orange paint on a six-foot-square canvas. "What does it represent?"

"Is not obvious?" replied the neanderthal.

"Of course!" said Harry, turning his head this way and that. "It's daffodils, isn't it?"

"No."

"A sunset?"

"No."

"Field of barley?"

"No."

"I give up."

"Closest yet, Mr. Flex. If you have to ask, then you *never* understand. To neanderthal, sunset is only finish-day. Van Gogh's *Green Rye* is merely poor depiction of a field. The only sapien painters we truly understand are Pollock and Kandinsky; they speak our language. Our paintings are not for you."

I looked at the small gathering of neanderthals who were

staring at Zorf's abstract paintings with wonderment. But Harry, a bullshitter to the end, had not yet given up hope.

"Can I have another guess?" he asked Zorf, who nodded.

He stared at the canvas and screwed up his eyes.

"It's a—"

"Hope," said a voice close by. "It's hope. Hope for the future of neanderthal. It is the fervent wish—for *children*."

Zorf and all the other neanderthals turned to stare at the speaker. It was Granny Next.

"*Exactly* what I was about to say," said Flex, fooling no one but himself.

"The esteemed lady shows understanding beyond her species," said Zorf, making a small grunting noise that I took to be laughter. "Would lady sapien like to add to our painting?"

This was indeed an honor. Granny Next stepped forward, took the proffered brush from Zorf, mixed a subtle shade of turquoise and made a few fine brushstrokes to the left of center. There was a gasp from the neanderthals, and the women in the group hastily placed veils over their faces while the men—including Zorf—raised their heads and stared at the ceiling, humming quietly. Gran did likewise. Flex, Cordelia and I looked at one another, confused and ignorant of neanderthal customs. After a while the staring and humming stopped, the women raised their veils and they all ambled slowly over to Gran and smelled her clothes and touched her face gently with their large hands. Within a few minutes it was all over; the neanderthals returned to their seats and were staring at Zorf's paintings again.

"Hello, young Thursday!" said Gran, turning to me. "Let's find somewhere quiet to have a chat!"

We walked off towards the church organ and sat on a pair of hard plastic chairs.

"What did you paint on his picture?" I asked her, and Gran smiled her sweetest smile.

"Something a bit controversial," she confided, "yet *supportive*. I have worked with neanderthals in the past and know many of their ways and customs. How's hubby?"

"Still eradicated," I said glumly.

"Never mind," said Gran seriously, touching my chin so I would look into her eyes. "*Always* there is hope. You'll find, as I did, that it's really *very* funny the way things turn out."

"I know. Thanks, Gran."

"Your mother will be a tower of strength—never be in any doubt of that."

"She's here if you want to see her."

"No, no," said Gran hurriedly, "I expect she's a little busy. While we're here," she went on, changing the subject without drawing breath, "can you think of any books that might be included in the 'ten most boring classics'? I'm about ready to go."

"Gran!"

"Indulge me, young Thursday!"

I sighed.

"How about *Paradise Lost*?"

Gran let out a loud groan.

"Awful! I could hardly walk for a week afterwards—it's enough to put anyone off religion for good!"

"*Ivanhoe*?"

"Pretty dull but redeemable in places. It isn't in the top ten, I think."

"*Moby-Dick*?"

"Excitement and action interspersed with mind-numbing dullness. Read it twice."

"*A la recherche du temps perdu*?"

"English or French, its sheer tediousness is undiminished."

"*Pamela*?"

"Ah! Now you're talking. Struggled through *that* when a teenager. It might have had resonance in 1741, but today the only resonance it possesses is the snores that emanate from those deluded enough to attempt it."

"How about *A Pilgrim's Progress?*"

But Gran's attention had wandered.

"You have visitors, my dear. Look over there past the stuffed squid inside the piano and just next to the Fiat 500 carved from frozen toothpaste."

There were two people in ill-fitting dark suits who looked very out of place. They were clearly SpecOps but *not* Dedmen and Walken. It looked as though SO-5 had suffered another mishap. I asked Gran if she would be all right on her own and walked across to meet them. I found them looking dubiously at a flattened tuba on the ground entitled *The Indivisible Thriceness of Death.*

"What do you think?" I asked them.

"I don't know," began the first agent nervously. "I'm . . . I'm . . . not really up on art."

"Even if you were, it wouldn't help here," I replied dryly. "SpecOps-5?"

"Yes, how did—"

He checked himself quickly and rummaged for a pair of dark glasses.

"I mean, *no.* Never heard of SpecOps, much less SpecOps-5. Don't exist. Oh *blast.* I'm not very good at this, I'm afraid."

"We're looking for someone named Thursday Next," said his partner in a very obvious whisper from the side of her mouth, adding, in case I didn't get the message, "*Official* business."

I sighed. Obviously, SO-5 were beginning to run out of volunteers. I wasn't surprised.

"What happened to Dedmen and Walken?" I asked them.

"They were—" began the first agent but the second nudged him in the ribs and announced instead:

"Never heard of them."

"*I'm* Thursday Next," I told them, "and I think you're in more danger than you realize. Where did they get you from? SO-14?"

They took their sunglasses off and looked at me nervously.

"I'm from SO-22," said the first. "The name's Lamme. This is Slorter; she's from—"

"—SO-28," said the woman. "Thank you, Blake, I can talk, you know—and let me handle this. You can't open your mouth without putting your foot in it."

Lamme sank into a sulky silence.

"SO-28? You're an income tax assessor?"

"So what if I am?" retorted Slorter defiantly. "We all have to risk things for advancement."

"I know that only too well," I replied, steering them towards a quiet spot next to a model of a matchstick made entirely out of bits of the houses of Parliament. "Just so long as you know what you're getting into. What happened to Walken and Dedmen?"

"They were reassigned," explained Lamme.

"You mean dead?"

"No," exclaimed Lamme with some surprise. "I mean reas— Oh my goodness! Is *that* what it means?"

I sighed. These two weren't going to last the day.

"Your predecessors are both dead, guys—and the ones before that. Four agents gone in less than a week. What happened to Walken's case notes? Accidentally destroyed?"

"Don't be ridiculous!" laughed Lamme. "When recovered they were *totally* intact—they were then put through the shedder by a new member of staff who mistook it for a photocopier."

"Do you have *anything at all* to go on?"

"As soon as they realized it was a shredder, I—sorry, *they* stopped and we were left with these."

He handed two half documents over. One was a picture of a young woman striding out of a shop laden down with carrier bags and parcels. Her face, tantalizingly enough, was the part that had been destroyed by the shredder. I turned the picture over. On the back was a penciled note: "A.H. leaves Dorothy Perkins having shopped with a stolen credit card."

"The 'A.H.' means Acheron Hades," explained Lamme in a confident tone. "We were allowed to read part of his file. He can lie in thought, deed and action."

"I know. I wrote it. But this *isn't* Hades. Acheron doesn't resolve on film."

"Then who is it that we're after?" asked Slorter.

"I have no idea. What was on the other document?"

This was simply a handwritten page of notes, compiled by Walken about whoever it was they were watching. I read:

". . . 9:34: Contact with suspect at Camp Hopson sales. 11:03: Elevenses of carrot juice and flapjack—leaves without paying. 11:48: Dorothy Perkins. 12:57: Lunch. 14:45: Continues shopping. 17:20: Argues with manager of Tammy Girl about returned leg warmers. 17:45: Lost contact. 21:03: Reestablished contact at the HotBox nightclub. 23:02: A.H. leaves the HotBox with male companion. 23:16: Contact lost. . . ."

I put down the sheet.

"It's not exactly how I'd describe the work of a master criminal, now is it?"

"No," replied Slorter glumly.

"What were your orders?"

"Classified," announced Lamme, who was getting the hang of SpecOps-5 work, right at the point I didn't want him to.

"Stick to you like glue," said Slorter, who understood the situation a lot better, "and reports every half hour sent to SO-5 HQ in three separate ways."

"You're being used as live bait," I told them. "If I were you I'd go back to SO-23 and -28 just as quick as your legs can carry you."

"And miss all this?" asked Slorter, replacing her dark glasses and looking every bit the part. SO-5 would be the highest office for either of them. I hoped they lived long enough to enjoy it.

By ten-thirty the exhibition was pretty much over. I sent Gran home in a cab fast asleep and a bit tipsy. Saveloy tried to kiss me goodnight but I was too quick for him, and Duchamp$_{2924}$ had managed to sell an installation of his called *The Id Within VII— in a Jar, Pickled.* Zorf refused to sell any paintings to anyone who couldn't see what they were, but to neanderthals who *could* see what they were he gave them away, arguing that the bond between a painting and an owner should not be sullied by anything as obscenely sapien as cash. The flattened tuba was sold too, the new owner asking Joffy to drop it round to him, and if he wasn't at home to just slip it under the door. I went home via Mum's place to collect Pickwick, who hadn't come out of the airing cupboard the entire time I was in Osaka.

"She insisted on being fed in there," explained my mother, "and the trouble with the other dodos! Let one in and they *all* want to follow!"

She handed me Pickwick's egg wrapped in a towel. Pickwick hopped up and down in a very aggravated manner and I had to show her the egg to keep her happy, then we both drove home to my apartment at the same sedate twenty miles per hour and the egg was safely placed in the linen cupboard with Pickwick sitting on it in a cross mood, very fed up with being moved about.

# 22.

## Travels with My Father

The first time I went traveling with my father was when I was much younger. We attended the opening night of *King Lear* at the Globe in 1602. The place was dirty and smelly and slightly rowdy, but for all that, not unlike a lot of other opening nights I had attended. We bumped into someone named Bendix Scintilla, who was, like my father, a lonely traveler in time. He said he hung around in Elizabethan England to avoid ChronoGuard patrols. Dad said later that Scintilla had been a truly great fighter for the cause but his drive had left him when they eradicated his best friend and partner. I knew how he felt but did not do as he did.

THURSDAY NEXT,
*Private Diaries*

**D**AD TURNED UP for breakfast. I was just flicking through that morning's copy of *The Toad* at the kitchen table when he arrived. The big news story was the volte-face in Yorrick Kaine's fortunes. From being a sad politically dead no-hoper he was polling ahead of the ruling Teafurst party. The power of Shakespeare. The world suddenly stopped, the picture on the TV froze up and the sound became a dull hum, the same tone and pitch as it was the moment Dad arrived. He had the power to stop the clock like this; time ground to a halt when he visited me. It was a hard-won skill—for him there was no return to normality.

"Hello, Dad," I said brightly. "How are things?"

"Well, it depends," he replied. "Have you heard of Winston Churchill yet?"

"Not yet."

"Blast!" he muttered, sitting down and raising his eyebrows at the newspaper headline: *Chimp Merely Pet, Claims Croquet Supremo.* "How's your mother?"

"She's well. Is the world still going to end next week?"

"Looks like it. Does she ever talk about me?"

"All the time. I got this report from SpecOps forensics."

"Hmm," said my father, donning his glasses and reading the report carefully. "Carboxy-methyl-cellulose, phenylalanine and hydrocarbons. Animal fat? Doesn't make any sense at all!"

He handed back the report.

"I don't get it," he said quietly, sucking the end of his spectacles. "That cyclist lived and the world *still* ended. Maybe it's not him. Trouble is, nothing else happened at that particular time and place."

"Yes it did," I said in a sober voice.

"What?"

I picked up the evidence bag with the pink goo inside.

"You gave me this."

Dad snapped his fingers.

"That must be it. My handing you the bag of slime was the key event and *not* the death of the cyclist. Did you tell anyone where that pink goo came from?"

"No one."

He thought for a bit.

"Well," he said at last, "unlike hindsight, avoiding Armageddons is not an exact science. We may have to let events lead us for a while until we can figure it out. How is everything else going?"

"Goliath eradicated Landen," I replied glumly.

"Who?"

"My husband."

"Oh!" he said, suddenly thoughtful. "Any particular reason?"

"Goliath want Jack Schitt out of 'The Raven.' "

"Ah!" he exclaimed. "The old blackmail routine. I'm sorry to hear that, sweetpea. But listen, don't be downhearted. We have a saying about reactualizing eradicatees that goes like this: 'No one is truly dead until they are forgotten.' "

"So," I answered slowly, "if I forgot about him, then he *would* be gone?"

"Precisely," remarked my father, helping himself to some coffee. "That's why I'm having so much trouble reactualizing Churchill and Nelson—I have to find someone who remembers them as they were so I can figure out where things might have gone awry." He laughed for a moment and then got up.

"Well, get dressed, we're leaving!"

"Where to?"

"Where?" he exclaimed. "Why, to get your husband back, of course!"

This *was* good news. I quickly dashed into the bedroom to pull some clothes on while Dad read the paper and had a bowl of cereal.

"Schitt-Hawse told me they had the summer of 1947 sewn up so tight not even a transtemporal gnat could get in there," I told him, breathless from preparation.

"Then," replied my father thoughtfully, "we will have to out-smart them! They will expect us to arrive at the right time and the right place—but we won't. We'll arrive at the right place but at the *wrong* time, then simply wait. Worth a try, wouldn't you say?"

I smiled.

"Definitely!"

I was conscious of a series of rapid flashes and there we

were in a blacked-out Humber Snipe, driving alongside a dark strip of water on a moonlit night. In the distance I could see searchlights crisscross the sky and the distant thump-thump-thump of a bombing raid.

"Where are we?" I asked.

Dad changed down a gear.

"Approaching Henley-on-Thames in occupied England, November 1946."

I looked out at the river again, an uncomfortable feeling starting to develop in the pit of my stomach.

"Is this . . . is this where Landen—you know—in the car accident?"

"This is *where* it happens, but not *when.* If I were to jump straight there, Lavoisier would be on to us like a shot. Ever played Kick the Can?"

"Sure."

"It's a bit like that. Guile, stealth, patience—and a small amount of cheating. Okay, we're here."

We had reached an area of the road where there was a sharp bend. I could see how an inattentive motorist might easily misjudge the road and end up in the river. I shivered.

We got out and Dad walked across the road to where a small group of silver birches stood amidst a tangle of dead bracken and brambles. It was a good place to observe the bend in the road; we were barely ten yards away. Dad laid down a plastic carrier bag he had brought and we sat on the grass, leaning up against the smooth bark of a large birch.

"Now what?"

"We wait for six months."

"*Six months?* Dad, are you crazy? We can't sit here for six months!"

"So little time, so much to learn," mused my father. "Do you want a sandwich? Your mother leaves them out for me every morning. I'm not mad keen on corned beef and custard, but it has a sort of eccentric charm—and it does fill a hole."

"Six months?" I repeated.

He took a bite from his sandwich.

"Lesson one in time travel, Thursday. First of all, we are *all* time travelers. The vast majority of us manage only one day per day. Now if we accelerate ourselves like *so*—"

The clouds gathered speed above our heads and the trees shook faster in the light breeze; by the light of the moon I could see that the pace of the river had increased dramatically; a convoy of lorries sped past us in sudden accelerated movement.

"This is about twenty days per day—every minute compressed into about three seconds. Any slower and we would be visible. As it is, an outside observer might *think* he saw a man and woman sitting at the bottom of these trees, but if he looked again we would be gone. Ever thought you saw someone, then looked again only to find them gone?"

"Sure."

"ChronoGuard traffic moving through, most likely."

The dawn was breaking and presently a German Wehrmacht patrol found our abandoned car and dashed around looking for us before a breakdown truck appeared and took the car away. More cars rushed along the road and the clouds sped rapidly across the sky.

"Pretty, isn't it?" said my father. "I miss all this, but I have so little time these days. At fifty daypers we would still have to wait a good three or four days for Landen's accident; I've a dental appointment, so we're going to have to pick it up a bit."

The clouds sped faster; cars and pedestrians were nothing more than blurs. The shadow of the trees cast by the sun traversed rapidly and lengthened in the afternoon sun; pretty soon it was evening and the clouds were tinged with pink before the rapidly gathering gloom overtook the day and the stars appeared, followed by the moon, which arced rapidly across the sky. The stars spun around the pole star as the sky grew bluer with the early dawn and the sun began its rapid climb in the east.

"Eight and one-half thousand daypers," explained my father. "This is my favorite bit. Watch the leaves!"

The sun now rose and set in under ten seconds. Pedestrians were invisible to us as we were to them, and a car had to be parked for at least two hours for us to see it at all. But the leaves! They turned from green to brown as we watched, the outer branches a blur of movement, the river a soft undulating mirror without so much as a ripple. The plants died off as we watched, the sky grew more overcast and the spells of dark were now much longer than the light. Flecks of light showed along the road where traffic moved, and opposite us an abandoned Kübelwagen was rapidly stripped of spares and then dumped upside down in the river.

"I'd never get bored of this, Dad. Do you travel like this all the time?"

"Never this slow. This is just for tourists. We usually approach speeds of ten billion or more daypers; if you want to go backwards you have to go faster still!"

"Go backwards by going forwards faster?" I queried, confounded by the illogicality of it.

"That's enough for now, sweetpea. Just enjoy yourself and watch."

I pulled myself closer to him as the air grew chilly and a heavy blanket of snow covered the road and forest around us.

"Happy New Year," said my father.

"Snowdrops!" I cried in delight as green shoots nuzzled through the snow and flowered, their heads angling towards the low sun. Then the snow was gone and the river rose again and small amounts of detritus gathered around the upturned Kübelwagen, which rusted as we watched. The sun flashed past us higher and higher in the sky and soon there were daffodils and crocuses.

"Ah!" I said in surprise as a shoot from a small shrub started to grow up my trouser leg.

"Train them *away* from your body," explained my father, diverting the course of a bramble trying to ensnare him with the palm of his hand. My own shoot pushed against my hand like a small green worm and moved off in another direction. I did the same with the others that threatened me, but Dad went one further and with a practiced hand trained his bramble into a pretty bow.

"I've known students literally rooted to the spot," explained my father. "It's where the phrase comes from. But it can be fun, too. We had an operative named Jekyll who once trained a four-hundred-year-old oak into a heart as a present for her boyfriend."

The air was warmer now, and as my father checked his chronograph again we started to decelerate. The six months we had spent there had passed in barely thirty minutes. By the time we had returned to one day per day, it was night again.

"I don't see anyone, do you?" he hissed.

I looked around; the road was deserted. I opened my mouth to speak but he put a finger to his lips. At that moment a Morris 8 saloon appeared around the corner and drove rapidly down the road. It swerved to avoid a fox, skidded sideways off the road and landed upside down in the river. I wanted to get up, but my father held me with a pinched grip. The driver of the car—who I assumed was Billden—broke the surface of the river, then quickly dived back to the car and resurfaced a few moments later with a woman. He dragged her to the bank and was just about to return to the submerged vehicle when a tall man in a greatcoat appeared from nowhere and placed his hand on Billden's arm.

"Now!" said my father and we dashed from the safety of the copse.

"Leave him!" yelled my father. "Leave him to do what he has to do!"

My father grabbed the interloper, and with a sharp cry the man vanished. Billden looked confused and made a run for the river, but in a few short moments a half-dozen ChronoGuard had dropped in, Lavoisier amongst them. One of the agents rugby-tackled Landen's father before he could return to rescue Landen. I yelled, *"NO!"* and pulled out my gun and aimed it at the man who held Billden.

I yelled, *"NO!"* and pulled out my gun and aimed it at the man who held Billden.

I yelled, *"NO!"* and pulled out my gun and aimed it at the man who held Billden.

I yelled, *"NO!"* and pulled out my gun and aimed it at the man who held Billden.

I yelled, *"NO!"* and pulled out my gun and aimed it at the man who held Billden.

I yelled, *"NO!"* and pulled out my gun and aimed it at the man who held Billden.

I yelled, *"NO!"* and pulled out my gun and aimed it at the man who held Billden.

I yelled, *"NO!"* and pulled out my gun and aimed it at the man who held Billden.

I yelled, *"NO!"* and pulled out my gun and aimed it at the man who held Billden.

I yelled, *"NO!"* and pulled out my gun and aimed it at the man who held Billden.

I yelled, *"NO!"* and pulled out my gun and aimed it at the man who held Billden.

I yelled, *"NO!"* and pulled out my gun and aimed it at the man who held Billden.

I yelled, *"NO!"* and pulled out my gun and aimed it at the man who held Billden.

I yelled, *"NO!"* and pulled out my gun and aimed it at the man who held Billden.

The next thing I knew I was disarmed, sitting on the ground and feeling shocked and disoriented after my brief enloopment. It was how I imagine a stuck record might feel. Two SO-12 operatives stared at me while my father and Lavoisier talked in angry voices close by. Billden was breathing heavily and sobbing into the damp earth, holding his still-unconscious wife.

"Bastards!" I spat. "My husband's in there!"

"*So* much to learn," muttered Lavoisier as I got to my feet and stood by my father's side. "The infant Parke-Laine is *not* your husband, he is an accident statistic—or not. It rather depends on your father."

"A lackey for the Goliath Corporation, Lavoisier?" said Dad quietly. "You disappoint me."

"Greater need prevails, Colonel. If you'd handed yourself in I wouldn't have had to take these extreme measures. Besides, the ChronoGuard can't function without corporate sponsorship."

"And in return you do a few favors?"

"As I said, greater needs prevail. And before you start waving charges of corruption at me, this combined Goliath/Chrono-Guard operation has been fully sanctioned by the Chamber. Now, it's so simple even you can understand it. Give yourself up and your daughter can have her husband back—whether or not she decides to help Goliath. As you can see, I am in a *very* generous mood."

I looked at Dad and saw him bite his lip. He rubbed his temples and sighed. He had spent years fighting corruption in the ChronoGuard, and despite Landen's being so close to reactualization, I wasn't going to see Dad lose his liberty over either of us. What had he said?—"No one is truly dead until they are forgotten." Landen was still strong in my memory—we *would* have another chance.

As Dad opened his mouth to reluctantly agree, I said: "No."

"What?" exclaimed Lavoisier.

"No," I repeated. "Dad, don't do it—I'll get Jack Schitt out—or *something!*"

Dad smiled and rested his hand on my shoulder.

"Bah!" went Lavoisier. "Each as hideously self-righteous as the other!"

He nodded to his men, who raised their weapons. But Dad was quick. I felt him grasp my shoulder tightly and we were off. The sun rose quickly as we leapt forward in time, leaving Lavoisier and the others several hours away before they realized what had happened.

"Let's see if we can lose him!" muttered my father. "As for that Chamber stuff—bullshit. Landen's eradication was murder, pure and simple. In fact, it's just the sort of information I need to bring Lavoisier down!"

Days amounted to no more than brief flashes of alternate dark and light as we hurtled into the future. But the odd thing was, we didn't actually move physically from the place we were standing. The world just aged about us.

"We're not at full speed," Dad explained. "He might over-take me without thinking. Keep an eye out for—"

Lavoisier and his cronies appeared for no more than the briefest glimpse as they moved past us into the future. Dad stopped abruptly and I staggered slightly as we returned to real time. We moved off the road as a fifties-style truck drove past, horn blaring.

"What now?"

"I think we shook him off. Blast—!"

We were off again—Lavoisier had reappeared. We lost him for a moment but pretty soon he was back again, keeping pace with us, matching our speed as we moved through history. As Dad slowed down slightly, so did Lavoisier. As he accelerated, Lavoisier did the same. It was like a transtemporal game of follow the leader.

"I'm too old to fall for that one!" smiled Lavoisier.

Soon after, two of his cronies reappeared as each one found us and matched the speed we were moving through time.

"I knew you'd come," said Lavoisier triumphantly, walking towards us slowly as the time flashed past, faster and faster. A new road was built where we were standing, then a bridge, houses, shops. "Give yourself up. You'll have a fair trial, believe me."

The two other ChronoGuard operatives grabbed my father and held him tightly.

"I'll see you hang for this, Lavoisier! The Chamber would *never* sanction such an action. Give Landen back his life and I promise you I will say nothing."

"Well, that's just it, isn't it?" replied Lavoisier scornfully. "Who do you think they're going to believe? You, with your record, or me, third in command at the ChronoGuard? Besides, your clumsy attempt to get Landen back has covered any tracks I might have made getting rid of him!"

Lavoisier aimed his gun at my father. The two Chrono-Guards held on to Dad tightly to stop him accelerating away, and we buffeted slightly as he tried. Things, to say the least, looked bad. From the makes of the cars on the road I could see we were approaching the early eighties. It wouldn't be long before we arrived at 1985. I had a sudden thought. Wasn't there ChronoGuard industrial action happening sometime soon?

"Say," I said, "do you guys cross picket lines?"

The ChronoGuard agents looked at each other, then at the chronographs on their wrists, then at Lavoisier. The taller of the two was the first to speak.

"She's right, Mr. Lavoisier, sir. I don't mind bullying and

killing innocents, and I'll follow you beyond the crunch *normally*, but—"

"But what?" asked Lavoisier angrily.

"—but I *am* a loyal TimeGuild member. I don't cross picket lines."

"Neither do I," replied the other agent, nodding to his friend. "Likewise and truly."

Lavoisier smiled engagingly.

"Listen here, guys, I'll *personally* pay—"

"I'm sorry, Mr. Lavoisier," replied the operative with a hint of indignation, "but we've been instructed not to enter into any individual contracts."

And in an instant they were gone as December arrived and the world turned pink. What had once been the road was now a few inches of the same pink slime that Dad had shown me. We were beyond the 12th December 1985, and where before there had been growth, change, seasons, clouds, now there was nothing but a never-ending landscape of shiny opaque curd.

"Saved by industrial action!" said Dad, laughing. "Tell *that* to your friends at the Chamber!"

"Bravo," replied Lavoisier wryly. He lowered his pistol. Without his cronies to hold on to Dad and stop him escaping, there was little he could do. "Bravo. I think we should just say *au revoir*, my friends—until we meet again."

"Do we have to make it *au revoir*?" I asked. "What's wrong with *goodbye*?"

He didn't have time to answer as I felt Dad tense and we accelerated faster through the timestream. The pink slime was washed away, leaving only earth and rocks, and as I watched, the river moved away from us, meandered off into the flood plain and then swept under our feet and undulated back and forth like a snake before finally being replaced by a lake. We moved faster, and soon I could see the earth start to buckle as the crust bent and twisted under the force of plate tectonics. Plains dropped to make seas and mountains rose in their place. New vegetation reestablished itself as millions of years swept past in a matter of seconds. Vast forests grew and fell. We were covered, then uncovered, then covered again, now in a sea, now inside rock, now surrounded by an ice sheet, now a hundred feet in the air. More forests, then a desert, then mountains rose rapidly in the east, only to be scoured flat a few moments later.

"Well," said my father as we traveled through time, "Lavoisier in the pocket of Goliath. Who'd have thought it?"

"Dad?" I asked as the sun grew visibly bigger and redder. "How do we get back?"

"We don't go back," he replied. "We *can't* go back. Once the present has happened, that's it. We just carry on going until we return to where we started. Sort of like a roundabout. Miss an exit and you have to drive around again. There are just a few more exits and the roundabout is much, much, bigger."

"How much bigger?"

"A lot."

"How *much* of a lot?" I persisted.

"A lot of a lot. Quiet now—we're nearly there!"

And all of a sudden we weren't *nearly* there, we *were* there, back at breakfast in my apartment, Dad turning the pages of the newspaper and me running out from my bedroom having just got dressed. I stopped in mid-stride and sat down at the table, feeling deflated.

"Well, we tried, didn't we?" said my father.

"Yes Dad," I replied, staring at the floor, "we did. Thanks."

"Don't worry," he said kindly. "Even the finest eradications leave *something* behind for us to reactualize from. There is always a way—we just have to find it. Sweetpea, we *will* get him back—I'm not having my grandchild without a father."

His determination did reassure me, and I thanked him.

"Good!" he said, closing his newspaper. "By the way, did you manage to get any tickets for the Nolan Sisters concert?"

"I'm working on it."

"Good show. Well, time waits for no man, as we say—"

He squeezed my hand and was gone. The world started up again, the TV came back on, and there was a muffled plocking from Pickwick, who had managed to lock herself in the airing cupboard again. I let her out and she ruffled her feathers in an embarrassed fashion before going off in search of her water dish.

I went in to work, but there was precious little to do. We had a call from an enraged Mrs. Hathaway34, demanding to know when we were going to arrest the *unlick'd bear-whelp* who had cheated her, and another from a student who wanted to know whether we thought Hamlet's line was *this too too solid flesh* or *this too too sullied flesh,* or even perhaps *this two-toed swordfish.* Bowden spent the morning mouthing the lines for his routine, and by noon there had been two attempts to steal *Cardenio* from Vole Towers. Nothing serious; SO-14 had doubled the guard. This didn't concern SpecOps-27 in any way, so I spent the afternoon surreptitiously reading the Jurisfiction instruction manual, which felt a little like flicking through a girls' magazine during school. I was tempted to have a go at entering a work of fiction to try out a few of their "handy bookjumping tips" (page 28), but Havisham had roundly forbidden me from doing anything of the sort until I was more experienced. By the time I was ready to go home I had learned a few tricks about emergency book evacuation procedures (page 34) and read about the aims of the Bowdlerizers (page 62), who were a group of well-meaning yet censorious individuals hell bent on removing obscenities from fiction. I also read about Heathcliff's unexpected three-year career in Hollywood under the name of

Buck Stallion and his eventual return to the pages of *Wuthering Heights* (page 71), the forty-six abortive attempts to illegally save Beth from dying in *Little Women* (page 74), details of the Character Exchange Program (page 81), using holorimic verse to flush out renegade book people, or PageRunners as they were known (page 96), and how to use spelling mistakes, misprints and double negatives to signal to other PROs in case emergency book evacuation procedures (page 34) failed (page 105). But there weren't only pages of instructions. The last ten or so pages featured hollowed-out recesses which contained devices that were far too deep to have fitted in the book. One of the pages contained a device similar to a flare gun which had "Mk IV TextMarker" written on its side. Another page had a glass panel covering a handle like a fire alarm. A note painted on the glass read: *IN UNPRECEDENTED EMERGENCY\* BREAK GLASS*. The asterisk, I noted somewhat chillingly, related to the footnote: *\*Please note: personal destruction does NOT count as an unprecedented emergency*. I was just learning about writing brief descriptions of where you are by hand to enable you to get back (page 136) when it was time to clock off. I joined the general exodus and wished Bowden good luck with his routine. He didn't seem in the least nervous, but then he rarely did.

I got home to find my landlord on my doorstep. He looked around to make sure Miss Havisham was nowhere in sight, then said: "Time's up, Next."

"You said Saturday," I replied, unlocking the door.

"I said Friday," countered the man.

"How about I give you the money on Monday when the banks open?"

"How about if I take that dodo of yours and you live rent-free for three months?"

"How about you stick it in your ear?"

"It doesn't pay to be impertinent to your landlord, Next. Do you have the money or not?"

I thought quickly.

"No—but you said Friday, and it's not the end of Friday yet. In fact, I've got over six hours to find the cash."

He looked at me, looked at Pickwick, who had popped her head round the door to see who it was, then at his watch.

"Very well," he said. "But you'd better have the cash to me by midnight sharp or there'll be *serious* trouble."

And with a last withering look, he left me alone on the landing.

I offered Pickwick a marshmallow in a vain attempt to get her to stand on one leg. She stared vacantly at me, so after several more attempts I gave up, fed her and changed the paper in her basket before calling Spike at SO-27. It wasn't the perfect plan, but it did have the benefit of being the *only* plan, so on that basis alone I reckoned it was worth a try. I was eventually patched through to him in his squad car. I related my problem, and he told me his freelance budget was overstuffed at present as no one ever wanted to be deputized, so we arranged a ludicrously high hourly rate and a time and place to meet. As I put the phone down I realized I had forgotten to say that I preferred *not* to do any vampire work. What the hell. I needed the money.

# 23.

## Fun with Spike

VAN HELSING'S GAZETTE: "Did you do much SEB containment work?"

AGENT STOKER: "Oh yes. The capture of Supreme Evil Beings, or SEBs, as we call them, is the main bread-and-butter work for SO-17. Quite how there can be more than one Supreme Evil Being I have no idea. Every SEB I ever captured considered itself not only the worst personification of unadulterated evil that ever stalked the earth, but also the only personification of unadulterated evil that ever stalked the earth. It must have been quite a surprise—and not a little galling—to be locked away with several thousand other SEBs, all pretty much the same, in row upon row of plain glass jars at the Loathsome Id Containment Facility. I don't know where they came from. I think they leak in from elsewhere, the same way as a leaky tap drips water. [laughs] They should replace the washer."

AGENT "SPIKE" STOKER, SO-27 (ret.),
interviewed for *Van Helsing's Gazette*, 1996

THE INCIDENTS I am about to relate took place in the winter of the year 1985, at a place whose name even now, by reasons of propriety, it seems safer not to divulge. Suffice to say that the small village I visited that night was deserted, and had been for some time. The houses stood empty and vandalized, the pub, corner store, and village hall but empty shells. As I drove slowly into the dark village, rats scurried amongst the detritus and small pockets of mist appeared briefly in my headlights. I reached the old oak at the crossroads, stopped, switched off the lights and surveyed the morbid surroundings. I could hear nothing. Not a breath of wind gave life to the trees about me, no distant sound of humanity raised my spirits. It had not always been so. Once children played here, neighbors hailed neighbors with friendly greetings, lawn mowers buzzed on a Sunday afternoon, and the congenial crack of leather on willow drifted up from the village green. But no more. All lost one late winter's night not five years earlier, when the forces of evil rose and claimed the village and all that lived within. I looked about, my breath showing on the still night. By the manner in which the blackened timbers of the empty houses pierced the sky it seemed as though the memory of that night was still etched upon the fabric of the ruins. Parked close by was another car, and leaning against the door was the man who had brought me to this place. He was tall and muscular and had faced horrors that I, thankfully, would never have to face. He did this with his heart filled with courage and duty in equal measure, and, as I approached, a smile rose on his features, and he spoke.

"Quite a shithole, eh, Thurs?"

"You're not kidding," I replied, glad to be with company. "All kinds of creepy weirdness was running through my head just now."

"How have you been? Hubby still with an existence problem?"

"Still the same—but I'm working on it. What's the score here?"

Spike clapped his hands together and rubbed them.

"Ah, yes! Thanks for coming. This is one job I can't do on my own."

I followed his gaze towards the derelict church and surrounding graveyard. It was a dismal place even by SpecOps-17 standards, which tended to regard anything that is merely *dreary* as a good venue for a party. It was surrounded by two rows of high wire fences; no one had come or gone since the "troubles" ten years previously. The restless spirits of the condemned souls trapped within the churchyard had killed all plant life not only within the confines of the Dark Place but for a short distance all around it—I could see the grass wither and die not two yards from the inner fence, the trees standing lifeless in the moonlight. In truth, the wire fences were to keep the curious or just plain stupid out as much as to keep the undead in; a ring of burnt yew wood just within the outer wire was the last line of undead defense across which they could never move, but it didn't stop them trying. Occasionally a member of the Dark One's Legion of Lost Souls made it across the inner fence. Here they lumbered into the motion sensors affixed at ten-foot intervals. The undead might be quite good servants of the Dark One, but they were certainly crap when it came to electronics. They usually blundered around in the area between the fences until the early-morning sun or an SO-17 flamethrower reduced their lifeless husk to a cinder, and released the tormented soul to make its way through eternity in peace.

I looked at the derelict church and the scattered tombs of the desecrated graveyard and shivered.

"What are we doing? Torching the lifeless walking husks of the undead?"

"Well, no," replied Spike uneasily, moving to the rear of his car. "I wish it were as simple as that."

He opened the boot of his car and passed me a clip of silver bullets. I reloaded my gun and frowned at him.

"What then?"

"Dark forces are afoot, Thursday. Another Supreme Evil Being is pacing the earth."

"*Another?* What happened? Did he escape?"

Spike sighed.

"There have been a few cuts in recent years, and SEB transportation is now done by a private contractor. Three months ago they mixed up the consignment and instead of delivering him straight to the Loathsome Id Containment Facility, they left him at the St. Merryweather's Home for Retired Gentlefolk."

"TNN said it was Legionnaire's disease."

"That's the usual cover story. Anyhow, some idiot opened the jar and all hell broke loose. I managed to corner it, but getting the SEB transferred back to his jar is going to be tricky—and that's where *you* come in."

"Does this plan involve going in *there?*"

I pointed to the church. As if to make a point, two barn owls flew noiselessly from the belfry and soared close by our heads.

"I'm afraid so. We should be fine. There will be a full moon tonight, and they don't generally perambulate on the lightest of nights—it'll be easy as falling off a log."

"So what do I do?" I asked uneasily.

"I can't tell you for fear that he will hear my plan, but keep close and do precisely what I tell you. Do you understand? No matter what it is, you must do *precisely* what I tell you."

"Okay."

"Promise?"

"I promise."

"No, I mean you have to *really* promise."

"All right—I *really* promise."

"Good. I officially deputize you into SpecOps-17. Let's pray for a moment."

Spike dropped to his knees and muttered a short prayer under his breath—something about delivering us both from evil and how he hoped his mother would get to the top of the hip replacement waiting list, and that Cindy wouldn't drop him like a hot potato when she found out what he did. As for myself, I said pretty much what I usually said but added that if Landen was watching, could he please please please keep an eye out for me.

Spike got up.

"Ready?"

"Ready."

"Then let's make some light out of this darkness."

He pulled a green holdall from the back of the car and a pump-action shotgun. We walked towards the rusty gates and I felt a chill on my neck.

"Feel that?" asked Spike.

"Yes."

"He's close. We'll meet him tonight, I promise you."

Spike unlocked the gates, and they swung open with a squeak of long-unoiled hinges. Operatives generally used their flamethrowers through the wire; no one would trouble coming in here unless there was serious work to be done. He relocked the gates behind us and we walked through the undead no-go zone.

"What about the motion sensors?"

A beeper went off from his car.

"I'm pretty much the only recipient. Helsing knows what I'm doing; if we fail he'll be along tomorrow morning to clean up the mess."

"Thanks for the reassurance."

"Don't worry," replied Spike with a grin, "we won't fail!"

We arrived at the second gate. The musty smell of long-departed corpses reached my nostrils. It had been softened to the odor of rotted leaves by age, but it was still unmistakable. Once inside the inner gates we made our way swiftly to the lych-gate and walked through the crumbling structure. The churchyard was a mess. The graves had all been dug up, and the remains of those too far gone to be resurrected had been flung around the graveyard. They had been the fortunate ones. Those that were freshly dead had been press-ganged into a second career as servants of the Dark One—not something you would want to put on your CV, if you still had one.

"Untidy bunch, aren't they?" I whispered as we picked our way across the scattered human bones to the heavy oak door.

"I wrote Cindy some poetry," said Spike softly, rummaging in his pocket. "If anything happens, will you give it to her?"

"Give it to her yourself. Nothing's going to happen—you said so yourself. And don't say things like that; it gives me the wobblies."

"Right," said Spike, putting the poem back in his pocket. "Sorry."

He took a deep breath and grasped the handle, turned it and pushed open the door. The interior was not as pitch-black as I had supposed; the moonlight streamed in the remains of the large stained-glass windows and the holes in the roof. Although it was gloomy, we could still see. The church was in no better state than the graveyard. The pews had been thrown around and broken into matchwood. The lectern was lying in an untidy heap, and all sorts of vandalism of a chilling nature had taken place.

"Home away from home for His Supreme Evilness, wouldn't you say?" said Spike with a cheery laugh. He moved behind me and shut the heavy door, turning the large iron key in the lock and handing it to me for safekeeping.

I looked around but could see no one in the church. The door to the vestry was firmly locked, and I looked across at Spike.

"He doesn't appear to be here."

"Oh, he's here, all right—we just have to flush him out. Darkness can hide in all sorts of corners. We just need the right sort of fox terrier to worry it out of the rabbit hole—metaphorically speaking, of course."

"Of course. And where might this metaphorical rabbit hole be?"

Spike looked at me sternly and pointed to his temple.

"He's up here. He thought he could dominate me from within, but I've trapped him somewhere in the frontal lobes. I have some uncomfortable memories, and those help to screen him—trouble is, I can't seem to get him out again."

"I have someone like that," I replied, thinking of Hades barging into the tearoom memory with Landen.

"Oh? Well, forcing him out is going to be a bit tricky. I thought his home ground might make him emerge spontaneously, but it seems not. Hang on, let me have a go."

Spike leaned against the remains of a pew and grunted and strained for a few minutes, making some of the oddest faces as he tried to expel the spirit of the Evil One. It looked as if he were trying to force a bowling ball out of his left nostril. After a few minutes of exertions he stopped.

"Bastard. It's like trying to snatch a trout from a mountain stream with a boxing glove. Never mind. I have a plan B which shouldn't fail."

"The metaphorical fox terrier?"

"Exactly so. Thursday, draw your weapon."

"Now what?"

"Shoot me."

"Where?"

"In the chest, head, anywhere fatal—where did you think? In my foot?"

"You're joking!"

"Never been more serious."

"Then what?"

"Good point. I should have explained that first."

He opened the holdall to reveal a vacuum cleaner.

"Battery powered," explained Spike. "As soon as his spirit makes an appearance, suck him up."

"As simple as that?"

"As simple as that. SEB containment isn't rocket science, Thursday—it's just not for the squeamish. Now, kill me."

"Spike—!"

"What?"

"I can't do it!"

"But you promised—and what's more you *really* promised."

"If promising meant killing you," I replied in an exasperated tone, "I wouldn't have gone along with it!"

"SpecOps-17 work ain't no bed of roses, Thursday. I've had enough, and believe me, having this little nurk coiled up in my head is not as easy as it looks. I should have never let him in in the first place, but what's done is done. You have to kill me and kill me well."

"You're crazy!"

"Undoubtedly. But look around you. You followed me in here. Who's crazier? The crazy or the crazy who follows him?"

"Listen—" I began. "What's that?"

There was a thump on the church door.

"Blast!" replied Spike. "The undead. Not necessarily fatal, and severely handicapped by that slow swagger—but they can be troublesome if you get cornered. After you have killed me and captured Chuckles up here, you may have to shoot your way out. Take my keys; these two here are for the inner and outer gates. It's a bit stiff, and you have to turn it to the left—"

"I get the picture."

Another thump echoed the first. There was a crash from the vestry, and a shape moved past one of the lower windows.

"They are gathering!" said Spike ominously. "You'd better get a move on."

"I can't!"

"You *can,* Thursday. I forgive you. It's been a good career. Did you know that out of the three hundred and twenty-nine SpecOps-17 operatives who have ever been, only two ever made it to retirement age?"

"Did they tell you that when you joined?"

There was the sound of stone against stone as one of the graves from the floor was pushed aside. The undead who was thumping on the door was joined by another—and then another. Outside we could hear the noises of the *awakening.* Despite the moonlit night, the Evil One was calling to his servants—and they were coming running, or shambling, at the very least.

"Do it!" said Spike in a more urgent manner. "Do it *now* before it's too late!"

I raised my gun and pointed it at Spike.

*"Do it!"*

I increased the pressure on the trigger as a shaky form stood up from the open grave behind him. I pointed the gun at the figure instead—the pathetic creature was so far dried out it could barely move—but it sensed our presence and teetered in our direction anyway.

"Don't shoot it, shoot *me!*" said Spike with some alarm in his voice. "The job in hand, Thursday, *please!*"

I ignored him and pulled the trigger. The hammer fell harmlessly with a dull *thock.*

"Eh?" I said, rechambering the next round. Spike was quicker than I and loosed off a shot that disintegrated the head of the abomination, who then collapsed in a heap of dried skin and powdery bone. The sound of scrabbling increased from the door.

"God damn and blast, Next, why couldn't you do as I told you?!"

"What?"

"I put that dud on the top of your clip, idiot!"

"Why?"

He tapped his head.

"So I could trick Chuckles in here to come out—he's not going to stay in a host he thinks is about to croak! You pull the trigger, out he comes, dud bullet, Stoker lives, SEB sucked up—QED."

"Why didn't you tell me?" I asked, my temper rising.

"You had to *mean* to kill me! He might be the personification of all that is evil within the heart of man, but he's no fool."

"Oops."

"Oops indeed, knucklehead! Right, we'd better be out of here!"

"Isn't there a plan C?" I asked as we headed for the door.

"Shit no!" replied Spike as he fumbled with the key. "B is as high as I ever get!"

Another creature was arising from behind some upended tables that once held a harvest festival display; I caught it before it was even upright. I turned back to Spike, who had the key in the lock and was muttering something about how he wished he *was* working at SommeWorld™.

"Stay away from the door, Spike."

He recognized the serious tone in my voice. He turned to face the barrel of my automatic.

"Whoa! Careful, Thursday, that's the end that bites."

"It ends here and tonight, Spike."

"This is a joke, right?"

"No joke, Spike. You're right. I have to kill you. It's the only way."

"Er—steady on, Thursday—aren't you taking this just a *little bit* too seriously?"

"The Supreme Evil Being must be stopped, Spike—you said so yourself!"

"I know I *said* that, but we can come back tomorrow with a plan C instead!"

"There is no plan C, Spike. It ends now. Close your eyes."

"Wait!"

"Close them!"

He closed his eyes and I pulled the trigger and twitched my hand at the same time; the slug powered its way through three layers of clothing, grazed Spike's shoulder and buried itself in the wood of the old door. It did the trick; with a short and unearthly wail, a wispy entity like smoke emerged from Spike's nostrils and coalesced into the ethereal version of an old and long-unwashed dishcloth.

"Good work!" muttered Spike in a very relieved voice as he took a step sideways and started to fumble with the bag that contained the vacuum cleaner. "Don't let it get near you!"

I drew back as the wraithlike spirit moved in my direction.

"Fooled!" said a low voice. "Fooled by a mere mortal, how utterly, *utterly* depressing!"

The thumping had now increased and was also coming from the vestry door; I could see the hinge pins start to loosen in the powdery mortar.

"Keep him talking!" yelled Spike as he pulled out the vacuum cleaner.

"A *vacuum cleaner!*" sneered the low voice. "Spike, you insult me!"

Spike didn't answer but instead unwound the hose and switched the battery-powered appliance on.

"A vacuum cleaner won't hold me!" sneered the voice again.

"Do you really believe that I can be trapped in a bag like so much dust?"

Spike turned the vacuum cleaner on and sucked up the small spirit in a trice.

"He didn't seem that frightened of it," I murmured as Spike fiddled with the machine's controls.

"This isn't *any* vacuum cleaner, Thursday. James over at R&D dreamt it up for me. You see, unlike conventional vacuum cleaners, this one works on a dual cyclone principle that traps dust and evil spirits by powerful centrifugal force. Since there is no bag, there is no loss of suction—you can use a lower-wattage motor. There's a hose action—and a small brush for stair carpets."

"You find evil spirits in stair carpets?"

"No, but my stair carpets need cleaning just the same as anyone else's."

I looked at the glass container and could see a small vestige of white spinning round very rapidly. Spike deftly placed the lid on the jar and detached it from the machine. He held it up, and there inside was a very angry and now quite dizzy spirit of the Evil One—well and truly trapped.

"As I said," went on Spike, "it's not rocket science. You had me scared, though; I thought you really *were* going to kill me!"

"That," I replied, "was plan D!"

"Spike . . . you . . . you . . . you . . . *bastard!*" said the small voice from inside the jar. "You'll suffer the worst torments in hell for this!"

"Yeah, yeah," replied Spike as he placed the jar in the holdall, "you and all the rest."

He slung the bag round his body, replaced the spent cartridge in his shotgun with another from his pocket and flicked off the safety.

"Come on, those deadbeats are starting to get on my tits. Whoever nails the least is a sissypants."

We flung open the door to a bunch of very surprised dried corpses, who fell inwards in a large tangled mass of putrefied torsos and sticklike limbs. Spike opened fire first, and after we had dispatched that lot we dashed outside, dodged the slower of the undead and cut down the others as we made our way to the gates.

"The Cindy problem," I said as the head of a long-dead carcass exploded in response to Spike's shotgun. "Did you do as I suggested?"

"Sure did," replied Spike, letting fly at another walking corpse. "Stakes and crucifixes in the garage and all my back issues of *Van Helsing's Gazette* in the living room."

"Did she get the message?" I asked, surprising another walking corpse who had been trying to stay out of the action behind a tombstone.

"She didn't say anything," he replied, decapitating two dried cadavers, "but the funny thing is, I now find copies of *Sniper* magazine in the toilet—and a copy of *Great Underworld Hitmen* has appeared in the kitchen."

"Perhaps she's trying to tell *you* something?"

"Yes," agreed Spike, "but what?"

I bagged ten undead that night, but Spike only managed eight—so he was the sissypants. We partook of a haddock chowder with freshly baked bread at a roadside eatery and joked about the night's events while the SEB swore at us from his glass jar. I got my six hundred quid and my landlord didn't get Pickwick. All in all, it was a good evening well spent.

# 24.

## Performance-Related Pay,
## Miles Hawke & Norland Park

Performance-Related Pay was the bane of SpecOps as much then as it is now. How can your work be assessed when your job is so extraordinarily varied? I would love to have seen Officer Stoker's review panel listen to what he got up to. It was no surprise to anyone that they rarely lasted more than twenty seconds, and he was, as always, awarded an A++—"Exceptional service, monthly bonus recommended."

THURSDAY NEXT,
*A Life in SpecOps*

**D**OG-TIRED, I slept well that night and had expected to see Landen but dreamt of Humpty Dumpty, which was odd. I went in to work, avoided Cordelia again and then had to take my turn with the employment review board, which was all part of the SpecOps work-related pay scheme. Victor would have given us all A++, but sadly it wasn't conducted by him—it was chaired by the area commander, Braxton Hicks.

"Ah, Next!" he said jovially as I entered. "Good to see you. Have a seat, won't you?"

I thanked him and sat down. He looked at my performance file over the past few months and stroked his mustache thoughtfully.

"How's your golf?"

"I never took it up."

"Really?" he said with surprise. "You sounded most keen when we first met."

"I've been busy."

"Quite, quite. Well, you've been with us three months and on the whole your performance seems to be excellent. That *Jane Eyre* malarkey was a remarkable achievement; it did SpecOps the power of good and showed those bean counters in London that the Swindon office could hold its own."

"Thank you."

"No really, I mean it. All this PR work you've been doing. The network is very grateful to you, and more than that, *I'm* grateful to you. I could have been on the scrap heap if it wasn't for you. I'd really like to shake you by the hand and—I don't do this very often, y'know—put you up for membership of my golf club. *Full* membership, no less—the sort usually reserved for men."

"That's more than generous of you," I said, getting up to leave.

"Sit down, Next—that was just the friendly bit."

"There's more?"

"Yes," he replied, his demeanor changing abruptly. "*Despite* all of that, your conduct over the past two weeks has been less than satisfactory. I've had a complaint from Mrs. Hathaway$_{34}$ to say that you failed to spot her forged copy of *Cardenio*."

"I told her it was a forgery in no uncertain terms."

"That's *your* story, Next. I haven't located your report on the matter."

"I didn't think it was worth the trouble to write one, sir."

"We have to keep on top of paperwork, Next. If the new legislation on SpecOps accountability comes into force, we will be under severe scrutiny every time we so much as sneeze, so get used to it. And what's this about you hitting a neanderthal?"

"A misunderstanding."

"Hm. Is this also a misunderstanding?"

He laid a police charge sheet on the desk.

"*Permissioning a* ~~horse and carte~~ <u>car</u> *to be driven by personn of low moral turpithtude.* You lent your car to a lunatic driver, then helped her to escape the law. What on earth did you think you were doing?"

"The greater good, sir."

"No such thing," he barked back, handing me a SpecOps claim docket. "Officer Tillen at stores gave me this. It's your claim for a new Browning automatic."

I stared dumbly at the docket. My original Browning, the one I had looked after from first issue, had been left in a motorway services somewhere in a patch of bad time.

"I take this very seriously, Next. It says here you 'lost' SpecOps property in *unsanctioned* SO-12 work. Flagrant disregard for network property makes me very angry, Next. There is our budget to think of, you know."

"I thought it would come down to *that*," I murmured.

"What did you say?"

"I said: 'I'll retrieve it eventually, sir.' "

"Maybe so. But lost property has to come under the *monthly* current expenditure and not the *yearly* resupply budget. We've been a little stretched recently. Your escapade with *Jane Eyre* was successful but not without cost. All things considered, I am sorry but I will have to mark your performance as 'F—definite room for improvement.' "

"An F? Sir, I must protest!"

"Talk's over, Next. I'm truly sorry. This is quite outside my hands."

"Is this an SO-1 way of punishing me?" I asked indignantly. "You know I've never had anything lower than an A in all my eight years with the service!"

"Raising your voice does you no good at all, young lady," replied Hicks in an even tone, wagging his finger as a man might do to his spaniel. "This interview is over. I am sorry, believe me."

I didn't believe he was sorry for one moment—and suspected that he had been influenced from higher up. I sighed, got up, saluted and made for the door.

"Wait!" said Braxton. "There's something else."

I returned.

"Yes?"

"Keep your temper."

"Is that all?"

"No."

He handed over a packet of clothes in a polythene bundle.

"The department is now sponsored by the Toast Marketing Board. You'll find a hat, T-shirt and jacket in this package. Wear them when you can and be prepared for some corporate entertainment."

"Sir—!"

"Don't complain. If you hadn't eaten that toast on *The Adrian Lush Show* they never would have contacted us. Over a million quid in funding—not to be sniffed at with people like you soaking up the funds. Shut the door on the way out, will you?"

The morning's fun wasn't over. As I stepped out of Braxton's office I almost bumped into Flanker.

"Ah!" he said. "Next. A word with you, if you don't mind—?"

It wasn't a request—it was an order. I followed him into an empty interview room and he closed the door.

"Seems to me you're in such deep shit your eyes will turn brown, Next."

"My eyes are already brown, Flanker."

"Then you're halfway there already. I'll come straight to the point. You earned £600 last night."

"So?"

"The service takes a dim view of moonlighting."

"It was Stoker at SO-27," I told him. "I was deputized—all aboveboard."

Flanker went quiet. His intelligence-gathering had obviously let him down badly.

"Can I go?"

Flanker sighed.

"Listen, here, Thursday," he began in a more moderate tone of voice, "we need to know what your father is up to."

"What's the problem? Industrial action standing in the way of next week's cataclysmic event?"

"Freelance navigators will sort it out, Next."

He was bluffing.

"You have no more idea about the nature of the Armageddon than Dad, me, Lavoisier, or anyone else, do you?"

"Perhaps not," replied Flanker, "but we at SpecOps are far better suited to having no clue at all than you and that chronupt father of yours."

"Chronupt?" I said angrily, getting to my feet. "My father? That's a joke! What is your golden boy Lavoisier doing eradicating my husband, then?"

Flanker eyed me silently for a moment.

"That's a very serious accusation," he observed. "Have you any proof?"

"Of course not," I replied, barely able to conceal my rage. "Isn't that the point of eradication?"

"I have known Lavoisier for longer than I would care to forget," intoned Flanker gravely, "and I have never had anything but the highest regard for his integrity. Making wild accusations isn't going to help your cause one iota."

I sat down again and rubbed a hand across my face. Dad had been right. Accusing Lavoisier of any wrongdoing was pointless.

"Can I go?"

"I have nothing to hold you on, Next. But I'll find something. Every agent is on the make. It's just a question of digging deep enough."

---

"How did it go?" asked Bowden when I got back to the office.

"I got an F," I muttered, sinking into my chair.

"Flanker," said Bowden, trying on his *Eat More Toast* cap. "Has to be."

"How did the stand-up go?"

"Very well, I think," answered Bowden, dropping the cap in the bin. "The audience seemed to find it very funny indeed. So much so that they want me to come back as a regular— What are you doing?"

I slithered to the floor as quickly as I could and hid under the table. I would have to trust Bowden's quick wits.

"Hello!" said Miles Hawke as he walked into the room. "Has anyone seen Thursday?"

"I think she's at her monthly assessment meeting," replied Bowden, whose deadpan delivery was obviously as well suited to lying as it was to stand-up. "Can I take a message?"

"No, just ask her to get in contact, if she could."

"Why don't you stay and wait?" said Bowden. I kicked him under the table.

"No, I'd better run along," replied Miles. "Just tell her I dropped by, won't you?"

He walked off and I stood up. Bowden, *very* unusually for him, was giggling.

"What's so funny?"

"Nothing—why don't you want to see him?"

"Because I might be carrying his baby."

"You're going to have to speak up. I can hardly hear you."

"I might," I repeated in a hoarse whisper, "be carrying his *baby!*"

"I thought you said it was Land— What's the matter now?"

I had dropped to the ground again as Cordelia Flakk walked in. She was scanning the office for me in annoyance, hands on hips.

"Have you seen Thursday about?" she asked Bowden. "She's *got* to meet these people of mine."

"I'm really not sure where she is," replied Bowden.

"Really? Then who was it I saw ducking under this table?"

"Hello, Cordelia," I said from beneath the table. "I dropped my pencil."

"Sure you did."

I clambered out and sat down at my desk.

"I expected more from you, Bowden," said Flakk crossly, then turned to me: "Now, Thursday. We promised these two people they could meet you. Do you really want to disappoint them? *Your* public, you know."

"They're not my public, Cordelia, they're *yours*. You made them for me."

"I've had to keep them at the Finis for another night," implored Cordelia. "Costs are escalating. They're downstairs right now. I knew you'd be in for your assessment. How did you do, by the way?"

"Don't ask."

I looked at Bowden, who shrugged. Looking for some sort of rescue, I twisted on my seat to where Victor was running a possible unpublished sequel of *1984* entitled *1985* through the Prose Analyzer. All the other members of the office were busy on their various tasks. It looked like my PR career was just about to restart.

"All right," I sighed, "I'll do it."

"Better than hiding under the desk," said Bowden. "All that jumping around is probably not good for the baby."

He clapped his hand over his mouth, but it was too late.

"Baby?" echoed Cordelia. "What baby?"

"Thanks, Bowden."

"Sorry."

"Well, congratulations!" said Cordelia, hugging me. "Who is the lucky father?"

"I don't know."

"You mean you haven't told him yet?"

"No, I mean I don't know. My husband's, I hope."

"You're married?"

"No."

"But you said—?"

"Yes I did," I retorted as dryly as I could. "Confusing, isn't it?"

"This is *very* bad PR," muttered Cordelia darkly, sitting on the edge of the desk to steady herself. "The leading light of SpecOps knocked up in a bus shelter by someone she doesn't even know!"

"Cordelia, it's not like that—and I wasn't 'knocked up'—and who mentioned anything about bus shelters? Perhaps the best thing would be if you kept this under your hat and we pretend that *Bowden* never said anything."

"Sorry," muttered Bowden meekly.

Cordelia leaped to her feet.

"Good thinking, Next. We can tell everyone you have water retention or an eating disorder brought on by stress." Her face fell. "No, that won't work. *The Toad* will see through it like a shot. Can't you get married really quickly to someone? What about to Bowden? Bowden, would you do the decent thing for the sake of SpecOps?"

"I'm seeing someone over at SpecOps-13," replied Bowden hurriedly.

"Blast!" muttered Flakk. "Thursday, any ideas?"

But this was a part of Bowden I knew nothing about.

"You never told me you were seeing someone over at SO-13!"

"I don't have to tell you *everything*."

"But I'm your partner, Bowden!"

"Well, you never told me about Miles."

"Miles?" exclaimed Cordelia. "The oh-so-handsome-to-die-for Miles *Hawke?*"

"Thanks, Bowden."

"Sorry."

"That's *wonderful!*" exclaimed Cordelia, clapping her hands together. "A dazzling couple! 'SpecOps wedding of the year!' This is worth soooooo much coverage! Does he know?"

"No. And you're not going to tell him. And what's more—*Bowden*—it might not even be his."

"Which puts us back to square one again!" responded Cordelia in a huff. "Stay here, I'm going to fetch my guests. Bowden, don't let her out of your sight!"

And she was gone.

Bowden stared at me for a moment and then asked: "Do you really believe the baby is Landen's?"

"I'm hoping."

"You're not married, Thurs. You might think you are, but you're not. I looked at the records. Landen Parke-Laine died in 1947."

"*This* time he did. My father and I went—"

"You don't have a father, Thursday. There is no record of anyone on your birth certificate. I think maybe you should speak to one of the stressperts."

"And end up doing comedy stand-up, arranging pebbles or counting blue cars? No, thanks."

There was a pause.

"He *is* very handsome," said Bowden.

"Who?"

"Miles Hawke, of course."

"Oh. Yes, yes I know he is."

"Very polite, very popular."

"I know that."

"A child without a father—"

"Bowden, I'm not in love with him and it isn't his baby—okay?"

"Okay, okay. Let's forget it."

We sat there in silence for a bit. I played with a pencil and Bowden stared out of the window.

"What about the voices?"

"Bowden—!"

"Thursday, this is for your own good. You told me you heard them yourself, and officers Hurdyew, Tolkien and Lissning heard you talking and listening to someone in the upstairs corridor."

"Well, the voices have stopped," I said categorically. "Nothing like that will *ever* happen again.[1]

"Oh shit."[2]

"What do you mean, 'Oh shit'?"

"Nothing—just, well, that. I've got to use the ladies' room—would you excuse me?"

I left Bowden shaking his head sadly and was soon in the ladies'. I checked the stalls were empty and then said: "Miss Havisham, are you there?"[3]

"You must understand, Miss Havisham, that where I come

---

1. "Miss Next? Havisham speaking!"
2. *"I hope you didn't say what I thought I heard you say!"*
3. "I am here, young lady, but I am *shocked* by your coarse language!"

from customs are different from your own. People curse here as a matter of course."[4]

"I'll be there directly, ma'am!"

I bit my lip and rushed out of the ladies', grabbed my Jurisfiction travelbook and my jacket and was heading back when—

"Thursday!" went a loud and strident voice that I knew could only be Flakk's. "I've got the winners outside in the corridor—!"

"I'm sorry, Cordelia, but I *have* to go to the loo."

"Don't think I'm going to fall for *that* one again, do you?" she growled under her breath.

"It's true this time."

"And the book?"

"I always read on the loo."

She narrowed her eyes at me and I narrowed my eyes back.

"Very well," she said finally, "but I'm coming with you."

She smiled at the two lucky winners of her crazy competition, who were outside in the corridor. They smiled back through the half-glazed office door and we both trotted into the ladies'.

"Ten minutes," she said to me as I locked myself in a cubicle. I opened the book and started to read:

"Many were the tears shed by them in their last adieus to a place so much beloved. 'Dear, dear Norland!' said Marianne, as she wandered alone before the house, on the last evening of their being there. . . ."

The small melamine cubicle started to evaporate, and in its

4. "Really? Well, I will not hear it from my apprentices. But I forgive you, I suppose. I need you to attend to me right now. Norland Park, Chapter Five, paragraph one—you'll find it in the travelbook Mrs. Nakajima left for you."

place was a large park, bathed in the light of a dying sun, the haze softening the shadows and making the house glow in the failing light. There was a light breeze and in front of the house a lone girl dressed in a Victorian dress, bonnet and shawl. She walked slowly, gazing fondly at the—

"Do you always read aloud in the toilet?" asked Cordelia from behind the door.

The images evaporated in a flash and I was back in the ladies'.

"Always," I replied. "And if you don't leave me alone, I'll *never* be finished."

> ". . . when shall I cease to regret you!—when learn to feel a home elsewhere?—Oh! happy house, could you know what I suffer in now viewing you from this spot, from whence perhaps I may view you know more!—And you, ye well known trees!—But you will continue . . .*"*

The house came back again, the young woman talking quietly, matching her words to mine as I drifted into the book. I was now sitting not on a hard SpecOps standard toilet seat but a white-painted wrought-iron garden bench. I stopped reading when I was certain I was completely within *Sense and Sensibility* and listened to Marianne as she finished her speech:

> ". . . and insensible of any change in those who walk under your shade!—But who will remain to enjoy you?"

She sighed dramatically, clasped her hands to her breast and sobbed quietly for a moment or two. Then she took one long look at the large white-painted house and turned to face me.

"Hello!" she said in a friendly voice. "I haven't seen you around here before. Would you be working for Juris-thingummy-whatsit?"

"Don't we have to be careful as to what we say?" I managed to utter, looking around nervously.

"Goodness me *no!*" exclaimed Marianne with a delightful giggle. "The chapter is over, and besides, this book is written in the *third person.* We are free to do what we please until tomorrow morning, when we depart for Devon. The next two chapters are heavy with exposition—I hardly have anything to do, and I say even less! You look confused, poor thing! Have you been into a book before?"

"I went into *Jane Eyre* once."

Marianne frowned overdramatically.

"Poor, dear, sweet Jane! I would so *hate* to be a first-person character! Always on your guard, always having people reading your thoughts! Here we *do* what we are told but *think* what we wish. It is a much happier circumstance, believe me!"

"What do you know about Jurisfiction?" I asked.

"They will be arriving shortly," she explained. "Mrs. Dashwood might be beastly to Mama, but she understands self-preservation. We wouldn't want to suffer the same tragic fate as *Confusion and Conviviality,* now would we?"

"Is that Austen?" I queried. "I've not even heard of it!"

Marianne sat down next to me and rested her hand on my arm.

"Mama said it was *socialist collective,*" she confided in a hoarse whisper. "There was a revolution—they took over the entire book and decided to run it on the principle of every character having an equal part, from the Duchess to the cobbler! I ask you! Jurisfiction tried to save it, of course, but it was too far gone—not even Ambrose could do anything. The entire book was . . . *boojummed!*"

She said the last word so seriously that I would have laughed had she not been staring at me so intensely with her dark brown eyes.

"How I do talk!" she said at last, jumping up, clapping her hands and doing a twirl on the lawn. "*. . . and insensible of any change in those who walk under your shade . . .*"

She stopped and checked herself, placed her hand over her mouth and nose and uttered an embarrassed girlish giggle.

"What a loon!" she muttered. "I've said that already! Farewell, Miss, miss— I beg your pardon but I don't know your name!"

"It's Thursday—Thursday Next."

"What a strange name!"

She gave a small curtsy in a half-joking way.

"I am Marianne Dashwood, and I welcome you, Miss Next, to *Sense and Sensibility.*"

"Thank you," I replied. "I'm sure I shall enjoy it here."

"I'm sure you shall. We all enjoy it tremendously—do you think it shows?"

"I think it shows a great deal, Miss Dashwood."

"Call me Marianne, if it pleases you."

She stopped and thought for a moment, smiled politely, looked over her shoulder and then said:

"May I be so bold as to ask you a favor?"

"Of course."

She sat on the seat with me and stared into my eyes.

"Please, I wonder if I might be so bold as to ask when *your* own book is set."

"I'm not a bookperson, Miss Dashwood—I'm from the real world."

"Oh!" she exclaimed. "Please excuse me; I didn't mean to imply that you weren't real or anything. In that case, when, might I ask, is your own world set?"

I smiled at her strange logic and told her: 1985. She was pleased to hear this and leaned closer still.

"Please excuse the impertinence, but would you bring something back next time you come?"

"Such as—?"

"Mintolas. I simply *adore* Mintolas. You've heard of them, of course? A bit like Munchies but minty—and, if it's no trouble, a few pairs of nylon tights—and some AA batteries; a dozen would be perfect."

"Sure. Anything else?"

Marianne thought for a moment.

"Elinor would so *hate* me asking favors from a stranger, but I happen to know she has an inordinate fondness for Marmite—and some real coffee for Mama."

I told her I would do what I could. She thanked me profusely, pulled on a leather flying helmet and goggles that she had secreted within her shawl, held my hand for a moment and then was gone, running across the lawn.

# 25.

## Roll Call at Jurisfiction

**Boojum:** Term used to describe the total annihilation of a word/line/character/subplot/book/series. Complete and irreversible, the nature of a boojum is still the subject of some heated speculation. Some past members of Jurisfiction theorize that a Boojum might be a gateway to an "antilibrary" somewhere beyond the "imagination horizon." It is possible that the semimythical *Snark* may hold the key to decipher what is, at present, a mystery.

**Bowdlerizers:** A group of fanatics who attempt to excise obscenity and profanity from all texts. Named after Thomas Bowdler, who attempted to make Shakespeare "family reading" by cutting lines from the plays, believing by so doing that "the transcendental genius of the poet would undoubtedly shine with greater luster." Bowdler died in 1825, but his torch is still carried, illegally, by active cells eager to complete and extend his unfinished work at any cost. Attempts to infiltrate the Bowdlerizers have so far met with no success.

UNITARY AUTHORITY OF WARRINGTON CAT,
*The Jurisfiction Guide to the Great Library* (glossary)

**I** WATCHED MARIANNE until she was no longer in sight and then, realizing that her *"remain to enjoy you"* line was the *last* of Chapter Five and Chapter Six begins with the Dashwoods already embarked on their journey, I decided to wait and see what a chapter ending looks like. If I had expected a thunderclap or something equally dramatic, I was to be disappointed. Nothing happened. The leaves in the trees gently rustled, the occasional sound of a wood pigeon reached my ears, and before me a red squirrel hopped across the grass. I heard an engine start up and a few minutes later a biplane rose from the meadow behind the rhododendrons, circled the house twice and then headed off towards the setting sun. I rose and walked across the finely manicured lawn, nodded at a gardener who tipped his head in reply and made my way to the front door. Norland was never described in that much detail in *Sense and Sensibility*, but it was every bit as impressive as I thought it would be. The house was located within a broad sweeping parkland which was occasionally punctuated by mature oak trees. In the distance I could see only woods, and beyond that, the occasional church spire. Outside the front door there was a Bugatti 35B motorcar and a huge white charger saddled for battle, munching idly on some grass. A large white dog was attached to the saddle by a length of string, and it had managed to wrap itself three times around a tree.

I trotted up the steps and tugged on the bell pull. Within a few minutes a uniformed footman answered and looked at me blankly.

"Thursday Next," I said. "Here for Jurisfiction—Miss Havisham."

The footman, who had large bulging eyes and a curved head like a frog, opened the door and announced me simply by rearranging the words a bit:

"Miss Havisham, Thursday Next—here for Jurisfiction!"

I stepped inside and frowned at the empty hall, wondering quite who the footman thought he was actually announcing me to. I turned to ask him where I should go, but he bowed stiffly and walked—excruciatingly slowly, I thought—to the other side of the hall, where he opened a door and then stood back, staring at something above and behind me. I thanked him, stepped in and found myself in the central ballroom of the house. The room was painted in white and pale blue, and the walls, where not decorated with delicate plaster moldings, were hung with lavish gold-framed mirrors. Above me the glazed ceiling let in the evening light, but already I could see servants preparing candelabra.

It had been a long time since the Jurisfiction offices had been used as a ballroom. The floor space was liberally covered with sofas, tables, filing cabinets and desks piled high with paperwork. To one side a table had been set up with coffee urns, and tasty snacks were arrayed upon delicate china. There were two dozen or so people milling about, sitting down, chatting or just staring vacantly into space. I could see Akrid Snell at the far side of the room, speaking into what looked like a small gramophone horn connected by a flexible brass tube to the floor. I tried to get his attention, but at that moment—

"Please," said a voice close by, "draw me a sheep!"

I looked down to see a young boy of no more than ten. He had curly golden locks and stared at me with an intensity that was, to say the least, unnerving.

"Please," he repeated, "draw me a sheep."

"You had better do as he asks," said a familiar voice close by. "Once he starts on you he'll *never* let it go."

It was Miss Havisham. I dutifully drew the best sheep I could and handed the result to the boy, who walked away, very satisfied with the result.

"Welcome to Jurisfiction," said Miss Havisham, still limping slightly from her injury at Booktastic and once more dressed in her rotted wedding robes. "I won't introduce you to everyone straightaway, but there are one or two people you should know."

She took me by the arm and guided me towards a conservatively dressed lady who was attending to the servants as they laid out some food upon the table.

"This is Mrs. John Dashwood; she graciously allows us the use of her home. Mrs. Dashwood, this is Miss Thursday Next—she is my new apprentice."

I shook Mrs. Dashwood's delicately proffered hand, and she smiled politely.

"Welcome to Norland Park, Miss Next. You are fortunate indeed to have Miss Havisham as your teacher—she does not often take pupils. But tell me, as I am not so very conversant with contemporary fiction—what book are you from?"

"I'm not from a book, Mrs. Dashwood."

Mrs. Dashwood looked startled for a moment, then smiled even more politely, took my arm in hers, muttered a pleasantry to Miss Havisham about "getting acquainted" and steered me off towards the tea table.

"How do you find Norland, Miss Next?"

"Very lovely, Mrs. Dashwood."

"Can I offer you a Crumbobbilous cutlet?" she asked in a clearly agitated manner, handing me a sideplate and napkin and indicating the food.

"Or some tea?"

"No, thank you."

"I'll come straight to the point, Miss Next."

"You seem most anxious to do so."

She glanced furtively to left and right and lowered her voice.

"Does everyone *out there* think my husband and I are so *very* cruel, cutting the girls and their mother out of Henry Dashwood's bequest?"

She looked at me so *very* seriously that I wanted to smile.

"Well," I began—

"Oh I knew it!" gasped Mrs. Dashwood. She pressed the

back of her hand to her forehead in a dramatic gesture. "I told John that we should reconsider—I expect *out there* we are burnt in effigy, reviled for our actions, damned for all time?"

"Not at all," I said, attempting to console her. "Narratively speaking, without your actions there wouldn't be much of a story."

Mrs. Dashwood took a handkerchief from her cuff and dried her eyes, which, as far as I could see, had not even the smallest tear in them.

"You are so right, Miss Next. Thank you for your kind words—but if you hear anyone speaking ill of me, please tell them that it was my husband's decision—I tried to stop him, believe me!"

"Of course," I said, reassuring her. I made my excuses and left to find Miss Havisham.

"We call it *minor character syndrome*," explained Miss Havisham after I rejoined her. "Quite common when an essentially minor character has a large and consequential part. She and her husband have allowed us the use of this room ever since the trouble with *Confusion and Conviviality*. In return we make all Jane Austen books a matter of our special protection; we don't want anything like that to happen again. There is a satellite office in the basement of Elsinore castle run by Mr. Falstaff—that's him over there."

She pointed to an overweight man with a florid face who was in conversation with another agent. They both laughed uproariously at something Falstaff had said.

"Who is he talking to?"

"Vernham Deane, romantic lead in one of Daphne Farquitt's novels. Mr. Deane is a stalwart member of Jurisfiction, so we don't hold it against him—"

"WHERE IS HAVISHAM!?" bellowed a voice like thunder. The doors burst open and a very disheveled Red Queen hopped in. The whole room fell silent. Except, that is, for Miss Havisham, who said in an unnecessarily provocative tone:

"Bargain hunting just doesn't suit some people, now does it?"

The assembled Jurisfiction operatives, realizing that all they were witnessing was another round in a long and very personal battle, carried on talking.

The Red Queen had a large and painful-looking black eye, and two of her fingers were in a splint. The sales at Booktastic had not been kind to her.

"What's on your mind, your majesty?" asked Havisham in an even tone.

"Meddle in my affairs again," growled the Red Queen, "and I won't be responsible for my actions!"

I shuffled uncomfortably and wanted to move away from this embarrassing confrontation. But since I thought *someone* should be on hand to separate them if there was a fight, I remained where I was.

"Don't you think you're taking this a little too seriously, your majesty?" said Havisham, always maintaining due regal respect. "It was only a set of Farquitts, after all!"

"A *boxed* set!" replied the Red Queen coldly. 'You deliberately took the gift I planned to give to my own dear beloved husband. And do you know why?"

Miss Havisham pursed her lips and was silent.

*"Because you can't bear it that I'm happily married!"*

"Rubbish!" returned Miss Havisham angrily. "We beat you fair and square!"

"Ladies and, er, ladies and *majesties,* please!" I said in a conciliatory tone. "Do we have to argue here at Norland Park?"

"Ah yes!" said the Red Queen. "Do you know *why* we use *Sense and Sensibility?* Why Miss Havisham *insisted* on it, in fact?"

"Don't believe this," murmured Miss Havisham. "It's all poppycock. Her majesty is a verb short of a sentence."

"I'll tell you why," went on the Red Queen angrily, "because in *Sense and Sensibility* there are no strong father or husband figures!"

Miss Havisham was silent.

"Face the facts, Havisham. Neither the Dashwoods, the Steeles, the Ferrar brothers, Eliza Brandon *or* Willoughby have a father to guide them! Aren't you taking your hatred of men just a little too far?"

"Deluded," replied Havisham, then added after a short pause: "Well then, *your majesty,* since we are in a questioning vein, just what is it, *exactly,* that you rule over?"

The Red Queen turned scarlet—which was tricky, as she was *quite* red to begin with—and pulled a small dueling pistol from her pocket. Havisham was quick and *also* drew her weapon, and there they stood, quivering with rage, guns pointing at each other. Fortunately the sound of a bell tingling caught their attention and they both lowered their weapons.

"The Bellman!" hissed Miss Havisham as she took my arm and moved towards where a man dressed as a town crier stood on a low dais. *"Showtime!"*

The small group of people gathered around the crier; the Red Queen and Miss Havisham stood side by side, their argument seemingly forgotten. I looked around at the odd assortment of characters and wondered quite what I was doing here. Still, if I was to learn how to travel in books, I would have to know more. I listened attentively.

The Bellman put down his bell and consulted a list of notes.

"Is everyone here? Where's the Cat?"

"I'm over there," purred the Cat, sitting precariously atop one of the gold-framed mirrors.

"Good. Okay, anyone missing?"

"Shelley's gone boating," said a voice at the back. "He'll be back in an hour if the weather holds."

"O-kay," continued the Bellman. "Jurisfiction session number 40311 is now in session."

He tingled his bell again, coughed and consulted a clipboard.

"Item one is bad news, I'm afraid."

There was a respectful hush. He paused for a moment and picked his words carefully.

"I think we will all have to come to the conclusion that David and Catriona aren't coming back. It's been eighteen sessions now, and we have to assume that they've been . . . *boojummed.*"

There was a reflective pause.

"We remember David and Catriona Balfour as friends, colleagues, worthy members of our calling, protagonists in *Kidnapped* and *Catriona* and for all the booksploring they did—especially finding a way into Barchester, for which we will always be grateful. I ask for a minute's silence. To the Balfours!"

"The Balfours!" we all repeated. Then, heads bowed, we stood in silence. After a minute ticked by, the Bellman spoke again.

"Now, I don't want to sound disrespectful, but what we learn from this is that we must *always* sign the outings book so we know where you are—*particularly* if you are exploring new routes. Don't forget the ISBN numbers either—they weren't introduced *just* for cataloguing, now were they? Mr. Bradshaw's maps might have a traditionalist's charm about them—"

"Who's Bradshaw?" I whispered.

"*Commander* Bradshaw," explained Havisham. "Retired now but a wonderful character—did most of the booksploring in the early days."

"—but they are old and full of errors," continued the Bellman. "New technology is here to be used, guys. Anyone who wants to attend a training course on how ISBN numbers relate to transbook travel, see the Cat for details."

The Bellman looked around the room as if to reinforce the order, then unfolded a sheet of paper and adjusted his glasses.

"Right. Item two. New recruit. Thursday Next. Where are you?"

The assembled Prose Resource Operatives looked around the room before I waved a hand to get their attention.

"There you are. Thursday is apprenticed to Miss Havisham; I'm sure you'll all join me in welcoming her to our little band."

"Didn't like the way *Jane Eyre* turned out?" said someone in a hostile tone from the back. Everyone watched as a middle-aged man stood up and walked up to the Bellman's dais. There was silence.

"Who's that?" I hissed.

"Harris Tweed," replied Havisham. "Dangerous and arrogant but *quite* brilliant—for a man."

"Who approved her application?" asked Tweed.

"She didn't apply, Harris," replied the Bellman. "Her appointment was forshadowed long ago. Besides, her work within *Jane Eyre* ridding the book of the loathsome Hades is good enough testimonial for me."

"But she *altered* the book!" cried Tweed angrily. "Who's to say she wouldn't do the same again?"

"I did what I did for the best," I said in a loud voice, feeling I had to defend myself against Tweed. This startled him—I got the feeling no one really stood up to him.

"If it wasn't for Thursday we wouldn't *have* a book," said the Bellman. "A full book with a different ending is better than half a book without."

"That's not what the rules say, Bellman."

To my great relief, Miss Havisham spoke up.

"*Truly* competent Literary Detectives are as rare as truthful men, Mr. Tweed—you can see her potential as clearly as I can. Frightened of someone stealing your thunder, perhaps?"

"It's not that at all," protested Tweed. "But what if she were here for another reason altogether?"

"I shall vouch for her!" said Miss Havisham in a thunderous tone. "I call for a show of hands. If there is a majority amongst you who think my judgment poor, then put your hands up now and I will banish her back to where she came from!"

She said it with such a show of fierce temper that I thought that no one would raise a hand; in the event, only one did—Tweed himself, who, after reading the situation, judged that good grace was the best way in which to retire. He gave a wan half-smile, bowed and said: "I withdraw all objections."

I sighed a sigh of relief as Havisham nudged me in the ribs and gave me a wink.

"Good," said the Bellman as Tweed returned to his desk. "As I was saying, we welcome Miss Next to Jurisfiction and we don't want any of those silly practical jokes we usually play on new recruits—okay?"

He surveyed the room with a stern expression before returning to his list.

"Item two: There is an illegal PageRunner from Shakespeare, so this is a priority red. Perp's name is Feste; worked as a jester in *Twelfth Night*. Took flight after a debauched night with Sir Toby. Who wants to go after him?"

A hand went up in the crowd.

"Fabien? Thanks. You may have to stand in for him for a while; take Falstaff with you, but please, Sir John—stay out of sight. You've been allowed to stay in *Merry Wives,* but don't push your luck."

Falstaff got up, bowed clumsily, burped, and sat down again.

"Item three: Interloper in the Sherlock Holmes series by the name of Mycroft—turns up quite unexpectedly in *The Greek Interpreter* and claims to be his brother. Anyone know anything about this?"

I shrank lower, hoping that no one would have enough knowledge of my world to know we were related. Sly old Fox! So he *had* rebuilt the Prose Portal. I covered my mouth to hide a smile.

"No?" went on the Bellman. "Well, Sherlock seems to think he *is* his brother, and so far there is no harm done—but I think this would be a good opportunity to open up a way into the Sherlock Holmes series. Suggestions, anyone?"

"How about through 'The Murders in the Rue Morgue'?" suggested Tweed, to the accompaniment of laughter and cat-calls from around the room.

"Order! *Sensible* suggestions, please. Poe is out of bounds and will remain so. It's possible 'The Murders in the Rue Morgue' might open an avenue to *all* detective stories that came after it, but I won't sanction the risk. Now—any other suggestions?"

"*The Lost World*?"

There were a few giggles, but they soon stopped; this time Tweed was serious.

"Conan Doyle's other works might afford a link to the Sherlock Holmes series," he added gravely. "I know we can get into *The Lost World*. I just need to find a way to move beyond that."

There was an uncomfortable moment as the Jurisfiction agents muttered to one another.

"What's the problem?" I whispered.

"Adventure stories always bring the highest risks to anyone establishing a new route," hissed back Miss Havisham. "The worst you might expect from a romantic novel or domestic pot-boiler is a slapped face or a nasty burn from the Aga. Finding a way into *King Solomon's Mines* cost two agents' lives."

The Bellman spoke again.

"The last booksplorer who went into *The Lost World* was shot by Lord Roxton."

"Gomez was an amateur," retorted Tweed. "I can take care of myself."

The Bellman thought about this for a moment, weighed up the pros and cons and then sighed.

"Okay, you're on. But I want reports every ten pages, understand? Okay. Item four—"

There was a noise from two younger members of the service who were laughing about something.

"Hey, listen up, guys. I'm not just talking for my health."

They were quiet.

"Okay. Item four: nonstandard spelling. There have been some odd spellings reported in nineteenth- and twentieth-century texts, so keep your eyes open. It's probably just texters having a bit of fun, but it just *might* be the mispeling vyrus coming back to life."

There was a groan from the assembled agents.

"Okay, okay, keep your hair on—I only said 'might.' Samuel Johnson's dictionary cured it after the 1744 outbreak and Lavinia-Webster and the *OED* keep it all in check, but we have to be careful of any new strains. I know this is boring, but I want *every* misspelling you come across reported and given to the Cat. He'll pass it on to Agent Libris at Text Grand Central."

He paused for effect and looked at us sternly.

"We can't let this get out of hand, people. Okay. Item five: There are thirty-one pilgrims in Chaucer's *Canterbury Tales* but only twenty-four stories. Mrs. Cavendish, weren't you keeping an eye on this?"

"We've been watching *Canterbury Tales* all week," said a woman dressed in the most fabulously outrageous clothes, "and every time we look away, another story gets boojummed. Someone's getting in there and erasing the story from within."

"Deane? Any idea who's behind all this?"

Daphne Farquitt's romantic lead stood up and consulted a list.

"I think I can see a pattern beginning to emerge," he said. "*The Merchant's Wife* was the first to go, followed by *The Milliner's Tale*, *The Pedlar's Cok*, *The Cuckold's Revenge*, *The Maiden's Wonderful Arse* and, most recently, *The Contest of Farts*. *The Cook's Tale* is already half gone—it looks as though whoever is doing this has a problem with the healthy vulgarity of Chaucerian texts."

"In that case," said the Bellman with a grave expression, "it looks like we have an active cell of Bowdlerizers at work again. *The Miller's Tale* will be the next to go. I want twenty-four-hour surveillance, and we should get someone on the inside. Volunteers?"

"I'll go," said Deane. "I'll take the place of the host—he won't mind."

"Good. Keep me informed of your progress."

"I say!" said Akrid Snell, putting up his hand.

"What is it, Snell?"

"If you're going to be the host, Deane, can you get Chaucer to cool it a bit on the Sir Topaz story? He's issued a writ for libel, and not to put too fine a point on it, I think we could lose our trousers over this one."

Deane nodded, and the Bellman returned to his notes.

"Item six: Now *this* I regard as kind of serious, guys."

He held up an old copy of the Bible.

"In this 1631 printing, the seventh commandment reads: *Thou shalt commit adultery.*"

There was a mixture of shock and stifled giggles from the small gathering.

"I don't know who did this, but it's just not funny. Fooling around with internal Text Operating Systems might have a sort of mischievous appeal to it, but it's not big and it's not clever. The occasional bout of high spirits I might overlook, but this isn't an isolated incident. I've also got a 1716 edition that urges the faithful to *sin on more,* and a Cambridge printing from 1653 which tells us that *The unrighteous shall inherit the Kingdom of God.* Now listen, I don't want to be accused of having no sense of humor, but this is something that I *will not tolerate.* If I find out the joker who has been doing this, it'll be a month's enforced holiday inside *Ant & Bee.*"

"*Marlowe!*" said Tweed, making it sound like a cough.

"What was that?"

"Nothing. Bad cough—*sorry.*"

The Bellman stared at Tweed for a moment, laid down the offending Bible and looked at his watch.

"Okay, that's it for now. I'll be doing individual briefings in a few minutes. We thank Mrs. Dashwood for her hospitality, and Perkins—it's your turn to feed the Morlock."

There was a groan from Perkins. The group started to wander off and talk to one another. The Bellman had to raise his voice to be heard.

"We go off shift in eight bells, and listen up—!"

The assembled Jurisfiction staff stopped for a moment.

"Let's be *careful* out there."

The Bellman paused, tingled his bell and everyone returned to their tasks. I caught Tweed's eye; he smiled, made a pistol out of his hand and pointed it at me. I did the same back and he laughed.

"King Pellinore," said the Bellman to a disheveled white-haired whiskery gentleman in half-armor, "there has been a sighting of the Questing Beast in the backstory of *Middlemarch.*"

King Pellinore's eyes opened wide; he muttered something that sounded like "What what, hey hey?," then drew himself up to his full height, picked a helmet from a nearby table and clanked from the room. The Bellman ticked his list, consulted the next entry and turned to us.

"Next and Havisham," he said. "Something easy to begin with. Bloophole needs closing. It's in *Great Expectations,* Miss Havisham, so you can go straight home afterwards."

"Good," she exclaimed. "What do we have to do?"

"Page two," explained the Bellman, consulting his clipboard. "Abel Magwitch escapes—swims, one assumes—from a prison hulk with a 'great iron' on his leg. He'd sink like a stone. No Magwitch, no escape, no career in Australia, no cash to give to Pip, no 'expectations,' no story. He's got to have the shackles still on him when he reaches the shore so Pip can fetch a file to release him, so you're going to have to footle with the backstory. Any questions?"

"No," replied Miss Havisham. "Thursday?"

"Er—no also," I replied, my head still spinning after the Bellman's speech. I was just going to walk in Miss Havisham's shadow for a bit—which was, on reflection, a very good place to be.

"Good," said the Bellman, signing a docket and tearing it off. "Take this to Wemmick in stores."

He left us and called to Foyle and the Red Queen about a missing person named Cass in *Silas Marner.*

"Did you understand any of that?" asked Miss Havisham.

"Not really."

"Good!" smiled Miss Havisham. "Confused is *exactly* how all cadets to Jurisfiction should enter their first assignment!"

# 26.

## Assignment One: Bloophole Filled in *Great Expectations*

**Bloophole:** Term used to describe a narrative hole by the author that renders his/her work seemingly impossible. An unguarded bloophole may not cause damage for millions of readings, but then, quite suddenly and catastrophically, the book may unravel itself in a very dramatic fashion. Hence the Jurisfiction saying "A switch in a line can save a lot of time."

**TextMarker:** An emergency device that outwardly resembles a flare pistol. Designed by the Jurisfiction Design & Technology department, the TextMarker allows a trapped PRO to "mark" the text of the book they are within using a predesignated code of bold, italics, underlining, etc., unique to the agent. Another agent may then jump in at the right page to effect a rescue. Works well as long as the rescuer is looking for the signal.

UNITARY AUTHORITY OF WARRINGTON CAT,
*The Jurisfiction Guide to the Great Library* (glossary)

**M**ISS HAVISHAM had dispatched me to get some tea and meet her back at her desk, so I walked across to the refreshments.

"Good evening, Miss Next," said a well-dressed young man in plus fours and a sports jacket. He had a well-trimmed mustache and a monocle screwed into his eye; he smiled and offered me his hand to shake. "Vernham Deane, resident cad of *The Squire of High Potternews*, D. Farquitt, 246 pages, softcover £3.99."

I shook his hand.

"I know what you're thinking," he said sadly. "No one thinks much of Daphne Farquitt, but she sells a lot of books and she's always been pretty good to me—apart from the chapter where I ravish the serving girl at Potternews Hall and then callously have her turned from the house. I didn't want to, believe me."

He looked at me with the same earnestness that Mrs. Dashwood had exhibited when explaining *her* actions in *Sense and Sensibility*. It sounded as though a preordained life could be something of a nuisance.

"I've not read the book," I told him untruthfully, unwilling to get embroiled in Farquitt plot intricacies—I could be stuck here for days.

"Ah!" he said with some relief, then added: "You have a good teacher in Miss Havisham. Solid and dependable, but a stickler for rules. There are many shortcuts here that the more mature members either frown upon or have no knowledge of; will you permit me to show you around some time?"

I was touched by the courtesy.

"Thank you, Mr. Deane—I accept."

"Vern," he said. "Call me Vern. Listen, don't rely too heavily on the ISBN numbers. The Bellman's a bit of a technophile and although the ISBN Positioning System might *seem* to have its attractions, I should keep one of Bradshaw's maps with you as a backup at all times."

"I'll bear that in mind, Vern, thanks."

"And don't worry about old Harris. His bark is a lot worse than his bite. He looks down on me because I'm from a racy potboiler, but listen—I can hold my own against him any day!"

He poured some tea for us both before continuing.

"He was trained during the days when cadets were cast into *A Pilgrim's Progress* and told to make their own way out. He thinks all us young 'uns are soft as soap. Don't you, Tweed?"

He turned to meet my detractor.

Harris Tweed stood by with an empty coffee cup.

"What are you blathering about, Deane?" he asked, scowling like thunder.

"I was telling Miss Next here that you think we're all a bit soft."

Harris took a step closer, glared at Deane and then fixed me with his dark brown eyes. He was about fifty, graying, and had the sort of face that looked as though the skin had been measured upon a skull three sizes smaller before fitment.

"Has Havisham mentioned the Well of Lost Plots to you?" he asked.

"The Cat mentioned it. Unpublished books, I think he said."

"Not *just* unpublished. The Well of Lost Plots is where vague ideas ferment into sketchy plans. This is the Notion Nursery. The Word Womb. Go down there and you'll see plot outlines coalescing on the shelves like so many primordial life forms. The spirits of roughly sketched characters flit about the corridors in search of plot and dialogue before they are woven into the story. If they get lucky, the book finds a publisher and rises into the Great Library above."

"And if they're unlucky?"

"They stay in the basement. But there's more. Below the Well of Lost Plots is *another* basement. Subbasement twenty-seven. No one talks of it much. It's where deleted characters, poor plot devices, half-baked ideas and corrupt Jurisfiction agents go to spend a painful eternity. Just remember that."

I was stunned, so said nothing. Tweed glared at Deane, scowled at me, filled up his coffee cup and left. As soon as he was out of earshot, Vernham turned to me and said: "Old wives' tales. There's no such thing as basement twenty-seven."

"Sort of like using the Jabberwock to frighten children, yes?"

"Well, not really," replied Deane thoughtfully, "because there is a Jabberwock. Frightfully nice fellow—good at fly-fishing and plays the bongos. I'll introduce you sometime."

I heard Miss Havisham calling my name.

"I'd better go," I told him.

Vern looked at his watch.

"Of course. Goodness, is that the time? Well, hey-ho, see you about!"

Despite Vern's assurances about Harris Tweed's threats I still felt uneasy. Was jumping into a copy of Poe from my side enough of a misdemeanor to attract Tweed's ire? And how much training would I need before I could even *attempt* to rescue Jack Schitt? I returned to Miss Havisham deep in thought about Jurisfiction and Landen and bookjumping. I noticed her desk was as far from the Red Queen's as one could get and laid her tea in front of her.

"What do you know about subbasement twenty-seven?" I asked her.

"Old wives' tales," replied Havisham, concentrating on the report she was filing. "One of the other PROs trying to frighten you?"

"Sort of."

I looked around while Miss Havisham busied herself. There seemed to be a lot of activity in the room; PROs melted in and out of the air around me with the Bellman moving around, reading instructions from his clipboard. My eyes alighted on a shiny horn that was connected to a polished wood-and-brass device on the desk by a flexible copper tube. It reminded me of a very old form of gramophone—something that Thomas Edison might have come up with.

Miss Havisham looked up, saw I was trying to read the instructions on the brass plaque and said: "It's a footnoterphone. We use them to communicate. Book-to-book or external calls, their value is incalculable. Try it out if you wish."

I took the horn and looked inside. There was a cork plug pushed into the end attached to a short chain. I looked at Miss Havisham.

"Just give the title of the book, page, character, and if you really want to be specific, line and word."

"As simple as that?"

"As simple as that."

I pulled out the plug and heard a voice say: "Operator services. Can I help you?"

"Oh! yes—er, book-to-book, please." I thought of a novel I had been reading recently and chose a page and line at random. "*It Was a Dark and Stormy Night,* page 156, line four."

"Trying to connect you. Thank you for using FNP Communications."

There were a few clicking noises and I heard a man's voice saying: "*. . . and our hearts, though stout and brave, still like muffled . . .*"

The operator came back on the line.

"I'm sorry, we had a crossed line. You are through now, caller. Thank you for using FNP Communications."

Now all I could hear was the low murmur of conversation above the sound of engines of a ship. At a loss to know what to say I just gabbled: "Antonio?"

There was the sound of a confused voice, and I hurriedly replaced the plug.

"You'll get the hang of it," said Havisham kindly, putting her report down. "Paperwork! My goodness. Come along, we've got to visit Wemmick in the stores. I like him, so *you'll* like him. I won't expect you to do much on this first assignment—just stay close to me and observe. Finished your tea? We're off!"

I hadn't, of course, but Miss Havisham grabbed my elbow and before I knew it we were back in the huge entrance lobby near the Boojumorial. Our footsteps rang out on the polished floor as we crossed to one side of the vestibule, where a small counter not more than six feet wide was set into the deep red marble wall. A battered notice told us to take a number and we would be called.

"Rank must have its privileges!" cried Miss Havisham gaily as she walked to the front of the queue. A few of the Jurisfiction agents looked up, but most were too busy swotting up on their passnotes, cramming for their impending destinations.

Harris Tweed was in front of us, kitting up for his trip into *The Lost World.* On the counter before him there was a complete safari suit, knapsack, binoculars and revolver.

"—and one Rigby .416 sporting rifle, plus sixty rounds of ammunition."

The storekeeper laid a mahogany rifle box on the counter and shook his head sadly.

"Are you *sure* you wouldn't prefer an M-16? A charging stegosaurus can take some stopping, I'll be bound."

"An M-16 would be sure to raise suspicions, Mr. Wemmick. Besides, I'm a bit of a traditionalist at heart."

Mr. Wemmick sighed, shook his head and handed the clipboard to Tweed for him to sign. Harris grunted his thanks to Mr. Wemmick, signed the top copy, had the docket stamped and returned to him before he gathered up his possessions, nodded respectfully at Miss Havisham, ignored me and then murmured, ". . . *long, dark, wood-paneled corridor lined with bookshelves* . . ." before vanishing.

"Good day, Miss Havisham!" said Mr. Wemmick politely as soon as we stepped up. "And how are we this day?"

"In health, I think, Mr. Wemmick. Is Mr. Jaggers quite well?"

"Quite well to my way of thinking, I should say, Miss Havisham, quite well."

"This is Miss Next, Mr. Wemmick. She has joined us recently."

"Delighted!" remarked Mr. Wemmick, who looked every bit the way he was described in *Great Expectations*. That is to say, he was short, had a slightly pockmarked face, and had been that way for about forty years.

"Where are you two bound?"

"Home!" said Miss Havisham, laying the docket on the counter.

Mr. Wemmick picked up the piece of paper and looked at it for a moment before disappearing into the storeroom and rummaging noisily.

"The stores are indispensable for our purposes, Thursday. Wemmick quite literally writes his own inventory. It all has to be signed for and returned, of course, but there is very little that he doesn't have. Isn't that so, Mr. Wemmick?"

"Exactly so!" came a voice from behind a large pile of Turkish costumes and a realistic rubber bison.

"By the way, can you swim?" asked Miss Havisham.

"Yes."

Mr. Wemmick returned with a small pile of items.

"Life vests—life preserving, for the purpose of—two. Rope—in case of trouble—one. Life belt—to assist Magwitch buoyancy—one. Cash—for incidental expenses—ten shillings and fourpence. Cloak—for disguising said agents Next and Havisham, heavy-duty, black—two. Packed supper—two. Sign here."

Miss Havisham picked up the pen and paused before signing.

"We'll need my boat, Mr. Wemmick," she said lowering her voice.

"I'll footnoterphone ahead, Miss H," said Wemmick, winking broadly. "You'll find it on the jetty."

"For a man you are not bad at all, Mr. Wemmick!" said Miss Havisham. "Thursday, gather up the equipment!"

I picked up the heavy canvas bag.

"Dickens *is* within walking distance," explained Havisham,

"but it's better practice for you if you jump us straight there—there are over fifty thousand miles of shelf space."

"Ah—okay, I know how to do that," I muttered, putting down the bag, taking out my travel book and flicking to the passage about the library.

"Hold on to me as you jump, and think *Dickens* as you read."

So I did, and within a trice we were at the right place in the library.

"How was that?" I asked, quite proudly.

"Not bad," said Havisham. "But you forgot the bag."

"Sorry."

"I'll wait while you get it."

So I read myself back to the lobby, retrieved the bag to a few friendly jibes from Deane, and returned—but by accident to where a series of adventure books for plucky girls by Charles *Pickens* were stored. I sighed, read the library passage again and was soon with Miss Havisham.

"This is the outings book," she said without looking up from one of the reading desks. "Name, destination, date, time—I've filled it in already. Are you armed?"

"Always. Do you expect any trouble?"

Miss Havisham drew out her small pistol, released the twin barrels, pivoted it upwards and gave me one of her more serious stares.

"I *always* expect trouble, Thursday. I was on HPD—Heathcliff Protection Duty—in *Wuthering Heights* for two years, and believe me, the ProCaths tried everything. I personally saved him from assassination eight times."

She extracted a spent cartridge, replaced it with a live one and locked the barrels back into place.

"But *Great Expectations*? Where's the danger there?"

She rolled up her sleeve and showed me a livid scar on her forearm.

"Things can turn pretty ugly even in *Toytown*," she explained. "Believe me, Larry is no lamb—I was lucky to escape with my life."

I must have been looking nervous, because she said: "Everything okay? You can bail out whenever you want, you know. Say the word and you'll be back in Swindon before you can say 'Mrs. Hubbard.' "

It wasn't a threat. She was giving me a way out. I thought of Landen and the baby. I'd survived the book sales and *Jane Eyre* with no ill effects—how hard could "footling" with the backstory of a Dickens novel be? Besides, I needed all the practice I could get.

"Ready when you are, Miss Havisham."

She nodded, rolled down her sleeve again, pulled *Great Expectations* from the bookshelf and opened it on one of the reading desks.

"We need to go in *before* the story really begins, so this is *not* a standard bookjump. Are you paying attention?"

"Yes, Miss Havisham."

"Good. I've no desire to go through this more than once. First, read us into the book."

I opened the book and read aloud from the first page, making quite sure I had hold of the bag this time:

"... Ours was the marsh country, down by the river, within, as the river wound, twenty miles of the sea. My first most vivid and broad impression of the identity of things, seems to me to have been gained on a memorable raw afternoon toward evening. At such a time I found out for certain that this bleak place overgrown with nettles was the churchyard; and that Philip Pirrip, late of this parish, and also Georgiana wife of the above, were dead and buried; and that Alexander, Bartholomew, Abraham, Tobias, and

Roger, infant children of the aforesaid, were also dead and buried; and that the dark flat wilderness beyond the churchyard, intersected with dikes and mounds and gates, with scattered cattle feeding on it, was the marshes; and that the low leaden line beyond was the river; and that the distant savage lair from which the wind was rushing was the sea; and that the small bundle of shivers growing afraid of it all, and beginning to cry, was Pip. . . ."

And there we were, in amongst the gravestones at the beginning of *Great Expectations*, the chill and dampness in the air, the fog drifting in from the sea. On the far side of the graveyard a small boy was crouched among the weathered stones, talking to himself as he stared at two gravestones set to one side. But there was someone else there. In fact, there were a *group* of people, digging away at an area just outside the churchyard walls. They were illuminated in the fading light by two electric lamps powered by a small generator that hummed to itself some distance away.

"Who are they?" I whispered.

"Okay," hissed Havisham, not hearing me straightaway, "now we jump to wherever we want by— What did you say?"

I nodded in the direction of the group. One of their number pushed a wheelbarrow along a plank and dumped it onto a large heap of spoil.

"Good heavens!" exclaimed Miss Havisham, walking briskly toward the small group. "It's Commander Bradshaw!"

I trotted after her and I soon saw that the digging was of an archaeological nature. Pegs were set in the ground and joined by lengths of string, delineating the area in which the volunteers were scraping with trowels, all trying to make as little noise as possible. Sitting on a folding safari seat was a man dressed like a big game hunter. He wore a safari suit and pith helmet and sported both a monocle and a large and bushy mustache. He was also barely three feet tall. When he got up from his chair, he was shorter.

" 'pon my word, it's the Havisham girlie!" he said in a hoarse whisper. "You're looking younger every time I see you!"

Miss Havisham thanked him and introduced me. Bradshaw shook me by the hand and welcomed me to Jurisfiction.

"What are you up to, Trafford?" asked Havisham.

"Archaeology for the Charles Dickens Foundation, m'girl. A few of their scholars are of the belief that *Great Expectations* began not in this churchyard but in Pip's house when his parents were still alive. There is no manuscriptual evidence, so we thought we'd have a little dig around the environs and see if we could pick up any evidence of previously overwritten scenes."

"Any luck?"

"We've struck a reworked idea that ended up in *Our Mutual Friend*, a few dirty limericks and an unintelligible margin squiggle—but nothing much."

Havisham wished him well, and we said our goodbyes and left them to their dig.

"Is that unusual?"

"You'll find around here that there is not much that *is* usual," replied Havisham. "It's what makes this job so enjoyable. Where did we get to?"

"We were going to jump into the pre-book backstory."

"I remember. To jump forwards we have only to concentrate on the page number or, if you prefer, a specific event. To go backwards *before* the first page we have to think of *negative* page numbers or an event that we assume had happened before the book began."

"How do I picture a negative page number?"

"Visualize something—an albatross, say."

"Yes?"

"Okay, now take the albatross away."

"Yes?"

"Now take *another* albatross away."

"How can I? There are no albatrosses left!"

"Okay; imagine I have lent you an albatross to make up your seabird deficit. How many albatrosses have you now?"

"None."

"Good. Now relax while I take my albatross back."

I shivered as a coldness swept through me and for a fleeting moment an empty vaguely albatross-shaped void opened and closed in front of me. But the strange thing was, for that briefest moment I *understood* the principle involved—but then it was gone like a dream upon waking. I blinked and stared at Havisham.

"That," she announced, "was a negative albatross. Now you try it—only use page numbers instead of albatrosses."

I tried hard to picture a negative page number, but it didn't work and I found myself in the garden of Satis House, watching two boys square up for a fight. Miss Havisham was soon beside me.

"What are you doing?"

"I'm trying—"

"You are *not,* my girl. There are two sorts of people in this world, doers and tryers. You are the latter and I am trying to make you the former. Now concentrate, girl!"

So I had another attempt at the negative page number idea and this time found myself in a curious tableau *resembling* the graveyard in Chapter One but with the graves, wall and church little more than cardboard cutouts. The two featured characters, Magwitch and Pip, were also very two-dimensional and as still as statues—except that their eyes swiveled to look at me as I jumped in.

"Oi," hissed Magwitch between clenched teeth, not moving a muscle. "Piss off."

"I'm sorry?"

"Piss *off!*" repeated Magwitch, this time more angrily.

I was just pondering over all this when Havisham caught up with me, grabbed my hand and jumped to where we were meant to be.

"What was that?" I asked.

"The frontispiece. You're not a natural at this, are you?"

"I'm afraid not," I replied, feeling like a bit of a clot.

"Never mind," said Miss Havisham in a kindlier tone, "we'll make a Prose Resource Operative out of you yet."

We walked down the darkened jetty to where Havisham's boat was moored. But it wasn't any old boat. It was a polished-wood and gleaming-chrome Riva. I stepped aboard the beautifully built motor launch and stowed the gear as Miss Havisham sat in the skipper's seat.

Miss Havisham seemed to take on a new lease of life when confronted by anything with a powerful engine. I cast off when she ordered me to and pushed off into the oily black waters of the Thames. The boat rocked slightly as I sat down next to Havisham, who fired up the twin Chevrolet petrol engines with a throaty growl and then gently piloted our way into the darkness of the river. I pulled two cloaks from the bag, donned one and took the other to Miss Havisham, who was standing at the helm, the wind blowing through her gray hair and tugging at her tattered veil.

"Isn't this a bit anachronistic?" I asked.

"Officially *yes*," replied Havisham, weaving to avoid a small jolly-boat, "but we're actually in the backstory minus one day, so I could have brought in a fleet of Harrier jump jets and the entire Ringling Brothers circus and no one would be any the wiser. If we had to do this any time *during* the book then we'd be stuck with whatever was available—which can be a nuisance."

We were moving upriver against a quickening tide. It had gone midnight and I was glad of the cloak. Billows of fog blew in from the sea and gathered in great banks that caused Miss Havisham to slow down; within twenty minutes the fog had closed in and we were alone in the cold and clammy darkness. Miss Havisham shut down the engines and doused the navigation lights, and we gently drifted in with the tide.

"Sandwich and soup?" said Miss Havisham, peering in the picnic basket.

"Thank you, ma'am."

"Do you want my wagonwheel?"

"I was about to offer you mine."

We heard the prison ships before we saw them, the sound of men coughing and cursing and the occasional shout of fear. Miss Havisham started the engines and idled slowly in the direction of the sounds. Then the mist parted and we could see the prison hulk appear in front of us as a large black shape that rose from the water, the only light visible the oil lamps that flickered through the gunports. The old man-of-war was secured fore and aft by heavily rusted anchor chains against which flotsam had collected in a tangle. After checking the name of the ship Miss Havisham slowed down and stopped the engines. We drifted down the flanks of the prison hulk, and I used the boathook to fend us off. The gunports were above us and out of reach, but as we moved silently down the ship we came across a homemade rope draped from a window on the upper gun deck. I quickly fastened the boat to a projecting ring, and the motor launch swung around and settled facing the current.

"Now what?" I hissed.

Miss Havisham pointed to the life preserver, and I quickly tied it onto the end of the homemade rope.

"That's it?" I asked.

"That's it," replied Miss Havisham. "Not much to it, is there? Wait—! Look there!"

She pointed to the side of the prison hulk, where a strange creature had attached itself to one of the gunports. It had large batlike wings folded untidily across the back of its body, which was covered by patchy tufts of matted fur. It had a face like a fox, sad brown eyes and a long thin beak that was inserted deep into the wood of the gunport. It was oblivious to us both and made quiet sucky noises as it fed.

Miss Havisham raised her pistol and fired. The bullet struck close by the strange creature, which uttered a startled cry of "Gawk!," unfolded its large wings and flew off into the night.

"Blast!" said Miss Havisham, lowering her gun and pushing the safety back on. "Missed!"

The noise had alerted the guards on the deck.

"Who's there?" yelled one. "You had better be on the king's business or by St. George you'll feel the lead from my musket!"

"It's Miss Havisham," replied Havisham in a vexed tone, "on Jurisfiction business, Sergeant Wade."

"Begging your pardon, Miss Havisham," replied the guard apologetically, "but we heard a gunshot!"

"That was me," yelled Havisham. "You have grammasites on your ship!"

"Really?" replied the guard, leaning out and looking around. "I don't see anything."

"It's gone now, you dozy idiot," said Havisham to herself, quickly adding: "Well, keep a good lookout in future—if you see any more I want to know about them *immediately!*"

Sergeant Wade assured her he would, bade us both good-night, then disappeared from view.

"What on earth is a grammasite?" I asked, looking nervously about in case the odd-looking creature should return.

"A parasitic life form that live inside books and feed on

grammar," explained Havisham. "I'm no expert, of course, but that one looked suspiciously like an adjectivore. Can you see the gunport it was feeding on?"

"Yes."

"Describe it to me."

I looked at the gunport and frowned. I had expected it to be old or dark or wooden or rotten or wet, but it wasn't. But then it wasn't sterile or blank or empty either—it was simply a gunport, nothing more nor less.

"The adjectivore feeds on the adjectives *describing* the noun," explained Havisham, "but it generally leaves the noun intact. We have verminators who deal with them, but there are not enough grammasites in Dickens to cause any serious damage—yet."

"How do they move from one book to the next?" I asked, wondering if Mycroft's bookworms weren't some sort of grammasite-in-reverse.

"They seep through the covers using a process called oozemosis. That's why individual bookshelves are never more than six feet long in the library—you'd be well advised to follow the same procedure at home. I've seen grammasites strip a library to nothing but indigestible nouns and page numbers. Ever read Sterne's *Tristram Shandy*?"

"Yes."

"Grammasites."

"I have a lot to learn," I said softly.

"Agreed," replied Havisham. "I'm trying to get the Cat to write an updated travelbook that includes a bestiary, but he has a lot to do in the library—and holding a pen is tricky with paws. Come on, let's get out of this fog and see what this motor launch can do."

As soon as we were clear of the prison ship, Havisham started the engines and slowly powered back the way we had come, once again keeping a careful eye on the compass but even so nearly running aground six times.

"How did you know Sergeant Wade?"

"As the Jurisfiction representative in *Great Expectations* it is my business to know everybody. If there are any problems, then they must be brought to my attention."

"Do all books have a rep?"

"All the ones that have been brought within the controlling sphere of Jurisfiction."

The fog didn't lift. We spent the rest of that cold night steering in amongst the moored boats at the side of the river. Only when dawn broke did we see enough to manage a sedate ten knots.

We returned the boat to the jetty and Havisham insisted I jump us both back to her room at Satis House, which I managed to accomplish at the first attempt, something that helped me recover some lost confidence over the debacle with the frontispiece. I lit some candles and saw her to bed before returning alone to the stores, and Wemmick. I had the second half of the docket signed, filled out a form for a missing life vest and was about to return home when a very scratched and bruised Harris Tweed appeared from nowhere and approached the counter where I was standing. His clothes were tattered and he had lost one boot and most of his kit. It looked like *The Lost World* hadn't really agreed with him. He caught my eye and pointed a finger at me.

"Don't say a word. Not a *single* word!"

Pickwick was still awake when I got in even though it was nearly 6 a.m. There were two messages on the answer machine—one from Cordelia, and another from a *very annoyed* Cordelia.

# 27.

## Landen and Joffy Again

George Formby was born George Hoy Booth in Wigan in 1904. He followed his father into the music hall business, adopted the ukulele as his trademark and by the time the war broke out was a star of variety, pantomime and film. During the first years of the war, he and his wife, Beryl, toured extensively for ENSA, entertaining the troops as well as making a series of highly successful movies. By 1942 he and Gracie Fields stood alone as the nation's favorite entertainers. When invasion of England was inevitable, many influential dignitaries and celebrities were shipped out to Canada. George and Beryl elected to stay and fight, as George put it, "to the last bullet on the end of Wigan pier!" Moving underground with the English resistance and various stalwart regiments of the Local Defense Volunteers, Formby manned the outlawed "Wireless St. George" and broadcast songs, jokes and messages to secret receivers across the country. Always in hiding, always moving, the Formbys used their numerous contacts in the north to smuggle allied airmen to neutral Wales and form resistance cells that harried the Nazi invaders. Hitler's order of 1944 to "have all ukuleles and banjos in England burnt" was a clear indication of how serious a threat he was considered to be. George's famous comment after peace was declared, "ee, turned out nice again!," became a national catchphrase. In postwar republican England he was made nonexecutive president for life, a post he held until his assassination.

JOHN WILLIAMS,
*The Extraordinary Career of George Formby*

**I**T WAS AFTER two or three days of plain LiteraTec work and a dull weekend without Landen that I found myself lying awake and staring at the ceiling, listened to the clink-clink of milk bottles and the click-click of Pickwick's feet on the linoleum as she meandered around the kitchen. Sleep patterns never came out quite right in reengineered species; no one knew why. There had been no *major* coincidences over the past few days, although on the night of Joffy's exhibition the two SpecOps-5 agents who had been assigned to watch Slorter and Lamme died in their car as a result of carbon monoxide poisoning. It seemed their car had a faulty exhaust. Lamme and Slorter had been following me around very indiscreetly for the past two days. I just let them get on with it; they weren't bothering me—or my unseen assailant. If they had, they'd as likely as not be dead.

But there was more than just SO-5 to worry about. In three days the world would be reduced to a sticky mass of sugar and proteins—or so my father said. I had seen the pink and gooey world for myself, too, but then I had *also* seen myself shot at Cricklade Skyrail station, so the future wasn't *exactly* immutable—thank goodness. There had been no advance on the forensic report; the pink slime matched to no known chemical compound. Coincidentally, next Thursday was also the day of the general election, and Yorrick Kaine looked set to make some serious political gain thanks to his "generous" sharing of *Cardenio*. Mind you, he was still taking no chances—the first public unveiling of the text was not until the day *after* the election. The thing was, if the pink gunge got a hold, Yorrick Kaine could have the shortest career as a prime minister ever. Indeed, next Thursday could be the last Thursday for all of us.

I closed my eyes and thought of Landen. He was there as I best remembered him: seated in his study with his back to me, oblivious to everything, writing. The sunlight streamed in through the window and the familiar clacketty-clack of his old Underwood typewriter sounded like a fond melody to my ears.

He stopped occasionally to look at what he had written, make a correction with the pencil clenched between his teeth, or just pause for pause's sake. I leaned on the doorframe for a while and smiled to myself. He mumbled a line he had written, chuckled to himself and typed faster for a moment, hitting the carriage return with a flourish. He typed quite animatedly in this fashion for about five minutes until he stopped, took out the pencil and slowly turned to face me.

"Hey, Thursday."

"Hey, Landen. I didn't want to disturb you; shall I—?"

"No, no," he said hurriedly, "this can wait. I'm just pleased to see you. How's it going out there?"

"Boring," I told him despondently. "After Jurisfiction, SpecOps work seems as dull as ditchwater. Flanker at SO-1 is still on my back, I can feel Goliath breathing down my neck, and this Lavoisier character is using me to get to Dad."

"Can I do anything to help?"

So I sat on his lap and he massaged the back of my neck. It was heaven.

"How's Junior?"

"Junior is smaller than a broadbean—little more to the left—but making himself known. The Lucozade keeps the nausea at bay most of the time; I must have drunk a swimming pool of it by now."

There was a pause.

"Is it mine?" he asked.

I held him tightly but said nothing. He understood and patted my shoulder.

"Let's talk about something else. How are you getting along at Jurisfiction?"

"Well," I said, blowing my nose loudly, "I'm not a natural at this bookjumping lark. I want you back, Land, but I'm only going to get one shot at 'The Raven,' and I need to get it right. I've not heard from Havisham for nearly three days—I don't know when the next assignment will be."

Landen shook his head slowly.

"Sweetness, I don't want you to go into 'The Raven.' "

I looked up at him.

"You heard me. Leave Jack Schitt where he is. How many people would have died for him to make a packet out of that plasma rifle scam? One thousand? Ten thousand? Listen, your memory may grow fuzzy, but I'll still be here, the good times—"

"But I don't want just the good times, Land. I want *all* the times. The shitty ones, the arguments, that annoying habit you had of always trying to make the next filling station and running out of petrol. Picking your nose, farting in bed. But more than that, I want the times that haven't happened yet—the future. *Our* future! I *am* getting Schitt out, Land—make no mistake about that."

"Let's talk about something else *again*," said Landen. "Listen—I'm a bit worried about someone trying to kill you with coincidences."

"I can look after myself."

He looked at me solemnly.

"I don't doubt it for one moment. But I'm only alive in your memories—and some mewling and puking ones of my mum's I suppose—and without you I'm nothing at all, *ever*—so if whoever is juggling with entropy gets lucky next time, you and I are both for the high jump—but at least you get a memorial and a SpecOps regulation headstone."

"I see your point, however muddled you might make it. Did you see how I manipulated coincidences in the last entropic lapse to find Mrs. Nakajima? Clever, eh?"

"Inspired. Now, can you think of *any* linking factor—except the intended victim—that connects the three attacks?"

"No."

"Are you sure?"

"Positive. I've thought it through a thousand times. Nothing."

Landen thought for a moment, tapped a finger on his temple and smiled.

"Don't be so sure. I've been having a little peek myself, and, well, I want to show you something."

And there we were, on the platform of the Skyrail station at South Cerney. But it wasn't a moving memory, like the other ones I had enjoyed with Landen, it was frozen like a stilled video image—and like a stilled video image, it wasn't very good; all blurry and a bit jumpy.

"Okay, what now?" I asked as we walked along the platform.

"Have a look at everyone. See if there is anyone you recognize."

I stepped onto the shuttle and walked round the players in the fiasco, who were frozen like statues. The faces that were most distinct were the neanderthal driver-operator, the well-heeled woman, the woman with Pixie Frou-Frou and the woman with the crossword. The rest were vague shapes, generic female human forms and little else—no mnemonic tags to make them unique. I pointed them out.

"Good," said Landen, "but what about her?"

And there she was, the young woman sitting on the bench in the station, doing her face in a makeup mirror. We walked closer and I looked intently at the nondescript face that loomed dimly out of my memory.

"I only glimpsed her for a moment, Land. Slightly built, mid-twenties, red shoes. So what?"

"She was here when you arrived, she's on the southbound platform, all trains go to all stops—yet she *didn't* get the Skyrail. Suspicious?"

"Not really."

"No," said Landen, sounding crestfallen, "not exactly a smoking gun, is it? Unless," he smiled, "unless you look at this."

The Skyrail station folded back to be replaced by the area near the Uffington white horse on the day of the picnic. I looked up nervously. The large Hispano-Suiza automobile was hanging motionless in the air not fifty feet up.

"Anything spring to mind?" asked Landen.

I looked around carefully. It was another bizarre frozen vignette. Everyone and everything was there—Major Fairwelle, Sue Long, my old croquet captain, the mammoths, the gingham tablecloth, even the bootleg cheese. I looked at Landen.

"Nothing, Land."

"Are you sure? Look again."

I sighed and scanned their faces. Sue Long, an old school friend whose boyfriend set his own trousers on fire for a bet; Sarah Nara, who lost her ear at Bilohirsk on a training accident and ended up marrying General Spottiswode; croquet pro Alf Widdershaine, who taught me how to "peg out" all the way from the forty-yard line. Even the previously unknown Bonnie Voige was there, and—

"Who's this?" I asked, pointing at a shimmering memory in front of me.

"It's the woman who called herself Violet De'ath," answered Landen. "Does she seem familiar?"

I looked at her blank features. I hadn't given her a second thought at the time, but something about her *was* familiar.

"Sort of," I responded. "Have I seen her somewhere before?"

"You tell me, Thursday," Landen said, shrugging. "It's *your* memory. But if you want a clue, look at her shoes."

And there they were. Bright red shoes that just *might* have been the same ones on the girl at the Skyrail platform.

"There's more than one pair of red shoes in Wessex, Land."

"You're right," he observed. "I did say it was a long shot."

I had an idea, and before Landen could say another word we were in the square at Osaka with all the Nextian-logoed Japanese, the fortune-teller frozen in mid-beckon, the crowd around us an untidy splash of visual noise that is the way crowds appear to the mind's eye, the logos I remembered jutting out in sharp contrast to the unremembered faces. I peered through the crowd as I anxiously searched for anything that might resemble a young European woman.

"See anything?" asked Landen, hands on hips and surveying the strange scene.

"No," I replied. "Wait a minute, let's come in a bit earlier."

I took myself back a minute and there she was, getting up from the fortune-teller's chair the moment I first saw him. I walked closer and looked at the vague shape. I squinted at her feet. There, in the haziest corner of my mind, was the memory I was looking for. The shoes were *definitely* red.

"It's her, isn't it?" asked Landen.

"Yes," I murmured, staring at the wraithlike figure in front of me. "But it doesn't help; none of these memories are strong enough for a positive ID."

"Perhaps not on their *own,*" observed Landen. "But since I've been in here I've figured out a few things about how your memory works. Try and *superimpose* the images."

I thought of the woman on the platform, placed her across the vague form in the market and then added the specter who had called herself De'ath. The three images shimmered for a bit before they locked together. It wasn't great. I needed more. I pulled from my memory the half-shredded picture that Lamme and Slorter had shown me. It fitted perfectly, and Landen and I stared at the result.

"What do you think?" asked Landen. "Twenty-five?"

"Possibly a little older," I muttered, looking closer at the amalgam of my attacker, trying to fix it in my memory. She had plain features, a small amount of makeup and blond hair cut in an asymmetric bob. She didn't look like a killer. I ran through all the information I had—which didn't take long. The failed SpecOps-5 investigations allowed me a few clues: the recurring name of Hades, the initials A.H., the fact that she *did* resolve on pictures. Clearly it wasn't Acheron in disguise, but perhaps—

"Oh, *shit*."

"What?"

"It's Hades."

"It can't be. You killed him."

"I killed *Acheron*. He had a brother named Styx—why couldn't he have a sister?"

We exchanged nervous looks and stared at the mnemonograph in front of us. Some of her features *did* seem to resemble Acheron now that I stared at her. Like Hades, she was tall and her lips were thin. That alone would not have been enough; after all, many people are tall with thin lips, and few, if any, are evil geniuses. But her eyes were unmistakable—they had a sort of brooding *darkness* to them.

"No wonder she's pissed off with you," murmured Landen. "You killed her brother."

"Thanks for that, Landen," I replied. "Always know how to relax a girl."

"Sorry. So we know the H in A.H. is *Hades*—what about the A?"

"The Acheron was a tributary of the river Styx," I said quietly. "As was the Phlegethon, Cocytus, Lethe—and *Aornis*."

I'd never felt so depressed at having identified a suspect before. But something was niggling at me. There was something here that I *couldn't* see, like listening to a TV from another room. You hear dramatic music but you have no idea what's going on.

"Cheer up," smiled Landen, rubbing my shoulder, "she's ballsed it up three times already—it might never happen!"

"There's something *else*, Landen."

"What?"

"Something I've forgotten. Something I never remembered. Something about—I don't know."

"It's no good asking me," replied Landen. "I may *seem* real to you, but I'm not—I'm only here as your *memory* of me. I can't know any more than you do."

Aornis had vanished and Landen was starting to fade.

"You've got to go now," he said in a hollow-sounding voice. "Remember what I said about Jack Schitt."

"Don't go!" I yelled. "I want to stay here for a bit. It's not much fun out here at the moment, I think it's Miles's baby, Aornis wants to kill me and Goliath and Flanker—"

But it was too late. I'd woken up. I was still in bed, undressed, bedclothes rumpled. The clock told me it was a few minutes past nine. I stared at the ceiling in a forlorn mood, wondering how I could really have got myself into such a mess, and then wondering if there was anything I could have done to prevent it. I decided, on the face of it, probably not. This, to my fuddled way of thinking, I took to be a positive sign, so I slipped on a T-shirt and shuffled into the kitchen, filled the kettle and put some dried apricots in Pickwick's bowl after trying and failing once again to get her to stand on one leg.

I shook the entroposcope just in case—was thankful to find everything normal—and was just checking the fridge for some fresh milk when the doorbell rang. I trotted out to the hall, picked up my automatic from the table and asked: "Who is it?"

"Open the door, Doofus."

I put the gun away and opened the door. Joffy smiled at me as he entered and raised his eyebrows at my disheveled state.

"Half day today?"

"I don't feel like working now that Landen's gone."

"Who?"

"Never mind. Coffee?"

We walked into the kitchen. Joffy patted Pickwick on the head, and I emptied the old grounds out of the coffee jug. He sat down at the table.

"Seen Dad recently?"

"Last week. He was fine. How much did you make on the art sale?"

"Over £2,000 in commission. I thought of using the cash to repair the church roof but then figured, what the hell—I'll just blow it on drink, curry and prostitutes."

I laughed.

"Sure you will, Joff."

I rinsed some mugs and stared out of the window.

"What can I do for you, Joff?"

"I came round to pick up Miles's things."

I stopped what I was doing and turned to face him.

"Say that again."

"I said I'd come—"

"I *know* what you said, but, but—how do you know Miles?"

Joffy laughed, saw I was serious, frowned at me and then remarked: "He *said* you didn't recognize him that night at Vole Towers. Is everything okay?"

I shrugged. "Not really, Joff—but tell me: How do you know him?"

"We're going out, Thurs—surely you can't have forgotten?"

"You and Miles?"

"Sure! Why not?"

This was *very* good news indeed.

"Then his clothes are in my apartment because—"

"—we borrow it every now and then."

I tried to grasp the facts.

"You borrow my apartment because it's . . . secret—?"

"Right. You know how old-fashioned SpecOps are when it comes to their staff fraternizing with clerics."

I laughed out loud and wiped away the tears that had sprung to my eyes.

"Sis?" said Joffy, getting up. "What's the matter?"

I hugged him tightly.

"Nothing's the matter, Joff. Everything's *wonderful!*—I'm not carrying his baby!"

"Miles?" said Joff. "Wouldn't know how. Wait a minute, sis—you've got a bun in the oven? Who's the father?"

I smiled through my tears.

"It's Landen's," I said with a renewed confidence. "By God it's Landen's!"

And I jumped up and down overwhelmed by the sheer joy of the fact, and Joffy, who had nothing better to do, joined me in jumping up and down until Mrs. Scroggins in the apartment below banged on the ceiling with a broom handle.

"Sister dearest," said Joffy as soon as we had stopped, "who in St. Zvlkx's name is Landen?"

"Landen Parke-Laine," I gabbled happily. "The Chrono-Guard eradicated him, but something *other* happened and I still have his child, so it's all *meant* to come out right, don't you see? And I *have* to get him back because if Aornis *does* get to me then he'll *never* exist ever ever ever—and neither will the baby and I can't stand that idea and I've been farting around for too long so I'm going to go into 'The Raven' no matter what—because *if I don't I'm going to go nuts!*"

"I'm more than happy for you," said Joffy slowly. "You've

completely lost your tiny doofus-like mind, but I'm very happy for you, in spite of it."

I ran into the living room, rummaged across my desk until I found Schitt-Hawse's calling card and rang the number. He answered in less than two rings.

"Ah, Next," he said with a triumphant air. "Changed your mind?"

"I'll go into 'The Raven' for you, Schitt-Hawse. Double-cross me and I'll maroon both you and your half brother in the worst Daphne Farquitt novel I can find. Believe me, I can do it—and will do it, if necessary."

There was a pause.

"I'll send a car to pick you up."

The phone went dead and I placed the receiver back on the cradle. I took a deep breath, shooed Joffy out of the door once he had collected Miles's stuff, then had a shower and got dressed. My mind was set. I would get Landen back, no matter what the risks. I was still lacking a coherent plan, but this didn't bother me that much—I seldom did.

# 28.

## "The Raven"

"The Raven" was undoubtedly Edgar Allan Poe's finest and most famous poem, and was his own personal favorite, being the one he most liked to recite at poetry readings. Published in 1845, the poem drew heavily on Elizabeth Barrett's "Lady Geraldine's Courtship," something he acknowledged in the original dedication but had conveniently forgotten when explaining how he wrote "The Raven" in his essay "The Philosophy of Composition"—the whole affair tending to make nonsense of Poe's attacks on Longfellow as a plagiarist. A troubled genius, Poe also suffered the inverse cash/ fame law—the more famous he became, the less money he had. "The Gold Bug," one of his most popular short stories, sold over 300,000 copies but netted him only $100. With "The Raven" he fared even worse. Poe's total earnings for one of the greatest poems in the English language were a paltry $9.

MILLON DE FLOSS,
*Who Put the Poe in Poem?*

THE DOORBELL RANG as I was putting my shoes on. But it wasn't Goliath. It was Agents Lamme and Slorter. I was really quite glad to see that they were still alive; perhaps Aornis didn't regard them as a threat. I wouldn't.

"Her name's Aornis Hades," I told them as I hopped up and down, trying to pull my other shoe on, "sister of Acheron.

Don't even *think* of tackling her. You know you're close when you stop breathing."

"Wow!" exclaimed Lamme, patting his pockets for a pen. "*Aornis* Hades! How did you figure that out?"

"I glimpsed her several times over the past few weeks."

"You must have a good memory," observed Slorter.

"I have help."

Lamme found a pen, discovered it didn't work and borrowed a pencil off his partner. The point broke. I lent him mine.

"What was her name again?"

I spelled it out for him and he wrote it down so slowly it was painful.

"Good!" I said once they had finished. "What are you guys doing here, anyway?"

"Flanker wants a word."

"I'm busy."

"You're not busy anymore," replied Slorter, looking very awkward and wringing her hands. "I'm sorry about this—but you're under arrest."

"What for *now*?"

"Possession of an illegal substance."

This was an interesting development. He'd obviously not found the cause of tomorrow's Armageddon and was attempting a little framing to make me compliant. I had thought he would try something of the sort, but now wasn't the time. I had a appointment in "The Raven" I needed to keep.

"Listen, guys, I'm not just busy, I'm *really* busy, and Flanker sending you along with some bullshit trumped-up charge is just wasting your time and mine."

"It's *not* trumped up," said Slorter, holding out an arrest warrant. "It's cheese. *Illegal* cheese. SO-1 found a block of flattened cheese under a Hispano-Suiza with your prints all over it.

It was part of a cheese seizure, Thursday. It should have been consigned to the furnaces."

I groaned. It was just what Flanker wanted. A simple internal charge that usually meant a reprimand—but could, if needed, result in a custodial sentence. A solid gold arm-twister, in other words. Before the two agents could even draw breath I had slammed the door in their faces and was heading out the fire escape. I heard them yell at me as I ran out onto the road, just in time to be picked up by Schitt-Hawse. It was the first and last time I would ever be pleased to see him.

So there I was, unsure if I had just got out of the frying pan and into the fire or out of the fire and into the frying pan. I had been frisked for weapons and a wire and they had taken my automatic, keys and Jurisfiction travelbook. Schitt-Hawse drove and I was sitting in the backseat—wedged tightly between Chalk and Cheese.

"I'm kind of glad to see you, in a funny sort of way."

There was no answer, so I waited ten minutes and then asked: "Where are we going?"

This didn't elicit a response either, so I patted Chalk and Cheese on the knees and said: "You guys been on holiday this year?"

Chalk looked at me for a moment, then looked at Cheese and answered: "We went to Majorca," before he lapsed back into silence.

An hour later we arrived at Goliath's Research & Development Facility at Aldermaston. Surrounded by triple fences of razor wire and armed guards patrolling with full-sized sabertooths, the complex was a labyrinth of aluminum-clad windowless buildings and concrete bunkers interspersed with electrical substations and large ventilation ducts. We were waved through the gate and parked in a layby next to a large marble Goliath logo where Chalk, Cheese and Schitt-Hawse offered up a short prayer of contrition and unfailing devotion to the corporation. That done, we were on our way again past thousands of yards of pipework, buildings, parked military vehicles, trucks and all manner of junk.

"Be honored, Next," said Schitt-Hawse. "Few are blessed with seeing this far into the workings of our beloved corporation."

"I feel more humbled by the second, Mr. Schitt-Hawse."

We drove on to a low building with a domed concrete roof. This was of an even higher security than the main entrance, and Chalk, Cheese and Schitt-Hawse had to have their half-windsor tie knots scanned for verification. The guard on duty opened a heavy blast door that led to a brightly lit corridor which in turn contained a row of elevators. We descended to lower ground twelve, went through another security check and then along a shiny corridor past doors either side of us that had brass placards screwed to the polished wood explaining what went on inside. We walked past *Electronic Computing Engines, Tachyon Communications, Square Peg in a Round Hole* and stopped at *The Book Project*. Schitt-Hawse opened the door and we entered.

The room was quite like Mycroft's laboratory apart from the fact that the devices seemed to have been built to a much higher degree of quality and had actually cost some money. Where my uncle's machines were held together with baler twine, cardboard and rubber solution glue, the machines in here had all been crafted from high-quality alloys. All the testing apparatus looked brand-new, and there was not an atom of dust anywhere. It was chaos—but *refined* chaos. There were about a half-dozen technicians, all of whom seemed to have a certain pallid disposition as though they spent most of their life indoors, and they looked at us curiously as we walked in—I don't suppose they saw many strange faces. In the middle of the room was a doorway a little like a walk-through metal detector; it was tightly wrapped with thousands of yards of fine copper wire. The wire ended in a tight bunch the width of a man's arm that led away to a large machine that hummed and clicked to itself. As we walked in, a technician pulled a switch, there was a crackle and a puff of smoke, and everything went dead. It *was* a Prose Portal, but more relevant to the purposes of this narrative, it didn't work.

I pointed to the copper-bound doorway in the middle of the room. It had started to smoke, and the technicians were now trying to put it out with $CO_2$ extinguishers.

"Is that *thing* meant to be a Prose Portal?"

"Sadly, yes," admitted Schitt-Hawse. "As you may or may not know, all we managed to synthesize was a form of curdled stodgy gunge from volumes one to eight of *The World of Cheese.*"

"Jack Schitt said it was cheddar."

"Jack always tended to exaggerate a little, Miss Next. This way."

We walked past a large hydraulic press which was rigged in an attempt to open one of the books that I had seen at Mrs. Nakajima's apartment. The steel press groaned and strained but the book remained firmly shut. Further on a technician was valiantly attempting to burn a hole in another book, with similar poor results, and after that another technician was looking at an X-ray photograph of the book. He was having a little trouble as two or three thousand pages of text and numerous other "enclosures" all sandwiched together didn't lend themselves to easy examination.

"What do these books do, Next?"

I was in no mood for a show-and-tell; I was here to get Landen back, nothing more.

"Do you want me to get Jack Schitt out or not?"

He stared at me for a moment before dropping the subject and walking on past several other experiments, down a short corridor and through a large steel door to another room that contained a table, chair—and Lavoisier. He was reading the copy of *The Poems of Edgar Allan Poe* as we entered. He looked up.

"Monsieur Lavoisier, I understand you already know Miss Next?" asked Schitt-Hawse.

"We did some time together," I replied slowly, staring at Lavoisier, who seemed a great deal older and distinctly ill at ease with the situation. I got the impression he didn't like Goliath any more than I did. He didn't say anything; he just nodded his head in greeting, shut the book and rose to his feet. We stood in silence for a moment.

"So go on," said Schitt-Hawse finally, "do your booky stuff, and Lavoisier will reactualize your husband as though nothing had happened. No one will ever know he had gone—except you, of course."

I bit my lip. This was one of the biggest chances I was ever likely to take. I would try and capitalize on Lavoisier's apparent dislike of Goliath—after all, the ChronoGuard had no interest in Landen or Jack Schitt—and there was more than one way to trap my father. I was going to have to risk it.

"I need more than just your promise, Schitt-Hawse."

"It's not *my* promise, Next—it's a Goliath Guarantee. Believe me, it's riveted iron."

"So was the *Titanic*," I replied. "In my experience a Goliath Guarantee guarantees *nothing*."

He stared at me and I stared back.

"Then what do you want?" he asked.

"One: I want Landen reactualized as he was. Two: I want my

travelbook back and safe conduct from here. Three: I want a signed confession admitting that you employed Lavoisier to eradicate Landen."

I gazed at him steadily, hoping my audacity would strike a positive nerve.

"One: Agreed. Two: You get the book back *afterwards*. You used it to vanish in Osaka, and I'm not having that again. Three: I can't do."

"Why not?" I asked. "Bring Landen back and the confession is irrelevant, because it never happened—but I can use it if you *ever* try anything like this again."

"Perhaps," put in Lavoisier, "you would accept this as a token of my intent."

He handed me a brown hard-back envelope. I opened it and pulled out a picture of Landen and me at our wedding.

"I have nothing to gain from your husband's eradication and everything to lose, Miss Next. Your father, well, I'll get to him eventually. But you have the word of a commander in the ChronoGuard—if that's good enough."

I looked at Lavoisier, then at Schitt-Hawse, then at the photo. It was the one that used to sit on the mantelpiece at my mother's house.

"Where did you get this?"

"In another time, another place," replied Lavoisier. "And at considerable personal risk to myself, I assure you. Landen is nothing to us, Miss Next—I am only here to help Goliath. Once done I can leave them to their nefarious activities—and not before time."

Schitt-Hawse shuffled slightly and glared at Lavoisier. It was clear they mistrusted each other deeply; it could only work to my advantage.

"Then let's do it," I said finally. "But I need a sheet of paper."

"Why?" asked Schitt-Hawse.

"Because I have to write a detailed description of this charming dungeon to be able to get *back*, that's why."

Schitt-Hawse nodded to Chalk, who gave me a pen and paper, and I sat down and wrote the most detailed description that I could. The travelbook said that five hundred words was adequate for a solo jump, a thousand words if you were to bring anyone with you, so I wrote fifteen hundred just in case. Schitt-Hawse looked over my shoulder as I wrote, checking I wasn't writing another destination.

"I'll take that back, Next," said Schitt-Hawse, retrieving the pen as soon as I had finished. "Not that I don't trust you or anything."

I took a deep breath, opened the copy of *The Poems of Edgar Allan Poe* and read the first verse to myself:

> Once upon a midnight dreary, while I pondered weak and
>     weary,
> O'er a plan to venge myself upon that cursed Thursday
>     Next—
> This Eyre affair, so surprising, gives my soul such loath
>     despising,
> Here I plot my temper rising, rising from my jail of text.
> "Get me out!" I said, advising, "Pluck me from this jail of
>     text—
> or I swear I'll wring your neck!"

He was still pissed off, make no mistake about *that*. I read on:

> Ah, distinctly I remember it was in my bleak September
> when that loathsome SpecOps member tricked me through
>     "The Raven's" door.
> Eagerly I wished the morrow would release me from this
>     sorrow,

then a weapon I will borrow, Sorrow *her* turn to explore—
I declare that obnoxious maiden who is little but a
    whore—
darkness hers—for evermore!

"Still the same old Jack Schitt," I murmured.

"I won't let him lay a finger on you, Miss Next," assured Schitt-Hawse. "He'll be arrested before you can say ketchup."

So, gathering my thoughts, I offered my apologies to Miss Havisham for being an impetuous student, cleared my mind and throat and then read the words out loud, large as life and clear as a bell.

There was a distant rumble of thunder and the flutter of wings close to my face. An inky blackness fell and a wind sprang up and whistled about me, tugging at my clothes and flicking my hair into my eyes. A flash of lightning briefly illuminated the sky about me, and I realized with a start that I was high above the ground, hemmed in by clouds filled with the ugly passion of a tempest in full spate. The rain struck my face with a sudden ferocity, and I saw in the feeble moonlight that I was being swept along close to a large storm cloud, illuminated from within by bolts of lightning. Just when I thought that perhaps I had made a *very* big mistake by attempting this feat without proper instruction, I noticed a small dot of yellow light through the swirling rain. I watched as the dot grew bigger until it wasn't a dot but an oblong, and presently this oblong became a window, with frames, and glass, and curtains beyond. I flew closer and faster, and just when I thought I must collide with the rain-splashed glass I was *inside,* wet to the skin and quite breathless.

The mantel clock struck midnight in a slow and steady

rhythm as I gathered my thoughts and looked around. The furniture was of highly polished dark oak, the drapes a gloomy shade of purple, and the wall coverings, where not obscured by bookshelves or morbid mezzotints, were a dismal brown color. For light there was a solitary oil lamp that flickered and smoked from a poorly trimmed wick. The room was in a mess; the bust of Pallas lay shattered on the floor, and the books that had once graced the shelves were now scattered about the room with their spines broken and pages torn. Worse still, some books had been used to rekindle the fire; a choked profusion of blackened paper had fallen from the grate and now covered the hearth. But to all of this I paid only the merest attention. Before me was the poor narrator of "The Raven" himself, a young man in his mid-twenties seated in a large armchair, bound and gagged. He looked at me imploringly and mumbled something behind the gag as he struggled with his bonds. As I removed the gag the young man burst forth in speech as though his life depended upon it:

" *'Tis some visitor,"* he said urgently and rapidly, *"tapping at my chamber door—only this and nothing more!"*

And so saying, he disappeared from view into the room next door.

"Damn you, Sebastian!" said a chillingly familiar voice from the adjoining room. "I would pin you to your chair if this poetical coffin had seen so fit as to furnish me with hammer and nails—!"

But the speaker stopped abruptly as he entered the room and saw me. Jack Schitt was in a wretched condition. His previously neat crew cut had been replaced by straggly hair and his thin features were now covered with a scruffy beard; his eyes were wide and haunted and hung with dark circles from lack of sleep. His sharp suit was rumpled and torn, his diamond tiepin lacking in luster. His arrogant and confident manner had given way to a lonely desperation, and as his eyes met mine I saw tears spring up and his lips tremble. It was, to a committed Schitt-hater like myself, a joyous spectacle.

"Thursday!" he croaked in a strangled cry. "Take me back! Don't let me stay one more second in this vile place! The endless clock striking midnight, the tap-tap-tapping, the raven—oh my good God, the *raven!*"

He fell to his knees and sobbed as the young man bounded happily back into the room and started to tidy up as he muttered: " *'Tis some visitor entreating entrance at my chamber door—!*"

"I'd be more than happy to leave you here, Mr. Schitt, but I've cut a deal. C'mon, we're going home."

I grasped the Goliath agent by the lapel and started to read the description of the vault back at Goliath R&D. I felt a tug on my body and another rush of wind, the tapping increased, and I just had time to hear the student say, *"Sir or Madam, truly your forgiveness I implore . . ."* when we found ourselves back in the Goliath lab at Aldermaston. I was pleased with this, as I hadn't thought it would be that easy, but all my feelings of self-satisfaction vanished when, instead of being arrested, Jack was hugged warmly by his half brother.

"Jack—!" said Schitt-Hawse happily. "Welcome back!"

"Thank you, Brik—how's Mum?"

"She had to have her hip done."

"Again—?"

"Wait a minute!" I interrupted. "How about *your* part of the deal?"

The two Schitts stopped chattering for a moment.

"All in good time, Miss Next," murmured Schitt-Hawse with an unpleasant grin. "We need you to do one or two *other* small jobs before your husband is reactualized."

"The hell I will," I said angrily, taking a step forward as Chalk put a massive hand on my shoulder. "What happened to the riveted-iron Goliath Guarantee?"

"Goliath don't do promises," replied Schitt-Hawse slowly as Jack stood blinking stupidly. "The profit margin is too low. I want you to remain our guest for a while—a woman with your talents is far too useful to lose. You may actually quite like it here."

"Lavoisier!" I yelled, turning to the Frenchman. "*You* promised! The word of a commander in the ChronoGuard—!"

He stared at me coldly.

"After what you did to me," he said tersely, "this is the most glorious revenge possible. I hope you rot in hell."

"What did I ever do to you?"

"Oh, nothing *yet*," he replied, readying himself to leave, "but you *will*."

I stared at him coldly. I didn't know what I was going to do to him, but I hoped it was painful.

"Yes," I replied in a quieter voice, "you can count on it."

He walked from the room without looking back.

"Thank you, monsieur!" shouted Schitt-Hawse after him. "The wedding picture was a touch of genius!"

I leaped forward to grab Schitt-Hawse but was pinned down by Chalk and Cheese. I struggled long, hard—and hopelessly. My shoulders sagged and I stared at the ground. Landen had been right. I should have walked away.

"I want to wring her ghost upon the floor," said Jack Schitt, staring in my direction, "to still this beating of my heart. Mr. Cheese, your weapon."

"No, Jack," said Schitt-Hawse. "Miss Next and her unique attributes could open up a large and *highly* profitable market to exploit."

Schitt rounded on his half brother.

"Do you have any idea of the fantastic terrors I've just been through? Tapping—I mean *trapping*—me in 'The Raven' is something Next is *not* going to live to regret. No, Brik, the bookslut *will* surcease my sorrow—!"

Schitt-Hawse held Jack by the shoulders and shook him.

"Snap out of that 'Raven' talk, Jack. You're home now. Listen: The bookslut is potentially worth *billions*."

Schitt stopped and gathered his thoughts.

"Of course," he murmured finally. "A vast untapped resource of consumers. How much useless rubbish do you think we can offload on those ignorant masses in nineteenth-century literature?"

"Indeed," replied Schitt-Hawse, "and our unreprocessed waste—*finally* an effective disposal location. *Untold* riches await the corporation. And listen—if it doesn't work out, *then* you can kill her."

"When do we start?" asked Schitt, who seemed to be growing stronger by the second in the life-giving warmth of corporate avarice.

"It depends," said Schitt-Hawse, looking at me, "on Miss Next."

"I'd sooner die," I told them. I meant it, too.

"Oh!" said Schitt-Hawse. "Hadn't you heard? As far as the outside world is concerned you're dead already! Did you think you could see all that was going on here and live to tell the tale?"

I tried to think of some sort of way to escape, but there was nothing to hand—no weapon, no book, nothing.

"I really haven't decided," continued Schitt-Hawse in a patronizing tone, "whether you fell down a lift shaft or blundered into some machinery. Do you have any preferences?"

And he laughed a short and very cruel laugh. I said nothing. There didn't seem to be anything I *could* say.

"I'm afraid, my girl," said Schitt-Hawse as they started to file out the vault door, taking my travelbook with them, "that you are a guest of the corporation for the rest of your natural life. But it won't all be bad. We *will* be willing to reactualize your husband. You won't actually meet him again, of course, but he will be alive—so long as you cooperate, and you will, you know."

I glared at the two Schitts.

"I will never help you, as long as I have breath in my lungs."

Schitt-Hawse's eyelid twitched.

"Oh, you'll help us, Next—if not for Landen, then for your child. Yes, we know about that. We'll leave you for now. And you needn't bother looking for any books in here to pull your vanishing trick—we made *quite* sure there were none!"

He smiled again and stepped out of the vault. The door slammed shut with a reverberating boom that shook me to the core. I sat down on one of the chairs, put my head in my hands and cried tears of frustration, anger—and loss.

# 29.

## Rescued

Miss Havisham's extraction of Thursday from the Goliath vault is the stuff that legends are built on. The thing was, not only had no one ever done it before, no one had even *thought* of doing it before. It put them both on the map and earned Havisham her eighth cover on the Jurisfiction trade paper, *Movable Type,* and Thursday her first. It cemented the bond between them. In the annals of Jurisfiction there were notable partnerships such as Beowulf & Sneed, Falstaff & Tiggywinkle, Voltaire & Flark. That night Havisham & Next emerged as one of the greatest pairings Jurisfiction would ever see. . . .

UNITARY AUTHORITY OF WARRINGTON CAT,<br>
Jurisfiction Journals

**T**HE MOST NOTICEABLE THING about being locked in a vault twelve floors below ground at the Goliath R&D lab was not the isolation, but the *silence.* There was no hum of air-conditioning, no odd snatch of conversation heard through the door, nothing. I thought about Landen, about Miss Havisham, Joffy, Miles and then the baby. What, I wondered, did Schitt-Hawse have in store for him? I got up and paced around the vault, which was lit by harsh striplights. There was a large mirror on the wall that I had to assume was some kind of watching gallery. There was a toilet and shower in a room behind, and a bedroll and a few toiletries in a locker that someone had left out for me.

I spent twenty minutes searching the few nooks and crannies of the room, hoping to find a discarded trashy novel or something that might effect me an escape. There was nothing—not so much as a pencil shaving, let alone a pencil. I sat on the only chair, closed my eyes and tried to visualize the library and remember the description in my travelbook, and I even recited aloud the opening passage to *A Tale of Two Cities*, something I had learned at school many years ago. My bookjumping skills were nonexistent without a text to read from, but there was nothing to lose, so I tried every quote, passage and poem I had ever committed to memory from Ovid to de la Mare. When I ran out of those I switched to limericks—and ended up telling Bowden's jokes out loud. Nothing. Not so much as a flicker.

I unrolled the bedroll, lay on the floor and closed my eyes, hoping to remember Landen again and discuss the problem with him. It wasn't to be. At that moment the ring that Miss Havisham had given me grew almost unbearably hot, there was a sort of *fworpish* noise, and a figure was standing next to me.

It was Miss Havisham, and she didn't look terribly pleased. Before I could tell her how relieved I was to see her she pointed a finger at me and said: "You, young lady, are in a *lot* of trouble!"

"Tell me about it."

This wasn't the sort of careless remark she liked to hear from me, and she certainly expected me to jump to my feet when she arrived, so she rapped me painfully on the knee with her stick.

"Ow!" I said, getting the message and rising. "Where did you spring from?"

"Havishams come and go as they please," she replied imperiously. "Why on earth didn't you tell me?"

"I—I didn't think you'd approve of me leaping into a book

on my own—especially not Poe," I muttered sheepishly, expecting a tirade of abuse—Vesuvius, in fact. But it didn't happen. Miss Havisham's ire was from *quite* a different direction.

"I couldn't care less about *that*," remarked Miss Havisham haughtily. "What you do in your own time to cheap reprints is no concern of mine!"

"Oh," I said, contemplating her stern features and trying to figure out what I *had* done wrong.

"You should have said *something!*" she said, taking another pace towards me.

"About the baby?" I stammered.

"No, idiot—about *Cardenio!*"

"*Cardenio?*"

There was a faint clank from the door as someone fiddled with the lock. Havisham's arrival, it seemed, had been observed.

"It'll be Chalk and Cheese," I told her. "You'd better jump out of here."

"Absolutely not!" replied Havisham. "We go together. You might be a complete and utter imbecile, but you *are* my responsibility. Trouble is, fourteen feet of concrete is slightly daunting—I'm going to have to *read* us out. Quick, pass me your travelbook!"

"They took it from me."

The door opened and Schitt-Hawse entered; he was grinning fit to burst.

"Well, well," he said, "lock up a bookjumper and another soon joins her!"

He took one look at Havisham's old wedding dress and put two and two together.

"Goodness! Is that . . . Miss Havisham?"

As if in answer, Havisham whipped out her small pistol and fired it in his direction. Schitt-Hawse gave a yelp and leaped back out the door, which clanged shut.

"We need a book," said Miss Havisham grimly. "Anything will do—even a pamphlet."

"There's nothing in here, Miss Havisham."

She looked around.

"Are you sure? There must be *something*!"

"I've looked—there's nothing!"

Miss Havisham raised an eyebrow and looked me up and down.

"Take off your trousers, girl—and don't say 'what?' in that impudent manner. Do as you're told."

So I did, and Havisham turned the garment over in her fingers as she searched for something.

"There!" she cried triumphantly as the door opened and a hissing gas canister was lobbed in. I followed her gaze but she had found only—*the washing label*. I must have looked incredulous, for she said in an offended manner: "It's enough for me!" and then repeated out loud: "*Wash inside out, wash and dry separately, wash inside out, wash and dry separately . . .*"

We surfed in on the pungent smell of washing detergent and overheated iron. The landscape was dazzling white and was without depth; my feet were firmly planted on ground, yet I could see nothing but white surrounding my shoes when I looked down, the same as the view above me and to either side. Miss Havisham, whose dirty dress seemed even more shabby than usual in the white surroundings, was looking around the lone inhabitants of this strange and empty world: five bold icons the size of garden sheds that stood neatly in a row like standing stones. There was a crude tub with the number 60 on it, an iron shape, a tumble-dryer shape and a couple of others that I wasn't too sure about. I touched the first icon, which felt warm to the touch and very comforting; they all seemed to be made of compressed cotton.

"What were you saying about *Cardenio*?" I asked, still wondering why she was so angry.

"Yes, yes, *Cardenio*," she replied crossly, examining the large washing icons with interest. "Just how likely was it for a pristine copy of a missing play to just pop up out of the blue like that?"

"You mean," I said, the penny finally dropping, "it's a Great Library copy?"

"Of *course* it's a library copy. That fog-headed pantaloon Snell only just reported it, and we need your help to get it back— What are these big shape things?"

"Iconographic *representations* of washing instructions," I told her as I put my trousers back on.

"Hmm," responded Miss Havisham. "This could be tricky. We're inside a washing label, but there are none of those in the library—we need to jump into a book which *is*. I can do it without text, but I need a target book to head for. Is there a book written about washing labels?"

"Probably," I replied, "but I've no idea what it might be called." I had an idea. "Does it have to be a book about washing labels?"

Havisham raised an eyebrow, so I carried on.

"Washing machine instructions *always* carry these icons, explaining what they mean."

"Hmm," said Miss Havisham thoughtfully. "Do *you* have a washing machine?"

Fortunately, I did—and more fortunately still, it was one of the things that had survived the sideslip. I nodded excitedly.

"Good. Now, more important, do you know the make and model?"

"Hoover Electron 1000—no! *800* Deluxe—I think."

"Think? You *think*? You'd better be sure, girl, or you and I will be nothing more than carved names on the Boojumorial! Now. Are you *sure*?"

"Yes," I said confidently. "Hoover Electron 800 Deluxe."

She nodded, placed her hands on the tub icon and concentrated hard, teeth clenched and her face red with the effort. I took hold of her arm, and after a moment or two in which I could feel Miss Havisham shake with exertion, we had jumped out of the washing label and into the Hoover instructions.

*"Don't allow the drain hose to kink as this could stop the machine from emptying,"* said a small man in a blue Hoover boiler suit standing next to a brand-new washing machine. We were standing in a sparkling clean washroom that was barely ten feet square. It had neither windows nor door—just a belfast sink, tiled floor, hot and cold inlet taps and a single plug on the wall. For furniture a bed was pushed against the corner, and next to it was a chair, table and cupboard.

*"Do remember that to start a program you must pull out the program control knob.* Sorry," he said, "I'm being read at the moment. I'll be with you in a sec. *If you have selected white nylon, minimum iron, delicate or . . ."*

"Thursday—!" said Miss Havisham, who suddenly seemed weak at the knees and whose face had turned the same color as her wedding dress. "That took quite some—"

I just managed to catch her as she collapsed; I gently laid her down on the small truckle bed.

"Miss Havisham? Are you okay?"

She patted my arm encouragingly, smiled and closed her eyes. I could see she was pleased with herself—even if the jump had worn her out.

I pulled the single blanket over her, sat on the edge of the low bed, pulled my hair tie out and rubbed my scalp. My trust in Havisham was implicit, but it was still a bit unnerving to be stuck in Hoover instructions.

*". . . until the drum starts to rotate. Your machine will empty*

*and spin to complete the program. . . .* Hello!" said the man in the boiler suit. "The name's Cullards—I don't often get visitors!"

"Thursday Next," I told him, shaking his hand. "This is Miss Havisham of Jurisfiction."

"Goodness!" said Mr. Cullards, scratching his shiny bald head and smiling impishly. "Jurisfiction, eh? You *are* off the beaten track. The only visitor I've had was—excuse me— *Control setting D: Whites economy, lightly soiled cotton or linen articles which are color-fast to boiling*—was the time we had a new supplement regarding woolens—but that would have been six or seven months ago. Where *does* the time go?"

He seemed a cheerful enough chap. He thought for a moment and then said: "Would you like a cup of tea?"

I thanked him and he put the kettle on.

"So what's the news?" asked Mr. Cullards, rinsing out his one and only cup. "Any idea when the new washing machines are due out?"

"I'm sorry," I said, "I have no idea—"

"I'm about ready to move on to something a bit more modern. I started on vacuum cleaner instructions but was promoted to Hoovermatic T5004, then transferred to the Electron 800 after twin-tub obsolescence. They asked me to take care of the 1100 Deluxe, but I told them I'd sooner wait until the Logic 1300 came out."

I looked around at the small room.

"Don't you ever get bored?"

"Not at all!" said Cullards, pouring the hot water into the teapot. "Once I've put in my ten years I'm eligible to apply for work in *all* domestic appliance instructions: food mixers, liquidizers, microwaves—who knows, if I work *really* hard I could make it into television or wireless. *That's* the future for an ambitious manual worker. Milk and sugar?"

"Please."

He leaned closer.

"Management have this idea that only young 'uns should do Sound & Vision instructions, but they're wrong. Most of the kids in VCR manuals barely do six months in Walkmans before they're transferred. It's little wonder no one can understand them."

"I never thought of that before," I confessed.

We chatted for the next half hour. He told me he had begun French and German classes so he could apply for work in multilingual instructions, then confided in me his fondest feelings for Tabitha Doehooke, who worked for Kenwood Mixers. We were just talking about the sociological implications of labor-saving devices within the kitchen and how they related to the women's movement when Miss Havisham stirred.

"Compeyson—!" she muttered without waking. "You lying, stealing, thieving, hound of a . . ."

"Miss Havisham?" I asked.

She stopped mumbling and opened her eyes.

"Next, my girl," she gasped. "I need—"

"Yes?" I asked, leaning closer.

"—a cup of tea."

"Can do!" said Mr. Cullards cheerfully, pouring out a fresh cup. Miss Havisham sat up, drank three cups of tea and also ate the biscuit that Cullards was reserving for his birthday next May. I introduced the Hoover instructionalist, and Miss Havisham nodded politely before announcing we would have to be off.

We said our goodbyes and Mr. Cullards made me promise I would clean out the powder dispenser on my washer; in an unguarded moment I had let slip I had yet to do so, despite the washer's being nearly three years old.

*     *     *

The short trip to the nonfiction section of the Great Library was an easy jump for Miss Havisham, and from there we *fworped* back into her dingy ballroom in *Great Expectations*, where the Cheshire Cat and Harris Tweed were waiting for us, talking to Estella. The Cat seemed quite relieved to see us both, but Harris simply scowled.

"Estella!" said Miss Havisham abruptly. "*Please* don't talk to Mr. Tweed."

"Yes, Miss Havisham," replied Estella meekly.

Havisham replaced her trainers with the less comfortable wedding shoes.

"I have Pip waiting outside," said Estella slightly nervously. "If you will excuse me mentioning it—ma'am is a paragraph *late*."

"Dickens can just flannel for a bit longer," replied Havisham. "I must finish with Miss Next."

She turned to me with a grim look; I thought I'd better say something to soothe her—I hadn't yet seen Havisham lose her temper and I was in no hurry to do so.

"Thank you for my rescue, ma'am," I said quickly. "I'm very grateful to you."

"Humph!" replied Miss Havisham. "Don't expect salvation from me every time you get yourself into a jam, my girl. Now, what's all this about a *baby?*"

The Cheshire Cat, sensing trouble, vanished abruptly on the pretext of some "cataloguing," and even Tweed mumbled something about checking *Lorna Doone* for grammasites and went too.

"Well?" asked Havisham again, peering at me quite intensely.

I didn't feel quite as frightened of her as I once did, so I thought I should come clean and tell her everything. I told her all about Landen's eradication, the offer from Goliath, Jack

Schitt in "The Raven" and even Mycroft's Prose Portal. Just for good measure I finished up by telling her how much I was in love with Landen and how I'd do *anything* to get him back.

"For love? Pah!" she answered, dismissing Estella with a wave of her hand in case the young woman got any odd ideas. "And what, in your tragically limited experience, is *that?*"

She didn't seem to be losing her temper, so, emboldened, I continued: "I think you know, ma'am. You were in love once, I believe?"

"Stuff and nonsense, girl!"

"Isn't the pain you feel *now* the equal to the love you felt *then?*"

"You're coming perilously close to contravening my Rule Two!"

"I'll tell you what love is," I told her. "It is blind devotion, unquestioning self-humiliation, utter submission, trust and belief against yourself and against the whole world, giving up your whole heart and soul to the smiter!"

"That was quite good," said Havisham, looking at me curiously. "Could I use that? Dickens won't mind."

"Of course."

"I think," said Miss Havisham after a few moments of deliberation, "that I shall categorize your complex marital question under *widowed*, which sits with me well enough. Upon reflection—and quite possibly against my better judgment— you may stay as my apprentice. That's all. You are needed to help retrieve *Cardenio*. Go!"

So I left Miss Havisham in her darkened chamber with all the trappings of her wedding that never was. In the few days I had known her I had learned to like her a great deal, and hoped someday I might repay her kindness and match her fortitude.

# 30.

## *Cardenio* **Rebound**

**PageRunner:** Any character who is out of his or her book and moves through the backstory (or more rarely the plot) of another book. PageRunners may be lost, vacationing, part of the Character Exchange Program or criminals, intent on mischief. (See: Bowdlerizers)

**Texters:** Slang term given to a relatively harmless PageRunner (q.v.) (usually juvenile) who surfs from book to book for adventure and rarely appears in the frontstory but does, on occasion, cause small changes to text and/or plot lines.

UNITARY AUTHORITY OF WARRINGTON CAT,
*The Jurisfiction Guide to BookJumping* (glossary)

HARRIS TWEED and the Cheshire Cat took me back to the library. We sat on a bench in front of the Boojumorial and Harris stared at me while the Cat—who was nothing if not courteous—went to get me a pasty from the snack bar just next to Mr. Wemmick's storeroom.

"Where did she find you?" snapped Harris. I was getting used to his aggressive mannerisms by now. If he thought as little of me as he made out, then I wouldn't be here at all.

The Cat popped his head up between us and said: "Hot or cold pasty?"

"Hot, please."

"Okay then," he said, and vanished again.

I explained Havisham's leap from the Goliath vault to the washing label; Tweed was clearly impressed. He had been apprenticed to Commander Bradshaw many years previously, and Bradshaw's accuracy in bookjumping was as poor as Havisham's was good—hence the commander's interest in maps.

"A washing label. Now that *is* impressive," mused Harris. "Not many PROs would even attempt to jump blind into less than a hundred words. Havisham took quite a risk with you, Miss Next. Cat, what do you think?"

"I think," said the Cat, handing me a steaming hot pasty, "that you've forgotten the Moggilicious cat food you promised, hmm?"

"Sorry," I replied. "Next time."

"Okay," said the Cat.

"Right," said Harris. "To business. Tell me, who are the chief players in *Cardenio's* discovery?"

"Well," I began, "there's Lord Volescamper, an hereditary peer. He *said* he found it in his library. Amiable chap—bit of a duffer. Then there's Yorrick Kaine, a Whig politician who hopes to use the free distribution of the play to sway the Shakespeare vote in his favor at tomorrow's election."

"I'll see if I can find which book they're from—if at all," said the Cat, and vanished.

"Is that really likely?" I asked. "Volescamper has been around since before the war, and Kaine has been on the political scene for at least five years."

"It means nothing, Miss Next," replied Harris impatiently. "Mellors had a wife and family in Slough for two decades and Heathcliff worked in Hollywood for three years under the name of Buck Stallion—no one suspected a thing in either case."

"But *Cardenio,*" I asked, "it *is* the library's copy, yes?"

"Without a doubt. Despite elaborate security arrangements,

someone managed to swipe it from under the Cat's whiskers—he's very upset about it."

"Did you say *fig*, or *whig*?" inquired the Cat, who had reappeared.

"I said *Whig*," I replied. "And I wish you wouldn't keep appearing and vanishing so suddenly: you make one quite giddy."

"All right," said the Cat; and this time he vanished quite slowly, beginning with the end of his tail, and ending with his grin.

"He doesn't *seem* terribly upset," I observed.

"Looks can be deceptive—in the Cat's case, trebly so. We heard about *Cardenio* only yesterday. It nearly gave the Bellman a fit. He was all for putting together one of his madcap and typically Boojum-ridden expeditions. As soon as I found out that Kaine was going to make *Cardenio* public property, I knew we had to act and act fast."

"But listen," I said, my head spinning slightly with all this new intelligence, "why is it so important that *Cardenio* remain lost? It's a *brilliant* play."

"I wouldn't expect you to understand," replied Tweed crossly, "but believe me, there are extremely good reasons why *Cardenio* must stay lost. Listen, it's no accident that only seven out of Aeschylus' hundred or so plays survive, or that *Paradise Lost Once More* will never be known."

"Why?"

"Don't ask," replied Tweed shortly. "And besides, if the rest of the bookworld figures out there is something to gain by swiping library books, then we could be in one hell of a state."

"Okay," I returned, quite used to secretive policing divisions at SpecOps, "so why am I here?"

"Clearly, this is no place for an apprentice, but you know the layout of Vole Towers as well as having met the key suspects. Do you know where *Cardenio* is kept?"

"In a combination-and-key safe within the library itself."

"Good. But first we need to get in. Can you remember any of the other books in the library?"

I thought for a moment.

"There was a rare first edition of *Decline and Fall* by Evelyn Waugh."

"Come on then," he said abruptly. "No time for dawdling. We're off."

We took the elevator to Floor W of the library, found the copy we were looking for and were soon within the book, tiptoeing past a noisy party in the quad at Scone College. Tweed concentrated on the outward jump, and a few moments later we were standing inside the locked library at Vole Towers.

"Cat," said Harris, looking around at the untidy library, "you there?"[1]

"A simple 'Yes' will do. Send the safecrackers in by way of a first of *Decline and Fall*. If they come across Captain Grimes, they are not to lend him money *on any account*. Anything on Volescamper or Kaine?"[2]

"Blast!" exclaimed Tweed. "Too much to hope they'd be stupid enough to use their own names."

Two men suddenly appeared next to us, and Harris pointed them in the direction of the safe. One wore a fine evening dress; the other was attired in a more sober woolen suit and carried a holdall that once opened revealed an array of beautifully crafted safecracking tools. After running an expert eye over the safe for a few moments the elder of the two removed his jacket, took

1. "Loud and clear, whiskers pressed, fed and watered, boots on and laced, ready to—"
2. "Not yet—none of the names appear in the register of fictioneers—I'm just going through the reams of unpublished characters from the Well of Lost Plots—it might take some time."

the stethoscope proffered to him by his companion and listened to the safe as he gently turned the combination wheel.

"Is that Raffles?" I whispered. "The gentleman thief?"

Harris nodded, checking his watch.

"With his assistant, Bunny. If anyone can, they can."

"So who do you think stole *Cardenio*?"

"A good one for tricky questions, aren't you, Next? We have a suspect list as long as your arm—there are several million possible contenders in the bookworld, and any one of them could have gone rogue, jumped out of their book, swiped *Cardenio* and legged it over here."

"So how do you tell whether someone is an impostor or not?"

Harris looked at me.

"With great difficulty. Do you think I belong here, in your world?"

I looked at the short man with the elegant tweed herringbone suit and touched him gently on the chest with a finger. He was as real to me as anyone I had ever met, either within books or without. He breathed, smiled, scowled—how was I meant to tell?

"I don't know. Are you from a 1920s detective novel?"

"Wrong," replied Harris. "I'm as real as you are. I work three days a week for Skyrail as a signals operator. But how could I *prove* that? I could just as easily be a minor character in an obscure novel somewhere. The only sure way to tell would be to place me under observation for two months—that's about the limit any bookperson can stay outside their book. But enough of this. Our first priority is to get the manuscript back. After that, we can start figuring out who is who."

"There's no quicker way?"

"Only one other that I know of. No bookperson is going to take a bullet; if you try and shoot one, chances are they'll jump."

"It sounds a bit like testing for witches. If they sink and drown, they're innocent—"

"It's not ideal," said Harris gruffly. "I'm the first to admit that."

Within half an hour Raffles had worked out the combination and now turned his attention to the secondary locking mechanism. He was slowly drilling a hole above the combination knob, and the quiet squeaking of the drill bit seemed inordinately loud to our heightened nerves. We were staring at him and silently urging him to go faster when a noise from the library's heavy door made us turn. Harris and I leaped to either side as the unlocking wheel spun to draw the steel tabs from the slots in the iron frame, and the door swung slowly open. Raffles and Bunny, well used to being disturbed, silently gathered up their tools and hid beneath a table.

"The manuscript will be released to the publishers first thing tomorrow morning," said Kaine as he and Volescamper strolled in. Tweed pointed his automatic at them, and they jumped visibly. I pushed the door shut behind them and spun the locking mechanism.

"What is the meaning of this?" said Volescamper in an outraged voice. "Miss Next? Is that you?"

"As large as life, Volescamper. I'm sorry, I have to search you."

The two of them meekly acquiesced to a searching; they were unarmed, but Yorrick Kaine had turned a deep shade of crimson during the process.

"Thieves!" he spat. "How dare you!"

"No," replied Harris, beckoning them further into the room and signaling for Raffles to continue with his work, "we have only come to retrieve *Cardenio*—something that does not belong to either of you."

"Now look here, I don't know what you're talking about," began Volescamper, who was visibly outraged. "This house is surrounded by SO-14 agents—there is no escape. And as for you, Miss Next, look here, I am deeply disappointed by your perfidy!"

"What do you reckon?" I said to Harris. "His indignation *seems* real."

"It does—but he has less to gain from this than Kaine."

"You're right—my money's on Kaine."

"What are you *talking* about?!" demanded Kaine angrily. "The manuscript belongs to literature—how do you think you can sell something like this on the open market? You may think you can get away with it, but I will die before I allow you to remove the literary heritage that belongs to all of us!"

"Well, I don't know," I added. "Kaine is pretty convincing too."

"Remember, he's a politician."

"Of course," I returned, snapping my fingers. "I'd forgotten. What if it's neither?"

I didn't have time to answer as there was a crash from somewhere near the front of the house and the sound of an explosion. A low guttural moan reached our ears, followed by the terrified scream of a man in mortal terror. A shiver ran up my spine and I could see that everyone else in the room had felt it too. Even the implacable Raffles paused for a moment before returning to work with just a little bit more urgency.

"Cat!" exclaimed Harris. "What's going on?"[3]

"The Questing Beast?" exclaimed Tweed. "The *Glatisant*? Summon King Pellinore *immediately*."[4]

"The Questing Beast?" I asked. "Is that bad?"

"Bad?" replied Harris. "It's the *worst*. Think loathsome, think repulsive, think evil, think of escape. The Questing Beast was

3. "I hope I'm mistaken but you've got the Questing Beast approaching from the southeast—one hundred yards and closing."
4. "He's in *Middlemarch* at the moment. I'll try him on the footnoterphone—but you know how deaf he is."

born in the oral tradition *before* books; an amalgam of every dark and fetid horror that ever sprang from the most depraved recesses of the human imagination—all rolled into one foul-smelling package. It has many names, but its goal is always the same: death and destruction. As soon as it comes through the door anyone still in here will be stone cold dead."

"*Through* the vault door?"

"There is no barrier yet created that can withstand the Questing Beast, except a Pellinore—they have hunted it for years!"

Harris turned to Kaine and Volescamper.

"But there's one thing it does tell us. One of you *is* fictional. One of you has invoked the Questing Beast. I want to know who it is!"

Kaine and Volescamper looked at Tweed, then at me, at each other and finally at the steel door as we heard another low moan. The light machine gun at the front door fell silent and a splintering of wood met our ears as the Questing Beast forced its way through the main entrance and moved its odious form closer to the library.

"Cat!" yelled Tweed again. "Where's that King Pellinore I asked for?"[5]

"Keep trying," muttered Tweed. "We've still got a few minutes. Next—have *you* any ideas?"

For once, I didn't. With loathsome creatures from the id *outside,* a fictional person pretending to be real *inside* and me in the middle wondering quite what I was doing here in the first place, creative thought wasn't exactly high on my agenda. I mumbled an apology and shook my head.

There was a crunching sound as the Questing Beast made its

5. "He's not answering. Do you know, this reminds me of the time the Demogorgon met Medusa in the 1923 Miss Loathsome competition—"

way down the corridor amidst screams of terror and sporadic rifle fire.

"Raffles?" yelled Tweed. "How long?"

"Two minutes, old chum," replied the safecracker without pausing or looking up. He had finished drilling the hole, made a small cup out of clay and stuck it against the side of the safe and was now pouring in what looked like liquid nitrogen.

The battle outside seemed to increase in ferocity. There were shouts, concussions from grenades, screams and the rattle of automatic weaponry until, after an almighty crash that shook the ceiling lights and toppled books from their shelves, all was quiet.

We looked at one another. Then a gentle tap rang out, like the tip of a spear struck against the other side of the steel door. There was a pause, then another.

"Thank goodness!" said Tweed in relief. "King Pellinore must have arrived and seen it off. Next, open the door."

But I didn't. Suspicious of loathsome beasts from the deepest recesses of the human imagination, I stayed my hand. It was as well that I did. The next blow was harder. The blow following *that* was harder still; the vault door shook.

"Blast!" exclaimed Tweed. "Why is there *never* a Pellinore around when you need one? Raffles, we don't have much time—!"

"Just a few minutes more . . ." replied Raffles quietly, tapping the safe door with a hammer while Bunny pulled on the brass handle.

Tweed looked at me as the library door buckled under another heavy blow; a split opened up in the steel, and the locking wheel sheared off and dropped to the ground. It wasn't a question of *if* the Glatisant got in, it was a question of *when*.

"Okay," said Tweed reluctantly, grabbing my elbow in anticipation of a jump, "that's it. Raffles, Bunny, out of here!"

"Just a few moments longer . . ." replied the safecracker with his usual calm. Raffles was used to fine deadlines and didn't like to give up on a safe, no matter what the possible consequences.

The steel door buckled once more and the rent in the steel grew wider as the Questing Beast charged it with a deafening crash. Books fell off the shelves in a cloud of dust and a foul odor began to fill the air. Then, as the Questing Beast readied itself for another blow, I had the one thing that had eluded me for the past half hour. *An idea.* I pulled Tweed close to me and whispered in his ear.

"No!" he said. "What if—?"

I explained again, he smiled and I began:

"So one of you is fictional," I announced, looking at them both.

"And we have to find out who it is," remarked Tweed, leveling his pistol in their direction.

"Might it be Yorrick Kaine—" I added, staring at Kaine, who glared back at me, wondering what we were up to,

"—failed right-wing politician—"

"—with a cheery enthusiasm for war—"

"—and putting a lid on civil liberties?"

Tweed and I bantered lines back and forth for as long as we dared, faster and faster, the blows from the beast outside matching the blows from Raffles's hammer within.

"Or perhaps it is Volescamper—"

"—lord of the *old* realm, who wants—"

"—to try and get—"

"—back into power with the help—"

"—of his friends at the Whig party?"

"*But* the important thing is, in all this dialogue—"

"—that has pitched back and forth between—"

"—the two of us, a *fictional* person—"

"—might have lost track of which one of us is talking."

"And do you know, in all the excitement, *I kind of forgot myself!*"

There was another crash against the door. A splinter of steel flew off and zipped past my ear. The doors were almost breached; with the next blow the abomination would be upon us.

"So you're going to have to ask yourselves one simple question: *Which one of us is speaking now?*"

"You are!" yelled Volescamper, pointing—correctly—at me. Kaine, revealing his fictional roots by his inability to follow undedicated dialogue, pointed his finger—at *Tweed*.

He corrected himself quickly, but it was too late for the politician, and he knew it. He scowled at the two of us, trembling with rage. His charming manner seemed to desert him as we sprang the trap; suaveness gave way to snarling, smooth politeness to clumsy threats.

"Now listen," growled Kaine, trying to regain control of the situation, "you two are in way over your heads. Try to arrest me and I can make things *very* difficult for you—one footnoterphone call from me and the pair of you will spend the next eternity on grammasite watch inside the *OED*."

But Tweed was made of stern stuff, too.

"I've closed bloopholes in *Dracula* and *Biggles Flies East*," he replied evenly. "I don't frighten easily. Call off the Glatisant and put your hands on your head."

"Leave *Cardenio* here with me—if only until tomorrow," added Kaine, changing tack abruptly and forcing a smile. "In return I can give you *anything* you want. Power, cash—an earldom, Cornwall, character exchange into Hemingway—you name it, Kaine will provide!"

"You have nothing of any value to bargain with, Mr. Kaine," Tweed told him, his hand tightening on his pistol. "For the last time—"

But Kaine had no intention of being taken, alive or otherwise. He cursed us both to a painful excursion in the twelfth circle of hell and melted from view as Tweed fired. The slug buried itself harmlessly in a complete set of bound *Punch* magazines. At the same time the steel doors burst open. But instead of a pestilential hell-beast conjured from the depths of mankind's most degenerate thoughts, only an icy rush of air entered, bringing with it the lingering smell of death. The Questing Beast had vanished as quickly as its master, back to the oral tradition and any books unfortunate enough to feature it.

"Cat!" yelled Tweed as he reholstered his gun. "We've got a PageRunner. I need a bookhound ASAP!"[6]

Volescamper sat down on a handy chair and looked bewildered.

"You mean," he stammered incredulously, "look here, Kaine was—?"

"—entirely fictional—yes," I replied, laying a hand on his shoulder.

"You mean *Cardenio* didn't belong to my grandfather's library after all?" he asked, his confusion giving way to sadness.

"I'm sorry, Volescamper," I told him. "Kaine stole the manuscript. He used your library as a front."

"And if I were you," added Tweed in a less kindly aside, "I should just go upstairs and pretend you slept all through this. You never saw us, never heard us, you know *nothing* of what happened here."

"Bingo!" cried Raffles as the handle on the safe turned, shattering the frozen lock inside and creaking open. Raffles handed me the manuscript before he and Bunny vanished back to their own book with only the thanks of Jurisfiction to show for the night's efforts—a valuable commodity on their side of the law.

6. "Coming up!"

I passed *Cardenio* to Tweed. He rested a reverential hand on the play and smiled a rare smile.

"An undedicated dialogue trap, Next—quick thinking. Who knows, we might make a Jurisfiction agent of you yet."

"Well, thank—"

"Cat!" bellowed Tweed again. "Where's that blasted bookhound?"[7]

A large and sad-looking bloodhound appeared from nowhere, looked at us both lugubriously, made a sort of hopeless doggy-sigh and then started to sniff the books scattered on the floor in a professional manner. Tweed snapped a lead on the dog's collar.

"If I was the sort of person to apologize," he conceded, straining at the leash of the bookhound, who had locked onto the scent of one of Kaine's expletives, "I would. Join me in the hunt for Kaine?"

It was tempting, but I remembered Dad's prediction—and there was Landen to think of.

"I have to save the world tomorrow," I announced, surprising myself by just how matter-of-fact I sounded. Tweed, on the other hand, didn't seem in the least surprised.

"Oh!" he said. "Well, another time, then. On sir, seek, *away!*"

The bookhound gave an excited bark and leaped forward; Tweed hung grimly to the leash and they both disappeared into fine mist and the smell of hot paper.

"I suppose," said Lord Volescamper, interrupting the silence in a glum voice, "that this means I won't be in Kaine's government after all?"

"Politics is overrated," I told him.

"Perhaps you're right," he agreed, getting up. "Well, goodnight,

7. "Any second now, Tweedy."

Miss Next. I didn't see anything, didn't hear anything, is that right?"

"Nothing at all."

Volescamper sighed and looked at the shattered remains of the interior of his house. He picked his way to the twisted steel door and turned to face me.

"Always was a heavy sleeper. Look here, pop round for tea and scones one day, why don't you?"

"Thank you, sir. I shall. Goodnight."

Volescamper gave me a desultory wave and was soon out of sight. I smiled to myself at the revelation of Kaine's fictional identity; I reckoned that not being a real person had to present a pretty good obstacle to being prime minister, but I couldn't help wondering just how much power he *did* wield within the world of fiction—and whether I had heard the last of him. After all, the Whig party was still in existence, with or without their leader. Still, Tweed was a professional, and I had other things to deal with.

I looked down the corridor, past the twisted doors. The front of Vole Towers, was virtually destroyed; the ceiling had collapsed and rubble lay strewn around where the Glatisant had fought the very finest of SO-14. I picked my way through the twisted door and down the corridor, where deep gouges had been scraped in the floor and walls by the leaden hide of the beast. The remaining SpecOps-14 operatives had all pulled back to regroup, and I slipped out in the confusion. Nine good men fell to the Questing Beast that night. The officers would all be awarded the SpecOps Star for Conspicuous Bravery in the Face of Other.

As I walked along the gravel drive away from what remained of Vole Towers, I could see a white charger galloping towards me, the warrior on its back holding a sharpened lance while behind him a dog barked excitedly. I waved King Pellinore to a halt.

"Ah!" he said, raising his visor and peering down at me. "The Next girl! Seen the Questin' Beast, what what?"

"I'm afraid you've missed it," I explained. "Sorry."

"Dem shame," announced Pellinore sadly, parking the lance in his stirrup. "Dem shame indeed, eh? I'll find it, you know. It is the lot of the Pellinores, to go a-mollocking for the beastly beast. Come, sir—away!"

He spurred his steed and galloped off across the parkland of Vole Towers, the horse's hooves throwing great divots of grass high in the air, the large white dog running behind them, barking furiously.

I returned to my apartment after giving an anonymous tip-off to *The Mole*, suggesting that they confirm the ongoing existence of *Cardenio*. The fact that I still had the apartment verified once and for all that Landen hadn't been returned. I had been a fool to think that Goliath would honor their part of the deal. I sat in the dark for a while, but even fools need rest, so I went to sleep *under* the bed as a precaution, which was just as well—at 3 a.m. Goliath turned up, had a good look around and then left. I stayed hidden as a further precaution and was glad of this also, because SpecOps turned up at 4 a.m. and did exactly the same. Confident now of no further interruptions, I crawled out from my hiding place and climbed into bed, sleeping heavily until ten the next morning.

# 31.

## Dream Topping

Ever since calories and "sugar intake" were discovered, the realm of the pudding has suffered intensely. There was a day when one could honestly and innocently enjoy the sheer pleasure of a good sticky toffee pudding; when ice cream was nice cream and bakewell tart really was baked well. Tastes change, though, and the world of the sweet has often been sour, having to go through some dramatic overhaulage in order to keep pace. Whilst a straightforward sausage and a common kedgeree maintain their hold on a nation's culinary choices, the pudding has to stay on its toes to tantalize our tastebuds. From low fat through to no fat, from sugar-free through to taste-free; what the next stage is we can only wait and see. . . .

CILLA BUBB,
*Don't Desert Your Desserts*

I PEERED CAUTIOUSLY from the window as I ate my breakfast and could see a black SpecOps Packard on the street corner, doubtless waiting for me to make an appearance. Across the road from them was another car, this time the unmistakable deep blue of Goliath; Mr. Cheese leaned against the bonnet, smoking. I switched on the telly and caught the news. The break-in at Vole Towers had been heavily censored, but it was reported that an unknown "agency" had gained entrance to the building, killed a number of SO-14 agents and made off with

*Cardenio.* Lord Volescamper had been interviewed and maintained that he had been "sound asleep" and knew nothing. Yorrick Kaine was still reported as "missing," and early exit polls from the day's election had shown that Kaine and the Whigs had not to have lived up to expectations. Without *Cardenio,* the powerful Shakespeare lobby had returned their allegiances to the current administration, who had promised to postpone, with the help of the ChronoGuard, the eighteenth-century demolition of Shakespeare's old Stratford home.

I allowed myself a wry smile at Kaine's dramatic fall but felt sorry for the officers who had had to face the Questing Beast. I walked through to the kitchen. Pickwick looked at me and then at her empty supper dish with an accusing air.

"Sorry," I muttered as I poured her some dried fruit.

"How's the egg?"

"*Plock-plock,*" said Pickwick.

"Well," I replied, "suit yourself. I was only asking."

I made another cup of tea and sat down to have a think. Dad had said the world was going to end this evening, but whether that was *really* going to happen or not, I had no idea. As for me, I was wanted by SpecOps *and* Goliath; I was going to have to either outwit them or lie very low for a long time. I spent most of the day pacing my apartment, trying to figure out the best course of action. I wrote out my account of what had happened and hid it behind the fridge, just in case. I expected Dad to turn up, but the hours ticked by and everything carried on as normal. The Goliath and SpecOps vehicles were relieved by two others at midday, and as dusk drew on I became more desperate. I couldn't stay trapped inside my own apartment forever. Bowden and Joffy I could trust—and perhaps Miles, too. I elected to sneak out and use a public phonebox to call Bowden and was just about to open the door when someone pressed the intercom buzzer downstairs. I quickly ducked out of my apartment and started to run down the staircase. If I reached the bottom and made my way out through the service entrance I might be able to slip away. Then, disaster. One of the tenants was about to leave at that precise moment and opened the door for whoever it was. I heard a brusque voice.

"Here for Miss Next—SpecOps."

I cursed Mrs. Scroggins as she replied: "Fourth floor, second on the left!"

The fire escape was out the front in full view of SpecOps and Goliath, so I ran all the way back upstairs to my flat, only to find that in my hurry I had locked myself out. There was nowhere to hide except behind a potted rubber plant about seven sizes too small, so I pushed open the letterbox and hissed: "Pickwick!"

She wandered out into the hall from the living room and stared at me, head cocked on one side.

"Good. Now listen. I know that Landen said you were really bright, and if you don't do this I'm going to be looped and you're going to be put in a zoo. Now, I need you to find my keys."

Pickwick stared at me dubiously, took two steps closer and then relaxed and plocked a bit.

"Yes, yes, it's me. All the marshmallows you can eat, Pickers, but I need my keys. My *keys.*"

Pickwick obediently stood on one leg.

"Shit," I muttered.

"Ah, Next!" said a voice behind me. I stopped, rested my head against the door and let the letterbox snap shut.

"Hello, Cordelia," I said softly without turning round.

"Well, you *have* been giving us the runaround, haven't you?"

I paused, turned and stood up. But Cordelia wasn't with any other SpecOps types—she was with a couple, the winners of her competition. Perhaps things were not quite as bad as I thought. I put my arm around her shoulder and walked her out of earshot.

"Cordelia—"

"Dilly."

"Dilly—"

"Yes, Thurs?"

"What's the word over at SpecOps?"

"Well, darling," answered Cordelia, "the order for your arrest is still only within SpecOps—Flanker is hoping you'll give yourself up. Goliath are telling anyone who will listen that you stole some highly sensitive industrial secrets."

"It's all bullshit, Cordelia."

"I know *that,* Thursday. But I've a job to do. Are you going to meet my people now?"

I had nothing to lose, so we returned to where the two of them were looking at a brochure for the Gravitube.

"Thursday Next, this is James and Catia Plummer, visitors to Swindon for their honeymoon."

"Congratulations," I said, shaking their hands and adding: "Swindon for a honeymoon, eh? You must live only for pleasure."

Cordelia elbowed me and scowled.

"I'd invite you in for a coffee," I explained, "but I've locked myself out."

James rummaged in his pocket and produced a set of keys.

"Are these yours? I found them on the path outside."

"I don't think that's very likely."

But they *were* my keys—a set I had lost a few days earlier. I unlocked the door.

"Come on in. That's Pickwick. Stay away from the windows; there are a few people I don't want to meet outside."

They shut the door behind them and I walked through to the kitchen.

"I was married once," I said as I looked out of the kitchen window. I needn't have worried; the two cars and their occupants were in the same place. "And I hope to be again. Did you tie the knot in Swindon?"

"No," replied Catia. "We were going to have a blessing in the Church of Our Blessed Lady of the Lobsters, but—"

"But what?"

"We were late and missed the appointment."

"Ah," I replied, pausing to consider just how *wholly unlikely* it was that James had found my keys when other passing residents had missed them.

"Can I ask you a question, Miss Next?" asked James.

"Call me Thursday. Hang on a minute."

I nipped into the living room to fetch the entroposcope and shook it as I walked back in.

"Well, Thursday," continued James, "I was wondering—"

"Shit!" I exclaimed, looking at the swirling pattern within the rice and lentils. "It's happening again!"

"I think your dodo is hungry," observed Catia, as Pickwick performed her "starving dodo" routine for her on the kitchen floor.

"It's a scam for a marshmallow," I replied absently. "You can give her one if you want. The jar is on top of the fridge."

Catia put down her bag and reached up for the glass jar.

"Sorry, James, you were saying?"

"Here it is. Who do you—"

But I wasn't listening. I was looking out of the kitchen window. Below me, sitting on the wall at the entrance to the apartment block, was a woman in her mid-twenties. She was dressed in slightly garish clothes and was reading a fashion magazine.

"Aornis?" I whispered. "Can you hear me?"

The figure turned to look at me as I said the words, and my scalp prickled. It was *her,* no doubt about it. She smiled, waved and pointed to her watch.

"It's her," I mumbled. "Goddamned sonofabitch—it's her!"

"—and that's my question," concluded James.

"I'm sorry, James, I wasn't listening."

I shook the entroposcope, but the pulses were no more patterned than before—whatever the danger was, we weren't quite there yet.

"You had a question, James?"

"Yes," he said, slightly annoyed. "I was wondering—"

"Look out!" I shouted, but it was too late. The glass marshmallow jar had slipped from Catia's grasp and fell heavily on the worktop—right on top of the small evidence bag full of the pink goo from beyond the end of the world. The jar didn't break, but the bag *did,* and Catia, myself, Cordelia and James were splattered in gooey slime. James got the worst of it—a huge gob went right in his face.

"Ugh!"

"Here," I said, handing him a Seven Wonders of Swindon tea towel, "use this."

"What *is* that gick?" asked Cordelia, dabbing at her clothes with a damp cloth.

"I wish I knew."

But James licked his lips and said: "I'll tell you what this is. It's Dream Topping."

"Dream Topping?" I queried. "Are you sure?"

"Yes. Strawberry flavor. Know it anywhere."

I put a finger in the goo and tasted it. No mistake, it *was* Dream Topping. If only forensics had looked at the big picture instead of staring at molecules, they might have figured it out for themselves. But it got me thinking.

"Dream Topping?" I wondered out loud, looking at my watch. There were eighty-seven minutes of life left on the planet. "How could the world turn to Dream Topping?"

"It's the sort of thing," piped up James, "that Mycroft might know."

"You," I said, pointing a finger at the pudding-covered individual, "are a genius."

What had Mycroft said before he left about his R&D work at ConStuff? Miniaturized machines, *nanomachines* barely bigger than a cell, building food protein out of nothing more than garbage? Banoffee pie from landfills? Perhaps there was going to be an accident. After all, what *stopped* nanomachines from making banoffee pie once they had started? I looked out of the window. Aornis had gone.

"Do you have a car?" I asked.

"Sure," said James.

"You're going to have to take me over to ConStuff. Dilly, I need your clothes."

Cordelia looked suspicious.

"Why?"

"I've got watchers. Three in, three out—they'll think I'm you."

"No way on earth," replied Cordelia indignantly. "Unless you agree to do *all* my interviews and press junkets."

"At my first appearance I'll have my head lopped off by Goliath or SpecOps—or both."

"Perhaps that's so," replied Cordelia slowly, "but I'd be a fool to pass on an opportunity as good as this. All the interviews and appearances I request for *a year*."

"Two months, Cordelia."

"Six."

"Three."

"Okay," she sighed, "three months—but you have to do *The*

*Thursday Next Workout Video* and talk to Harry about the *Eyre Affair* film project."

"Deal."

So Cordelia and I switched clothes. It felt very odd to be wearing her large pink sweater, short black skirt and high heels.

"Don't forget the Peruvian love beads," said Cordelia, "and my gun. Here."

"Excuse me, Miss Flakk," said James in a slightly indignant tone. "You promised I could ask Miss Next a question."

Flakk pointed a finely manicured fingertip at him and narrowed her eyes. "Listen here, buster. You're both on SpecOps business right now—a bonus I'd say. Any complaints?"

"Er—no, I guess not," stammered James.

I led them outside, past the Goliath and SpecOps agents waiting for me. I made some expansive Cordelia-like moves and they barely gave us a second glance. We were soon in James's hired Studebaker, and I directed him across town as I switched back to my own clothes.

"Thursday?" asked James.

"Yes?" I replied, looking around to see if I could see Aornis and shaking the entroposcope. Entropy seemed to be holding at the "slightly odd" mark.

"Who is the father of Pickwick's egg?"

I get asked some odd questions sometimes. But he was driving me across town, so I thought I would show him some slack.

"I think it was one of the feral dodos down at the park," I explained. "I caught Pickwick doing a sort of coy come-hither dodo thing a month back, with a large male near the bandstand. Pickwick's amour plocked noisily outside the house for a week, but I didn't know anything had actually *happened*. Does that answer your question?"

"I guess."

"Good. Okay, pull up over there. I'll walk the rest of the way."

They dropped me by the side of the road, and I thanked them before running up the street. It was already quite dark and the streetlamps were on. It didn't look like the world was about to end in twenty-six minutes, but then I don't suppose it ever does.

# 32.

## The End of Life
## as We Know It

After failing to get Landen back, dealing with Armageddon didn't really hold the same sort of *excitement* for me that it would later. They always say the first time you save the world is the hardest—personally I have *always* found it tricky, but this time, I don't know. Perhaps Landen's loss numbed my mind and immunized me against panic. Perhaps the distraction actually helped.

THURSDAY NEXT,
*Private Diaries*

**C**ONSOLIDATED USEFUL STUFF was situated in a large complex on the airfield at Stratton. There was a guardhouse, but I had coincidence on my side—as I walked into the security building all three guards had been called away on some errand or other, and I was able to slip through unnoticed. I rubbed my arm, which had inexplicably twinged with pain, and followed the signs toward MycroTech Developments. I was just wondering how to get into the locked building when a voice made me jump.

"Hello, Thursday!"

It was Wilbur, Mycroft's boring son.

"No time to explain, Will—I need to get into the nanotechnology lab."

"Why?" asked Wilbur, fumbling with his keys.

"There's going to be an accident."

"Absolutely *impossible!*" he scoffed, throwing the doors open to reveal a mass of spinning red lights and the raucous sounding of a klaxon.

"Heavens!" exclaimed Wilbur. "Do you think it's meant to be doing that?"

"Call someone."

"Right."

He picked up the phone. Predictably enough, it was dead. He tried another but they were *all* dead.

"I'll get help!" he said, tugging at the doorknob, which came off in his hand. "What the—"

"Entropy's decreasing by the second, Will. Are you using Dream Topping in any of your nanomachines?"

He led me to a cabinet where a tiny drop of pink goo was suspended in midair by powerful magnets.

"There she is. The first of her kind. Still experimental, of course. There are a few problems with the discontinuation command string. Once it starts changing organic matter into Dream Topping, *it won't stop.*"

I looked at my watch and noticed that there were barely twelve minutes left.

"What's keeping it from working at the moment?"

"The magnetic field keeps the nanodevice immobilized, the refrigeration system is set below its activation temperature of minus ten degrees—what was that?"

The lights had flickered.

"Power grid failure."

"No problem, Thursday—there are three backup generators. They can't *all* fail at the same time, that would be too much of a—"

"—coincidence, yes, I know. But they will. And when they do, that coincidence will be the biggest, the best—and the last."

"Thursday, that's not possible!"

"*Anything* is possible right now. We're in the middle of an isolated high-coincidental localized entropic field decreasement."

"We're in a *what?*"

"We're in a pseudoscientific technobabble."

"Ah!" replied Wilbur, having witnessed quite a few at Mycro-Tech Developments. "One of *those.*"

"What happens when the final backup fails, Wilbur?"

"The nanodevice will be expelled into the atmosphere," said Wilbur grimly. "It is programmed to make strawberry-flavored pudding mix and will continue to do so as long as it has organic material to work with. You, me, that table over there—then when someone comes to let us out in the morning, the machine will get to work on the outside."

"How quickly?"

"Well," said Wilbur, thinking hard, "the device will make replicas of itself to carry out the work even faster, so the more organic material is swallowed up, the faster the process becomes. The entire planet? I'd give it about a week."

"And nothing can stop it?"

"Nothing I know of," he replied sadly. "The best way to stop this is to not allow it to start—sort of a minimum entry requirement for man-made disasters, really."

"Aornis!" I shouted at the top of my voice. "*Where the hell are you?*"

There was no reply.

"*AORNIS!*"

And then she answered. But it was from such an unexpected quarter that I cried out in fright. She spoke to me—*from my memory.* It was as though a barrier had been lifted in my mind. The day on the Skyrail platform. The moment I first set eyes on Aornis. I thought it had only been a glimpse, but it wasn't. We had spoken together for several minutes as I waited for the shuttle. I cast my mind back and read the newly recovered memories as my palms grew sweaty. The answers had been there all along.

"Hello, Thursday," said the young woman on the bench, dabbing her nose with a powder compact.

I walked over to her.

"You know my name?"

"I know a lot more than that. My name is Aornis Hades. You killed my brother."

I tried not to let my surprise show.

"Self-defense, Miss Hades. If I could have taken him alive, I would have."

"No member of the Hades family has been taken alive for over eighty-three generations."

I thought about the twin puncture, the Skyrail ticket, all the chance happenings to get me on the platform.

"Are you manipulating coincidences, Hades?"

"Of course!" she replied as the shuttle hissed into the station. "You're going to get on that shuttle and be shot accidentally by an SO-14 marksman. An ironic end, don't you think? Shot by one of your own?"

"What if I don't get on the Skyrail? What if I take you in right here and now?"

Aornis sniggered at my naïveté.

"Dear Acheron was a fine and worthy Hades despite the fact he killed his brother—something Mother was very cut up about—but he was never truly *au fait* with some of the family's more diabolical attributes. You'll get on that train, Thursday—*because you won't remember anything about this conversation!*"

"Don't be ridiculous!" I laughed, but Aornis returned to her powder compact and I *had* got on the train.

\*         \*         \*

"What is it?" asked Wilbur, who had been staring at me as the memories of Aornis came flooding back.

"Recovered memories," I replied grimly as the lights flickered. The first backup generator had failed. I checked my watch. There were six minutes to go.

"Thursday?" murmured Wilbur, lower lip trembling. "I'm frightened."

"Me too, Will. Quiet a sec."

And I thought back to my next meeting with Aornis. At Uffington, when she posed as Violet De'ath. On this occasion we had been in company, so she hadn't said anything, but the next time, when I was in Osaka, she had sat next to me on the bench, just after the fortune-teller was struck by lightning.

"Clever trick," she said, arranging her shopping bags so they wouldn't fall over, "using the coincidence in that way. Next time you won't be so lucky—and while we're on the subject, how did you get out of the jam on the Skyrail?"

I really didn't want to answer her questions.

"What are you doing to me?" I demanded instead. "What are you doing to my *head*?"

"A simple recollection erasure, Thursday. I'm a mnemenomorph. My particular edge is that I am instantly forgettable—you will *never* capture me because you will forget that we ever met. I can erase your memory of me so instantaneously I am rendered invisible. I can walk where I please, steal what I wish—I can even murder in broad daylight."

"Very clever, Hades."

"Please, call me Aornis—I'd like us to be pals."

She pushed her hair behind her ear and looked at her nails for a moment before asking: "I saw a beautiful cashmere sweater just now; it's available in turquoise or emerald. Which do you think would suit me better?"

"I have no idea."

"I'll get them both," she replied after a moment of reflection. "It's on a stolen credit card, after all."

"Enjoy your game, Aornis, it won't be forever. I defeated your brother—I'll do the same to you."

"And how do you propose to do that?" she sneered. "When you can't recollect anything about our meetings at all? My dear, you won't even remember *this* one—until I want you to!"

And she gathered up her bags and walked off.

The lights in the nanotechnology lab flickered again. Wilbur and I looked at one another as the second backup generator failed. He tried the phones again in desperation, but everything was still dead. Death by coincidence. What a way to go. But it was now, with only two minutes to go, that Aornis lifted the last barrier and I clearly remembered the *last* occasion she and I had faced each other. It had occurred not twenty minutes before at the ConStuff reception. It hadn't been empty at all; Aornis had been there, waiting for me—ready to deliver the *coup de grâce*.

"Well!" she exclaimed as I walked in. "Figured this one out, did you?"

"Damn you, Hades!" I retorted, reaching for my pistol. She caught my wrist and pulled me into a painful half nelson with surprising speed.

"Listen to me," she whispered in my ear while holding my arm locked tightly behind me. "There's going to be an accident in the nanotechnology lab. Your uncle hoped to feed the world, when in fact he will be the father of its destruction. The irony is so heavy you could cut it with a knife!"

"Wait—!" I said, but she pulled my arm up harder and I yelped.

"I'm talking, Next. *Never* interrupt a Hades when they're

talking. You will die for what you have done to our family, but just to show I'm not a total fiend, I will allow you one last heroic gesture, something your pathetic self-righteous character seems to crave. At precisely six minutes before the accident, you will begin to remember all our little chats together."

I struggled, but she held me tight.

"You'll remember this meeting last. So here's my offer. Take your pistol and turn it upon yourself—and I'll spare the planet."

"And if I don't?" I shouted. "You'll die too!"

"No," she laughed, "I know you'll do it. *Despite* the baby. Despite *everything*. You're a good person, Next. A *fine* human being. It will be your downfall. I'm counting on it."

She leaned forwards and whispered in my ear.

"They're wrong, you know, Thursday. Revenge is *so* sweet!"


"Thursday?" asked Wilbur. "Are you all right?"

"No, not really," I muttered as I saw the clock tick into the final minute. Acheron was nothing compared to Aornis, either in his powers or his sense of humor. I'd messed with the Hades family and now I was paying the price.

I pulled out my automatic as the clock ticked into the last half minute.

"If Landen ever comes back, tell him I love him."

Twenty seconds.

"If *who* ever comes back?"

"Landen. You'll know him when you see him. Tall, one leg, writes daft books and had a wife named Thursday who loved him beyond comprehension."

Ten seconds.

"So long, Wilbur."

I closed my eyes and placed the gun to my temple.

# 33.

## The Dawn of Life
## as We Know It

Three billion years ago the atmosphere on earth had stabilized to what scientists referred to as A-II. The relentless hammering of the atmosphere had created the ozone layer, which in turn now stopped new oxygen from being produced. A new and totally different mechanism was needed to kick-start the young planet into the living green ball that we know and enjoy today.

DR. LUCIANO SPAGBOG,
*How I Think Life Began on Earth*

"NO NEED FOR THAT," said my father, gently taking the gun from my hand and laying it on the table. I don't know whether he purposely arrived late to increase the drama, but there he was. He hadn't frozen time—I think he was done with that. Whenever he had appeared in the past he had always been smiles and cheeriness, but today he was different. And he looked, for the first time ever, *old*. Perhaps eighty—maybe more.

He thrust his hand inside the nanodevice container as the final generator failed. The small blob of nanotechnology fell on his hand, and the emergency lights flicked on, bathing us all in a dim green glow.

"It's cold," he said. "How long have I got?"

"It has to warm up first," replied Wilbur glumly. "Three minutes?"

"I'm sorry to disappoint you, sweetpea, but self-sacrifice is *not* the answer."

"It was all I had left, Dad. Me alone or me *and* three billion souls."

"You don't get to make that decision, Thursday, *but I do*. You've got a lot of good work to do, and your son, too. Me, I'm just glad that it all ends before I become so enfeebled as to be useless."

"Dad—!"

I felt the tears start to roll down my cheeks. There was so much I wanted to ask him. There always is.

"It all seems so clear to me now!" he said, smiling as he cupped his hand so none of the all-consuming Dream Topping would fall to the ground. "After several million years of existence I finally realized my purpose. Will you tell your mother there was *absolutely nothing* between me and Emma Hamilton?"

*"Oh—Dad! Don't, please!"*

"And tell Joffy I forgive him for breaking the windows of the greenhouse."

I hugged him tightly.

"I'll miss you. And your mother of course, and Sévé, Louis Armstrong, the Nolan Sisters—which reminds me, did you get any tickets?"

"Third row, but—but—I don't suppose you'll need them now."

"You never know," he murmured. "Leave my ticket at the box office, will you?"

"Dad, there must be *something* we can do for you, surely?"

"No, my darling, I'm going to be out of here pretty soon. *The Great Leap Forward*. The thing is, I wonder where to? Was there anything in the Dream Topping that shouldn't have been there?"

"Chlorophyll."

He smiled and sniffed the carnation in his buttonhole. "Yes,

I thought as much. It's all *very* simple, really—and quite ingenious. Chlorophyll is the key— Ow!"

I looked at his hand. His skin and flesh were starting to swirl as the wayward nanodevice thawed enough to start work, devouring, changing and replicating with ever-increasing speed.

I looked at him, wanting to ask a hundred questions but not knowing where to start.

"I'm going three billion years in the past, Thursday, to a planet with only the *possibility* of life. A planet waiting for a miraculous event, something that has not happened, as far as we know it, anywhere else in the universe. In a word, *photosynthesis*. An oxidizing atmosphere, sweetpea—the ideal way to start an embryonic biosphere."

He laughed.

"It's funny the way things turn out, isn't it? All life on earth descended from the organic compounds and proteins contained within Dream Topping."

"And the carnation. And you."

He smiled at me.

"Me. Yes. I thought this might be the ending, *the Big One*— but in fact it's really only just the beginning. And I'm it. Makes me feel all sort of, well, *humble*."

He touched my face with his good hand and kissed me on the cheek.

"Don't cry, Thursday. It's how it happens. It's how it has *always* happened, always *will* happened. Take my chronograph; I'm not going to need it anymore."

I unstrapped the heavy watch from his good wrist as the smell of artificial strawberries filled the room. It was Dad's hand. It had almost completely changed to pudding. It was time for him to go, and he knew it.

"Goodbye, Thursday. I never could have wished for a finer daughter."

I composed myself. I didn't want his last memory of me to be of a sniveling wretch. I wanted him to see I could be as strong as he was. I pursed my lips and wiped the tears from my eyes.

"Goodbye, Dad."

He winked at me.

"Well, time waits for no man, as we say."

He smiled again and started to fold and collapse and spiral into a single dot, much like water escaping from a plughole. I could feel myself tugged into the event, so I took a step back as my father vanished into himself with a very quiet *plop* as he traveled into the deep past. A final gravitational tug dislodged one of my shirt buttons; the wayward pearl fastener sailed through the air and was caught in the small rippling vortex. It vanished from sight, and the air rocked for a moment before settling down to that usual state that we refer to as *normality*.

My father had gone.

The lights flickered back on as entropy returned to normal. Aornis's boldly audacious plan for revenge had backfired badly. She had, perversely enough, actually *given* us all life. And after all that talk about irony. She'd probably be kicking herself all the way to TopShop. Dad was right. It *is* funny the way things turn out.

I sat through the Nolan Sisters concert that evening with an empty seat beside me, glancing at the door to see if he would arrive. I hardly even heard the music—I was thinking instead of a lonely foreshore on a planet devoid of any life, a person who had once been my father sloughing away to his component parts. Then I thought of the resultant proteins, now much replicated and evolved, working on the atmosphere. They released oxygen and combined hydrogen with carbon dioxide to form simple food molecules. Within a few hundred million years the atmosphere would be full of free oxygen; aerobic life could begin—and a couple of billion years after that, something slimy would start wriggling onto land. It was an inauspicious start, but now there was a sort of family pride attached to it. He wasn't just *my* father but *everyone's* father. As the Nolans performed "Goodbye Nothing to Say," I sat in quiet introspection, regretting, as children always do upon the death of a parent, all the things we never said nor ever did. But my biggest regret was far more mundane: Since his identity and existence had been scrubbed by the ChronoGuard, I never knew, nor ever asked him—*his name*.

# 34.

# The Well of Lost Plots

**Character Exchange Program:** If a character from one book looks suspiciously like another from the same author, more than likely, they are. There is a certain degree of economy that runs through the bookworld, and personages from one book are often asked to stand in for others. Sometimes a single character may play another in the same book, which lends a comedic tone to the proceedings if they have to talk to themselves. Margot Metroland once told me that playing the same person over and over and over again was as tiresome as "an actress condemned to the same part in a provincial repertory theater for eternity with no holiday." After a spate of illegal PageRunning (q.v.) by bored and disgruntled bookpeople, the Character Exchange Program was set up to allow a change of scenery. In any year there are close to ten thousand exchanges, few of which result in any major plot or dialogue infringements. The reader rarely suspects anything at all.

UNITARY AUTHORITY OF WARRINGTON CAT,
*The Jurisfiction Guide to the Great Library* (glossary)

**I** SLEPT OVER at Joffy's place. I say slept, but that wasn't entirely accurate. I just stared at the elegantly molded ceiling and thought of Landen. At dawn I crept quietly out of the vicarage, borrowed Joffy's Brough Superior motorcycle and rode into Swindon as the sun crept over the horizon. The bright rays of a new day usually filled me with hope, but that morning I could think only of unfinished business and an uncertain future. I rode through the empty streets, past Coate and up the Marlborough road towards my mother's house. She had to know about Dad, however painful the news might be, and I hoped she would take solace, as I did, in his final selfless act. I would go to the station and hand myself in to Flanker afterwards. There was a good chance that SO-5 would believe my account of what happened with Aornis, but I suspected that convincing SO-1 of Lavoisier's chronuption might take a lot more. Goliath and the two Schitts were a worry, but I was sure I would be able to think of *something* to keep them off my back. Still, the world hadn't ended yesterday, which was a big plus—and Flanker couldn't exactly charge me with "failing to save the planet *his* way," no matter how much he might want to.

As I approached the junction outside Mum's house I noticed a car that looked suspiciously Goliathesque parked across the street, so I rode on and did a wide circuit, abandoning the motorcycle two blocks away and treading noiselessly down the back alleys. I skirted around another large dark blue Goliath motorcar, climbed over the fence into Mum's garden and crept past the vegetable patch to the kitchen door. It was locked, so I pushed open the large dodo flap and crawled inside. I was just about to switch on the lights when I felt the cold barrel of a gun pressed against my cheek. I started and almost cried out.

"Lights stay *off*," growled a husky woman's voice, "and don't make any sudden moves."

I dutifully froze. A hand snaked into my jacket and removed Cordelia's pistol. DH-82 was fast asleep in his basket; the idea of being a fierce guard-Taswolf had obviously not entered his head.

"Let me see you," said the voice again. I turned and looked into the eyes of a woman who had departed more rapidly into middle age than years alone might allow. I noticed that her gun arm wavered slightly, she had a slightly florid appearance and her hair had been clumsily brushed and pulled into a bun. But for all that it was clear she had once been beautiful; her eyes were bright and cheerful, her mouth delicate and refined, her bearing resolute.

"What are you doing here?" she demanded.

"This is my mother's house."

"Ah!" she said, giving a slight whisper of a smile and raising an eyebrow. "You must be Thursday."

She returned her pistol to a holster that was strapped to her thigh beneath several layers of her large brocade dress and started to rummage in the cupboards.

"Do you know where your mother keeps the booze?"

"Suppose you tell me who *you* are?" I demanded, my eyes alighting on the knife block as I searched for a weapon—just in case.

The woman didn't give me an answer, or, at least, not to the question I'd asked.

"Your father told me Lavoisier eradicated your husband."

I halted my surreptitious creep towards the carving knives.

"You know my father?" I asked in some surprise.

"I do so hate that term *eradicated*," she announced grimly, searching in vain amongst the tinned fruit for anything resembling alcohol. "It's murder, Thursday—nothing less. They killed my husband, too—even if it did take three attempts."

"Who?"

"Lavoisier and the French revisionists."

She thumped her fist on the kitchen top as if to punctuate her anger and turned to face me.

"You have memories of your husband, I suppose?"

"Yes."

"Me too," she sighed. "I wish to heaven I hadn't, but I have. Memories of things that *might* have happened. Knowledge of the loss. It's the worst part of it."

She opened another cupboard door, revealing still more tinned fruit.

"I understand your husband was barely two years old—mine was forty-seven. You might think that makes it better, but it doesn't. The petition for his divorce was granted and we were married the summer following Trafalgar. Nine years of glorious life as Lady Nelson—then I wake up one morning in Calais, a drunken, debt-ridden wretch, and with the revelation that my one true love died a decade ago, shot by a sniper's bullet on the quarterdeck of the *Victory*."

"I know who you are," I murmured. "You're Emma Hamilton."

"I *was* Emma Hamilton," she replied sadly. "Now I'm a broke out-of-timer with a dismal reputation, no husband and a thirst the size of the Gobi."

"But you still have your daughter?"

"Yes," she groaned, "but I never told her I was her mother."

"Try the end cupboard."

She moved down the counter, rummaged some more and found a bottle of cooking sherry. She poured a generous helping into one of my mother's teacups. I looked at the saddened woman and wondered if I'd end up the same way.

"We'll sort out Lavoisier eventually," muttered Lady Hamilton sadly, downing the cooking sherry. "You can be sure of that."

"We?"

She looked at me and poured another generous—even by my mother's definition—cup of sherry.

"Me—and your father, of course."

I sighed. She obviously hadn't heard the news.

"That's what I came to talk to my mother about."

"What did you come to talk to me about?"

It was my mother. She had just walked in wearing a quilted dressing gown with her hair sticking in all directions. For someone usually so suspicious of Emma Hamilton, she seemed quite cordial and even wished her good morning—although she swiftly removed the sherry from the counter and replaced it in the cupboard.

"You early bird!" she cooed. "Do you have time to take DH-82 to the vet's this morning? His boil needs lancing again."

"I'm kind of busy, Mum."

"Oh!" she exclaimed, sensing the seriousness in my voice. "Was that business at Vole Towers anything to do with you?"

"Sort of. I came over to tell you—"

"Yes?"

"That Dad has—Dad is—Dad was—"

Mum looked at me quizzically as my father, large as life, strode into the kitchen.

"—is making me feel *very* confused."

"Hello, sweetpea!" said my father, looking considerably younger than the last time I saw him. "Have you been introduced to Lady Hamilton?"

"We had a drink together," I said uncertainly. "But—you're—you're—*alive!*"

He stroked his chin and replied: "Should I be something else?"

I thought for a moment and furtively shook my cuff down to hide his ChronoGraph on my wrist.

"No—I mean, that is to say—"

But he had twigged me already.

"Don't tell me! I don't want to know!"

He stood next to Mum and placed an arm round her waist. It was the first time I had seen them together for nearly seventeen years.

"But—"

"You mustn't be so *linear,*" said my father. "Although I try to visit only in *your* chronological order, sometimes it's not possible."

He paused.

"Did I suffer much pain?"

"No—none at all," I lied.

"It's funny," he said as he filled the kettle, "I can recall everything up until final curtain minus ten, but after that it's all a bit fuzzy—I can vaguely see a rugged coastline and the sunset on a calm ocean, but other than that, nothing. I've seen and done a lot in my time, but my entry and exit will *always* remain a mystery. It's better that way. Stops me getting cold feet and trying to change them."

He spooned some coffee into the Cafetiere. I was glad to see that I had only witnessed Dad's death and not the end of his life, as the two, I learned, are barely related at all.

"How are things, by the way?" he asked.

"Well," I began, unsure of where to start, "the world didn't end yesterday."

He looked at the low winter sun that was shining through the kitchen windows.

"So I see. Good job too. An Armageddon right now might have been awkward. Have you had any breakfast?"

"Awkward? Global destruction would be *awkward?*"

"Decidedly so. *Tiresome* almost," replied my father thoughtfully. "The end of the world could *really* louse up my plans. Tell me, did you manage to get me a ticket to the Nolans' concert last night?"

I thought quickly.

"Er—no, Dad—sorry. They'd all sold out."

There was another pause. Mum nudged her husband,

who looked at her oddly. It looked as if she wanted him to say something.

"Thursday," she began when it became obvious that Dad wasn't going to take her cue, "your father and I think you should take some leave until our *first* grandchild is born. Somewhere safe. Somewhere *other*."

"Oh yes!" added Dad with a start. "With Goliath, Aornis and Lavoisier after you, the herenow is not *exactly* the best place to be."

"I can look after myself."

"I thought I could too," grumbled Lady Hamilton, gazing longingly at the cupboard where the cooking sherry was hidden.

"I *will* get Landen back," I replied resolutely.

"Perhaps *now* you might be physically up to it—but what happens in six months' time? You need a break, Thursday, and you need to take it now. Of course, you must fight—but fight with a level playing field."

"Mum?"

"It makes sense, darling."

I rubbed my head and sat on one of the kitchen chairs. It *did* seem to be a good idea.

"What have you in mind?"

Mum and Dad exchanged looks.

"I could downstream you to the sixteenth century or something, but good medical care would be hard to come by. Upstreaming is too risky—and besides, SO-12 would soon find you. No, if you're going to go anywhere, it will have to be *sideways*."

He came and sat down next to me.

"Henshaw at SO-3 owes me a favor. Between the two of us we could slip you sideways into a world where Landen *doesn't* drown aged two."

"You could?" I replied, suddenly perking up.

"Sure. But steady on. It's not so simple. A lot will be . . . *different*."

My euphoria was short-lived. A prickle rose on my scalp.

"How different?"

"*Very* different. You won't be in SO-27. In fact, there won't be any SpecOps at all. The Second World War will finish in 1945 and the Crimean conflict won't last much beyond 1854."

"I see. No Crimean War? Does that mean Anton will still be alive?"

"It does."

"Then let's do it, Dad."

He laid a hand on mine and squeezed it.

"There's more. It's your decision, and you have to know *precisely* what is involved. *Everything* will be gone. All the work you've ever done, all the work you *will* do. There will be no dodos or neanderthals, no Willspeak machines, no Gravitube—"

"No Gravitube? How do people get around?"

"In things called *jetliners*. Large passenger aircraft that can fly seven miles high at three-quarters of the speed of sound—some even faster."

It was plainly a ridiculous idea, and I told him.

"I know it's far-fetched, sweetpea, but you'll never know any different. The Gravitube will seem as impossible there as jetliners do here."

"What about mammoths?"

"No—but there will be ducks."

"Goliath?"

"Under a different name."

I was quiet for a moment.

"Will there be *Jane Eyre*?"

"Yes," sighed my father. "Yes, there will always be *Jane Eyre*."

"And Turner? Will he still paint *The Fighting Temeraire*?"

"Yes, and Carravaggggio will be there too, although his name will be spelt more sensibly."

"Then what are we waiting for?"

My father was silent for a moment.

"There's a catch."

"What sort of catch?"

He sighed.

"Landen will be back, but you and he won't have met. Landen won't even *know* you."

"But I'll know him. I can introduce myself, can't I?"

"Thursday, you're not part of this. You're outside of it. You'll still be carrying Landen's child, but you won't know the sideslip has ever happened. You will remember nothing about your old life. If you want to go sideways to see him, then you'll have to have a new past and a new present. Perversely enough, to be able to see him, you *cannot* have any recollection of him—nor he of you."

"That's some catch," I observed.

"It's the second-best there is," Dad agreed.

I thought for a moment.

"So I won't be in love with him?"

"I'm afraid not. You might have a small residual memory—feelings that you can't explain for someone you've never met."

"Will I be confused?"

"Yes."

He looked at me with an earnest expression. They all did. Even Lady Hamilton, who had been moving quietly towards the sherry, stopped and was staring at me. It was clear that making myself scarce was something I had to do. But having zero recollection of Landen? I didn't really have to think very hard.

"No, Dad. Thanks, but no thanks."

"I don't think you understand," he intoned, using his paternal go-to-your-room-young-lady voice. "In a year's time you can come back and everything will be as right as—"

"*No.* I'm not losing any more of Landen than I have already."

I had an idea.

"Besides, I do have somewhere I can go."

"Where?" inquired my father. "Where could you possibly go that Lavoisier couldn't find you? Backwards, forwards, sideways, otherways—there isn't anywhere else!"

I smiled.

"You're wrong, Dad. There *is* somewhere. A place where no one will ever find me—not even you."

"Sweetpea—!" he implored. "It is *imperative* that you take this seriously! Where will you go?"

"I'll just," I replied slowly, "lose myself in a good book."

Despite their pleading, I bade farewell to Mum, Dad and Lady Hamilton, crept out of the house and sped to my apartment on Joffy's motorbike. I parked outside the front door in clear defiance of the Goliath and SpecOps agents who were still waiting for me. I ambled slowly in; it would take them twenty minutes or more to report to base and then get up the stairs and break down the door—and I really only needed to pack a few things. I still had my memories of Landen, and they would sustain me until I got him back. Because I *would* get him back—but I needed time to rest and recuperate and bring our child into the world with the minimum of fuss, bother and interruptions. I packed four tins of Moggilicious cat food, two packets of Mintolas, a large jar of Marmite and two dozen AA batteries into a large holdall along with a few changes of clothing, a picture of my family and the copy of *Jane Eyre* with the bullet lodged in the cover. I placed a sleepy and confused Pickwick and her egg into the holdall and zipped up the bag so that only her head stuck out. I then sat and waited on a chair in front of the door with a copy of *Great Expectations* on my lap. I wasn't a natural bookjumper, and without my travelbook I was going to need the fear of capture to help catapult me through the boundaries of fiction.

I started to read at the first knock on the door and continued through the volley of shouts for me to open up, past the muffled thuds and the sound of splintered wood, until finally, as the door fell in, I melted into the dingy interior of *Great Expectations* and Satis House.

Miss Havisham was understandably shocked when I explained what I needed, and even more shocked at the sight of Pickwick, but she consented to my request and cleared it with the Bellman— on the proviso that I'd continue with my training. I was hurriedly inducted into the Character Exchange Program and given a secondary part in an unpublished book deep within the Well of Lost Plots—the woman I was replacing had for some time wanted to take a course in drama at the Reading Academy of Dramatic Arts, so it suited her equally well. As I wandered down to subbasement six, Exchange Program docket in hand made out to someone named Briggs, I felt more relaxed than I had for weeks. I found the correct book sandwiched between the first draft of an adventure in the Tasman Sea and a vague notion of a comedy set in Bomber Command. I picked it up, took it to one of the reading tables and quietly read myself into my new home.

I found myself on the banks of a reservoir somewhere in the home counties. It was summer and the air smelt warm and sweet after the wintry conditions back home. I was standing on a wooden jetty in front of a large and seemingly derelict flying boat, which rocked gently in the breeze, tugging on the mooring ropes. A woman had just stepped out of a door in the high-sided hull; she was holding a suitcase.

"Hello!" she shouted, running up and offering me a hand. "I'm Mary. You must be Thursday. My goodness! What's that?"

"A dodo. Her name's Pickwick."

"I thought they were extinct."

"Not where I come from. Is this where I'm going to live?" I was pointing at the shabby flying boat dubiously.

"I know what you're thinking," smiled Mary proudly. "Isn't she just the most beautiful thing ever? Short Sunderland; built in 1943 but last flew in '54. I'm midway converting her to a houseboat, but don't feel shy if you want to help out. Just keep the bilges pumped out, and if you can run the number three engine once a month I'd be very grateful."

"Er—okay," I stammered.

"Good. I've left a rough précis of the story taped to the fridge, but don't worry too much—since we're not published you can do pretty much what you want. Any problems, ask Captain Nemo who lives on the *Nautilus* two boats down, and don't worry, Jack might seem gruff to begin with, but he has a heart of gold, and if he asks you to drive his Austin Allegro, make sure you depress the clutch fully before changing gear. Did the Bellman supply you with all the necessary paperwork and fake IDs?"

I patted my pocket, and she handed me a scrap of paper and a bunch of keys.

"Good. This is my footnoterphone number in case of emergencies, these are the keys to the flying boat and my BMW. If someone named Arnold calls, tell him he had his chance and he blew it. Any questions?"

"I don't think so."

She smiled.

"Then we're done. You'll like it here. It's pretty odd. I'll see you in about a year. So long!"

She gave a cheery wave and walked off up the dusty track. I looked across the lake at the faraway dinghies, then watched a pair of swans beating their wings furiously and pedaling the water to take off. I sat down on a rickety wooden seat and let Pickwick out of the bag. It wasn't home but it looked pleasant enough. Landen's reactualization was in the uncharted future, along with Aornis's and Goliath's comeuppance—but all in good time. I would miss Mum, Dad, Joffy, Bowden, Victor and maybe even Cordelia. But it wasn't *all* bad news—at least this way I wouldn't have to do *The Thursday Next Workout Video.*

As my father said, it's funny the way things turn out.

\*

**Thursday Next returns in**

*The Well of Lost Plots*

Spring 2004